Lyman Copeland Draper, Reuben G. Thwaites, Alexander Scott
Withers, William Powers, William Hacker

Chronicles of Border Warfare

A history of the settlement by the whites, of north-western Virginia, and of the

Indian wars and massacres in that section of the state

Lyman Copeland Draper, Reuben G. Thwaites, Alexander Scott Withers, William Powers, William Hacker

Chronicles of Border Warfare
A history of the settlement by the whites, of north-western Virginia, and of the Indian wars and massacres in that section of the state

ISBN/EAN: 9783337343606

Printed in Europe, USA, Canada, Australia, Japan

Cover: Foto ©Andreas Hilbeck / pixelio.de

More available books at **www.hansebooks.com**

Chronicles of Border Warfare

OR, A

History of the Settlement by the Whites, of North-Western Virginia, and of the Indian Wars and Massacres in that section of the State

WITH

REFLECTIONS, ANECDOTES, &c.

BY

ALEXANDER SCOTT WITHERS

A New Edition

EDITED AND ANNOTATED BY

REUBEN GOLD THWAITES

Secretary of the Wisconsin Historical Society, editor of "Wisconsin Historical Collections," and author of "The Colonies, 1492–1750," "Historic Waterways," "Story of Wisconsin," etc.

With the addition of a Memoir of the Author, and several Illustrative Notes

BY THE LATE

LYMAN COPELAND DRAPER

Author of "King's Mountain and Its Heroes," "Autograph Collections of the Signers," etc.

REPRINTED 1961
McCLAIN PRINTING COMPANY
PARSONS, W. VA.

CINCINNATI
THE ROBERT CLARKE COMPANY
1895

CONTENTS.

(iii)

EDITOR'S PREFACE.

It is sixty-four years since the original edition of Withers's *Chronicles of Border Warfare* was given to the public. The author was a faithful recorder of local tradition. Among his neighbors were sons and grandsons of the earlier border heroes, and not a few actual participants in the later wars. He had access, however, to few contemporary documents. He does not appear to have searched for them, for there existed among the pioneer historians of the West a respect for tradition as the prime source of information, which does not now obtain; to-day, we desire first to see the documents of a period, and care little for reminiscence, save when it fills a gap in or illumines the formal record. The weakness of the traditional method is well exemplified in Withers's work. His treatment of many of the larger events on the border may now be regarded as little else than a thread on which to hang annotations; but in most of the local happenings which are here recorded he will always, doubtless, remain a leading authority—for his informants possessed full knowledge of what occurred within their own horizon, although having distorted notions regarding affairs beyond it.

The *Chronicles* had been about seven years upon the market, when a New York youth, inspired by the pages of Doddridge, Flint, and Withers, with a fervid love for border history, entered upon the task of collecting documents and traditions with which to correct and amplify the lurid story which these authors had outlined. In the prosecution of this undertaking, Lyman C. Draper became so absorbed with the passion of collecting that he found little opportunity for literary effort, and in time his early facility in this direction became dulled. He was the most successful of collectors of materials for Western history, and as such did a work which must earn for him the lasting gratitude of American historical students; but un-

fortunately he did little more than collect and investigate,
and the idea which to the last strongly possessed him, of
writing a series of biographies of trans-Alleghany pioneers,
was never realized. He died August 26, 1891, having accomplished wondrous deeds for the Wisconsin Historical
Society, of which he was practically the founder, and for
thirty-three years the main stay; in the broader domain of
historical scholarship, however, he had failed to reach his
goal. His great collection of manuscripts and notes, he
willed to his Society, which has had them carefully classi-
fied and conveniently bound—a lasting treasure for historians of the West and Southwest, for the important frontier
period between about 1740 and 1816.

Dr. Draper had exhibited much ability as an editor,
in the first ten volumes of the *Wisconsin Historical Collections.* In 1890, the Robert Clarke Company engaged him,
as the best living authority on the details of Western border
history, to prepare and edit a new edition of Withers. He
set about the task with interest, and was engaged in the
active preparation of "copy" during his last months on
earth; indeed, his note upon page 123 of this edition is
thought to have been his final literary work. He had at
that time prepared notes for about one-fourth of the book,
and had written his "Memoir of the Author."

The matter here rested until the autumn of 1894,
when the publishers requested the present writer to take
up the work where his revered friend had left it, and see
the edition through the press. He has done this with
some reluctance, conscious that he approached the task
with a less intimate knowledge of the subject than his
predecessor; nevertheless he was unwilling that Dr. Draper's notes on the early pages should be lost, and has
deemed it a labor of love to complete the undertaking upon
which the last thoughts of the latter fondly dwelt.

In the preparation of his own notes, the editor has
had the great advantage of free access to the Draper Manuscripts; without their help, it would have been impossible to throw further light on many of the episodes treated
by the author. The text of Withers has been preserved
intact, save that where errors have obviously been typo-

graphical, and not intended by the author, the editor has corrected them—perhaps in a dozen instances only, for the original proof-reading appears to have been rather carefully done. The pagination of the original edition has in this been indicated by brackets, as [54]. In the original, the publisher's "Advertisement" and the "Table of Contents" were bound in at the end of the work,—see collation in Field's *Indian Bibliography*,—but evidently this was a make-shift of rustic binders in a hurry to get out the long-delayed edition, and the editor has taken the liberty to transfer them to their proper place; also, while preserving typographical peculiarities therein, to change the pagination in the "Contents" to accord with the present edition. In order clearly to indicate the authorship of notes, those by Withers himself are unsigned; those by Dr. Draper are signed "L. C. D."; and those by the present writer, "R. G. T."

REUBEN GOLD THWAITES.

Madison, Wis.,
   February, 1895.

MEMOIR OF THE AUTHOR.

BY LYMAN COPELAND DRAPER.

In 1831, an interesting volume appeared from the press of Joseph Israel, of Clarksburg, in North Western Virginia, prepared by Alexander Scott Withers, on the border wars of the West. It was well received at the time of its publication, when works on that subject were few, and read with avidity by the surviving remnant of the participators in the times and events so graphically described, and by their worthy descendants.

Historians and antiquarians also received it cordially, universally according it high praise. Mann Butler, the faithful historian of Kentucky, declared that it was "a work to which the public was deeply indebted," composed, as it was, with "so much care and interest." The late Samuel G. Drake, the especial historian of the Red Man, pronounced it "a work written with candor and judgment." The late Thomas W. Field, the discriminating writer on *Indian Bibliography*, says: "Of this scarce book, very few copies are complete or in good condition. Having been issued in a remote corner of North-Western Virginia, and designed principally for a local circulation, almost every copy was read by a country fireside until scarcely legible. Most of the copies lack the table of contents. The author took much pains to be authentic, and his chronicles are considered by Western antiquarians, to form the best collection of frontier life and Indian warfare, that has been printed."

Of such a work, now difficult to procure at any price, a new edition is presented to the public. In 1845, the writer of this notice visited the Virginia Valley, collecting materials on the same general subject, going over much the same field of investigation, and quite naturally, at that early period, indentifying very large the sources of Mr. Withers's information, thus making it possible to reproduce his work with new lights and explanations, such as generally give pleasure and interest to the intelligent reader of border history.[1]

In 1829, a local antiquary, of Covington, a beautiful little village nestling in a high mountain valley near the head of James River, in Alleghany County, Virginia, gathered from the aged pioneers still lingering on the shores of time, the story of the primitive settlement and border wars of the Virginia Valley. Hugh Paul Taylor, for such was his name, was the precursor, in all that region, of the school of historic gleaners, and published in the nearest village paper, *The Fincastle Mirror*, some twenty miles away, a series of articles, over the signature of " Son of Cornstalk," extending over a period of some forty stirring years, from about 1740 to the close of the Revolutionary War. These articles formed at least the chief authority for several of the earlier chapters of Mr. Withers's work. Mr. Taylor had scarcely molded his materials into shape, and put them into print, when he was called hence at an early age, without having an opportunity to revise and publish the results of his labors under more favorable auspices.

Soon after Mr. Taylor's publication, Judge Edwin S. Duncan, of Peel Tree, in then Harrison, now Barbour County, West Virginia, a gentleman of education, and well fitted for such a work, residing in the heart of a region rife with the story of Indian wars and hair-breadth escapes, made a collection of materials, probably including Mr. Taylor's sketches, with a view to a similar work ; but his professional pursuits and judicial services interposed to preclude the faithful prosecution of the work, so he turned over to Mr. Withers his historic gatherings, with

---

[1] The venerable Mark L. Spotts, an intelligent and long-time resident of Lewisburg, West Virginia, writes, in December, 1890: " I had an old and particular friend, Mr. Thomas Matthews, of this place, who, many years ago, conceived the idea of preparing and publishing a revised edition of Withers's *Border Warfare*, and no doubt had collected many facts looking to such a publication ; but the old man's health gave way, he died, and his widow moved away, and what became of his notes, I can not say—perhaps destroyed."—L. C. D.

such suggestions, especially upon the Indian race, as by
his studies and reflections he was enabled to offer.

Other local gleaners in the field of Western history, particularly Noah Zane, of Wheeling, John Hacker, of the
Hacker's Creek settlement, and others, freely furnished
their notes and statements for the work. Mr. Withers,
under these favorable circumstances, became quite well
equipped with materials regarding especially the first settlement and Indian wars of the region now comprising
West Virginia; and, to a considerable extent, the region
of Staunton and farther southwest, of the French and Indian War period, together with Dunmore's War, and the
several campaigns from the western borders of Virginia
and Pennsylvania into the Ohio region, during the Revolutionary War.

Alexander Scott Withers, for his good services in the
field of Western history, well deserves to have his name
and memory perpetuated as a public benefactor. Descending, on his father's side, from English ancestry, he was the
fourth child of nine, in the family of Enoch K. and Jennet
Chinn Withers, who resided at a fine Virginia homestead,
called Green Meadows, half a dozen miles from Warrenton, Fauquier county, Virginia, where the subject of this
sketch was born on the 12th of October, 1792—on the
third centennial anniversary of the discovery of America
by Columbus. His mother was the daughter of Thomas
Chinn and Jennet Scott—the latter a native of Scotland,
and a first cousin of Sir Walter Scott.

Passing his early years in home and private schools,
he became from childhood a lover of books and knowledge. He read Virgil at the early age of ten; and, in
due time, entered Washington College. and thence entered the law department of the venerable institution of
William and Mary, where Jefferson, Monroe, Wythe, and
other Virginia notables, received their education.

Procuring a license to practice, he was admitted to
the bar in Warrenton, where for two or three years he
practiced his profession. His father dying in 1813, he
abandoned his law practice, which he did not like, because he could not overcome his diffidence in public

speaking; and, for quite a period, he had the management of his mother's plantation.

In August, 1815, he was united in marriage with Miss Melinda Fisher, a most estimable lady, a few months his junior; and about 1827, having a growing family, he looked to the Great West for his future home and field of labor, and moved to West Virginia, first locating temporarily in Bridgeport, in Harrison County, and subsequently settling near Clarksburg in the same county, where he devoted much time in collecting materials for and writing his *Chronicles of Border Warfare.*

The publisher, Joseph Israel, who took a deep interest in the work, as his "Advertisement" of it suggests, must have realized ample recompense for the work, as he had subscribers for the full edition issued; yet, from some cause, he failed pecuniarily, and Mr. Withers got nothing whatever for his diligence and labor in producing it, save two or three copies of the work itself. He used to say, that had he published the volume himself, he would have made it much more complete, and better in every way; for he was hampered, limited, and hurried—often correcting proof of the early, while writing the later chapters. Mr. Israel, the publisher, died several years ago.

After this worthy but unremunerative labor, Mr. Withers turned his attention to Missouri for a suitable home for his old age. He was disappointed in his visit to that new state, as the richer portions of the country, where he would have located, were more or less unhealthy. So he returned to West Virginia, and settled near Weston, a fine, healthful region of hills and valleys, where he engaged in agricultural pursuits, in which he always took a deep interest. He also served several years as a magistrate, the only public position he ever filled.

The death of his wife in September, 1853, broke sadly into his domestic enjoyments; his family were now scattered, and his home was henceforward made with his eldest daughter, Mrs. Jennet S. Tavenner, and her husband, Thomas Tavenner, who in 1861 removed to a home adjoining Parkersburg, in West Virginia. Here our author lived a retired, studious life, until his death, which occurred, after a few days' illness, January 23, 1865, in the seventy-third year of his age.

Mr. Withers had no talent for the acquisition of wealth; but he met with marked success in acquiring knowledge. He was an admirer of ancient literature, and to his last days read the Greek classics in the original. A rare scholar, a lover of books, his tastes were eminently domestic; he was, from his nature, much secluded from the busy world around him. Nearly six feet high, rather portly and dignified, as is shown by his portrait, taken when he was about sixty years of age—he was kind and obliging to all, and emphatically a true Virginia gentleman of the old school. His sympathies during the War of Secession, were strongly in favor of the Union cause, the happy termination of which he did not live to witness. His son, Henry W. Withers, served with credit during the war in the Union service in the Twelfth Virginia Regiment.

Mr. Withers was blessed with two sons and three daughters—one of the sons has passed away; the other, Major Henry W. Withers, resides in Troy, Gilmer county, West Virginia; Mrs. Tavenner still lives at Parkersburg; Mrs. Mary T. Owen, at Galveston, Texas, and Mrs. Elizabeth Ann Thornhill, in New Orleans.

CHRONICLES

OF

BORDER WARFARE,

OR

A HISTORY

OF THE

SETTLEMENT BY THE WHITES,

OF NORTH-WESTERN VIRGINIA:

AND

OF THE INDIAN WARS AND MASSACRES,

IN THAT SECTION OF THE STATE,

WITH

REFLECTIONS, ANECDOTES, &c.

BY ALEXANDER S. WITHERS.

CLARKSBURG, VA.

PUBLISHED BY JOSEPH ISRAEL,

1831

WESTERN DISTRICT OF VIRGINIA, *to wit:*

 Be it remembered, That on the twenty-sixth day of January, in the Fifty-fifth year of the Independence of the United States of America, JOSEPH ISRAEL, of the said District, hath deposited in this Office, the title of a Book, the right whereof he claims as Proprietor, in the words following, To wit:

"Chronicles of Border Warfare, or a history of the settlement, by the whites, of North-Western Virginia: and of the Indian wars and massacres, in that section of the State; with reflections, anecdotes, &c.—By ALEXANDER S. WITHERS, 1831," in conformity to the act of Congress of the United States, entitled "An act for the encouragement of learning, by securing the copies of maps, charts and books, to the Authors and Proprietors of such copies, during the times therein mentioned; and also to an act, entitled "An act for the encouragement of learning, by securing the copies of maps, charts and books, to the Authors and Proprietors of such copies, during the times therein mentioned, and extending the benefits thereof to the arts of Designing, Engraving and Etching historical and other prints."

JASPER YEATES DODDRIDGE,
Clerk of the Western District of Virginia.

(xiv)

ADVERTISEMENT.

The "Chronicles of Border Warfare" are now completed and presented to the public. Circumstances, over which the publisher had no control, have operated to delay their appearance beyond the anticipated period; and an apprehension that such might be the case, induced him, when issuing proposals for their publication, not positively to name a time at which the work would be completed and ready for delivery.

This delay, although unavoidable, has been the source of regret to the publisher, and has added considerably to the expenditure otherwise necessarily made, in attempting to rescue from oblivion the many interesting incidents, now, for the first time recorded. To preserve them from falling into the gulph of forgetfulness, was the chief motive which the publisher had in view; and should the profits of the work be sufficient to defray the expenses, actually incurred in its preparation and completion, he will be abundantly satisfied. That he will be thus far remunerated, is not for an instant doubted,—the subscription papers having attached to them, as many names as there are copies published.

In regard to the manner of its execution, it does not perhaps become him to speak. He was attentive to his duties, and watched narrowly the press; and if typographical errors are to be found, it must be attributed to the great difficulty of preventing them, even when the author is at hand to correct each proof sheet. They are however, certainly few, and such as would be likely to escape observation.

JOSEPH ISRAEL, Publisher.

CONTENTS.

CHAPTER I.

It is highly probable that the continent of America was known to the Ancient Carthaginians, and that it was the great island Atalantis, of which mention is made by Plato, who represents it as larger than Asia and Africa. The Carthaginians were a maritime people, and it is known that they extended their discoveries beyond the narrow sphere which had hitherto limited the enterprise of the mariner. And although Plato represents Atalantis as having been swallowed by an earthquake, and all knowledge of the new continent, if any such ever existed, was entirely lost, still it is by no means improbable, that it had been visited by some of the inhabitants of the old world, prior to its discovery by Columbus in 1492. The manner of this discovery is well known, as is also the fact that Americo Vespucci, a Florentine, under the authority of Emmanuel king of Portugal, in sailing as far as Brazil discovered the main land and gave name to America.

These discoveries gave additional excitement to the adventurous spirit which distinguished those times, and the flattering reports made of the country which they had visited, inspired the different nations of Europe, with the desire of reaping the rich harvest, which the enlightened and enterprising mind of Columbus, had unfolded to their view. Accordingly, as early as March 1496, (less than two years after the discovery by Columbus) a commission was granted by Henry VII king of England, to John Cabot and his three sons, empowering them to sail under the English banner in quest of new discoveries, and in the event of their success to take possession, in the name of

(1)

the king of England, of the countries thus discovered and not inhabited by *Christian people.*

The expedition contemplated in this commission was never carried into effect. But in May 1498 Cabot with his son Sebastian, embarked on a voyage to attain the desired object, and succeeded in his design so far as to effect a discovery of [4] North America, and although he sailed along the coast from Labrador to Virginia, yet it does not now appear that he made any attempt either at settlement or conquest.

This is said to have been the first discovery ever made of that portion of our continent which extends from the Gulph of Mexico to the North pole; and to this discovery the English trace their title to that part of it, subsequently reduced into possession by them.[1]

As many of the evils endured by the inhabitants of the western part of Virginia, resulted from a contest between England and France, as to the validity of their respective claims to portions of the newly discovered country, it may not be amiss to take a general view of the discoveries and settlements effected by each of those powers.

After the expedition of Cabot, no attempt on the part of England, to acquire territory in America, seems to have been made until the year 1558. In this year letters patent were issued by Queen Elizabeth, empowering Sir Humphrey Gilbert to " discover and take possession of such remote, heathen, and barbarous lands, as were not actually possessed by any *christian prince or people.*" Two expeditions, conducted by this gentleman terminated unfavorably. Nothing was done by him towards the accomplishment of the objects in view, more than the taking possession of the island of New Foundland in the name of the English Queen.

In 1584 a similar patent was granted to Sir Walter

---

[1] The author errs somewhat in his review of the voyages of the Cabots. In 1497, John set out to reach Asia by way of the north-west, and sighted Cape Breton, for which the generous king gave him £10 and blessed him with " great honours." In 1498, Sebastian's voyage was intended to supplement his father's; his exploration of the coast extended down to the vicinity of Chesapeake Bay.—R. G. T.

Raleigh, under whose auspices was discovered the country south of Virginia. In April of that year he dispatched two vessels under the command of Amidas and Barlow, for the purpose of visiting, and obtaining such a knowledge of the country which he proposed to colonize, as would facilitate the attainment of his object. In their voyage they approached the North American continent towards the Gulph of Florida, and sailing northwardly touched at an island situate on the inlet into Pamlico sound, in the state of North Carolina. To this island they gave the name of Wocoken, and proceeding from thence reached Roanoke near the mouth of Albemarle sound. After having remained here some weeks, and obtained from the natives the best information which they could impart concerning the country, Amidas and Barlow returned to England.

In the succeeding year Sir Walter had fitted out a squadron of seven ships, the command of which he gave to Sir Richard [5] Grenville. On board of this squadron were passengers, arms, ammunition and provisions for a settlement. He touched at the islands of Wocoken and Roanoke, which had been visited by Amidas and Barlow, and leaving a colony of one hundred and eight persons in the island of Roanoke, he returned to England. These colonists, after having remained about twelve months and explored the adjacent country, became so discouraged and exhausted by fatigue and famine, that they abandoned the country. Sir Richard Grenville returning shortly afterwards to America, and not being able to find them, and at a loss to conjecture their fate, left in the island another small party of settlers and again set sail for England.

The flattering description which was given of the country, by those who had visited it, so pleased Queen Elizabeth, that she gave to it the name of Virginia, as a memorial that it had been discovered in the reign of a Virgin Queen.

Other inefficient attempts were afterwards made to colonize North America during the reign of Elizabeth, but it was not 'till the year 1607, that a colony was permanently planted there. In December of the preceding year a small vessel and two barks, under the command of captain Newport, and having on board one hundred and five men, destined to remain, left England. In April they were driven by a storm into Chesapeak bay, and after a fruitless attempt to land at Cape Henry, sailed up the Powhatan (since called James) River, and on the 13th of May 1607, debarked on the north side of the river at a place to which they gave the name of Jamestown. From this period the country continued in the occupancy of the whites, and remained subject to the crown of Great Britain until the war of the revolution.

A new charter which was issued in 1609 grants to "the treasurer and company of the adventurers, of the city of London for the first colony of Virginia, in absolute property the lands extending from Point Comfort along the sea coast two hundred miles to the northward, and from the same point, along the sea coast two hundred miles to the southward, and up into the land throughout from sea to sea, west and north-west; and also all islands lying within one hundred miles of the coast of both seas of the precinct aforesaid." Conflicting charters, granted to other corporations, afterwards narrowed her limits; that she has been since reduced to her present comparatively small extent of territory, is attributable exclusively [6] to the almost suicidal liberality of Virginia herself.

On the part of France, voyages for the discovery and colonization of North America were nearly contemporaneous with those made by England for like objects. As early as the year 1540, a commission was issued by Francis 1st for the establishment of Canada.[1] In 1608, a French fleet, under the command of Admiral Champlaine, arrived

---

[1] This refers to the explorations of Jacques Cartier. But as early as 1534 Cartier sailed up the estuary of the St. Lawrence "until land could be seen on either side;" the following year he ascended the river as far as the La Chine rapids, and wintered upon the island mountain there which he named Mont Real. It was in 1541 that he made his third voyage, and built a fort at Quebec. The author's reference, a few lines below, to a "Spanish sailor" in the St. Lawrence, is the result of confusion over Cartier's first voyages; Cortereal was at Newfoundland for the Portuguese in 1500; and Gomez for Spain in 1525.—R. G. T.

in the St. Lawrence and founded the city of Quebec. So
successful were her attempts to colonize that province,
that, notwithstanding its proximity to the English colonies, and the fact that a Spanish sailor had previously entered the St. Lawrence and established a port at the mouth
of Grand river—neither of those powers seriously contested the right of France to its possession.—Yet it was
frequently the theatre of war; and as early as 1629 was
subdued by England. By the treaty of St. Germains in
1632 it was restored to France, as was also the then province of Acadie, now known as Nova Scotia. There is no
doubt but that this latter province was, by priority of
settlement, the property of France, but its principal town
having been repeatedly reduced to possession by the English, it was ceded to them by the treaty of Utrecht in
1713.

To the country bordering the Mississippi river, and its
tributary streams, a claim was made by England, France
and Spain. The claim of England (based on the discovery
by the Cabots of the eastern shore of the United States,)
included all the country between the parallels of latitude
within which the Atlantic shore was explored, extending
westwardly to the Pacific ocean—a zone athwart the continent between the thirtieth and forty-eighth degrees of
North latitude.

From the facility with which the French gained the
good will and friendly alliance of the Natives in Canada,
by intermarrying with, and assimilating themselves to the
habits and inclinations of, these children of the forest, an
intimacy arose which induced the Indians to impart freely
to the French their knowledge of the interior country.
Among other things information was communicated to
them, of the fact that farther on there was a river of great
size and immense length, which pursued a course opposite
to that of the St. Lawrence, and emptied itself into an
unknown sea. It was conjectured that it must necessarily
flow either into the Gulph of Mexico, or the South Sea;
and in 1673 Marquette and Joliet, French missionaries,
together with five other men, commenced a journey

[7] from Quebec to ascertain the fact and examine the country bordering its shores.

From lake Michigan they proceeded up the Fox river nearly to its source; thence to Ouisconsin; down it to the Mississippi, in which river they sailed as far as to about the thirty-third degree of north latitude. From this point they returned through the Illinois country to Canada.

At the period of this discovery M. de La Salle, a Frenchman of enterprise, courage and talents but without fortune, was commandant of fort Frontignac. Pleased with the description given by Marquette and Joliet, of the country which they had visited, he formed the determination of examining it himself, and for this purpose left Canada in the close of the summer of 1679, in company with father Louis Hennepin and some others.[1] On the Illinois he erected fort Crevecœur, where he remained during the winter, and instructing father Hennepin, in his absence to ascend the Mississippi to its sources, returned to Canada. M. de La Salle subsequently visited this country, and establishing the villages of Cahokia and Kaskaskia, left them under the command of M. de Tonti, and going back to Canada, proceeded from thence to France to procure the co-operation of the Ministry in effecting a settlement of the valley of the Mississippi. He succeeded in impressing on the minds of the French Ministry, the great benefits which would result from its colonization, and was the first to suggest the propriety of connecting the settlements on the Mississippi with those in Canada by a cordon of forts; a measure which was subsequently attempted to be carried into effect.

With the aid afforded him by the government of France, he was enabled to prepare an expedition to accomplish his object, and sailing in 1684 for the mouth of the Mississippi, steered too far westward and landed in the province of Texas, and on the banks of the river Guadaloupe. Every exertion which a brave and prudent man

[1] The author wrote at too early a date to have the benefit of Parkman's researches. La Salle had probably discovered the Ohio River four years before the voyage of Joliet and Marquette.--R. G. T.

could make to effect the security of his little colony, and conduct them to the settlement in Illinois, was fruitlessly made by him. In reward for all his toil and care he was basely assassinated; the remnant of the party whom he was conducting through the wilderness, finally reached the Arkansas, where was a settlement of French emigrants from Canada. The colonists left by him at the bay of St. Bernard were mostly murdered by the natives, the remainder were carried away by the Spaniards in 1689.

[8]   Other attempts made by the French to colonize the Mississippi near the Gulph of Mexico, were for some time unavailing. In an expedition for that purpose, conducted by M. Ibberville, a suit of armor on which was inscribed Ferdinand de Soto, was found in the possession of some Indians. In the year 1717 the spot, on which New Orleans now stands, was selected as the centre of the settlements, then first made in Louisiana, and the country continued in the possession of France until 1763. By the treaty of Paris in that year, she ceded to Great Britain, together with Canada her possessions east of the Mississippi, excepting only the island of New Orleans—this and her territory on the west bank of that river were transferred to Spain.

The title of Spain to the valley of the Mississippi, if made to depend on priority of discovery, would perhaps, to say the least, be as good as that of either of the other powers. Ferdinand de Soto, governor of Cuba, was most probably the first white man who saw that majestic stream.

The Spaniards had early visited and given name to Florida. In 1528 Pamphilo de Narvaez obtained a grant of it, and fitting out an armament, proceeded with four or five hundred men to explore and settle the country. He marched to the Indian village of Appalachas, when he was attacked and defeated by the natives. The most of those who escaped death from the hands of the savages, perished in a storm, by which they were overtaken on their voyage home. Narvaez himself perished in the wreck, and was succeeded in his attempt at colonization by de Soto.

Ferdinand de Soto, then governor of Cuba, was a man of chivalrous and enterprising spirit, and of cool, deliberate courage. In his expedition to Florida, although attacked by the Indians, immediately on his landing, yet, rather seeking than shunning danger, he penetrated the interior, and crossing the Mississippi, sickened and died on Red river. So frequent and signal had been the victories which he had obtained over the Indians, that his name alone had become an object of terror to them ; and his followers, at once to preserve his remains from violation, and prevent the natives from acquiring a knowledge of his death, enclosed his body in a hollow tree, sunk it in the Red river and returned to Florida.

Thus, it is said, were different parts of this continent discovered ; and by virtue of the settlements thus effected, by [9] those three great powers of Europe, the greater portion of it was claimed as belonging to them respectively, in utter disregard of the rights of the Aborigines. And while the historian records the colonization of America as an event tending to meliorate the condition of Europe, and as having extended the blessings of civil and religious liberty, humanity must drop the tear of regret, that it has likewise forced the natives of the new, and the inhabitants of a portion of the old world, to drink so deeply from the cup of bitterness.

The cruelties which have been exercised on the Aborigines of America, the wrong and outrage heaped on them from the days of Montezuma and Guatimozin, to the present period, while they excite sympathy for their sufferings, should extenuate, if not justify the bloody deeds, which revenge prompted the untutored savages to commit. Driven as they were from the lands of which they were the rightful proprietors—Yielding to encroachment after encroachment 'till forced to apprehend their utter annihilation—Witnessing the destruction of their villages, the prostration of their towns and the sacking of cities adorned with spendid magnificence, who can feel surprised at any attempt which they might make to rid the country of its invaders. Who, but must applaud the spirit which prompted them, when they beheld their prince a captive, the blood of their nobles staining the earth with its crimson dye, and the Gods of their adoration scoffed and derided, to aim at the destruction of their oppressors.—When Mexico, "with her tiara of proud towers," became the theatre in which foreigners were to revel in rapine and in murder, who can be astonished that the valley of Otumba resounded with the cry of "Victory or Death?" And yet, resistance on their part, served but as a pretext for a war of extermination; waged too, with a ferocity, from the recollection of which the human mind involuntarily revolts, and with a success which has forever blotted from the book of national existence, once powerful and happy tribes.

But they did not suffer alone. As if to fill the cup of oppression to the brim, another portion of the human family were reduced to abject bondage, and made the unwilling cultivators of those lands, of which the Indians had been dispossessed. Soon after the settlement of North America was commenced, the negroes of Africa became an article of commerce, and from subsequent importations and natural [10] increase have become so numerous as to excite the liveliest apprehensions in the bosom of every friend to this country. Heretofore they have had considerable influence on the affairs of our government; and recently the diversity of interest, occasioned in Virginia, by the possession of large numbers of them in the country east of the blue ridge of mountains, seemed for a while to threaten the integrity of the state.—Happily this is now passing away, but how far they may effect the future destines of America, the most prophetic ken cannot foresee. Yet, although the philanthopist must weep over their unfortunate situation, and the patriot shudder in anticipation of a calamity which it may defy human wisdom to avert; still it would be unfair to charge the existence of slavery among us to the policy of the United States, or to brand their present owners as the instruments of an evil which they cannot remove. And while others boast that they are free from this dark spot, let them remember, that but for them our national escutcheon might have been as pure and unsullied as their own.[1]

---

[1] It is said, that Georgia, at an early period of her colonial exist-

We are indebted to the Dutch for their introduction into Virginia, and to the ships of other than slave holding communities, for their subsequent unhallowed transportation to our shores. Yet those who were mainly instrumental in forging the chains of bondage, have since rendered the condition of the negro slave more intolerable by fomenting discontent among them, and by "scattering fire brands and torches," which are often not to be extinguished but in blood.

Nothwithstanding those two great evils which have resulted from the discovery and colonization of America, yet to these the world is indebted for the enjoyment of many and great blessings. They enlarged the theatre of agricultural enterprise, and thus added to the facilities of procuring the necessaries of life. They encouraged the industry of Europeans, by a dependence on them for almost every species of manufacture, and thus added considerably to their population, wealth and happiness; while the extensive tracts of fertile land, covering the face of this country and inviting to its bosom the enterprising [11] foreigner, has removed a far off any apprehension of the ill effects arising from a too dense population.

In a moral and political point of view much good has likewise resulted from the settlement of America. Religion, freed from the fetters which enthralled her in Europe, has shed her benign influence on every portion of our country. Divorced from an adulterous alliance with state, she has here stalked forth in the simplicity of her founder; and with "healing on her wings, spread the glad tidings of salvation to all men." It is true that religious intolerance and blind bigotry, for some time clouded our horizon, but they were soon dissipated; and when the sun arose which ushered in the dawn of our national existence scarce a speck could be seen to dim its lustre. Here too was

---

ence, endeavored by legislative enactment to prevent the importation of slaves into her territory, but that the King of England invariably negatived those laws, and ultimately Oglethorpe was dismissed from office, for persevering in the endeavor to accomplish so desirable an object. It is an historical fact that slaves were not permitted to be taken into Georgia, for some time after a colony was established there.

reared the standard of civil liberty, and an example set, which may teach to the nations of the old world, that as people are really the source of power, government should be confided to them. Already have the beneficial effects of this example been manifested, and the present condition of Europe clearly shows, that the lamp of liberty, which was lighted here, has burned with a brilliancy so steady as to have reflected its light across the Atlantic. Whether it will be there permitted to shine, is somewhat problematical. But should a "holy alliance of legitimates" extinguish it, it will be but for a season. Kings, Emperors and Priests cannot succeed much longer in staying the march of freedom. The people are sensibly alive to the oppression of their rulers—they have groaned beneath the burden 'till it has become too intolerable to be borne; and they are now speaking in a voice which will make tyrants tremble on their throne.

[12] INTRODUCTION.

Chapter II.

When America was first visited by Europeans, it was found that its inhabitants were altogether ignorant of the country from which their ancestors had migrated, and of the period at which they had been transplanted to the new world. And although there were among them traditions seeming to cast a light upon these subjects, yet when thoroughly investigated, they tended rather to bewilder than lead to any certain conclusion. The origin of the natives has ever since been a matter of curious speculation with the learned; conjecture has succeeded conjecture, hypothesis has yielded to hypothesis, as wave recedes before wave, still it remains involved in a labyrinth of inexplicable difficulties, from which the most ingenious mind will perhaps never be able to free it.

In this respect the situation of the aborigines of America does not differ from that of the inhabitants of other portions of the globe. An impenetrable cloud hangs over the early history of other nations, and defies the researches of the learned in any attempt to trace them to their origin. The attempt has nevertheless been repeatedly made; and philosophers, arguing from a real or supposed conformity of one people to another, have vainly imagined that they had attained to certainty on these subjects. And while one has in this manner, undertaken to prove China to have been an Egyptian colony, another, pursuing the same course of reasoning, has, by way of ridicule, shewn how easily a learned man of Tobolski or Pekin might as satisfactorily prove France to have been a Trojan, a Greek or even an Arabian colony; thus making manifest the utter futility of endeavoring to arrive at certainty in this way.[1]

[1] "If a learned man of Tobolski or Pekin were to read some of our books, he might in this way demonstrate, that the French are descended

[13] Nor is this to be at all wondered at, when we reflect on the barbarous state of those nations in their infancy, the imperfection of traditionary accounts of what had transpired centuries before, and in many instances the entire absence of a written language, by which, either to perpetuate events, or enable the philosopher by analogy of language to ascertain their affinity with other nations. Conjectural then as must be every disquisition as to the manner in which this continent was first peopled, still however, as many men eminent for learning and piety have devoted much labor and time to the investigation of the subject, it may afford satisfaction to the curious to see some of those speculations recorded. Discordant as they are in many respects, there is nevertheless one fact as to the truth of which they are nearly all agreed; Mr. Jefferson is perhaps the only one, of those who have written on the subject, who seems to discredit the assertion that

---

from the Trojans. The most ancient writings, he might say, and those in most esteem in France, are romances: these were written in a pure language, derived from the ancient Romans, who were famous for never advancing a falsehood. Now upwards of twenty of these authentic books, affirm that Francis, the founder of the monarchy of the Franks, was son to Hector. The name of Hector has ever since been preserved by this nation; and even in the present century one of the greatest generals was called Hector de Villars.

"The neighboring nations (he would continue,) are so unanimous in acknowledging this truth, that Ariosto, one of the most learned of the Italians, owns in his Orlando, that Charlemagne's knights fought for Hector's helmet. Lastly, there is one proof which admits of no reply; namely, that the ancient Franks to perpetuate the memory of the Trojans, their ancestors, built a new city called Troye, in the province of Champagne; and these modern Trojans have always retained so strong an aversion to their enemies, the Greeks, that there is not at present four persons in the whole province of Champagne, who will learn their language; nay, they would never admit any Jesuits among them; probably because they had heard it said, that some of that body used formerly to explain Homer in their public schools."

Proceeding in this manner, M. de Voltaire shows how easily this hypothesis might be overturned; and while one might thus demonstrate that the Parisians are descended from the Greeks, other profound antiquarians might in like manner prove them to be of Egyptian, or even of Arabian extraction; and although the learned world might much puzzle themselves to decide the question, yet would it remain undecided and in uncertainty.—*Preface to the Life of Peter the Great.*

America was peopled by emigrants from the old world. How well the conjecture, that the eastern inhabitants of Asia were descendants of the Indians of America can be supported by any knowledge which is possessed of the different languages spoken by the Aborigines, will be for others to determine. "Neque confirmare argumentis, neque refellere, in animo est; ex ingenio suo, quisque demat vel addat fidem."

Among those who have given to the world their opinions on the origin of the natives of America, is Father Jos. Acosta, a Jesuit who was for some time engaged as a missionary among them. From the fact that no ancient author has made mention of the [14] compass, he discredits the supposition that the first inhabitants of this country found their way here by sea. His conclusion is that they must have found a passage by the North of Asia and Europe which he supposes to join each other; or by those regions which lie southward of the straits of Magellan.

Gregorio Garcia, who was likewise a missionary among the Mexicans and Peruvians, from the traditions of those nations, and from the variety of characters, customs, languages and religion, observable in the new world, has formed the opinion that it was peopled by several different nations.

John de Laet, a Flemish writer, maintains that America received its first inhabitants from Scythia or Tartary, and soon after the dispersion of Noah's grand-sons. The resemblance of the northern Indians, in feature, complexion and manner of living, to the Scythians, Tartars, and Samojedes, being greater than to any other nations.

Emanuel de Moraez, in his history of Brazil, says that this continent was wholly peopled by the Carthagirians and Israelites. In confirmation of this opinion, he mentions the discoveries which the Carthaginians are known to have made beyond the coast of Africa. The progress of these discoveries being stopped by the Senate of Carthage, those who happened to be in the newly discovered countries, cut off from all communication with their countrymen, and being destitute of many of the necessaries of life, easily fell into a state of barbarism.

George de Huron, a Dutch writer on this subject, considering the short space of time which elapsed between the creation of the world and the deluge, maintains that America could not have been peopled before the flood. He likewise supposes that its first inhabitants were located in the north; and that the primitive colonies extended themselves over the whole extent of the continent, by means of the Isthmus of Panama. It is his opinion that the first founders of these Indian colonies were Scythians; that the Phœnicians and Carthaginians subsequently got to America across the Atlantic, and the Chinese across the Pacific ocean, and that other nations might have landed there by one of these means, or been thrown on the coast by tempest: since through the whole extent of the continent, both in its northern and southern parts there are evident marks of a mixture of the northern nations with those who have come from other places.

[15] He also supposes that another migration of the Phœnicians took place during a three years voyage made by the Tyrian fleet in the service of king Solomon. He asserts, on the authority of Josephus, that the port at which this embarkation was made, lay in the Mediterranean. The fleet, he adds, went in quest of Elephants' teeth and Peacocks, to the western coast of Africa, which is Tarshish, then for gold to Ophir, which is Haite or the Island of Hispaniola. In the latter opinion he is supported by Columbus, who, when he discovered that Island, thought he could trace the furnaces in which the gold had been refined.

Monsieur Charlevoix, who travelled through North America, is of opinion that it received its first inhabitants from Tartary and Hyrcania. In support of this impression he says that some of the animals which are to be found here, must have come from those countries: a fact which would go to prove that the two hemispheres join to the northward of Asia. And in order to strengthen this conjecture, he relates the following story, which he says was told to him by Father Grollon, a French Jesuit, as matter of fact.

Father Grollon said, that after having labored some

time in the missions of New France, he passed over to China.   One day as he was travelling in Tartary he met a Huron woman whom he had known in Canada.   He asked her by what adventure she had been carried into a country so very remote from her own; she replied that having been taken in war, she was conducted from nation to nation, until she reached the place where she then was.

Monsieur Charlevoix narrates another circumstance of a similar kind.   He says that he had been assured, another Jesuit had met with a Floridian woman in China.   She also had been made captive by certain Indians, who gave her to those of a more distant country, and by these again she was given to those of another nation, 'till having been successively passed from country to country, and after having travelled through regions extremely cold, she at length found herself in Tartary.   Here she had married a Tartar, who had attended the conquerors in China, and with whom she then was.

Arguing from these facts and from the similarity of several kinds of wild beasts which are found in America, with those of Hyrcania and Tartary, he arrives at what he deems, a [16] rational conclusion, that more than one nation in America had Scythian or Tartarian extraction.

Charlevoix possessed a good opportunity of becoming acquainted with the character and habits of the American Indians.   His theory however has been controverted by some, possessing equal advantages of observation.   Mr. Adair, an intelligent gentleman who resided among the nations during the space of forty years, and who became well acquainted with their manners, customs, religion, traditions and language, has given to them a very different origin.   But perfect soever as may have been his knowledge of their manners, customs, religion and traditions, yet it must be admitted that any inquiry into these, with a view to discover their origin, would most probably prove fallacious.   A knowledge of the primitive language, alone can cast much light on the subject.   Whether this knowledge can ever be attained, is, to say the least, very questionable—Being an unwritten language, and subject to change for so many centuries, it can scarcely be supposed now to bear much, if any affinity, to what it was in its purity.

Mr. Adair says, that from the most exact observation he could make during the long time which he traded among the Indians, he was forced to believe them lineally descended from the Israelites, either when they were a maritime power, or soon after the general captivity; most probably the latter.

He thinks that had the nine tribes and a half, which were carried off by Shalmanezer, king of Assyria, and which settled in Media, remained there long, they would, by intermarrying with the nations of that country, from a natural fickleness and proneness to idolatry, and from the force of example, have adopted and bowed before the Gods of the Medes and Assyrians; and have carried them along with them. But he affirms that there is not the least trace of this idolatry to be discovered among the Indians: and hence he argues that those of the ten tribes who were the forefathers of the natives, soon advanced eastward from Assyria and reached their settlements in the new continent, before the destruction of the first Temple.

In support of the position that the American Indians are thus descended, Mr. Adair adduces among others the following arguments:

1st, *Their division into tribes.*

"As each nation has its particular symbol, so each tribe has [17] the badge from which it is denominated. The Sachem is a necessary party in conveyances and treaties, to which he affixes the mark of his tribe. If we go from nation to nation among them, we shall not find one, who does not distinguish himself by his respective family. The genealogical names which they assume, are derived either from the names of those animals whereof the cherubim is said in revelation to be compounded; or from such creatures as are most similar to them. The Indians bear no religious respect to the animals from which they derive their names; on the contrary they kill them whenever an opportunity serves.

"When we consider that these savages have been upwards of twenty centuries without the aid of letters to

2

carry down their traditions, it can not be reasonably expected, that they should still retain the identical names of their primogenial tribes: their main customs corresponding with those of the Israelites, sufficiently clear the subject. Moreover they call some of their tribes by the names of the cherubinical figures, which were carried on the four principal standards of Israel."

2nd, *Their worship of Jehovah.*

" By a strict, permanent, divine precept, the Hebrew nation was ordered to worship at Jerusalem, Jehovah the true and living God, who by the Indians is styled ' *Yohewah.*' The seventy-two interpreters have translated this word so as to signify, *Sir, Lord, Master,* applying to mere earthly potentates, without the least signification or relation to that great and awful name, which describes the divine presence."

3rd, *Their notions of a theocracy.*

"Agreeably to the theocracy or divine government of Israel, the Indians think the deity to be the immediate head of the state. All the nations of Indians have a great deal of religious pride, and an inexpressible contempt for the white people. In their war orations they used to call us *the accursed people,* but flatter themselves with the name of the *beloved people,* because their supposed ancestors were, as they affirm, under the immediate government of the Deity, who was present with them in a peculiar manner, and directed them by Prophets, while the rest of the world were aliens to the covenant.'[1] When the old Archi-

---

[1] In a small work entitled "Ancient History of the Six Nations," written by David Cusick, an educated Indian of the Tuscarora village, frequent mention is made of the actual presence among them, of Tarenyawagua, or Holder of the Heavens, who guided and directed them when present, and left rules for their government, during his absence. Several miracles performed by him are particularly mentioned. It likewise speaks of the occasional visits of Angels or 'agents of the Superior power' as they are called by Cusick; and tells of a visitor who came among the Tuscaroras long anterior to the discovery of America by Columbus. "He appeared to be a very old man, taught them many things, and informed them that the people beyond the great water had killed their Maker, but that he rose again. The old man died among them and they buried him—soon after some person went to the grave and found that he had risen; he was never heard of afterwards."

magus, or any of their Magi, is [18] persuading the people at
their religious solemnities, to a strict observance of the old
beloved or divine speech, he always calls them the *beloved or
holy people,* agreeably to the Hebrew epithet, *Ammi,* (my
people) during the theocracy of Israel. It is this opinion,
that God has chosen them out of the rest of mankind, as
his peculiar people, which inspires the white Jew, and the
red American, with that steady hatred against all the
world except themselves, and renders them hated and de-
spised by all."

5th, *Their language and dialects.*

"The Indian language and dialects appear to have the
very idiom and genius of the Hebrew. Their words and
sentences are expressive, concise, emphatical, sonorous
and bold; and often both the letters and signification are
synonymous with the Hebrew language." Of these Mr.
Adair cites a number of examples.

6th, *Their manner of counting time.*

"The Indians count time after the manner of the Hebrews. They divide the year into spring, summer, autumn
and winter. They number their year from any of these
four periods, for they have no name for a year; and they
subdivide these and count the year by lunar months, like
the Israelites who counted time by moons, as their name
sufficiently testifies.

"The number and regular periods of the religious feasts
among the Indians, is a good historical proof that they
counted time by and observed a weekly Sabbath, long
after their arrival in America. They began the year at
the appearance of the first new moon of the vernal equi-
nox, according to the ecclesiastical year of Moses. 'Till
the seventy years captivity [19] commenced, the Israelites
had only numeral names for their months, except Abib
and Ethanim; the former signifying a *green ear of corn,*
the latter *robust or valiant;* by the first name the Indians
as an explicative, term their passover, which the trading
people call *the green corn dance.*"

7th, *Their prophets or high priests.*

"In conformity to, or after the manner of the Jews, the
Indians have their prophets, high priests, and others of a

religious order.   As the Jews have a Sanctum Sanctorum,
so have all the Indian nations. There they deposit their consecrated vessels—none of the laity daring to approach that
sacred place.   The Indian tradition says, that their forefathers were possessed of an extraordinary divine spirit by
which they foretold future events; and that this was transmitted to their offspring, provided they obeyed the sacred
laws annexed to it.[1]   [20] *Ishtoallo* is the name of all their

---

[1] In confirmation of this tradition among the Indians, the following
somewhat singular circumstance related by Mr. Carver, may with propriety be adduced:

While at Grand Portage, from the number of those who were
there and the fact that the traders did not arrive as soon as was expected, there was a great scarcity of provisions, and much consequent
anxiety as to the period of their arrival. One day, Mr. Carver says,
that while expressing their wishes for the event, and looking anxiously
to ascertain if they could be seen on the Lake, the chief Priest of the
Kilistines told them that he would endeavor in a conference with the
GREAT SPIRIT, to learn at what time the traders would arrive: and the
following evening was fixed upon for the spiritual conference.

When every preparation had been made, the king conducted Mr.
Carver to a spacious tent, the covering of which was so drawn up as to
render visible to those without, every thing which passed within. Mr.
Carver being seated beside the king within the tent, observed in the
centre a place of an oblong shape, composed of stakes stuck at intervals in
the ground, forming something like a coffin, and large enough to contain
the body of a man. The sticks were far enough from each other to admit a distinct view by the spectators, of what ever passed within them;
while the tent was perfectly illuminated.

When the Priest entered, a large Elk-skin being spread on the
ground, he divested himself of all his clothing, except that around his
middle, and laying down on the skin enveloped himself (save only his
head) in it. The skin was then bound round with about forty yards
of cord, and in that situation he was placed within the ballustrade of
sticks.

In a few seconds he was heard to mutter, but his voice, gradually
assuming a higher tone, was at length extended to its utmost pitch,
and sometimes praying, he worked himself into such an agitation as
to produce a foaming at the mouth. To this succeeded a speechless
state of exhaustion, of short duration; when suddenly springing on
his feet, and shaking off the skin, as easily as if the bands with
which it had been lashed around him, were burned asunder, he addressed the company in a firm and audible voice: "My Brothers,
said he, the Great Spirit has deigned to hold a talk with his servant.
He has not indeed told me when the traders will be here; but to-
morrow when the sun reaches the highest point in the heavens, a canoe

priestly order and their pontifical office descends by inheritance to the eldest. There are traces of agreement, though chiefly lost, in their pontifical dress. Before the Indian Archimagus officiates in making the supposed holy fire for the yearly atonement of sin, the *Sagan* clothes him with a white ephod, which is a waistcoat without sleeves. In resemblance of the Urim and Thummim the American Archimagus wears a breastplate made of a white conch-shell, with two holes bored in the middle of it, through which he puts the ends of an otter-skin strap; and fastens a buck-horn white button to the outside of each; as if in imitation of the precious stones of the Urim."

In remarking upon this statement of Mr. Adair, Faber, a learned divine of the church of England, has said, that Ishtoallo (the name according to Adair of the Indian priests) is most probably a corruption of *Ish-da-Eloah,* a man of God, (the term used by the Shunemitish woman in speaking of Elisha;) and that *Sagan* is the very name by which the Hebrews called the deputy of the High Priest, who supplied his office and who performed the functions of it in the absence of the high priest, or when any accident had disabled him from officiating in person.

8th, Their festivals, fasts and religious rites.

" The ceremonies of the Indians in their religious worship, [21] are more after the Mosaic institution, than of Pagan imitation. This could not be the fact if a majority of the old nations were of heathenish descent. They are utter strangers to all the gestures practiced by Pagans in their religious rites. They have likewise an appellative, which with them is the mysterious, essential name of God; the *tetragrammaton,* which they never use in common

---

will arrive, the people in that canoe will inform us when the traders will arrive."

Mr. Carver adds that on the next day at noon a canoe was descried on the lake at the distance of about three miles,—completely verifying the prediction of the High Priest, in point of time. From the people on board this canoe they learned that the traders would be at the portage on the second day thereafter, at which time they actually did arrive.

speech. They are very particular of the time and place, when and where they mention it, and this is always done in a very solemn manner. It is known that the Jews had so great and sacred regard for the four lettered, divine name, as scarcely ever to mention it, except when the High Priest went into the sanctuary for the expiation of sins."

Mr. Adair likewise says that the American Indians, like the Hebrews, have an ark in which are kept various holy vessels, and which is never suffered to rest on the bare ground. "On hilly ground, where stones are plenty, they always place it on them, but on level land it is made to rest on short legs. They have also a faith, in the power and holiness of their ark, as strong as the Israelites had in theirs. It is too sacred and dangerous to be touched by any one, except the chieftain and his waiter. The leader virtually acts the part of a priest of war protempore, in imitation of the Israelites fighting under the divine military banner."

Among their other religious rites the Indians, according to Adair, cut out the sinewy part of the thigh; in commemoration, as he says, of the Angel wrestling with Jacob.

12th, Their abstinence from unclean things.

" Eagles of every kind are esteemed by the Indians to be unclean food; as also ravens, crows, bats, buzzards and every species of owl. They believe that swallowing gnats, flies and the like, always breed sickness. To this that divine sarcasm alludes 'swallowing a camel and straining at a gnat.'" Their purifications for their Priests, and for having touched a dead body or other unclean thing, according to Mr. Adair, are quite Levitical. He acknowledges however, that they have no traces of circumcision; but he supposes that they lost this rite in their wanderings, as it ceased among the Hebrews, during the forty years in the wilderness.

15th, Their cities of refuge.

" The Israelites had cities of refuge for those who killed persons unawares. According to the same particular divine [22] law of mercy, each of the Indian nations has a house or town of refuge, which is a sure asylum to protect a man-slayer, or the unfortunate captive, if they can but once enter into it. In almost every nation they have peaceable towns, called ancient holy, or white towns. These seem to have been towns of refuge; for it is not in the memory of man, that ever human blood was shed in them, although they often force persons from thence and put them to death elsewhere."

16th, *Their purifications and ceremonies preparatory.*

" Before the Indians go to war they have many preparatory ceremonies of purification and fasting like what is recorded of the Israelites."

21st, *Their raising seed to a deceased brother.*

" The surviving brother, by the Mosaic law, was to raise seed to a deceased brother, who left a widow childless. The Indian custom looks the very same way; but in this as in their law of blood, the eldest brother can redeem."

With these and many arguments of a like kind, has Mr. Adair endeavored to support the conjecture, that the American Indians are lineally descended from the Israelites; and gravely asks of those who may dissent from his opinion of their origin and descent, to inform him how they came here, and by what means they formed the long chain of rites and customs so similar to those of the Hebrews, and dissimilar to the rites and customs of the pagan world.

Major Carver, a provincial officer who sojourned some time with the Indians and visited twelve different nations of them, instead of observing the great similarity, mentioned by Adair as existing between the natives and Hebrews, thought he could trace features of resemblance between them and the Chinese and Tartars; and has undertaken to shew how they might have got here. He says,

"Although it is not ascertained certainly, that the continents of Asia and America join each other, yet it is proven that the sea which is supposed to divide them, is full of islands the distance from which to either continent, is comparatively trifling. From these islands a communication with the main land could be more readily effected than from any other point." " It is very evident that the manners and customs of the American Indians, resemble that of the Tartars; and I have no doubt that in some future era, it will be reduced to a certainty that in some of the wars between the Chinese and Tartars, a part [23] of the inhabitants of the northern provinces were driven from their country and took refuge in some of these islands, and from thence found their way to America. At different periods each nation might prove victorious, and the conquered by turns fly before the conquerors; and hence might arise the similitude of the Indians to all these people, and that animosity which exists among so many of their tribes."

After remarking on the similarity which exists between the Chinese and Indians, in the singular custom of shaving or plucking out the hair leaving only a small spot on the crown of the head; and the resemblance in sound and signification which many of the Chinese and Indian words bear to each other, he proceeds, "After the most critical inquiry and mature deliberation, I am of opinion that America received its first inhabitants from the northeast, by way of the islands mentioned as lying between Asia and America. This might have been effected at different times and from different parts: from Tartary, China, Japan or Kamschatka, the inhabitants of these countries resembling each other, in color, feature and shape."

Other writers on this subject, coinciding in opinion with Carver, mention a tradition which the Indians in Canada have, that foreign merchants clothed in silk formerly visited them in great ships: these are supposed to have been Chinese, the ruins of Chinese ships having been found on the American coast. The names of many of the American kings, are said to be Tartar; and Tartarax, who reigned formerly in Quivira, means the Tartar. Manew, the founder of the Peruvian empire, most probably came from the Manchew Tartars. Montezuma, the title of the emperors of Mexico, is of Japanese extraction; for according to some authors it is likewise the appellation of the Japanese Monarch. The plant Ginseng, since found in America, where the natives termed it

Garentoguen, a word of the same import in their language, with Ginseng in the Tartar, both meaning THE THIGHS OF A MAN.

Dr. Robertson is decidedly of opinion, that the different tribes of American Indians, excepting the Esquimaux, are of Asiatic extraction. He refers to a tradition among the Mexicans of the migration of their ancestors from a remote country, situated to the north-west of Mexico, and says they point out their various stations as they advanced into the interior provinces, which is precisely the route they must have held, if they had been emigrants from Asia.

Mr. Jefferson, in his notes on Virginia, says, that the passage from Europe to America was always practicable, even to the imperfect [24] navigation of the ancient times; and that, from recent discoveries, it is proven, that if Asia and America be separated at all it is only by a narrow streight. "Judging from the resemblance between the Indians of America and the eastern inhabitants of Asia, we should say that the former are descendants of the latter, or the latter of the former, except indeed the Esquimaux, who, from the same circumstance of resemblance. and from identity of language, must be derived from the Greenlanders. A knowledge of their several languages would be the most certain evidence of their derivation which could be produced. In fact it is the best proof of the affinity of nations, which ever can be referred to."

After regretting that so many of the Indian tribes have been suffered to perish, without our having collected and preserved the general rudiments of their language, he proceeds,

"Imperfect as is our knowledge of the tongues spoken in America, it suffices to discover the following remarkable fact. Arranging them under the radical ones to which they may be palpably traced, and doing the same by those of the red men of Asia, there will be found probably twenty in America, for one in Asia, of those radical languages; so called because if ever they were the same, they have lost all resemblance to one another. A separation into dialects may be the work of a few ages only, but

for two dialects to recede from one another, 'till they have
lost all vestiges of their common origin, must require an
immense course of time; perhaps not less than many people give to the age of the earth. A greater number of
those radical changes of language having taken place
among the red men of America proves them of greater an-
tiquity than those of Asia.

Indian traditions say, that " in ancient days the Great
Island appeared upon the big waters, the earth brought
forth trees, herbs and fruits: that there were in the world
a good and a bad spirit, the good spirit formed creeks and
rivers on the great island, and created numerous species
of animals to inhabit the forests, and fishes of all kinds to
inhabit the water. He also made two beings to whom he
gave living souls and named them Ea-gwe-howe, (real
people). Subsequently some of the people became giants
and committed outrages upon the others. After many
years a body of Ea-gwe-howe people encamped on the
bank of a majestic stream, which they named, Kanawaga
(St. Lawrence.) After a long time a number of foreign
people sailed from a part unknown, but unfortunately the
winds drove them off and they ultimately landed on the
southern part of the great island and many of the crew
perished. Those who survived, selected a place for residence, erected fortifications, became a numerous people
and extended their settlements." [1]

Thus various and discordant are the conjectures respecting the manner in which this continent was first
peopled. Although some [25] of them appear more
rational and others, yet are they at best but hypothetical
disquisitions on a subject which will not now admit of
certainty. All agree that America was inhabited long anterior to its discovery by Columbus, and by a race of human beings, who, however numerous they once were, are
fast hastening to extinction; some centuries hence and
they will be no more known. The few memorials, which
the ravages of time have suffered to remain of them, in
those portions of the country from which they have been

---

[1] Indian traditions by Cusick.

long expelled; have destruction dealt them by the ruthless hand of man. History may transmit to after ages, the fact that they once were, and give their " local habitation and their name." These will probably be received as the tales of fiction, and posterity be at as much loss to determine, whether they ever had an existence, as we now are to say from whence they sprang.

> " I have stood upon Achilles' tomb
> And heard Troy doubted. Time will doubt of Rome."

INTRODUCTION.

CHAPTER III.

The aborigines of America, although divided into many different tribes, inhabiting various climates, and without a community of language, are yet assimilated to each other in stature and complexion, more strikingly than are the inhabitants of the different countries of Europe. The manners and customs of one nation, are very much the manners and customs of all; and although there be peculiarities observable among all, yet are they fewer and less manifest than those which mark the nations of the old world, and distinguish them so palpably from each other. A traveller might have traversed the country, when occupied exclusively by the natives, without remarking among them, the diversity which exists in Europe; or being impressed with the contrast which a visit across the Pyrennes would exhibit, between the affability and vivacity of a Frenchman at a theatre or in the Elysian fields, and the hauteur and reserve of a Spaniard at their bloody circus, when " bounds with one lashing spring the mighty brute."

[26] Nor is there much in savage life, calculated to inspire the mind of civilized man, with pleasurable sensations. Many of the virtues practised by them, proceed rather from necessity or ignorance than from any ethical principle existing among them. The calm composure with which they meet death and their stoical indifference to bodily pain, are perhaps more attributable to recklessness of life and physical insensibility,[1] than to fortitude or magnanimity; consequently they do not much heighten the zest of reflection, in contemplating their character. The christian and the philanthropist, with the benevolent

---

[1] It is said that the nerves of an Indian do not shrink as much, nor shew the same tendency to spasm, under the knife of the surgeon, as the nerves of a white man in a similar situation.

design of improving their morals and meliorating their condition, may profitably study every peculiarity and trait of character observable among them; it will facilitate their object and enable them the more readily to reclaim them from a life of heathenish barbarity, and to extend to them the high boons of civilization and christianity.

It has been observed that the different tribes of natives of North America, resemble each other very much in stature and complexion, in manners and customs; a general description of these will therefor be sufficient.

The stature of an Indian, is generally that of the medial stature of the Anglo Americans; the Osages are said to form an exception to this rule, being somewhat taller. They are almost universally straight and well proportioned; their limbs are clean, but less muscular than those of the whites, and their whole appearance strongly indicative of effeminacy. In walking, they invariable place one foot directly before the other—the toes never verging from a right line with the heel. When traveling in companies, their manner of marching is so peculiar as to have given rise to the expression, "*Indian file;*" and while proceeding in this way, each carefully places his foot in the vestige of the foremost of the party, so as to leave the impression of the footsteps of but one. They have likewise in their gait and carriage something so entirely different from the gait and carriage of the whites, as to enable a person to pronounce on one at a considerable distance. The hair of an Indian is also strikingly different from that of the whites. It is always black and straight, hangs loose and looks as if it were [27] oiled. There is a considerable resemblance in appearance, between it and the glossy black mane of a thoroughbred horse; though its texture is finer.

In the squaws there exist, the same delicacy of proportion, the same effeminacy of person, the same slenderness of hand and foot, which characterise the female of refined society; in despite too of the fact, that every laborious duty and every species of drudgery, are imposed on them from childhood. Their faces are broad, and between the eyes they are exceedingly wide; their cheek bones are high and the eyes black in both sexes—the noses of the women inclining generally to the flat nose of the African; while those of the men are more frequently aquiline than otherwise.

Instances of decrepitude and deformity, are rarely known to exist among them: this is probably owing to the manner in which they are tended and nursed in infancy. It is not necessary that the mother should, as has been supposed, be guilty of the unnatural crime of murdering her decrepid or deformed offspring—the hardships they encounter are too great to be endured by infants not possessed of natural vigor, and they sink beneath them.

Their countenances are for the most inflexible, stern and immovable. The passions which agitate or distract the mind, never alter its expression, nor do the highest ecstacies of which their nature is susceptible, ever relax its rigidity. With the same imperturbability of feature, they encounter death from the hand of an enemy, and receive the greetings of a friend.

In their intercourse with others, they seem alike insensible to emotions of pleasure and of pain; and rarely give vent to feelings of either. The most ludicrous scenes scarcely ever cause them to laugh, or the most interesting recitals draw from them more than their peculiar monosyllabic expression of admiration.

In conversation they are modest and unassuming; indeed taciturnity is as much a distinguishing trait of Indian character, as it ever was of the Roman. In their councils and public meetings, they never manifest an impatience to be heard, or a restlessness under observations, either grating to personal feeling or opposite to their individual ideas of propriety: on the contrary they are still, silent and attentive; and each is heard with the respect due to his years, his wisdom, his experience, or the fame which his exploits may have acquired him. [28] A loud and garrulous Indian is received by the others with contempt, and a cowardly disposition invariably attributed to him—

> "Bold at the council board,
> But in the field he shuns the sword,"

is as much and truly an apothegm with them as with us.

Their taciturnity and irrisibility however, are confined to their sober hours. When indulging their insatiate thirst for spirit, they are boisterous and rude, and by their obstreperous laughter, their demoniacal shrieks and turbulent vociferations, produce an appalling discord, such as might well be expected to proceed from a company of infernal spirits at their fiendish revels ; and exhibit a striking contrast to the low, monotonous tones used by them at other times.

There can be no doubt that the Indians are the most lazy, indolent race of human beings. No attempt which has ever been made to convert them into slaves, has availed much. The rigid discipline of a Spanish master, has failed to overcome that inertness, from which an Indian is roused only by war and the chase—Engaged in these, he exhibits as much activity and perseverance, as could be displayed by any one ; and to gratify his fondness for them, will encounter toils and privations, from which others would shrink. His very form indicates at once, an aptitude for that species of exercise which war and hunting call into action, and an unfitness for the laborious drudgery of husbandry and many of the mechanic arts. Could they have been converted into profitable slaves, it is more than probable we should never have been told, that "the hand of providence was visible in the surprising instances of mortality among the Indians, to make room for the whites."

In their moral character many things appear of a nature, either so monstrous as to shock humanity, or so absurd as to excite derision ; yet they have some redeeming qualities which must elicit commendation. And while we view with satisfaction those bright spots, shining more brilliantly from the gloom which surrounds them, their want of learning and the absence of every opportunity for refinement, should plead in extenuation of their failings and their vices. Some of the most flagrant of these, if not encouraged, have at least been sanctioned by the whites. In the war between the New England colonies and the Narragansetts, it was the misfortune of the brave Philip, after having witnessed the destruction of the

[29] greater part of his nation, to be himself slain by a Mohican. After his head had been taken off, Oneco, chief of the Mohicans, then in alliance with the colonists, claimed that he had a right to feast himself on the body of his fallen adversary. The whites did not object to this, but composedly looked on Oneco, broiling and eating the flesh of Philip—and yet cannibalism was one of their most savage traits of character.

This was a general, if not an universal custom among the Indians, when America became known to the whites. Whether it has yet entirely ceased is really to be doubted: some of those who have been long intimate with them, affirm that it has not; though it is far from being prevalent.

The Indians are now said to be irritable; but when Europeans first settled among them, they were not more irascible than their new neighbors. In their anger however, they differ very much from the whites. They are not talkative and boisterous as these are, but silent, sullen and revengeful. If an injury be done them, they never forget, they never forgive it. Nothing can be more implacable than their resentment—no time can allay it—no change of circumstances unfix its purpose. Revenge is to them as exhilarating, as the cool draught from the fountain, to the parched and fevered lips of a dying man.

When taking vengeance of an enemy, there is no cruelty which can be exercised, no species of torture, which their ingenuity can devise, too severe to be inflicted. To those who have excited a spirit of resentment in the bosom of an Indian, the tomahawk and scalping knife are instruments of mercy. Death by the faggot—by splinters of the most combustible wood, stuck in the flesh and fired—maiming and disemboweling, tortures on which the soul sickens but to reflect, are frequently practiced. To an enemy of their own color, they are perhaps more cruel and severe, than to the whites. In requiting upon him, every refinement of torture is put in requisition, to draw forth a sigh or a groan, or cause him to betray some symptom of human sensibility. This they never effect. An Indian neither shrinks from a knife, nor

winces at the stake; on the contrary he seems to exult
in his agony, and will mock his tormentors for the leniency
and mildness of their torture.[1]

[30] Drinking and gambling are vices, to which the
Indians, as well as the whites, are much addicted. Such
is their fondness for spirit of any kind that they are rarely
known to be sober, when they have it in their power to
be otherwise. Neither a sense of honor or of shame has
been able to overcome their propensity for its use; and
when drunk, the ties of race, of friendship and of kindred
are too weak, to bind their ferocious tempers.

In gambling they manifest the same anxiety, which
we see displayed at the card table of the whites. The
great difference seems to be, that we depend too frequently
on sleight and dexterity; whereas while they are shaking
their gourd neck of half whited plumbstones, they only
use certain *tricks* of conjuration, which in their simplicity
they believe will ensure them success. To this method of
attaining an object, they have frequent recourse. Superstition is the concomitant of ignorance. The most enlightened, are rarely altogether exempt from its influence—with the uninformed it is a master passion, swaying
and directing the mind in all its operations.

In their domestic economy, Indians are, in some respects, like the rude of all countries. They manifest but
little respect for the female; imposing on her not only the

---

[1] A Narraganset, made prisoner by Maj. Talcott in 1679, begged to
be delivered to the Mohicans that he might be put to death in their
own way. The New Englanders complying with his request, preparations were made for the tragical event. "The Mohicans, formed a
circle, and admitting within it as many of the whites as chose to witness
their proceedings, placed the prisoner in the centre. One of the Mohicans,
who had lost a son in the late engagement, with a knife cut off the
PRISONER'S EARS! then his NOSE! and then the FINGERS off each hand!
after the lapse of a few moments, his EYES WERE DUG OUT, AND THEIR
SOCKETS FILLED WITH HOT EMBERS!! All this time the prisoner instead
of bewailing his fate, seemed to surpass his tormentors in expressions of
joy. At length when exhausted with loss of blood and unable to stand,
his executioner closed the tragic scene by beating out his brains with a
tomahawk."—*Indian Wars, by Trumbull.*.

3

duties of the hut, but also the more laborious operations of husbandry; and observing towards them the hauteur and distance of superior beings.

There are few things, indeed, which mark with equal precision, the state of civilization existing in any community, as the rank assigned in it to females. In the rude and barbarous stages of society, they are invariably regarded as inferior beings, [31] instruments of sensual gratification, and unworthy the attention and respect of men. As mankind advance to refinement, females gradually attain an elevation of rank, and acquire an influence in society, which smoothes the asperities of life and produces the highest polish, of which human nature is susceptible.

Among the Indians there is, however rude they may be in other respects, a great respect always paid to female chastity. Instances in which it has been violated by them, if to be found at all, are extremely few. However much the passion of revenge may stimulate to acts of cruelty, the propensities of nature never lead them to infringe the virtue of women in their power.

The general character of the Indians, was more estimable, when they first became known to Europeans, than it is at present. This has been ascribed to the introduction of ardent spirits among them—other causes however, have conspired to produce the result.

The cupidity of those who were engaged in commerce with the natives, too frequently prompted them to take every advantage, for self aggrandizement, which they could obtain over the Indians. In the lucrative traffic carried on with them, the influence of honesty was not predominant—the real value of the commodity procured, was never allowed; while upon every article given in exchange, extortion alone affixed the price. These examples could not fail to have a deteriorating effect upon their untutored minds; and we find them accordingly losing their former regard for truth, honesty and fidelity; and becoming instead deceitful, dishonest and treacherous. Many of their ancient virtues however, are still practised by them.

The rights of hospitality are accorded to those who go among them, with a liberality and sincerity which would reflect credit on civilized man. And although it has been justly said that they rarely forgive an enemy, yet is it equally true that they never forsake their friends; to them they are always kind, generous and beneficent.

After the ceremony of introduction is over,[1] a captive enemy, [32] who is adopted by them, is also treated with the utmost humanity and attention. An Indian cheerfully divides his last morsel with an adopted son or brother; and will readily risk life in his defence. Such indeed, is the kindness which captives thus situated invariably receive, that they frequently regret the hour of their redemption, and refuse to leave their red brethren, to return and mingle with the whites. 1157699

As members of a community, they are at all times willing to devote their every faculty, for the good of the whole. The honor and welfare of their respective tribes, are primary considerations with them. To promote these, they cheerfully encounter every privation, endure every hardship, and face every danger. Their patriotism is of the most pure and disinterested character; and of those who have made us feel so sensibly, the horrors of savage warfare, many were actuated by motives which would reflect honor on the citizens of any country. The unfortunate Tecumseh was a remarkable example of the most ardent and patriotic devotion to his country.

Possessed of an acute and discerning mind, he witnessed the extending influence of the whites, with painful solicitude. Listening with melancholy rapture, to the traditionary accounts of the former greatness of his nation, and viewing in anticipation the exile or extinction of his race, his noble soul became fired with the hope that he might retrieve the fallen fortune of his country, and restore it to its pristine dignity and grandeur. His attachment to his tribe impelled him to exertion and every nerve was strained in its cause.

---

[1] Indians consider the running of the guantlet, as but the ceremony of an introduction; and say that it is "like the shake hands and howde do, of the whites."

Determined if possible to achieve the independence of
his nation, and to rid her of those whom he considered
her oppressors, he formed the scheme of uniting in hostility against the United States, all the tribes dwelling
east of the Mississippi river. In the prosecution of this
purpose, he travelled from Mackinaw to Georgia,[1] and with
wonderful adroitness practised on the different feelings of
his red brethren. Assuming at times the character of a
prophet, he wrought powerfully on their credulity and superstition.—Again, depending on the force of oratory, the
witchery of his eloquence drew many [33] to his standard.
But all was in vain—His plans were entirely frustrated.
He had brought none of his auxiliaries into the field ; and
was totally unprepared for hostilities, when his brother,
the celebrated Shawanese prophet, by a premature attack
on the army under Gen. Harrison, at an inauspicious moment, precipitated him into a war with the United States.

Foiled by this means, Tecumseh joined the standard
of Great Britain in the war of 1812 ; and as a Brigadier
General in her army, lost his life, bravely supporting the
cause which he had espoused. He deserved a better fate ;
and but for prejudice which is so apt to dim the eye and
distort the object, Tecumseh would, most probably, be
deemed a martyr for his country, and associated in the
mind with the heroes of Marathon and Thermopylæ.

To contemplate the Indian character, in a religious
point of view, is less gratifying than to consider it in regard to the lesser morals. At the period of the settlement
of Western Virginia, excepting the Moravians, and a few
others who had been induced by the zeal and exertions of
Roman catholic missionaries to wear the cross, the Indians
north west of the Ohio river, were truly heathens. They
believed indeed in a First Cause, and worshiped the Good
Spirit; but they were ignorant of the great truths of
Christianity, and their devotions were but superstitious
acts of blind reverence. In this situation they remain

---

[1] While performing this tour, Tecumseh carried a RED STICK, the
acceptance of which was considered a joining of his party—Hence those
Indians who were hostile to the United States, were denominated RED
STICKS.

generally at the present day, notwithstanding the many laudable endeavors which have been made to christianize them.

Perhaps there was never a tribe in America, but believed in the existence of a Deity; yet were their ideas of the nature and attributes of God, not only obscure, but preposterous and absurd. They believe also in the existence of many inferior deities, whom they suppose to be employed as assistants in managing the affairs of the world, and in inspecting the actions of men. Eagles and Owls are thought by some to have been placed here as observers of the actions of men; and accordingly, when an eagle is seen to soar about them by day, or an owl to perch near them at night, they immediately offer sacrifice, that a good report may be made of them to the Great Spirit.

They are likewise believers in the immortality of the soul; and have such an idea of a future state of existence, as accords with their character and condition here. Strangers to [34] intellectual pleasures, they suppose that their happiness hereafter will consist of mere sensual gratifications; and that when they die, they will be translated to a delightful region, where the flowers never fade, nor the leaves fall from the trees; where the forests abound in game, and the lakes in fish, and where they expect to remain forever, enjoying all the pleasures which delighted them here.[1]

---

[1] Pope has very finely expressed the leading articles of religion among the Indians in the following lines.

> Lo, the poor Indian! whose untutor'd mind
> Sees God in clouds, or hears him in the wind;
> His soul proud science never taught to stray
> Far as the Solar Walk or Milky Way;
> Yet simple nature to his hope has giv'n,
> Behind the cloud-topt hill an humbler heav'n;
> Some safer world in depth of woods embrac'd,
> Some happier island in the wat'ry waste;
> Where slaves once more their native land behold,
> No fiends torment. no Christians thirst for gold.
> To be, contents his natural desire,
> He asks no angel's wing, no seraph's fire:
> But thinks admitted to that equal sky,
> Kis faithful dog shall bear him company.

In consequence of this belief, when an Indian dies, and is buried, they place in the grave with him, his bow and arrows and such weapons as they use in war, that he may be enabled to procure game and overcome an enemy. And it has been said, that they grieve more for the death of an infant unable to provide for itself in the world of spirits, than for one who had attained manhood and was capable of taking care of himself. An interesting instance of this is given by Major Carver, and furnishes at once, affecting evidence of their incongruous creed and of their parental tenderness. Maj. Carver says:

"Whilst I remained with them, a couple whose tent was near to mine, lost a son about four years old. The parents were so inconsolable for its loss, and so much affected by its death, that they pursued the usual testimonies of grief with such uncommon vigor, as through the weight of sorrow and loss of blood, to occasion the death of the father. The mother, who had been hitherto absorbed in grief, no sooner beheld her husband expire, than she dried up her tears, and appeared cheerful and resigned.

"As I knew not how to account for so extraordinary a transition, I took an opportunity to ask her the reason of it. She replied, that as the child was so young when it died, and unable to support itself in the country of spirits, both she and her husband had been apprehensive that its situation would be far from pleasant; but no sooner did she behold its father depart for the same place, and who not only loved the child with the tenderest affection, but was a good hunter and [35] able to provide plentifully for its support, than she ceased to mourn. She added that she saw no reason to continue her tears, as the child was now happy under the protection of a fond father; and that she had only one wish remaining to be gratified, and that was a wish to be herself with them."[1]

In relation to the Indian antiquities so frequently met

<hr />

[1] The author's summary of Indian character is for the most part excellent, and in accord with more recent conclusions. See Chap. I. of *The Colonies*, in "Epochs of American History" (Longmans, 1892.)—R. G. T.

with in America, much doubt still exists. When and for
what purpose many of those vast mounds of earth, so
common in the western country, were heaped up, is matter of uncertainty. Mr. Jefferson has pronounced them to
be repositories of the dead; and many of them certainly
were designed for that purpose; perhaps all with which
he had become acquainted previous to the writing of his
notes of Virginia. Mr. Jefferson did not deem them
worthy the name of monuments. Since the country has
been better explored, many have been discovered justly
entitled to that appellation, some of which seem to have
been constructed for purposes other than inhumation.[1]
These are frequently met with in the valley of the Mississippi, and are said to extend into Mexico. The most celebrated works of this class, are believed to be those at Circleville in Ohio, which have so frequently been described,
and are justly considered memorials of the labor and perseverance of those by whom they were erected.

There is a tradition among the Indians of the north,
which if true would furnish a very rational solution to the
question, "for what purpose were they constructed?"
According to this tradition about "two thousand two
hundred years, before Columbus discovered America, the
northern nations appointed a prince, and immediately after,
repaired to the south and visited the GOLDEN CITY, the capital of a vast empire. After a time the emperor of the
south built many forts throughout his dominions, and extending them northwardly almost penetrated the lake
Erie. This produced much excitement. The people of
the north, afraid that they would be deprived of the country on the south side of the great lakes, determined to
defend it against the infringement of any foreign people;
long and bloody wars ensued which lasted about one hun-

---

[1] Gen. George Rogers Clark, an early and careful observer, scouted
the idea advanced by Noah Webster, in Carey's *American Museum*,
in 1789, that these extraordinary Western military defenses were the
work of De Soto. "As for his being the author of these fortifications,"
says Clark, "it is quite out of the question; they are more numerous
than he had men, and many of them would have required fifty thousand men for their occupancy." L. C. D.

dred years. The people of the north, being more skillful
in the use of bows and arrows, and capable of enduring
hardships which proved fatal to those of the south, gained
the conquest; and all the towns and forts, which had been
erected by their enemy, were totally destroyed and left in
a heap of ruins." [1]

The most considerable of those tumuli or sepulchral
mounds, which are found in Virginia, is that on the bottoms of Grave creek, near its entrance into the Ohio, about
twelve miles below Wheeling, and is the only large one in
this section of the country. Its diameter at the base, is
said to be one hundred yards, its perpendicular height
about eighty feet, and the diameter at its summit, forty-
five feet. Trees, of all sizes and of various kinds, are
growing on its sides; and fallen [36] and decayed timber,
is interspersed among them; a single white oak rises out
of a concavity in the centre of its summit.[2]

Near to Cahokia there is a group (of about two hundred) of these mounds, of various dimensions.[3] The largest
of these is said to have a base of eight hundred yards cir-
cumference, and an altitude of ninety feet. These and the
one mentioned as being on Grave creek and many smaller
ones in various parts of the country, were no doubt places
of inhumation.[4]—Many have been opened, and found to
contain human bones promiscuously thrown together. Mr.

---

[1] Indian traditions, by Cusick.

[2] This description, written by Withers in 1831, still holds good in
the main. The mound, which proves to have been a burial tumulus, is
now surrounded by the little city of Moundsville, W. Va., and is kept
inclosed by the owner as one of the sights of the place. The writer
visited it in May, 1894.—R. G. T.

[3] George Rogers Clark, who was repeatedly at Cahokia during the
period 1778-80, says: "We easily and evidently traced the town for
upwards of five miles in the beautiful plain below the present town of
Kahokia. There could be no deception here, because the remains of
ancient works were thick—the whole were mounds, etc." Clark's MS.
statement; Schoolcraft's *Indian Tribes*, IV., p. 135.—L. C. D.

[4] This mound was used, at least in part, for burial purposes. Nearly
fifty years ago, when the writer of this note explored this remarkable
artificial elevation of eighty feet in height, he found in the excavation
numerous beads of shell or bone, or both, ornaments of the dead buried
there.—L. C. D.

Jefferson supposed the one examined by him, (the diameter of whose base was only forty feet and height twelve) to contain the bones of perhaps a thousand human beings, of each sex and of every age. Others have been examined, in which were the skeletons of men of much greater stature, than that of any of the Indians in America, at the time of its discovery, or of those with whom we have since become acquainted.

It is a well known fact, that since the whites became settled in the country, the Indians were in the habit of collecting the bones of their dead and of depositing them in one general cemetery; but the earth and stone used by them, were taken from the adjacent land. This was not invariably the case, with those ancient heaps of earth found in the west. In regard to many of them, this singular circumstance is said to be a fact, that the earth, of which they are composed, is of an altogether different nature, from that around them; and must, in some instances, have been carried a considerable distance. The tellurine structures at Circleville are of this sort; and the material of which they were constructed, is said to be distinctly different, from the earth any where near to them.

The immensity of the size of these and many others, would induce the supposition that they could not have been raised by a race of people as indolent as the Indians have been, ever since a knowledge was had of them. Works, the construction of which would now require the concentrated exertions of at least one thousand men, aided by the mechanical inventions of later days, for several months, could hardly have been erected by persons, so subject to lassitude under labor as they are : unless indeed their population was infinitely greater than we now conceive it to have been. Admitting however, this density of population to have existed, other circumstances would corroborate the belief, that the country once had other inhabitants, than the progenitors of those who have been called, the aborigines of America: one of these circumstances is the uncommon size of many of the skeletons found in the smaller mounds upon the hills.

If the fact be, as it is represented, that the larger skele-

tons are invariably found on elevated situations, remote
from the larger water courses, it would tend to show that
there was a diversity of habit, and admitting their cotemporaneous existence, perhaps no alliance or intercourse
between those, whose remains they are, and the persons
by whom those large mounds and fortifications were
erected, [37] these being found only on plains in the contiguity of large streams or inland lakes; and containing
only the bones of individuals of ordinary stature.

Another and stronger evidence that America was occupied by others than the ancestors of the present Indians,
is to be found in those antiquities, which demonstrate that
iron was once known here, and converted to some of the
uses ordinarily made of it.

In graduating a street in Cincinnati, there was found,
twenty-five feet below the surface of the earth, a small
horse shoe, in which were several nails. It is said to present the appearance of such erosion as would result from
the oxidation of some centuries. It was smaller than
would be required for a common mule.[1]

Many are the instances of pieces of timber found,
various depths below the surface of the earth, with the
marks of the axe palpably visible on them.[2] A sword too,
said to have been enclosed in the wood of the roots of a
tree not less than five hundred years old, is preserved in
Ohio as a curiosity. Many other instances might, if necessary, be adduced to prove, that implements of iron were in
use in this country, prior to its occupation by the whites.
Now if a people once have the use of that metal, it is far

---

[1] This proves nothing. A silver medal of John Quincy Adams's administration, evidently presented to some Indian chief was, in 1894,
found in Wisconsin, twelve feet below the surface. Iron and silver tools
and ornaments, evidently made in Paris for the Indian trade, have been
found in Ohio and Wisconsin mounds. It is now sufficiently demon-
strated that the mound-builders were the ancestors of the aborigines
found in the country by the first white settlers, and that the mounds are
of various ages, ranging perhaps from three hundred to a thousand years.
Various *Reports* of the Bureau of Ethnology go into the matter with convincing detail.—R. G. T.

[2] Jacob Wolf, in digging a well on Hacker's creek, found a piece of
timber which had been evidently cut off at one end, twelve or thirteen
feet in the ground—marks of the axe were plainly distinguishable on it.

from probable that it will ever after be lost to them: the essential purposes to which it may be applied, would preserve it to them. The Indians however, 'till taught by the Europeans, had no knowledge of it.

Many of the antiquities discovered in other parts of the country, show that the arts once flourished to an extent beyond what they have ever been known to do among the Indians. The body found in the saltpetre cave of Kentucky, was wrapped in blankets made of linen and interwoven with feathers of the wild turkey, tastefully arranged. It was much smaller than persons of equal age at the present day, and had yellowish hair. In Tennessee many walls of faced stone, and even walled wells have been found in so many places, at such depths and under such circumstances, as to preclude the idea of their having been made by the whites since the discovery by Columbus.

[38] In this state too, have been found burying grounds, in which the skeletons seem all to have been those of pigmies: the graves, in which the bodies had been deposited, were seldom three feet in length; yet the teeth in the skulls prove that they were the bodies of persons of mature age.

Upon the whole there cannot be much doubt, that America was once inhabited by a people, not otherwise allied to the Indians of the present day, than that they were descendants of him, from whom has sprung the whole human family.

OF

BORDER WARFARE.

CHAPTER I.

At the time when Virginia became known to the whites, it was occupied by many different tribes of Indians, attached to different nations. That portion of the state lying north west of the Blue ridge, and extending to the lakes was possessed by the Massawomees. These were a powerful confederacy, rarely in amity with the tribes cast of that range of mountains; but generally harrassing them by frequent hostile irruptions into their country. Of their subsequent history, nothing is now known. They are supposed by some to have been the ancestors of the Six Nations. It is however more probable, that they afterwards became incorporated with these, as did several other tribes of Indians, who used a language so essentially different from that spoken by the Six Nations, as to render the intervention of interpreters necessary between them.

As settlements were extended from the sea shore, the Massawomees gradually retired; and when the white population reached the Blue ridge of mountains, the valley between it and the Alleghany, was entirely uninhabited. This delightful region of country was then only used as a hunting ground, and as a highway for belligerant parties of different nations, in their military expeditions against each other. In consequence of the almost continued hostilities between the northern and southern Indians, these expeditions were very frequent, and tended somewhat to retard the settlement of the valley, and render a residence

(44)

in it, for some time, insecure and unpleasant. Between the Alleghany mountains and the Ohio river, within the present limits of Virginia, there were some villages interspersed, inhabited by small numbers of Indians; the most [40] of whom retired north west of that river, as the tide of emigration rolled towards it. Some however remained in the interior, after settlements began to be made in their vicinity.

North of the present boundary of Virginia, and particularly near the junction of the Alleghany and Monongahela rivers, and in the circumjacent country the Indians were more numerous, and their villages larger. In 1753, when Gen. Washington visited the French posts on the Ohio, the spot which had been selected by the Ohio company, as the site for a fort, was occupied by Shingess, king of the Delawares; and other parts of the proximate country, were inhabited by Mingoes and Shawanees.[1] When the French were forced to abandon the position, which they had taken at the forks of Ohio, the greater part of the adjacent tribes removed farther west. So that when improvements were begun to be made in the wilderness of North Western Virginia, it had been almost entirely deserted by the natives; and excepting a few straggling hunters and warriors, who occasionally traversed it in quest of game, or of human beings on whom to wreak their vengeance, almost its only tenants were beasts of the forest.

In the country north west of the Ohio river, there were many warlike tribes of Indians, strongly imbued with feelings of rancorous hostility to the neighboring colonists. Among the more powerful of these were the Delawares, who resided on branches of Beaver Creek, Cayahoga, and

---

[1] King Shingiss was a famous village chief, "a terror to the frontier settlements of Pennsylvania." A brother, and later the successor of King Beaver, his camp was at the mouth of Beaver Creek, which empties into the Ohio twenty-six miles below "the forks" (site of Pittsburg). Christopher Gist visited him November 24, 1750. In 1759, when Fort Pitt was built, Shingiss moved up Beaver Creek to Kuskuskis on the Mahoning, and finally to the Muskingum. The land about the mouth of Beaver Creek is called "Shingis Old Town" in the Ft. Stanwix treaty, 1784.—R. G. T.

Muskingum; and whose towns contained about six hundred inhabitants—The Shawanees, who to the number of 300, dwelt upon the Scioto and Muskingum—The Chippewas, near Mackinaw, of 400—Cohunnewagos, of 300, and who inhabited near Sandusky—The Wyandots, whose villages were near fort St. Joseph, and embraced a population of 250—The Twightees, near fort Miami, with a like population—The Miamis, on the river Miami, near the fort of that name, reckoning 300 persons—The Pottowatomies of 300, and the Ottawas of 550, in their villages near to forts St. Joseph and Detroit,[1] and of 250, in the towns near Mackinaw. Besides these, there were in the same district of country, others of less note, yet equally inimical to the whites; and who contributed much to the annoyance [41] of the first settlers on the Ohio, and its tributaries.

There were likewise the Munsies, dwelling on the north branch of the Susquehanna, and on the Allegheny river—The Senecas, on the waters of the Susquehanna, Ontario and the heads of the Allegheny—The Cayugas, on Cayuga lake, and the Sapoonies, who resided in the neighborhood of the Munsies. In these tribes was an aggregate population of 1,380 souls, and they likewise aided in committing depredations on our frontiers.

Those who ventured to explore and occupy the south western portion of Virginia, found also in its vicinity some powerful and warlike tribes. The Cherokees possessed what was then, the western part of North Carolina and numbered 2,500—The Chicasaws, residing south of the Cherokees, had a population of 750—and the Catawbas, on the Catawba river in South Carolina with only 150 persons. These latter were remarkably adventurous, enterprising and courageous; and notwithstanding their remote situation, and the paucity of their numbers, frequently traversed the valley of Virginia, and even penetrated the country on the north branch of the Susque-

[1] The numbers here set down and those given below, are as they were ascertained by Capt. Hutchins, who visited the most of the tribes for purpose of learning their population in 1768.

hanna, and between the Ohio river and lake Erie, to wage
war upon the Delawares. Their success in many of these
expeditions, is preserved in the traditions of the Delawares, who continue to regard them as having used in
these wars, a degree of cunning and stratagem, to which
other tribes have never approached.[1]

Such were the numbers and positions of many of the
proximate Indians about the time settlements were begun
to be [42] made on the Monongahela river and its branches.
Anterior to this period, adventurers had explored, and
established themselves, in various parts of the valley between the Blue ridge and the Alleghany mountain. That
section of it, which was included within the limits of the
Northern-Neck, was the first to become occupied by the
whites. The facilities afforded by the proprietor for obtaining land within his grant, the greater salubrity of
climate and fertility of soil near to the Blue ridge, caused
the tide of emigration to flow rapidly towards the upper
country, and roll even to the base of that mountain. Settlements were soon after extended westwardly across the
Shenandoah, and early in the eighteenth century Winchester became a trading post, with sparse improvements
in its vicinity.

About this time Thomas Morlin, a pedlar trading
from Williamsburg to Winchester, resolved, in conjunction with John Salling a weaver also from Williamsburg,
to prosecute an examination of the country, beyond the

---

[1] A tradition among the Delawares says that formerly the Catawbas
came near one of their hunting camps and remaining in ambush at night
sent two or three of their party round the camp with Buffalo hoofs
fixed to their feet, to make artificial buffalo tracks and thus decoy the
hunters from their camp. In the morning the Delawares, discovering
the tracks and supposing them to have been made by buffaloes, followed them some time; when suddenly the Catawbas rose from their
covert, fired at and killed several of the hunters; the others fled, collected a party and went in pursuit of the Catawbas. These had brought
with them, rattle snake poison corked up in a piece of cane stalk; into
which they dipped small reed splinters, which they set up along their
path. The Delawares in pursuit were much injured by those poisoned
splinters, and commenced retreating to their camp. The Catawbas discovering this, turned upon their pursuers, and killed and scalped many
of them.

limits which had hitherto bounded the exploratory excursions of other adventurers. With this view, they travelled up the valley of the Shenandoah, and crossing James river and some of its branches, proceeded as far as the Roanoke, when Salling was taken captive by a party of Cherokees. Morlin was fortunate enough to elude their pursuit, and effect a safe retreat to Winchester.

Upon the return of the party by whom Salling had been captivated, he was taken to Tennessee where he remained for some years. When on a hunting expedition to the Salt licks of Kentucky, in company with some Cherokees to kill buffalo, they were surprised by a party of Illinois Indians, with whom the Cherokees were then at war, and by them Salling was again taken prisoner. He was then carried to Kaskaskia, when he was adopted into the family of a squaw whose son had been killed in the wars.

While with this nation of Indians, Salling frequently accompanied parties of them on hunting excursions, a considerable distance to the south. On several occasions he went with them below the mouth of the Arkansas, and once to the Gulph of Mexico. In one of those expeditions they met with a party of Spaniards, exploring the country and who needed an interpreter. For this purpose they purchased Salling of his Indian mother for three strands of beads and a Calumet. Salling attended them to the post at Crevecœur; from which [43] place he was conveyed to fort Frontignac: here he was redeemed by the Governor of Canada, who sent him to the Dutch settlement in New York, whence he made his way home after an absence of six years.[1]

---

[1] John Peter Salling, sometimes spoken of as Peter Adam Salling, was, if not of German birth, of German descent. With his brother Henry, he early settled in the forks of James River and North Branch, in the southern part of what is now Rockbridge county, Va. The details of his early explorations in the West are involved in doubt, but that he had such adventures there seems no good reason to doubt. It will be noticed that Withers omits the date; some writers have placed it at about 1724, but the probable time was 1738-40. His descendants told Draper (about 1850) that the family tradition was, that Salling and a son were employed by the governor of Virginia to explore the country

The emigration from Great Britain to Virginia was then very great, and at the period of Salling's return to Williamsburg, there were then many adventurers, who had but recently arrived from Scotland, and the north of England. Among these adventurers were John Lewis[1] and John

---

to the southwest; and when near the present Salem, Roanoke county, they were captured by Cherokees and carried to the Ohio River—one account says by way of the Tennessee, another by the New (Great Kanawha), their boat being made of buffalo skins. They appear by this tradition to have escaped, and in descending the Mississippi to have fallen into the hands of Spaniards. The son died, and the father was sent in a vessel bound for Spain, there to be tried as a British spy; but the Spaniard being captured by an English vessel, our hero was landed at Charleston, whence he reached his frontier home after an absence of over three years. This story differs in many details from the one in Kercheval's *History of the Valley of Virginia*, and also that in Withers's text, above. Salling kept a journal which was extant in 1745, for in the Wisconsin Historical Society's library is a diary kept by Capt. John Buchanan, who notes that in that year he spent two days in copying a part of it. In Du Pratz' *History of Louisiana* (London, 1774), Salling and one John Howard are said to have made this trip in 1742, and the authority is said to be a *Report of the Government of Virginia*. But Salling must have returned home by 1742, for his name is in the roll of Capt. John McDowell's militia company, and he was probably in the fight with the Indians (Dec. 14) that year, in which McDowell lost his life. In 1746, we found Salling himself a militia captain in the Rockbridge district of Augusta county. In September, 1747, he was cited to appear at court martial for not turning out to muster—and this is the last record we have of him. Descendants, named Sallee, now live in Kentucky and Tennessee.—R. G. T.

[1] John Lewis, the father of Gen. Andrew Lewis, was probably of Welsh descent, and born in 1678 in County Donegal, Ireland. About 1716 he married Margaret Lynn, of the famous Lynns of Loch Lynn, Scotland. In a dispute over his tenancy (1729), he killed a man of high station,—some say, his Catholic landlord,—and fled to Portugal, whence in 1731, after strange adventures, he emigrated to America, and was joined there by his family. Fearing to live near a sea-port he established himself on the frontier, in the Valley of Virginia, two miles east of the present site of Staunton. His house was of stone, built for defense, and in 1754 it successfully stood an Indian siege. Lewis was colonel of the Augusta county militia as early as 1743, presiding justice in 1745, and high sheriff in 1748. In 1751, then 73 years of age, he assisted his son Andrew, then agent of the Loyal Company, to explore and survey the latter's grant on Greenbrier River. It was because the old man became entangled in the thicket of greenbriers, that he gave this name to the stream. He died at his old fort homestead, February 1, 1762, aged 84

4

Mackey. Salling's return excited a considerable and very general interest, and drew around him many, particularly of those who had but lately come to America, and to whom the narrative of one, who had been nearly six years a captive among the Indians, was highly gratifying. Lewis and Mackey listened attentively to the description given of the country in the valley, and pleased with its beauty and fertility as represented by Salling, they prevailed on him to accompany them on a visit to examine it more minutely, and if found correspondent with his description to select in it situations for their future residence.

Lewis made choice of, and improved, a spot a few miles below Staunton, on a creek which bears his name—Mackey on the middle branch of the Shenandoah near Buffalogap; and Salling in the forks of James river, below the Natural Bridge, where some of his descendants still reside. Thus was effected the first white settlement ever made on the James river, west of the Blue ridge.[1]

In the year 1736, Lewis, being in Williamsburg, met with Benjamin Burden (who had then just come to the country as agent of Lord Fairfax, proprietor of the Northern Neck,) and on whom he prevailed to accompany him home. Burden remained at Lewis's the greater part of the summer, and on his return to Williamsburg, took with him a buffalo calf, which while hunting with Samuel[2] and Andrew Lewis (elder sons of John) they had caught and afterwards tamed. He presented this calf to Gov. Gooch, who thereupon entered on his journal, [44] an order, authorizing Burden to locate conditionally, any quantity of land not exceeding 500,000 acres on any of the waters of the Shen-

years. Some accounts state that he was a Presbyterian; he was, however, an Episcopalian.—R. G.T.

[1] Lewis soon afterwards obtained leave from Governor Gooch to locate 100,000 acres of land in separate parcels on the waters of the Shenandoah and James rivers; and when he would go out in search of good land to locate, Mackey would accompany him to hunt buffalo. The former amassed a large estate, while the latter lived and died in comparative poverty.

[2] As Col. John Lewis had no son Samuel, probably Thomas Lewis, the elder brother of Andrew, though near-sighted, may have engaged in buffalo hunting.—L. C. D.

andoah, or of James river west of the Blue ridge. The conditions of this grant were, that he should interfere with no previous grants—that he should settle 100 families, in ten years, within its limits; and should have 1000 acres adjoining each cabin which he should cause to be built, with liberty to purchase any greater quantity adjoining, at the rate of fifty pounds per thousand acres. In order to effect a compliance with one of these conditions, Burden visited Great Britian in 1737; and on his return to Virginia brought with him upwards of one hundred families of adventurers, to settle on his grant.[1] Amongst these adventurers were, John Patton, son-in-law to Benjamin Burden, who settled on Catawba, above Pattonsburg[2]—

[1] Of the origin of Benjamin Borden, Sr. (the name was mispronounced Burden, on the frontier), little is known. He was probably from New Jersey, and early became a fur trader on the Virginia frontier; later he was in Lord Fairfax's employ as a land agent. As such, he visited Governor Gooch and obtained from him several valuable tracts—one of them (October 3, 1734), Borden Manor, on Sprout run, Frederick county; another, 100,000 acres at the head of the James, on condition of locating thereon a hundred families. At the end of two years he had erected 92 cabins with as many families, and a patent was granted him November 8, 1739, for 92,100 acres. He died in 1742, before further development of his enterprise. His son Benjamin succeeded to his vast estate, but died of small-pox in 1753. In 1744, he married the widow of John McDowell, mentioned on the next page, who had been killed in the Indian fight of December 14, 1742.—R. G. T.

[2] The daughter of John Patton subsequently became the wife of Col. W. Preston, and the mother of James Patton Preston, late a governor of Virginia.

Comment by L. C. D.—This note of Mr. Withers, derived from Taylor's sketches (mentioned below), is erroneous both as to Patton and Preston. Col. Patton's first name was not John, but James, as both the records and his own autograph sufficiently attest. Neither did John Preston, nor his son Col. Wm. Preston, marry Col. Patton's daughter, but John Preston married his sister. Miss Elizabeth Patton, while crossing the Shannon in a boat, met the handsome John Preston, then a young ship carpenter, and an attachment grew out of their accidental meeting. But as Miss Patton belonged to the upper class of society, there was a wide gulf between their conditions, and a runaway match was the only way out of the difficulty. Gov. James Patton Preston was named after his granduncle. James Patton was born in County Londonderry, Ireland, in 1692. For many years he was a prosperous navigator, and crossed the Atlantic twenty-five times with "redemptioners" for Virginia; he was also an

Ephraim McDowell, who settled at Phoebe's falls—John, the son of Ephraim,[1] who settled at Fairfield, where Col. James McDowell now lives—Hugh Telford, who settled at the Falling spring, in the forks of James river—Paul Whitley, who settled on Cedar creek, where the Red Mill now is—Archibald Alexander, who settled on the North river, opposite Lexington—Andrew Moore, who settled adjoining Alexander—Sampson Archer, who settled at Gilmore's spring, east of the Bridge tavern, and Capt. John Matthews, who married Betsy Archer, (the daughter of Sampson) settled where Major Matthews lives, below the Natural bridge.

Among others who came to Virginia at this time, was an Irish girl named Polly Mulhollin. On her arrival she was hired to James Bell to pay her passage; and with whom she remained during the period her servitude was to continue. At its expiration she attired herself in the habit of a man; and with hunting shirt and mocasons, went into Burden's grant, for the purpose of making improvements and acquiring a title to land. Here she erected thirty cabins, by virtue of which she held one hundred acres adjoining each. When Benjamin Burden the younger, came on to make deeds to those who held cabin rights, he was astonished to see so many in the name of

officer in the royal navy in the wars with the Netherlands. Having obtained a grant of 120,000 acres above the Blue Ridge, he himself settled in Virginia in 1735. A man of wealth, enterprise and influence, he was a justice, sheriff, Indian treaty commissioner, and finally county lieutenant of Augusta. In 1755, he was killed by Indians while conveying ammunition to the borderers.

[1] Capt. John McDowell was of Scotch descent, and born in Ulster, Ireland, but in early manhood came to America, settling first in Pennsylvania, and then the Virginia Valley (autumn of 1737). He at once became one of Benjamin Borden's surveyors, and for five years made surveys on Borden's Manor. Becoming a captain in the Augusta militia, he was ordered to go out against a party of Northern Indians who, on the war-path against the Catawbas, had taken in the Virginia Valley on their way, and annoyed and plundered the white settlers. The savages were overtaken on the North Branch of James River, some fifteen miles from McDowell's place, and an engagement ensued (Dec. 14, 1742), in which McDowell and seven others lost their lives. The Indians escaped with small losses. This was the first battle between whites and Indians, in the Virginia Valley.—R. G. T.

Mulhollin. Investigation led to a discovery of the mystery, to the great mirth of the other claimants. She resumed her christian name and feminine dress, and many of [45] her respectable descendants still reside within the limits of Burden's grant.[1]

When in 1752 Robert Dinwiddie came over as governor of Virginia, he was accompanied by many adventurers; among whom was John Stuart,[2] an intimate friend of Dinwiddie, who had married the widow of John Paul (son of Hugh, bishop of Nottingham.) John Paul, a partizan of the house of Stuart, had perished in the siege of Dalrymple castle in 1745, leaving three children—John, who became a Roman catholic priest and died on the eastern shore of Maryland—Audley, who was for ten years an officer in the British colonial forces, — and Polly, who married Geo. Matthews, afterwards governor of Georgia. Mrs. Paul (formerly Jane Lynn, of the Lynns of Loch-Lynn, a sister to the wife of John Lewis) had issue, by

---

[1] This incident is well authenticated. See the deposition of Mrs. Mary Greenlee, preserved in the famous Borden land suit, among the court records of Augusta county, Va. Mrs. Greenlee was the sister of Capt. John McDowell, and among the very earliest settlers of that part of Augusta, now Rockbridge county. Mrs Greenlee's deposition is published in full in Peyton's *History of Augusta County, Va.* (Staunton, Va., 1882), pp. 69–74.—L. C. D.

[2] The late Charles A. Stuart, of Greenbrier, son of Col. John Stuart, after the appearance of Hugh Paul Taylor's sketches over the signature of "Son of Cornstalk," published in the *Staunton Spectator* of August 21, 1829, over the signature of "Son of Blue Jacket," a brief criticism, in the nature of some corrections regarding his own family, to this effect: That Mrs. Jane Paul was no relative of Mrs. Margaret Lewis, wife of Col. John Lewis; that her first husband, Mr. Paul—not John. but probably Hugh Paul—was apparently from the north of Ireland—their son Audley Paul was born before the migration of the family to Pennsylvania; Mr. Paul, Sr., it is said, became the pastor of the Presbyterian congregation of Chester, in that province; but as Chester was a Quaker settlement, it is more likely that he located in some Presbyterian community in that region, and there must have died. Mrs. Paul, for her second husband, married Col. David Stuart, also from Ireland, by whom she had John Stuart and two daughters. Mrs. Stuart's grandchild. Charles A. Stuart, resided many years in Augusta, representing that county in the State senate, subsequently removed back to Greenbrier county. where he died about 1850, at the age of about sixty-five years. He was a man of sterling qualities.—L. C. D.

Stuart, John, since known as Col. Stuart of Greenbrier, and Betsy, who became the wife of Col. Richard Woods of Albemarle.

The greater part of those, who thus ventured " on the untried being" of a wilderness life, were Scottish presbyterian dissenters; a class of religionists, of all others perhaps, the most remarkable for rigid morality. They brought with them, their religious principles, and sectional prepossessions; and acting upon those principles acquired for their infant colony a moral and devotional character rarely possessed by similar establishments. While these sectional prepossessions, imbibed by their descendants, gave to their religious persuasions, an ascendency in that section of country, which it still retains.

They were also men of industry and enterprise. Hunting, which too frequently occupies the time, of those who make the forest their dwelling place, and abstracts the attention from more important pursuits, was to them a recreation—not the business of life. To improve their condition, by converting the woods into fertile plains, and the wilderness into productive meadows, was their chief object. In the attainment of this, they were eminently successful. Their individual circumstances became prosperous, and the country flourishing.

The habits and manners of the primeval inhabitants of any country, generally give to it a distinctive character, which marks it through after ages. Notwithstanding the influx of strangers, bringing with them prejudices and prepossessions, at variance with those of the community in which they come; [46] yet such is the influence of example, and such the facility with which the mind imbibes the feelings and sentiments of those with whom it associates, that former habits are gradually lost and those which prevail in society, imperceptibly adopted by its new members.

In like manner, the moral and religious habits of those who accompanied Burden to Virginia, were impressed on the country which they settled, and entailed on it that high character for industry, morality and piety, which it still possesses, in an eminent degree.

At the time of the establishment of this settlement, all that part of Virginia lying west of the Blue ridge mountains, was included in the county of Orange. At the fall session, of the colonial legislature, in 1738, the counties of Frederick and Augusta were formed out of Orange—The country included within the boundaries of the Potomac river, on the north, the Blue ridge, on the east, and a line, to be run from the head spring of Hedgman, to the head spring of Potomac, on the south and west, to be the county of Frederick ; the remainder of the state west of the Blue ridge, to the utmost limits of Virginia to constitute Augusta. Within its limits were included, not only a considerable portion of Virginia as she now is, but an extent of territory out of which has been already carved four states, possessing great natural advantages, and the extreme fertility of whose soil, will enable them to support perhaps a more dense population, than any other portion of North America of equal dimensions. As the settlements were extended, subdivisions were made, 'till what was once Augusta county south east of the Ohio river, has been chequered on the map of Virginia, into thirty-three counties with an aggregate population ef 289,362.[1]

[1] The following table exhibits a list of the several counties west of the Blue ridge—the counties from which each was taken—when established—their area in square miles—population in 1830, and amount of taxation for the same year.

Counties.	From what taken.	When formed.	Area.	Population	Taxation.
Augusta,	Orange,	1738	948	19,925	6,734
Alleghany,	Bath, Botetourt and Monroe,	1822	521	2,816	526
Bath,	Augusta, Botetourt and Greenbrier,	1791	795	4,068	865
[47] Brooke,	Ohio,	1797	202	7,040	1,136
Berkeley,	Frederick,	1772	308	10,528	3,356
Botetourt,	Augusta,	1770	1057	16,354	3,809
Cabell,	Kanawha,	1809	1033	5,884	629
Frederick,	Orange,	1738	745	26,045	9,396
Greenbrier,	Botet't & Montg'ry,	1778	1409	9,059	1,716
Giles,	Montgomery, Monroe and Tazewell,	1806	935	5,300	541
Grayson,	Wythe,	1793	927	7,675	537

[48] About the year 1749 there was in the county of Frederick, a man subject to lunacy, and who, when laboring under the influence of this disease, would ramble a considerable distance into the neighboring wilderness. In one of these wanderings he came on some of the waters of Greenbrier river. Surprised to see them flowing in a westwardly direction, on his return to Winchester he made known the fact, and that the country abounded very

Counties.	From what taken.	When formed.	Area.	Popula- tion.	Taxa- tion.
Harrison,	Monongalia,	1784	1095	14,713	1,669
Hampshire,	Augusta & Fred'k,	1754	989	11,279	2,402
Hardy,	Hampshire,	1786	1156	5,700	2,633
Jefferson,	Berkeley,	1801	225	12,927	4,721
Kanawha,	Greenb'r & M'tg'ry,	1789	2090	9,334	1,453
Lewis,	Harrison,	1816	1754	6,241	630
Logan,	Giles, Kanawha, Ca- bell & Tazewell,	1824	2930	3,680	245
Lee,	Russell,	1793	512	9,461	789
Monongalia,	District of W. A'g'ta,	1776	721	14,056	1,492
Monroe,	Greenbrier,	1799	614	7,798	1,158
Morgan,	Berkeley and Hampshire,	1820	271	2,702	546
Montgomery,	Fincastle,	1777	1089	12,306	1,666
Mason,	Kanawha,	1804	904	6,534	915
Nicholas,	Kanawha, Greenbrier and Randolph,	1818	1431	3,338	373
Ohio,	District of W. A'g'ta,	1776	375	15,590	1,968
Preston,	Monongalia,	1818	601	5,144	441
Pendleton,	Augusta, Hardy and Rockingham,	1788	999	6,271	1,120
Pocahontas,	Bath, Pendleton and Randolph,	1821	794	2,542	405
Randolph,	Harrison,	1787	2061	5,000	644
Russell,	Washington,	1786	1370	6,717	739
Rockingham,	Augusta,	1778	833	20,663	5,056
Rockbridge,	Augusta & Botetourt,	1778	680	14,244	3,276
Scott,	Lee, Russell and Washington,	1814	624	5,712	503
Shehandoah,	Frederick,	1772	767	19,750	4,922
Tyler,	Ohio,	1814	855	4,308	757
Tazewell,	Russell & Wythe,	1799	1305	5,573	727
Washington,	Fincastle,	1777	1754	15,614	2,918
Wythe,	Montgomery,	1790	1998	12,163	2,178
Wood,	Harrison,	1799	1223	6,418	1,257
		Total,		378,293	76,848

much with different kinds of Game. In consequence of this information two men, recently from New England, visited the country and took up their residence on the Greenbrier river.

Having erected a cabin and being engaged in making some other improvements, an altercation arose, which caused Stephen Suel,[1] one of them, to forsake the cabin and abide for some time in a hollow tree not far from the improvement, which was still occupied by his old companion. They were thus situated in 1751, when John Lewis, of Augusta and his son Andrew were exploring the country; to whom Suel made known the cause of their living apart, and the great pleasure which he experienced now in their morning salutations, when issuing from their respective habitations; whereas when they slept under the same roof, none of those kindly greetings passed between them. Suel however did not long remain in the vicinity of Martin, the other of the two adventurers; he moved forty miles west of his first improvement, and soon after fell a prey to Indian ferocity. Martin is said to have returned to the settlements.

There was no other attempt made by the whites, to improve the Greenbrier country for several years. Lewis and his son thoroughly examined it; and when permission

---

[1] Little and Big Sewell mountains, dividing Fayette and Greenbrier counties, seem to perpetuate the name and memory of this early and adventurous pioneer. Col. John Stuart states, that Sewell's final settlement was forty miles west of his primitive one, and on a creek bearing his name originating in Sewell mountain, and flowing into Gauley. Col. Preston, in his *Register*, gives September, 1756, as the date of Stephen Sewell's death by the Indians, and Jackson's River as the locality.

Mrs. Anne Royall, in *Sketches of the History, Life and Manners of the United States*, (New Haven, 1826), p. 60, who visited the Greenbrier country in 1824, gives the name of Carver as Sewell's companion. "These two men," says Mrs. Royall, "lived in a cave for several years, but at length they disagreed on the score of religion, and occupied different camps. They took care, however, not to stay far from each other, their camps being in sight. Sewell used to relate that he and his friend used to sit up all night without sleep, with their guns cocked, ready to fire at each other. 'And what could that be for?' 'Why, because we couldn't agree.' 'Only two of you, and could you not agree—what did you quarrel about?' 'Why, about re-la-gin.' One of them, it seems, was a Presbyterian, and the other an Episcopalian."—L. C. D.

was given to the Greenbrier company (of which John Lewis was a member) to locate 100,000 acres, on the waters of this river, they became agents to make the surveys and locations. The war between France and England in 1754 checked their proceedings; and when they, on the restoration of peace, would have resumed them, they were interdicted by a royal proclamation, issued in 1761, commanding all those who had made settlements on the western waters to remove from them; and those who were engaged in making surveys to desist. Sound policy requiring, that a good understanding should be maintained with the Indians (who claimed the country) to prevent a further cooperation on their part with France.[1]

Previous to the issuing of this proclamation, some families had moved to Greenbrier and made two settlements—the one on Muddy creek, the other in the Big-Levels. These, disregarding the command of his royal majesty and rather regardless of their own safety, remained until they were destroyed by the Indians, in 1763.[2] From this time 'till 1769 Greenbrier was altogether uninhabited. Capt. John Stuart and a few other young men, then began to settle and improve the country; and al-

---

[1] An error as to date. King George's proclamation was dated Oct. 7, 1763. For full text, see *Wisconsin Historical Collections*, XI., pp. 46 et seq.—R. G. T.

[2] Thomas King, one of the ablest of the Iroquois chiefs, related an incident at an Indian conference held at Easton, Pa., Oct. 18, 1758, which may explain why the Indians evinced so much hostility against the Greenbrier settlements. "About three years ago," said Chief King, "eight Seneca warriors were returning from war, with seven prisoners and scalps with them; and, at a place called Greenbrier, they met with a party of soldiers, not less than one hundred and fifty, who kindly invited them to come to a certain store, saying they would supply them with provisions. Accordingly they travelled two days with them, in a friendly manner, and when they came to the house, they took their arms from the Senecas. The head men cried out, 'here is death; defend yourselves as well as you can,' which they did, and two of them were killed on the spot, and one, a young boy, was taken prisoner. This gave great offense; and the more so, as it was upon the warrior's road, and we were in perfect peace with our brethren. It provoked us to such a degree that we could not get over it. He wished the boy returned, if alive; and told his name, Squissatego." See Hazard's *Penna. Register*, V., p. 373; and *Penna. Records*, VIII., pp. 197-98.—L. C. D.

though attempts were subsequently made by the Indians to exterminate them, yet they ever after continued in possession of it.

[49] In the year 1756 settlements were also made on New river and on Holstein.[1] Among the daring adventurers who effected them, were Evan Shelby, William Campbell, William Preston and Daniel Boone, all of whom became distinguished characters in subsequent history. Thomas Walden,[2] who was afterwards killed on Clinch river and

---

[1] There were settlers on both New and Holston rivers prior to 1756 —Vause, Stalnacker and others on New River; and Stephen Holston, at least, on the river bearing his name, which was known as such anterior to April, 1748, when Dr. Walker, in his *Journal* of 1750, refers to it by that designation. But William Campbell did not settle on Holston until 1767; Wm. Preston settled in 1769; Evan Shelby and family in 1771; and, while Daniel Boone passed through that country as early, it is believed, as 1760, he never "settled" there.

A further notice of Stephen Holston, or Holstein, seems fitting in this connection. He was of an adventurous turn, and prior to 1748 had, during a hunt, discovered the river named after him. It was after this discovery that he settled on the Little Saluda, near Saluda Old Town, in South Carolina, where, in the summer of 1753, a party of Cherokees returning from a visit to Gov. Glen, at Charleston, behaved so rudely to Mrs. Holston, in her husband's absence, as to frighten her and her domestics away, fleeing several miles to the nearest settlement, when the house was robbed of utensils and corn, and two valuable horses were also taken. Holston and some of his neighbors settled on Holston's River, in what subsequently became Botetourt county: soon after this, they constructed canoes, and passed down the Holston into the Tennessee River, through the Muscle Shoals, and down the Ohio and Mississippi as far as Natchez. Returning from this notable adventure, his name became fixed to the noble stream which he discovered, and upon which he made the primitive settlement. His location on Holston was at the head spring of the Middle Fork; his log cabin was on the hill side some thirty rods from the spring. In 1774, one Davis occupied the place, and related that Holston had left several years before that date. On the breaking out of the Indian war in 1754, he seems to have retired with his family to Culpeper county, which was then not exempt from Indian forays; and Holston, about 1757, was captured by the Indians. But in due time he returned to the Holston country, served in the battle of Point Pleasant in 1774, on Christian's campaign against the Cherokees in 1776, and was reported in service in 1776 or 1777. As we hear no more of him, he probably did not long survive after this period.— L. C. D.

[2] The first name of Walden was not Thomas—Elisha Walden was his proper name. He was a son-in-law of William Blevins, and both

from whom the mountain dividing Clinch and Powel rivers derived its name, was likewise one of them. The lands taken up by them, were held as "*corn rights*"—each acquiring a title to an hundred acres of the adjoining land, for every acre planted in corn.

Nearly cotemporaneous with these establishments, was that at Galliopolis, on the north western bank of the Ohio, and below Point Pleasant, at the mouth of the Great Kenhawa. This was made by a party of French Jesuits, by whom the Indians were incited to make incursions, and commit the most enormous barbarities on the then frontiers.[1] This place and the mouth of Great Sandy were the chief points of rendezvous for the Ohio Indians. From

Walden and Blevins lived, in 1774, at the "Round-About" on Smith's River, two miles east of what is now Martinsville, Henry county, Virginia. He was then about forty years of age, nearly six feet in height, a rough frontiersman, and a noted hunter. He and several others, in 1761, penetrated into Powell's Valley, naming Walden's Mountain and Walden's Creek, and proceeded on through Cumberland Gap to Cumberland River, and a few miles beyond to the Laurel Mountain, where meeting a party of Indians, they returned. In subsequent years, Walden settled on Holston, about eighteen miles above Knoxville, where he was residing in 1796; a few years later, he removed to Powell's Valley, but soon after migrated to Missouri, where he lived hunting up to extreme old age. Save what is related from Haywood's *Hist. of Tennessee* about the trip of 1761, this information was communicated to the writer in 1849, by Maj. John Redd, of Henry county, Va., who personally knew the old hunter very well.—L. C. D.

[1] A curious misconception, this. Some of the founders of Marietta acquired in 1788 a large tract west and north of their own, and as a private speculation organized the Scioto Company. Joel Barlow, the poet, was sent to Paris to negotiate the sale of the lands. To the "Society of the Scioto," formed by him there, he sold three million acres, and France was deluged with rose-colored immigration pamphlets written by Barlow. In February, 1790, six hundred Frenchmen—chiefly professional men and small artisans from the large towns, with not an agriculturist among them—arrived in Alexandria, Va., *en route* for the Scioto. They found that the Society, not having paid for its lands, had forfeited its rights, and deeds granted to the intending settlers were void. Five hundred finally went west, and founded Gallipolis. Poor, not knowing how to work the soil, and simple folk with no notions of independence, they suffered from famine, Indians, and yellow fever. They finally repurchased their lands, and upon the cessation of the border war gained some strength; but Gallipolis was never more than a weakling until Americans and Germans came in and put it on its feet. —R. G. T.

the former of these places they would ascend the Kenhawa and Greenbrier rivers, and from thence crossing the mountains enter into Augusta; or after having ascended the Kenhawa, go up the New river, from which they would pass over to the James and Roanoke. From the mouth of Great Sandy they would ascend that river, and by the way of Bluestone fall over on the Roanoke and New river. From those two points, expeditions were frequently made by the Indians, which brought desolation and death into the infant settlements of the south west, and retarded their growth very much. In the spring of 1757 nearly the whole Roanoke settlement was destroyed by a party of Shawanees, who had thus made their way to it.

That portion of the valley of Virginia in which establishments were thus begun to be made, was at that time one continued forest; overspreading a limestone soil of great fertility; and intersected by rivers affording extensive bottoms of the most productive alluvial land. Indeed few rivers of equal size, are bordered with as wide and fertile levels of this formation of earth, as those which water that section of country: the Roanoke particularly affords large bodies of it, capable of producing in great abundance hemp, tobacco and the different kinds of grain usually grown. In the country generally, every species of vegetable, to which the climate was congenial, grew with great luxuriancy; while the calcareous nature of the soil, adapted it finely to the production of that kind of grain, to which European emigrants were mostly used.

The natural advantages of the country were highly improved by the persevering industry of its inhabitants. Its forests, felled by untiring labor, were quickly reduced to profitable cultivation, and the weeds which spontaneously sprang from the earth, were soon succeeded by the various grasses calculated to furnish the most nutritious food, for the lowing herds with which their farmers were early stocked; these yielded a present profit, and laid the sure foundation [50] of future wealth. Some of the most extensive and successful graziers of Virginia, now inhabit that country; and reap the rich reward of their management and industry, in the improved and more contiguous market of Richmond.

In the infancy of these establishments, their only market was at Williamsburg. Thither the early settlers *packed* their butter and poultry, and received in exchange salt, iron, and some of the luxuries of life; their beef and other stock was taken to the same place. In the process of time, as the country east of the Blue ridge became more improved, other markets were opened to them; and the facilities of communication were gradually increased. Their successors have already derived great advantage from those improvements; and the present generation will not only witness their farther extension, but most probably see the country first tenanted by Lewis and his cotemporaries, a great thoroughfare for the produce of several of the western states—a link of communication between the Chesapeak bay and the Gulph of Mexico.

[51] CHAPTER II.

The tract of country usually denominated North Western Virginia, includes the counties of Brook, Ohio, Tyler, Wood, Lewis, Randolph, Preston, Harrison and Monongalia, covering an area of 8,887 square miles, and having a population, according to the census of 1830, of 78,510 souls. These counties, with a portion of Pennsylvania then deemed to be within the limits of Virginia, constituted the district of West Augusta; and was the last grand division of the state, to become occupied by the whites. This was perhaps owing to natural causes, as well as to the more immediate proximity of hostile Indians.

The general surface of this district of country is very broken, its hills, though rich, are yet steep and precipitous, and the various streams which flow along their bases, afford but few bottoms; and these of too narrow and contracted dimensions to have attacted the adventurer, when more invited portions of the country, were alike open to his enterprise.—The Alleghany ridge of mountains, over which the eastern emigrant had to pass, presented too, no inconsiderable barrier to its earlier location; while the cold, bleak, inhospitable region, extending from the North Branch to the Cheat and Valley rivers, seemed to threaten an entire seclusion from the eastern settlements, and to render it an isolated spot, not easily connected with any other section of the state.

The first attempt on the part of the English to occupy the country contiguous to the Ohio river, was made in consequence of the measures adopted by the French to possess themselves of it. France had early become acquainted with the country, so far as to perceive the facility with which her possessions in the north, might, by means of a free communication down the valley of the Mississippi, be connected with those in the south. To preserve this communication uninterrupted, to acquire influence over the neighboring Indians and to prevent the occupancy and settlement by England of the country west [52] of the Alleghany mountains, the French were early induced to establish trading posts among the Indians on the Ohio, and to obtain and preserve possession of the country by the erection of a chain of forts to extend from Canada to Louisiana.[1]

To counteract those operations of the French, to possess herself of the country, to which she deemed her title to be good, and to enjoy the lucrative traffic which was then to be carried on with the Indians, England gave to an association of gentlemen in Great Britain and Virginia, (under the title of the Ohio Company,) liberty to locate and hold in their own right, 600,000 acres of land within the country then claimed by both England and France. In pursuance of this grant, steps were directly taken to effect those objects, by establishing trading houses among the Indians near the Ohio, and by engaging persons to make such a survey of the country, as would enable the grantees to effect a location of the quantity allowed them, out of the most valuable lands. The com-

---

[1] This is misleading. The author has told us, in the preceding chapter, of several attempts of English coast colonists to make trans-montane settlements, quite apart from thought of ousting the French. Englishmen had no sooner landed in America than they attempted to cross the western mountain barrier. Ralph Lane made the attempt in 1586, Christopher Newport and John Smith in 1606, and Newport himself in 1607. John Lederer, a German surgeon exploring for Governor Berkeley, of Virginia, reached the top of Blue Ridge in 1669, but did not descend the western slope. Two years later, Abraham Wood discovered the Great Kanawha. It is possible that the French Jesuit Le Moyne was on the Alleghany River as early as 1656. La Salle was probably at the Falls of the Ohio (Louisville) in 1669. But it was not until about 1700 that French and English fur-traders met in open rivalry on the Ohio. It was with no thought of the French that Governor Spottswood, of Virginia, passed over the Blue Ridge in 1714. The situation in short, was this: The English colonists early wanted the over-mountain country watered by the Ohio, but were too weak at first to hold for agricultural settlement lands so far from home, in the face of a savage foe. The French wanted the valley solely for the fur trade, but Iroquois opposition long kept them from entering; when at last they were able to do so, the English colonists had also grown strong enough to move in, and then ensued the long and bloody struggle in which New France fell.—R. G. T.

pany endeavored to complete their survey with all possible secrecy, and by inducing the Indians to believe their object to be purely commercial, to allay any apprehensions, which might otherwise arise, of an attempt to gain possession of the country.

The attempt to accomplish their purpose of territorial aggrandizement, with secrecy, was fruitless and unavailing.—The Pennsylvania traders, fearful that they would lose the profitable commerce carried on with the Indians, excited their jealousy by acquainting them with the real motive of the company; while the French actually seized, and made prisoners, of their traders, and opened and secured, by detachments of troops stationed at convenient situations, a communication from Presq' Isle to the Ohio river.

The Ohio company sent a party of men to erect a stockade fort at the confluence of the Monongahela and Alleghany rivers, which had been recommended by General Washington as a suitable position for the erection of fortifications.[1] This party of men was accompanied by a detachment of militia, which had been ordered out by the governor; but before they could effect their object, they were driven off by the French, [53] who immediately took possession of the place, and erected thereon Fort du Quesne. These transactions were immediately succeeded by the war, usually called Braddock's war, which put an end to the contemplated settlement, and the events of which are, for the most part, matter of general history. It may not however be amiss to relate some incidents connected with this war, which though of minor importance, may yet be interesting to some; and which have escaped the pen of the historian.

In Braddock's army there were two regiments of volunteer militia from Virginia.[2] One of these was com-

---

[1] In the journal (drawn up for the inspection of Gov. Dinwiddie) of the events of his mission to the commander of the French forces on the Ohio; this was the first of those splendid acts of a public nature, performed by Gen. Washington.

[2] Only five companies of the first Virginia regiment served on Brad-

manded by Col. Russel of Fairfax; the other by Col. Fry, and was from Shenandoah and James rivers. In this latter regiment there was a company from Culpepper, commanded by Capt. Grant, (afterwards known as a considerable land holder in Kentucky) and of which John Field (who was killed in the battle at Point Pleasant) was a lieutenant. There was likewise in this regiment, a company of riflemen, from Augusta, commanded by Capt. Samuel Lewis, (the eldest son of John Lewis, who, with Mackey and Salling, had been foremost in settling that country) who was afterwards known' as Col. Samuel Lewis of Rockingham.[1] In this company was also contained the five brothers of Capt. Lewis. Andrew, afterwards Gen. Lewis of Botetourt—Charles, afterwards Col. Lewis, who was likewise killed at Point Pleasant— William, John and Thomas. Among their compatriots in arms, were the five sons of Capt. John Matthews, (who had accompanied Burden to Virginia) Elihu Barkley, John McDowell,[2] Paul Whitly, James Bell, Patrick Lockard, and a number of others of the first settlers of Augusta, Rockbridge and Rockingham.

From the time the army crossed the Alleghany mountain, its movements were constantly watched by Indian

---

dock's campaign—hence there was no second regiment, nor any Colonel Russell engaged in that service; there was, however, at this period, a Colonel or Lieut.-Colonel William Russell, who emigrated from England when a young lawyer, to Virginia, about 1710, and settled in Culpeper, and by the readjustment of county lines he was thrown into the new county of Orange. He was a man of much prominence, and at one time was high sheriff of Orange; and apparently lieutenant-colonel of militia, and as such, in the early part of the French and Indian War, did some frontier service, though rather advanced in years at the time. In 1753, he was sent as a commissioner to pacify the Indians in the region where Pittsburg was subsequently located. He died October 18, 1757, aged about seventy-two years. His son of the same name served with reputation at the battle of Point Pleasant. and during the Revolutionary War, retiring at its close with the brevet rank of brigadier-general.—L. C. D.

[1] It has already been stated that Col. John Lewis's eldest son was Thomas, not Samuel.—L. C. D.

[2] Capt. John McDowell was killed in an engagement with the Indians, in December, 1742, and of course could not have served under either Andrew or Charles Lewis.—L. C. D.

spies, from Fort du Quesne; and as it approached nearer the point of destination, runners were regularly despatched, to acquaint the garrison with its progress, and manner of marching.—When intelligence was received that Braddock still moved in close order, the Indians laid the plan for surprising him, and carried it into most effectual execution with but little assistance from the French.[1]

[54] At the place where the English crossed the Monongahela river, there are about two acres of bottom land, bounded by the river on the east, and by a ledge of high cliffs on the west. Through these cliffs there is a considerable ravine, formed by the flowing of a small rivulet—On the summit, a wide prospect opens to the west, of a country whose base is level, but surface uneven. On this summit lay the French and Indians concealed by the prairie grass and timber, and from this situation, in almost perfect security, they fired down upon Braddock's men. The only exposure of the French and Indians, resulted from the circumstance of their having to raise their heads to peep over the verge of the cliff, in order to shoot with more deadly precision. In consequence, all of them who were killed in the early part of the action, were shot through the head.[2]

---

[1] James Smith, afterwards Col. Smith of Bourbon county in Kentucky, was then a prisoner at du Quesne. He says that the Indians in council planned the attack on Braddock's army and selected the ground from which to make it—that the assailants did not number more than 400 men, of whom but a small proportion were French. One of the Indians laughed when he heard the order of march in Braddock's army, and said "we'll shoot them down all as one pigeon." Washington beheld the event in fearful anticipation, and exerted himself in vain with Gen. Braddock, to alter the order of march.

[2] It is evident that the author never saw the site of Braddock's defeat, just below the mouth of Turtle Creek, for his description is quite inaccurate. June 30, 1755, the army, which had been following the Ohio Company's road from Will's Creek, *via* East Meadows, crossed the Youghiogheny and proceeding in a devious course struck the head of Turtle Creek, which was followed nearly to its mouth, whence a southern course was taken to avoid the steep hills. Reaching the Monongahela just below the mouth of the Youghiogheny, they crossed (July 9) to the west side, where there is a long, narrow bottom. Nearly opposite the mouth of Turtle Creek, and about four miles below the first crossing,

The companies, commanded by Capt. Grant and Lewis,[1] were the first to cross the river. As fast as they landed they formed, and proceeding up the ravine, arrived at the plain on the head of the rivulet, without having discovered the concealed enemy which they had just passed. So soon as the rear of Braddock's army had crossed the river, the enemy raised a heart rending yell, and poured down a constant and most deadly fire. Before General Braddock received his wound, he gave orders for the whole line to countermarch and form a phalanx on the bottom, so as to cover their retreat across the river. When the main column was wheeled, Grant's and Lewis' companies had proceeded so far in advance, that a large body of the enemy rushed down from both sides of the ravine, and intercepted

---

hills again closely approach the west bank, and the east side becomes the more favorable for marching. Here, only eight miles across country from Fort Duquesne, Braddock forded the second time, and in angling up the rather easy slope upon which is now built the busy iron-making town of Braddock, Pa., was obliged to pass through a heavily-wooded ravine. This was the place of the ambuscade, where his army was cut to pieces. Indians from the Upper Lakes, under the leadership of Charles Langlade, a Wisconsin fur-trader, were the chief participants in this affair, on the French side.—R. G. T.

[1] This statement about Capts. Grant and Lewis having taken part in the battle of the Monongahela, is altogether a mistake. It must have originated in some traditional account, and become confused in some way with Grant's defeat, three years later, in which Maj. James Grant and Maj. Andrew Lewis both took a prominent part. There is no record of any Capt. Grant in Braddock's army. Andrew Lewis, though a major, was still in command of his company, and at the time of Braddock's defeat was on detached service. Gov. Dinwiddie, writing to Maj. Lewis, July 8, 1755, says: "You were ordered to Augusta with your company to protect the frontier of that county;" and, in a letter of the same date, to Col. Patton, the Governor adds: "Enclosed you have a letter to Capt. Lewis, which please forward to him: *I think he is at Greenbrier.* Capt. Robt. Orme, aide-de-camp to Gen. Braddock, in his Journal appended to Sargent's *History of Braddock's Expedition*, states under date of April, 1755, that the Virginia troops having been clothed, were ordered to march to Winchester, for arming and drilling, and then adds: "Capt. Lewis was ordered with his company of Rangers to Greenbrier river, there to build two stockade forts, in one of which he was to remain himself and to detach to the other a subaltern and fifteen men. These forts were to cover the western settlers of Virginia from any inroads of Indians."—L. C. D.

them. A most deadly contest ensued. Those who intercepted Grant and Lewis, could not pass down the defile,
as the main body of Braddock's army was there, and it
would have been rushing into the midst of it, to inevitable destruction—the sides of the ravine were too steep and
rocky to admit of a retreat up them, and their only hope of
escape lay in cutting down those two companies and passing
[55] out at the head of the ravine. A dreadful slaughter
was the consequence. Opposed in close fight, and with
no prospect of security, but by joining the main army in
the bottom, the companies of Grant and Lewis literally
cut their way through to the mouth of the ravine. Many
of Lewis's men were killed and wounded, and not more
than half of Grant's lived to reach the river bank. Almost the only loss the enemy sustained was in this conflict.

The unfortunate result of the campaign of 1755, gave
to the French a complete ascendency over the Indians on
the Ohio. In consequence of this there was a general distress on the frontier settlements of Virginia. The incursions of the Indians became more frequent and were extended so far, that apprehensions existed of an irruption
into the country east of the Blue ridge.[1] This state of
things continued until the capture of Fort du Quesne in
1758, by Gen. Forbes.

In the regiment commanded by Washington in the
army of 1758, Andrew Lewis was a Major. With this
gentleman, Gen. Washington had become acquainted during the campaign of 1754, and had formed of him, as a
military man, the highest expectations; his conduct at the
defeat of Major Grant, realized those expectations, and
acquired for him a reputation for prudence and courage
which he sustained unimpaired, during a long life of public service.[2]

---

[1] The MS. Journal of Col. Charles Lewis, in possession of the Wisconsin Historical Society, covering the period from October 10 to December 27, 1755, is an unconsciously eloquent picture of the hardships of
life on the Virginia frontier, at this time.—R. G. T.

[2] After the capitulation of Fort Necessity, and while some of the
soldiers of each army were intermixed, an Irishman, exasperated with

Gen. Lewis was in person upwards of six feet high, finely proportioned, of uncommon strength and great activity. His countenance was stern and rather forbidding—his deportment distant and reserved; this rendered his person more awful than engaging. When he was at Fort Stanwich in 1768, as one of the commissioners from the colony of Virginia, to treat, in conjunction with commissioners from the eastern colonies, with the Six Nations, the Governor of New York remarked "that the earth seemed to tremble under his tread."

When the war of the revolution commenced, and General [56] Washington was commissioned commander in chief, he is said to have expressed a wish, that the appointment had been given to Gen. Lewis. Be this as it may, it is certain that he accepted the commission of Brigadier General at the solicitation of Washington; and when, from wounded pride[1] and a shattered constitution, he was induced to express an intention of resigning, Gen. Washington wrote him, entreating that he would not do so, and assuring him that justice should be done, as regarded his rank. Gen. Lewis, however, had become much reduced by disease, and did not think himself able, longer to endure the hardships of a soldier's life—he resigned his commission in 1780, and died in the county of Bedford, on the way to his home in Botetourt on Roanoke river.

When Major Grant, (who had been sent with a detachment for the purpose of reconnoitering the country about Fort du Quesne,) arrived in view of it, he resolved on attempting its reduction. Major Lewis remonstrated with him, on the propriety of that course, and endeavored to dissuade him from the attempt. Grant deemed it practicable to surprise the garrison and effect an easy con-

---

an Indian near him, " cursed the copper-coloured scoundrel" and raised his musket to shoot him. Gen. Lewis who had been twice wounded in the engagement, and was then hobbling on a staff, raised the Irishman's gun, as he was in the act of firing, and thus not only saved the life of the Indian, but probably prevented a general massacre of the Virginia troops.

[1] Congress had given to Gen. Stephens, and some others (whose senior Lewis had been in former services) commissions as Major Generals.

quest, and was unwilling that the provincial troops should divide with his Highland regulars the glory of the achievment—he therefore ordered Major Lewis two miles into the rear, with that part of the Virginia regiment then under his command.

Soon after the action had commenced, Lewis discovered by the retreating fire, that Grant was in an unpleasant situation, and leaving Capt. Bullet with fifty men to guard the baggage, hastened to his relief. On arriving at the battle ground, and finding Grant and his detachment surrounded by the Indians, who had passed his rear under covert of the banks of the Alleghany and Monongahela rivers, Major Lewis commenced a brisk fire and made so vigorous an attack on the Indians as to open a passage through which Grant and some few of his men effected an escape. Lewis and his brave provincials became enclosed within the Indian lines and suffered dreadfully. Out of eight officers five were killed, a sixth wounded and a seventh taken prisoner. Capt. Bullet, [57] who defended the baggage with great bravery and contributed much to save the remnant of the detachment, was the only officer who escaped unhurt.[1] Out of one

---

[1] Thomas Bullitt was a native of Prince William county, Virginia. He was appointed an ensign in Washington's first Virginia regiment, July 20, 1754, and promoted to a lieutenancy on October 30th following. It is said that he served in Braddock's defeat; but the records of the Virginia officers present do not include Lieut. Bullitt's name. He was, perhaps, with Capt. Lewis in the Greenbrier country, or on some other detached service. In May, 1756, he was stationed at Winchester; in July following, in command of Fort Frederick, on Jackson's River, and in November of that year, in command of Fort Cumberland. He was in active service in 1757, and early the next year we find him a captain; as such, he distinguished himself in checking the enemy and saving many of the fugitives at Grant's defeat, and shared in Gen. Forbes's successful expedition in the capture of Fort Du Quesne. In May, 1759, while guarding with one hundred men, fifteen wagons loaded with provisions for the westward, he was attacked and defeated by a strong party of French and Indians, losing thirty-five of his party killed and prisoners and all his wagons. In 1760, he was appointed a surveyor of a district bordering on the Ohio, and had much to do in early Kentucky exploration and surveys, making an early location and survey at the Falls of Ohio in 1773. In September, 1775, he was appointed adjutant-general of all the Virginia forces; and on the 9th of December following,

hundred and sixty-six men, sixty-two were killed on the spot and two were wounded.

Major Lewis was himself made prisoner; and although stripped by the Indians of every article of his clothing, and reduced to perfect nudity, he was protected from bodily injury by a French officer, who took him to his tent and supplied him with clothes. Grant who had wandered all night with five or six of his men, came in, on the morning after the engagement, and surrendered himself a prisoner of war.

While Grant and Lewis were prisoners, the former addressed a letter to Gen. Forbes giving a detailed account of the engagement and attributing the defeat to the ill conduct of the latter. This letter, (being inspected by the French who knew the falsehood of the charge it contained) was handed to Maj. Lewis. Exasperated at this charge, Lewis waited on Major Grant and in the interview between them, after having bestowed on him some abusive epithets, challenged him to the field. Grant declined to accept the invitation; and Lewis, after spitting in his face in the presence of several of the French officers, left him to reflect on his baseness.

After this defeat a council was held by the Indians to determine on the course proper for them to pursue. The most of them had come from about Detroit at the instance of the French commandant there, to fortify Fort du Quesne against an attack by Forbes—the hunting season had arrived and many of them were anxious to return to their town. The question which attracted their attention most seriously was, whether Gen. Forbes would then retreat or advance. As Grant had been most signally defeated, many supposed that the main arm would retire into winter quarters, as Dunbar had, after the battle on the Monongahela. The French expressed a different opinion, and endeavored to prevail on the Indians to remain and

---

he aided Colonel Woodford in defeating Capt. Fordyce and party at the Great Bridge. In March, 1776, Congress appointed him deputy adjutant-general of the Southern Department with the rank of lieutenant-colonel, and advanced him in May following to the full rank of colonel. He died while yet in service, in 1778.—L. C. D.

witness the result. This however they refused to do, and the greater part of them left du Quesne. Upon this the commandant of the fort, in order to learn the course which Gen. Forbes would pursue, and to impress upon the English, an idea that the French were in return preparing to attack them, ordered the remainder of the Indians, a number of Canadians and some French regulars to reconnoitre the route [58] along which Gen. Forbes would be most likely to march his army, to watch their motions and harrass them as much as possible; determining if they could not thus force him to abandon the idea of attacking Du Quesne during that campaign, they would evacuate the fort and retire into Canada.

When Major Grant with his men had been ordered on to Du Quesne, the main army had been left at Raystown, where it continued for some time; an advance was however posted at fort Ligonier. Between this vanguard and the detachment from Du Quesne there was a partial engagement, which resulted in the loss of some of the Maryland troops. Fort Ligonier was then closely watched by the French and Indians, and several of the sentinels were killed, before the point from which the fires were directed, was discovered; it was at length ascertained that parties of the enemy would creep under the bank of the Loyal Hanna till they could obtain a position from which to do execution. Some soldiers were then stationed to guard this point, who succeeded in killing two Indians, and in wounding and making prisoner of one Frenchman. From him the English obtained information that the greater part of the Indians had left Du Quesne, and that the fort was defenceless: the army then moved forward and taking possession of its ruins established thereon Fort Pitt.[1] The

---

[1] The French destroyed Fort Duquesne in November, 1758. During the winter following, Fort Pitt was erected by the English troops. In his *Journal of a Tour to the Ohio River* (1770), Washington says of it: "The fort is built on the point between the rivers Alleghany and Monongahela, but not so near the pitch of it as Fort Duquesne stood. It is five-sided and regular, two of which next the land are of brick; the others stockade. A moat encompasses it." Fort Pitt was invested by the Indians during Pontiac's War (1763). It was fully garrisoned until 1772, when a corporal and a few men were left as care-takers. In October of

country around began immediately to be settled, and several other forts were erected to protect emigrants, and to keep the Indians in awe.

Previous to this an attempt had been made by David Tygart and a Mr. Files to establish themselves on an upper branch of the Monongahela river.[1] They had been for some time frontier's men, and were familiar with the scenes usually exhibited on remote and unprotected borders; and nothing daunted by the cruel murders and savage enormities, which they had previously witnessed, were induced by some cause, most probably the uninterrupted enjoyment of the forest in the pursuit of game, to venture still farther into the wilderness. About the year 1754 these two men with their families arrived on the east fork of the Monongahela, and after examining the country, selected positions for their future residence. Files chose a spot on the river, at the mouth of a creek which still bears his name, where Beverly, the county seat of Randolph has been since established. Tygart settled a few miles farther up and also on the river. The valley in which they had thus taken up their abode, has been since called Tygart's [59] valley, and the east fork of the Monongahela, Tygart's-valley river.

----

that year, the property was sold, and several houses were built out of the material. In the course of the boundary dispute between Pennsylvania and Virginia, the latter colony took possession of the ruins, through Lord Dunmore's agent there, John Conolly.—R. G. T.

[1] The author overlooks the settlement made by Christopher Gist, the summer of 1753, in the town of Dunbar, Fayette county, Pa., two or three miles west of the Youghiogheny and some seventy miles northwest of Will's Creek; the site was doubtless selected by him in his trip of 1751-52. Washington, who visited him there in November, 1753, on the way to Fort Le Bœuf, calls it "Gist's new settlement," but the owner's name for his place was "Monongahela." It was the first settlement of which there is record, upon the Ohio Company's lands. Gist induced eleven families to settle near him; and on his journey home, in January, 1754, Washington met them going out to the new lands. The victory of the French over Washington, at Fort Necessity, in July, led to the expulsion from the region of all English-speaking settlers. The French commander, De Villiers, reports that he "burnt down all the settlements" on the Monongahela (from Redstone down), and in the vicinity of Gist's.—R. G. T.

The difficulty of procuring bread stuffs for their families, their contiguity to an Indian village, and the fact that an Indian war path passed near their dwellings, soon determined them to retrace their steps.[1] Before they carried this determination into effect, the family of Files became the victims of savage cruelty. At a time when all the family were at their cabin, except an elder son, they were discovered by a party of Indians, supposed to be returning from the South Branch, who inhumanly butchered them all.[2] Young Files being not far from the house and hearing the uproar, approached until he saw, too distinctly, the deeds of death which were doing; and feeling the utter impossibility of affording relief to his own, resolved if he could, to effect the safety of Tygart's family. This was done and the country abandoned by them.

Not long after this, Doctor Thomas Eckarly and his two brothers came from Pennsylvania and camped at the mouth of a creek, emptying into the Monongahela, 8 or 10 miles below Morgantown; they were Dunkards, and from that circumstance, the watercourse on which they fixed themselves for a while, has been called Dunkard's creek. While their camp continued at this place, these men were engaged in exploring the country; and ultimately settled on Cheat river, at the Dunkard bottom. Here they erected a cabin for their dwelling, and made such improvements as enabled them to raise the first year, a crop of corn sufficient for their use, and some culinary vegetables: their guns supplied them with an abundance of meat, of a flavor

[1] This trail was a continuation of the famous "Warrior Branch," which coming up from Tennessee passed through Kentucky and Southern Ohio, and threading the valley of Fish Creek crossed over to Dunkard's Creek and so on to the mouth of Redstone Creek.—R. G. T.

[2] In Col. Preston's MS. Register of Indian Depredations, in the Wisconsin Historical Society's library, it is stated that Robert Foyle, wife and five children, were killed on the Monongahela in 1754. Gov. Dinwiddie, in his speech to the Virginia house of burgesses in February, 1754, refers to this barbarous affair, giving the same number of the family destroyed; and the gazettes of that period state that Robert Foyle, together with his wife and five children, the youngest about ten years of age, were killed at the head of the Monongahela; their bodies, scalped, were discovered February 4th, and were supposed to have been killed about two months before.—L. C. D.

as delicious as the refined palate of a modern epicure could well wish. Their clothes were made chiefly of the skins of animals, and were easily procured: and although calculated to give a grotesque appearance to a fine gentleman in a city drawing room; yet were they particularly suited to their situation, and afforded them comfort.

Here they spent some years entirely unmolested by the Indians, although a destructive war was then raging, and prosecuted with cruelty, along the whole extent of our frontier. At length to obtain an additional supply of ammunition, salt and shirting, Doctor Eckarly left Cheat, with a pack of furs and skins, to visit a trading post on the Shenandoah. On his return, he stopped at Fort Pleasant, on the South Branch; and having communicated to its inhabitants the place of his residence, and the length of time he had been living there, he was charged with being in confederacy with the Indians, and probably at that instant a spy, examining the condition of the fort. In vain the Doctor protested his innocence and the fact that he had not even seen an Indian in the country; the suffering condition [59] of the border settlements, rendered his account, in their opinion improbable, and he was put in confinement.

The society, of which Doctor Eckarly was a member, was rather obnoxious to a number of the frontier inhabitants. Their intimacy with the Indians, although cultivated with the most laudable motives, and for noble purposes, yet made them objects at least of distrust to many. Laboring under these disadvantages, it was with difficulty that Doctor Eckarly prevailed on the officer of the fort to release him; and when this was done he was only permitted to go home under certain conditions—he was to be escorted by a guard of armed men, who were to carry him back if any discovery were made prejudicial to him. Upon their arrival at Cheat, the truth of his statement was awfully confirmed. The first spectacle which presented itself to their view, when the party came within sight of where the cabin had been, was a heap of ashes. On approaching the ruins, the half decayed, and mutilated bodies of the poor Dunkards, were seen in the yard; the hoops, on which their scalps

had been dried, were there, and the ruthless hand of desolation had waved over their little fields. Doctor Eckarly
aided in burying the remains of his unfortunate brothers,
and returned to the fort on the South Branch.

In the fall of 1758, Thomas Decker and some others
commenced a settlement on the Monongahela river, at the
mouth of what is now, Decker's creek. In the ensuing
spring it was entirely broken up by a party of Delawares
and Mingoes; and the greater part of its inhabitants murdered.

There was at this time at Brownsville a fort, then known
as Redstone fort, under the command of Capt. Paul.[1] One

---

[1] In 1750, the Ohio Company, as a base of operations and supplies,
built a fortified warehouse at Will's Creek (now Cumberland, Md.), on
the upper waters of the Potomac. Col. Thomas Cresap, an energetic
frontiersman, and one of the principal agents of the Company, was directed to blaze a pack-horse trail over the Laurel Hills to the Monongahela. He employed as his guide an Indian named Nemacolin, whose
camp was at the mouth of Dunlap Creek (site of the present Brownsville, Pa.), an affluent of the Monongahela. Nemacolin pointed out an
old Indian trace which had its origin, doubtless, in an over-mountain
buffalo trail; and this, widened a little by Cresap, was at first known as
Nemacolin's Path. It led through Little Meadows and Great Meadows—
open marshes grown to grass, and useful for feeding traders' and ex-
plorers' horses. Washington traveled this path in 1753, when he went
to warn the French at Fort Le Bœuf. Again, but widened somewhat,
it was his highway in 1754, as far north as Gist's plantation; and at Great
Meadows he built Fort Necessity, where he was defeated. Braddock
followed it in great part, in 1755, and henceforth it became known as
"Braddock's Road." The present National Road from Cumberland to
Brownsville, *via* Uniontown, differs in direction but little from Nemacolin's Path. For a map of Braddock's Road, see Lowdermilk's *History of
Cumberland, Md.,* p. 140. with description on pages 51, 52, 140–148. Ellis's
History of Fayette Co., Pa., also has valuable data.

The terminus of Nemacolin's Path was Dunlap's Creek (Brownsville). A mile-and-a-quarter below Dunlap's, enters Redstone Creek, and
the name "Redstone" became affixed to the entire region hereabout,
although "Monongahela" was sometimes used to indicate the pan-
handle between the Monongahela and the Youghiogheny. In 1752, the
Ohio Company built a temporary warehouse at the mouth of Dunlap's
Creek, at the end of the over-mountain trail. In 1754, Washington's advance party (Capt. Trent) built a log fort, called "The Hangard," at
the mouth of the Redstone, but this was, later in the year, destroyed by
the French officer De Villiers. In 1759, Colonel Burd, as one of the features of Forbes's campaign against Fort Duquesne, erected Fort Burd at
the mouth of Dunlap's, which was a better site. This fort was gar-

of Decker's party escaped from the Indians who destroyed the settlement, and making his way to Fort Redstone, gave to its commander the melancholy intelligence. The garrison being too weak to admit of sending a detachment in pursuit, Capt. Paul despatched a runner with the information to Capt. John Gibson, then stationed at Fort Pitt. Leaving the fort under the command of Lieut. Williamson, Capt. Gibson set out with thirty men to intercept the Indians, on their return to their towns.

In consequence of the distance which the pursuers had to go, and the haste with which the Indians had retreated, the expedition failed in its object; they however accidentally came on a party of six or seven Mingoes, on the head of Cross Creek in Ohio (near Steubenville)—these had been prowling about the river, below Fort Pitt, seeking an opportunity of committing depredations.[1] As Capt. Gibson passed the point of a small knoll, just after day break, he came unexpectedly upon them—some of them were lying down; the others were sitting round a fire, making thongs of green hides. Kiskepila or Little Eagle, a Mingo chief, headed the party. So soon as he discovered Capt. Gibson, he raised the war whoop and fired [61] his rifle—the ball passed through Gibson's hunting shirt and wounded a soldier just behind him. Gibson sprang forward, and swinging his sword with herculean force, severed the head of the Little Eagle from his body — two other Indians were shot down, and the remainder escaped to their towns on Muskingum.

When the captives, who were restored under the treaty of 1763, came in, those who were at the Mingo towns when the remnant of Kiskepila's party returned, stated that the Indians represented Gibson as having cut off the Little

---

risoned as late as the Dunmore War (1774), but was probably abandoned soon after the Revolutionary War. The name "Redstone Old Fort" became attached to the place, because within the present limits of Brownsville were found by the earliest comers, and can still be traced, extensive earthworks of the mound-building era.—R. G. T.

[1] Cross Creek empties into the Ohio through Mingo Bottom (site of Mingo Junction, O.). On this bottom was, for many years, a considerable Mingo village.—R. G T.

Eagle's head with a *long knife.* Several of the white persons were then sacrificed to appease the manes of Kiskepila; and a war dance ensued, accompanied with terrific
shouts and bitter denunciations of revenge on *"the Big knife
warrior."* This name was soon after applied to the Virginia militia generally; and to this day they are known
among the north,western Indians as the *"Long knives,"* or
"Big knife nation."[1]

---

[1] This statement, that Capt. Audley Paul commanded at Redstone,
and of his attempting to intercept a foraging Indian party, can not possibly be true. There was no fort, and consequently no garrison, at Redstone in 1758. It was not built 'till 1759, and then by Col. James Burd, of
the Pennsylvania forces. James L. Bowman, a native of Brownsville,
the locality of Redstone Old Fort, wrote a sketch of the history of that
place, which appeared in the *American Pioneer* in February, 1843, in which
he says: "We have seen it stated in a creditable work, that the fort was
built by Capt. Paul — doubtless an error, as the Journal of Col. Burd is
ample evidence to settle that matter." Col. Burd records in his Journal:
"Ordered, in Aug. 1759, to march with two hundred of my battalion to
the mouth of Redstone Creek, to cut a road to that place, and to erect
a fort." He adds: "When I had cut the road, and finished the fort," etc.

The other part of the story, about Capt. John Gibson commanding
at Fort Pitt in "the fall of 1758," is equally erroneous, as Gen. Forbes
did not possess himself of Fort Duquesne till Nov. 25th, 1758, within
five days of the conclusion of "fall" in that year; and Gen. Forbes commanded there in person until he left for Philadelphia, Dec. 3d following.
There is, moreover, no evidence that Gibson was then in service. The
story of his decapitating Kis-ke-pi-la, or the Little Eagle, if there was such
a person, or of his beheading any other Indian, is not at all probable.
He was an Indian trader for many years, and was made prisoner by the
Indians in 1763, and detained a long time in captivity.

Gibson could not by any such decapitating exploit, have originated
the designation of "Big Knife," or "Big Knife warrior," for this appellation had long before been applied to the Virginians. Gist says in his
Journal, Dec. 7th, 1750, in speaking of crossing Elk's Eye Creek — the
Muskingum — and reaching an Indian hamlet, that the Indians were all
out hunting; that "the old Frenchman, Mark Coonce, living there, was
civil to me; but after I was gone to my camp, upon his understanding I
came from Virginia, he called me *Big Knife.*" Col. James Smith, then a
prisoner with the Indians, says the Indians assigned as a reason why
they did not oppose Gen. Forbes in 1758, that if they had been only red
coats they could have subdued them; "but they could not withstand
Ash-a-le-co-a, or the *Great Knife,* which was the name they gave the
Virginians."—L. C. D.

Comment by R. G. T.—See note on p. 77, regarding erection of early
forts at Redstone. James Veech, in *Monongahela of Old,* says, "We know

These are believed to have been the only attempts to effect a settlement of North Western Virginia, prior to the close of the French war. The capture of Fort du Quesne and the erection and garrisoning of Fort Pitt, although they gave to the English an ascendency in that quarter; yet they did not so far check the hostile irruptions of the Indians, as to render a residence in this portion of Virginia, by any means secure.—It was consequently not attempted 'till some years after the restoration of peace in 1765.

---

that the late Col. James Paull served a month's duty in a drafted militia company in guarding Continental stores here [Fort Burd] in 1778." The term " Big Knives " or " Long Knives " may have had reference either to the long knives carried by early white hunters, or the swords worn by backwoods militia officers. See Roosevelt's *Winning of the West*, I., p. 197.

[62] CHAPTER III.

The destruction of the Roanoke settlement in the spring of 1757, by a party of Shawanees, gave rise to the campaign, which was called by the old settlers the " Sandy creek voyage." To avenge this outrage, Governor Dinwiddie ordered out a company of regulars (taken chiefly from the garrison at Fort Dinwiddie, on Jackson's river) under the command of Capt. Audley Paul; a company of minute-men from Boutetourt, under the command of Capt. William Preston; and two companies from Augusta, under Captains John Alexander[1] and William Hogg. In Capt. Alexander's company, John M'Nutt, afterwards governor of Nova Scotia, was a subaltern. The whole were placed under the command of Andrew Lewis.[2]

---

[1] Father of Dr. Archibald Alexander, sometime president of Hampden Sydney College in Virginia, and afterwards a professor at Princeton in New Jersey.

Comment by L. C. D.—He was the grandfather of Dr. Alexander.

[2] The attacks on the Roanoke settlement, mentioned by Withers, occurred in June and July, 1755 (not the spring of 1757, as he states); that on Greenbrier, in September following; and the expedition against the Shawnees did not take place in 1757, but in February and March, 1756. Diaries and other documents in the Wisconsin Historical Society's library prove this. Dr. Draper estimated that Lewis's force was about 263 whites and 130 Cherokees—418 in all. The several companies were officered by Peter Hogg, John Smith, William Preston, Archibald Alexander, Robert Breckenridge, Obadiah Woodson, John Montgomery, and one Dunlap. Two of Dr. Thomas Walker's companions in his Kentucky exploration of 1750, were in the expedition—Henry Lawless and Colby Chew. Governor Dinwiddie had stipulated in his note to Washington, in December, 1755, that either Col. Adam Stephen or Maj. Andrew Lewis was to command. Washington having selected the latter, disspatched him from Winchester about the middle of January, 1756, with orders to hurry on the expedition. To the mismanagement of the guides is attributed much of the blame for its failure. The interesting Journals of Capt. William Preston and Lieut. Thomas Norton are in the possession of the Wisconsin Historical Society.—R. G. T.

6

Beside the chastisement of the Indians, the expedition had for its object, the establishment of a military post at the mouth of the Great Sandy. This would have enabled them, not only to maintain a constant watch over marauding parties of Indians from that quarter; but to check the communication between them and the post at Galliopolis; and thus counteract the influence which the French there had obtained over them.[1]

The different companies detailed upon the Shawanee expedition, were required to rendezvous on the Roanoke, near to the present town of Salem in Bottetourt, where Col. Lewis was then posted. The company commanded by Capt. Hogg failed to attend at the appointed time; and Col. Lewis after delaying a week for its arrival, marched forward, expecting to be speedily overtaken by it.

To avoid an early discovery by the Indians, which would have been the consequence of their taking the more public route by the Great Kenhawa; and that they might fall upon the Indians towns in the valley of the Scioto, without being interrupted or seen by the French at Galliopolis, they took the route by the way of New river and Sandy. Crossing New river below the Horse-shoe, they descended it to the mouth of Wolf creek; and ascending this to its source, passed over to the head of Bluestone river; where they delayed another week awaiting the arrival of Capt. Hogg and his company.[2]—They then marched to the head of the north fork of Sandy, and continued down it to the great Burning Spring, where they

---

[1] But Gallipolis was not settled until 1790, as has been previously shown. Withers confounds the modern French town of Gallipolis, whose residents were the sad victims of Indian outrages rather than the abettors of them, with the old Shawnee town just below the mouth of the Scioto (site of Alexandria. O.). This fur-trading center was a village of log huts built by the French for the accommodation of their Shawnee allies, and was a center of frontier disturbances.—R. G. T.

[2] Preston's Journal does not lay much stress on Hogg's delay. Norton's Journal, speaking of Hogg, says, "common soldiers were by him scarcely treated with humanity," and he seems to have regularly over-ruled and disobeyed Lewis. There was much rancor in camp, and Norton writes of the Cherokee allies, "The conduct and concord that was kept up among the Indians might shame us, for they were in general quite unanimous and brotherly."—R. G. T.

also remained a day. Here the salt and provisions, which
had been conveyed [63] on pack horses, were entirely exhausted. Two buffaloes, killed just above the spring, were
also eaten while the army continued here; and their hides
were hung upon a beech tree. After this their subsistence was procured exclusively by hunting.

The army then resumed their march; and in a few
days after, it was overtaken by a runner with the intelligence that Capt. Hogg and his company were only a
day's march in the rear. Col. Lewis again halted; and
the day after he was overtaken by Hogg, he was likewise overtaken by an express from Francis Fauquier [1]
with orders for the army to return home; and for the dis-
banding of all the troops except Capt. Paul's regulars, [2]
who were to return to Fort Dinwiddie.

This was one of the first of Gov. Fauquier's official acts;
and it was far from endearing him to the inhabitants west
of the Blue ridge. They had the utmost confidence in
the courage and good conduct of Col. Lewis, and of the
officers and men under his command—they did not for an
instant doubt the success of the expedition, and looked
forward with much satisfaction, to their consequent exemption in a great degree, from future attacks from the
Indians. It was not therefore without considerable regret, that they heard of their countermanding orders.

Nor were they received by Lewis and his men with
very different feelings. They had endured much during
their march, from the inclemency of the weather; more
from the want of provisions—They had borne these hardships without repining; anticipating a chastisement of the
Indians, and the deriving of an abundant supply of provisions from their conquered towns—They had arrived
within ten miles of the Ohio river, and could not witness
the blasting of their expectations, without murmuring.
A council of war was held—disappointment and indigna-

---

[1] This expedition was sent out under the auspices of Gov. Dinwiddie—Fauquier did not become governor until 1758. No countermanding orders were sent.—L. C. D.

[2] Audley Paul was first lieutenant in Preston's company.—L. C. D.

tion were expressed in every feature. A majority of the
officers were in favor of proceeding to the Ohio river, under the expectation that they might fall in with some
of the enemy—they marched to the river and encamped
two nights on its banks. Discovering nothing of an
enemy, they then turned to retrace their steps through
pathless mountains, a distance of three hundred miles, in
the midst of winter and without provisions.

The reasons assigned by the friends of Gov. Fauquier,
for the issuing of those orders were, that the force detailed
by Gov. Dinwiddie, was not sufficient to render secure
an establishment at the contemplated point—near the Indian towns on the Scioto—within a few days journey of
several thousand warriors on the Miami—in the vicinity
of the hostile post at Galliopolis and so remote from the
settled part of Virginia, that they could not be furnished
with assistance, and supplied with provisions and military
stores, without incurring an expenditure, both of blood
and money, beyond what the colony could spare, for the
accomplishment of that object.

Had Capt. Hogg with his company, been at the place
of rendezvous at the appointed time, the countermanding orders of the governor [64] could not have reached the army,
until it had penetrated the enemy's country. What might
have been its fate, it is impossible to say—the bravery of
the troops—their familiar acquaintance with the Indian
mode of warfare—their confidence in the officers and the
experience of many of them, seemed to give every assurance of success—While the unfortunate result of many
subsequent expeditions of a similar nature, would induce
the opinion that the governor's apprehensions were perhaps prudent and well founded. That the army would
soon have had to encounter the enemy, there can be no
doubt; for although not an Indian had been seen, yet it
seems probable from after circumstances, that it had been
discovered and watched by them previous to its return.

On the second night of their march homeward, while
encamped at the Great falls, some of Hogg's men went
out on the hills to hunt turkeys, and fell in with a party
of Indians, painted as for war. As soon as they saw that

they were discovered, they fired, and two of Hogg's men were killed—the fire was returned and a Shawanee warrior was wounded and taken prisoner. The remaining Indians, yelling their war whoop, fled down the river.

Many of the whites, thinking that so small a party of Indians would not have pursued the army alone, were of opinion that it was only an advanced scout of a large body of the enemy, who were following them: the wounded Indian refused to give any information of their number or object. A council of war was convoked; and much diversity of opinion prevailed at the board. It was proposed by Capt. Paul to cross the Ohio river, invade the towns on the Scioto, and burn them, or perish in the attempt.[1] The proposition was supported by Lieut. M'Nutt, but overruled; and the officers, deeming it right to act in conformity with the governor's orders, determined on pursuing their way home. Orders were then given that no more guns should be fired, and no fires kindled in camp, as their safe return depended very much on silence and secrecy.

An obedience to this order, produced a very considerable degree of suffering, as well from extreme cold as from hunger. The pack horses, which were no longer serviceable (having no provisions to transport) and some of which had given out for want of provender, were killed and eaten. When the army arrived at the Burning spring, the buffalo hides, which had been left there on their way down, were cut into tuggs, or long thongs, and eaten by the troops, after having been exposed to the heat produced by the flame from the spring.—Hence they called it Tugg river—a name by which it is still known. After this the army subsisted for a while on beachnuts; but a deep snow

---

[1] Withers, deriving his information from Taylor's sketches, was misled as to any intention of establishing a fort at the mouth of the Kanawha; and also as to Paul's, or any one else's proposition to cross the Ohio, and invade the Shawnee towns. The only aim was, to reach the Upper Shawnee town.—L. C. D.

Comment by R. G. T.—"Upper Shawnee town" was an Indian village at the mouth of Old Town Creek, emptying into the Ohio from the north, 39 miles above the mouth of the Great Kanawha.

falling these could no longer be obtained, and the restrictions were removed.

About thirty men then detached themselves from the main body, to hunt their way home. Several of them were known to have perished from cold and hunger—others were lost and never afterwards [65] heard of; as they had separated into small parties, the more certainly to find game on which to live. The main body of the army was conducted home by Col. Lewis, after much suffering—the strings of their mocasons, the belts of their hunting shirts, and the flaps of their shot pouches, having been all the food which they had eaten for some days.[1]

A journal of this campaign was kept by Lieut. M'Nutt, a gentleman of liberal education and fine mind. On his return to Williamsburg he presented it to Governor Fauquier by whom it was deposited in the executive archives. In this journal Col. Lewis was censured for not having proceeded directly to the Scioto towns; and for imposing on the army the restrictions, as to fire and shooting, which have been mentioned.—This produced an altercation between Lewis and M'Nutt, which was terminated by a personal encounter.[2]

During the continuance of this war, many depredations were committed by hostile Indians, along the whole extent of the Virginia frontier. Individuals, leaving the forts on any occasion, scarcely ever returned; but were, almost always, intercepted by Indians, who were constantly prowling along the border settlements, for purposes of

---

[1] If such a journal ever existed, it passed into the hands of Gov. Dinwiddie, or possibly to Gov. Fauquier; but no reference to it is found among the *Dinwiddie Papers*, as published by the Virginia Historical Society; nor in the *Calendar of State Papers*, published by the State of Virginia. It is to be remarked, however, that few of the records of that period have been preserved by that State.—L. C. D.

[2] Shortly after, M'Nutt was appointed governor of Nova Scotia, where he remained until the commencement of the American revolution. In this contest he adhered to the cause of liberty, and joined his countrymen in arms under Gen. Gates at Saratoga. He was afterwards known as a meritorious officer in the brigade of Baron de Kalb, in the south—he died in 1811, and was buried in the Falling Spring church yard, in the forks of James river.

rapine and murder. The particulars of occurrences of this kind, and indeed of many of a more important character, no longer exist in the memory of man—they died with them who were contemporaneous with the happening of them.[1] On one occasion however, such was the extent of savage duplicity, and such, and so full of horror, the catastrophe resulting from misplaced confidence, that the events which marked it, still live in the recollection of the descendants of some of those, who suffered on the theatre of treachery and blood.

On the south fork of the South Branch of Potomac, in, what is now, the county of Pendleton, was the fort of Capt. Sivert.[2] In this fort, the inhabitants of what was

---

[1] Preston's MS. Register of the persons of Augusta county, Va., killed, wounded, captured by the Indians, and of those who escaped, from 1754 to May, 1758, is in the Wisconsin Historical Society's library. It is to be regretted that Col. Preston, whose opportunities were so good, did not continue the Register till the end of the Indian wars. It is a most valuable document as far as it goes, and supplies many dates and facts hitherto involved in doubt and obscurity.—L. C. D.

[2] Seybert's Fort was situated on the South Fork, twelve miles northeast of Franklin, in Pendleton County. At the time of this invasion, there was a fort located on the South Branch, garrisoned by Capt. James Dunlap and a company of rangers from Augusta county. Preston's Register states, that on the 27th of April, 1758, the fort at which Capt. Dunlap was stationed, was attacked and captured, the captain and twenty-two others killed; and, the next day, the same party, no doubt, attacked Seybert's Fort, killing Capt. Seybert and sixteen others, while twenty-four others were missing. Washington, at the time, placed the number as "about sixty persons killed and missing."

A gazette account, published at Williamsburg, May 5th ensuing, says: "The Indians lately took and burnt two forts, where were stationed one of our ranging companies, forty of whom were killed and scalped, and Lieut. Dunlap and nineteen missing."

Kercheval's *History of the Valley* gives some further particulars: That Seybert's Fort was taken by surprise; that ten of the thirty persons occupying it, were bound, taken outside; the others were placed on a log and tomahawked. James Dyer, a lad of fourteen, was spared, taken first to Logstown, and then to Chillicothe, and retained a year and ten months, when as one of an Indian party he visited Fort Pitt, and managed to evade his associates while there, and finally reached the settlements in Pennsylvania, and two years later returned to the South Fork. It is added by the same historian, as another tradition, that after the fort had been invested two days, and two of the Indians had been killed, the garrison agreed to surrender on condition of their lives being spared,

then called the " Upper Tract," all sought shelter from
the tempest of savage ferocity; and at the time the
Indians appeared before [66] it, there were contained
within its walls between thirty and forty persons of both
sexes and of different ages. Among them was Mr. Dyer,
(the father of Col. Dyer now of Pendleton) and his family.
On the morning of the fatal day, Col. Dyer and his sister
left the fort for the accomplishment of some object, and
although no Indians had been seen there for some time,
yet did they not proceed far, before they came in view of
a party of forty or fifty Shawanees, going directly towards
the fort. Alarmed for their own safety, as well as for the
safety of their friends, the brother and sister endeavored
by a hasty flight to reach the gate and gain admittance into
the garrison; but before they could effect this, they were
overtaken and made captives.

The Indians rushed immediately to the fort and commenced a furious assault on it. Capt. Sivert prevailed,
(not without much opposition,) on the besieged, to forbear
firing 'till he should endeavor to negotiate with, and buy
off the enemy. With this view, and under the protection
of a flag he went out, and soon succeeded in making the
wished for arrangement. When he returned, the gates
were thrown open, and the enemy admitted.

No sooner had the money and other articles, stipulated

---

which was solemnly promised. That when the gate was opened, the
Indians rushed in with demoniac yells, the whites fled, but were retaken, except one person; the massacre then took place, and ten were
carried off into captivity.

Still another tradition preserved by Kercheval, says the noted Delaware chief, Killbuck, led the Indians. Seybert's son, a lad of fifteen,
exhibited great bravery in the defense of the fort. Killbuck called out
to Capt. Seybert, in English, to surrender, and their lives should be
spared; when young Seybert at this instant, aimed his loaded gun at
the chief, and the father seized it, and took it from him, saying they
could not successfully defend the place, and to save their lives should
surrender, confiding in Killbuck's assurances. Capt. Seybert was among
the first of those sacrificed. Young Seybert was among the prisoners,
and told the chief how near he came to killing him. "You young
rascal," laughingly replied Killbuck, "if you had killed me, you would
have saved the fort, for had I fallen, my warriors would have immediately fled, and given up the siege in despair."—L. C. D.

to be given, been handed over to the Indians, than a most bloody tragedy was begun to be acted. Arranging the inmates of the fort, in two rows, with a space of about ten feet between them, two Indians were selected; who taking each his station at the head of a row, with their tomahawks most cruelly murdered almost every white person in the fort; some few, whom caprice or some other cause, induced them to spare, were carried into captivity, —such articles as could be well carried away were taken off by the Indians; the remainder was consumed, with the fort, by fire.

The course pursued by Capt. Sivert, has been supposed to have been dictated by timidity and an ill founded apprehension of danger from the attack. It is certain that strong opposition was made to it by many; and it has been said that his own son raised his rifle to shoot him, when he ordered the gates to be thrown open; and was only prevented from executing his purpose, by the interference of some near to him. Capt. Sivert was also supported by many, in the plan which he proposed to rid the fort of its assailants: it was known to be weak, and incapable of withstanding a vigorous onset; and [67] its garrison was illy supplied with the munitions of war. Experience might have taught them, however, the futility of any measure of security, founded in a reliance on Indian faith, in time of hostility; and in deep and bitter anguish, they were made to feel its realization in the present instance.

In the summer of 1761, about sixty Shawanee warriors penetrated the settlements on James river. To avoid the fort at the mouth of Looney's creek, on this river, they passed through Bowen's gap in Purgatory mountain, in the night; and ascending Purgatory creek, killed Thomas Perry, Joseph Dennis and his child and made prisoner his wife, Hannah Dennis. They then proceeded to the house of Robert Renix, where they captured Mrs. Renix, (a daughter of Sampson Archer) and her five children, William, Robert, Thomas, Joshua and Betsy—Mr. Renix not being at home. They then went to the house of Thomas Smith, where Renix was; and shot and scalped him and Smith; and took with them, Mrs. Smith and Sally Jew, a white servant girl.[1]

William and Audley Maxwell, and George Matthews, (afterwards governor of Georgia,) were then going to Smith's house; and hearing the report of the guns, supposed that there was a shooting match. But when they rode to the front of the house and saw the dead bodies of Smith and Renix lying in the yard, they discovered their mistake; and contemplating for a moment the awful spectacle, wheeled to ride back. At this instant several guns were fired at them; fortunately without doing any execution, except the cutting off the club of Mr. Matthews' cue. The door of the house was then suddenly opened; the Indians rushed out and raising the war cry, several of them fired—Audley Maxwell was slightly wounded in the arm.

It appeared afterwards, that the Indians had seen Matthews and the Maxwells coming; and that some of them had crowded into the house, while the others with the prisoners went to the north side of it, and concealed themselves behind some fallen timber. Mrs. Renix, after she was restored to her friends in 1766, stated that she was sitting tied, in the midst of four Indians, who laying their guns on a log, took deliberate aim at Matthews; the others firing at the Maxwells—The sudden wheeling of their horses no doubt saved the lives of all three.

The Indians then divided, and twenty of them taking the [68] prisoners, the plunder and some horses which they had stolen, set off by the way of Jackson's river, for

---

[1] The name is Renick. Robert Renick, who was killed on the occasion referred to, was a man of character and influence in his day. His name appears on Capt. John Smith's company roll of Augusta militia as early as 1742; and four years later, he was lieutenant of a mounted company of Augusta militia. Instead of 1761, the captivity of the Renick family occurred July 25, 1757, as shown by the Preston Register, which states that Renick and another were killed on that day—Mrs. Renick and seven children, and a Mrs. Dennis, captured; and the same day, at Craig's Creek, one man was killed and two wounded. The Renick traditions state that Mrs. Renick had only five children when taken; and one born after reaching the Indian towns; and corrects some other statements not properly related in Withers's narrative of the affair.—L. C. D.

the Ohio; the remainder started towards Cedar creek, with the ostensible view of committing farther depredations. But Matthews and the Maxwells had sounded the alarm, and the whole settlement were soon collected at Paul's stockade fort, at the Big spring near to Springfield. Here the women and children were left to be defended by Audley Maxwell and five other men; while the others, forming a party of twenty-two, with George Matthews at their head, set out in quest of the enemy.

The Indians were soon overtaken, and after a severe engagement, were forced to give ground. Matthews and his party followed in pursuit, as far as Purgatory creek; but the night being very dark in consequence of a continued rain, the fugitives effected an escape; and overtaking their comrades with the prisoners and plunder, on the next evening, at the forks of the James and Cowpasture rivers, proceeded to Ohio without further molestation.

When Matthews and his men, on the morning succeeding the engagement, returned to the field of battle, they found nine Indians dead; whom they buried on the spot. Benjamin Smith, Thomas Maury and the father of Sally Jew, were the only persons of Matthews' party, who were killed—these, together with those who had been murdered on the preceding day, were buried near the fork of a branch, in (what is now) the meadow of Thomas Cross sr.

In Boquet's treaty with the Ohio Indians, it was stipulated that the whites detained by them in captivity were to be brought in and redeemed. In compliance with this stipulation, Mrs. Renix was brought to Staunton in 1767 and ransomed, together with two of her sons, William, the late Col. Renix of Greenbrier, and Robert, also of Greenbrier—Betsy, her daughter, had died on the Miami. Thomas returned in 1783, but soon after removed and settled, on the Scioto, near Chilicothe. Joshua never came back; he took an Indian wife and became a Chief among the Miamies—he amassed a considerable fortune and died near Detroit in 1810.

Hannah Dennis was separated from the other captives,

and allotted to live at the Chilicothe towns.[1]   She learned
their language; painted herself as they do; and in many
respects conformed to their manners and customs.   She
was attentive to sick persons and was highly esteemed by
the Indians, as [69] one well skilled in the art of curing
diseases.   Finding them very superstitious and believers
in necromancy; she professed witchcraft, and affected to
be a prophetess.   In this manner she conducted herself,
'till she became so great a favorite with them, that they
gave her full liberty and honored her as a queen.   Notwithstanding this, Mrs. Dennis was always determined to
effect her escape, when a favorable opportunity should
occur; and having remained so long with them, apparently well satisfied, they ceased to entertain any suspicions
of such a design.

In June 1763, she left the Chilicothe towns, *ostensibly*
to procure herbs for medicinal purposes, (as she had before frequently done,) but *really* to attempt an escape.   As
she did not return that night, her intention became suspected; and in the morning, some warriors were sent in
pursuit of her.   In order to leave as little trail as possible,
she had crossed the Scioto river three times, and was just
getting over the fourth time 40 miles below the towns,
when she was discovered by her pursuers.   They fired at
her across the river without effect; but in endeavoring to
make a rapid flight, she had one of her feet severely cut
by a sharp stone.

The Indians then rushed across the river to overtake
and catch her, but she eluded them by crawling into the
hollow limb, of a large fallen sycamore.   They searched
around for her some time, frequently stepping on the log
which concealed her; and encamped near it that night.
On the next day they went on to the Ohio river, but finding no trace of her, they returned home.

Mrs. Dennis remained at that place three days, doc-

---

[1] In 1763-65, the great Shawnee village just below the mouth of the
Scioto (site of Alexandria, O.), was destroyed by floods.   Some of the
tribesmen rebuilt their town on a higher bottom just above the mouth
(site of Portsmouth, O.), while others ascended the Scioto and built
successively Old and New Chillicothe.—R. G. T.

toring her wound, and then set off for home. She crossed the Ohio river, at the mouth of Great Kenhawa, on a log of driftwood, travelling only during the night, for fear of discovery—She subsisted on roots, herbs, green grapes, wild cherries and river muscles—and entirely exhausted by fatigue and hunger, sat down by the side of Green-brier river, with no expectation of ever proceeding farther. In this situation she was found by Thomas Athol and three others from Clendennin's settlement, which she had passed without knowing it. She had been then upwards of twenty days on her disconsolate journey, alone, on foot—but 'till then, cheered with the hope of again being with her friends.

She was taken back to Clendennin's, where they kindly [70] ministered to her, 'till she became so far invig-orated, as to travel on horseback with an escort, to Fort Young on Jackson's river; from whence she was carried home to her relations.

In the course of a few days after Hannah Dennis had gone from Clendennins, a party of about sixty warriors came to the settlement on Muddy creek, in the county of Greenbrier. That region of country then contained no inhabitants, but those on Muddy creek, and in the Levels: and these are believed to have consisted of at least one hundred souls. The Indians came apparently as friends, and the French war having been terminated by the treaty of the preceding spring, the whites did not for an in-stant doubt their sincerity. They were entertained in small parties at different houses, and every civility and act of kindness, which the new settlers could proffer, were ex-tended to them. In a moment of the most perfect confi-dence in the innocense of their intentions, the Indians rose on them and tomahawked and scalped all, save a few women and children of whom they made prisoners.

After the perpetration of this most barbarous and bloody outrage, the Indians (excepting some few who took charge of the prisoners) proceeded to the settlement in the Levels. Here, as at Muddy creek, they disguised their horrid purpose, and wearing the mask of friendship,

were kindly received at the house of Mr. Clendennin.[1]
This gentleman had just returned from a successful hunt,
and brought home three fine elks—these and the novelty
of being with *friendly Indians*, soon drew the whole settlement to his house.   Here too the Indians were well
entertained and feasted on the fruit of Clendennin's hunt,
and every other article of provision which was there, and
could minister to their gratification.   An old woman, who
was of the party, having a very sore leg and having understood that Indians could perform a cure of any ulcer,
shewed it to one near her; and asked if he could heal it
—The inhuman monster raised his tomahawk and buried
it in her head.   This seemed to be the signal of a general
massacre and promptly was it obeyed—nearly every man of
the settlement was killed and the women and children
taken captive.

While this tragedy was acting, a negro woman, who
was [71] endeavoring to escape, was followed by her crying child.—To save it from savage butchery, she turned
round and murdered it herself.

Mrs. Clendennin, driven to despair by the cruel and
unprovoked murder of her husband and friends, and the
spoilation and destruction of all their property, boldly
charged the Indians with perfidy and treachery; and alleged that cowards only could act with such duplicity.
The bloody scalp of her husband was thrown in her face
—the tomahawk was raised over her head; but she did
not cease to revile them.   In going over Keeny's knot on
the next day, the prisoners being in the centre, and the
Indians in the front and rear, she gave her infant child to
one of the women to hold for a while.—She then stepped
into the thicket unperceived, and made her escape.   The
crying of the infant soon lead to a discovery of her flight
—one of the Indians observed that he could "bring the
cow to her calf," and taking the child by the heels, beat
out its brains against a tree.

Mrs. Clendennin returned that night to her home, a
distance of ten miles; and covering the body of her hus-

---

[1] Where Ballard Smith now resides.

band with rails and trash, retired into an adjoining corn field, lest she might be pursued and again taken prisoner. While in the corn field, her mind was much agitated by contending emotions; and the prospect of effecting an escape to the settlements, seemed to her dreary and hopeless. In a moment of despondency, she thought she beheld a man, with the aspect of a murderer, standing near her; and she became overwhelmed with fear. It was but the creature of a sickly and terrified imagination; and when her mind regained its proper tone, she resumed her flight and reached the settlement in safety.[1]

These melancholy events occurring so immediately after the escape of Hannah Dennis: and the unwillingness of the Indians that she should be separated from them, has induced the supposition that the party committing those dreadful outrages were in pursuit of her. If such were the fact, dearly were others made to pay the penalty of her deliverance.

This and other incidents, similar in their result, satisfied the whites that although the war had been terminated on the part of the French; yet it was likely to be continued with all its horrors, by their savage allies. This was then, and has since been, attributed to the smothered hostility of the French in [72] Canada and on the Ohio river; and to the influence which they had acquired over the Indians. This may have had its bearing on the event; but from the known jealousy entertained by the Indians, of the English Colonists; their apprehensions that they would be dispossessed of the country, which they then held (England claiming jurisdiction over it by virtue of the treaty of Paris;) and their dissatisfaction at the terms on which France had negotiated a peace, were in themselves sufficient to induce hostilities on the part of the Indians. Charity would incline to the belief that the continuance of the war was rightly attributable to these causes—the other reason assigned for it, supposing the existence of a

---

[1] Further particulars of this captivity are in Royall's *Sketches of History, Life, and Manners in U. S.* (New Haven, 1826), pp. 60–66.—R. G. T.

depravity, so deep and damning, as almost to stagger credulity itself.

In October, 1764, about fifty Delaware and Mingo warriors ascended the Great Sandy and came over on New river, where they separated; and forming two parties, directed their steps toward different settlements—one party going toward Roanoke and Catawba—the other in the direction of Jackson's river. They had not long passed, when their trail was discovered by three men, (Swope, Pack and Pitman) who were trapping on New river. These men followed the trail till they came to where the Indian party had divided; and judging from the routes which had been taken, that their object was to visit the Roanoke and Jackson's river settlements, they determined on apprizing the inhabitants of their danger. Swope and Pack set out for Roanoke and Pitman for Jackson's river. But before they could accomplish their object, the Indians had reached the settlements on the latter river, and on Catawba.

The Party which came to Jackson's river, travelled down Dunlap's creek and crossed James river, above Fort Young, in the night and unnoticed; and going down this river to William Carpenter's, where was a stockade fort under the care of a Mr. Brown, they met Carpenter just above his house and killed him. They immediately proceeded to the house, and made prisoners of a son of Mr. Carpenter, two sons of Mr. Brown¹ [73] (all small children)

---

¹ Carpenter's son (since Doctor Carpenter of Nicholas) came home about fifteen years afterwards— Brown's youngest son, (the late Col. Samuel Brown of Greenbrier) was brought home in 1769—the elder son never returned. He took an Indian wife, became wealthy and lived at Brown's town in Michigan. He acted a conspicuous part in the late war and died in 1815.

Comment by L. C. D.—Adam Brown, who was captured as mentioned in the above text and note, was thought by his last surviving son, Adam Brown, Jr., whom I visited in Kansas in 1868, to have been about six years old when taken; and he died, he thought, about 1817, at about seventy-five years of age. But these dates, and his probable age, do not agree; he was either older when taken, or not so old at his death. The mother was killed when the sons were captured, and the father and some others of the family escaped. The late William Walker, an educated Wyandott, and one woman—the others belonging to the house, were in the field at work. The Indians then dispoiled the house and taking off some horses, commenced a precipitate retreat—fearing discovery and pursuit.

When Carpenter was shot, the report of the gun was heard by those at work in the field; and Brown carried the alarm to Fort Young. In consequence of the weakness of this fort, a messenger was despatched to Fort Dinwiddie, with the intelligence. Capt. Paul (who still commanded there,) immediately commenced a pursuit with twenty of his men; and passing out at the head of Dunlap's creek, descended Indian creek and New river to Piney creek; without making any discovery of the enemy. On Indian creek they met Pitman, who had been running all the day and night before, to apprise the garrison at Fort Young of the approach of the Indians. Pitman joined in pursuit of the party who had killed Carpenter; but they, apprehending that they would be followed, had escaped to Ohio, by the way of Greenbrier and Kenhawa rivers.[1]

As Capt. Paul and his men were returning, they accidently met with the other party of Indians, who had been

and at one time territorial governor of Kansas, stated to me, that the Wyandotts never made chiefs of white captives. but that they often attained, by their merits, considerable consequence. It is, however, certain that Abraham Kuhn, a white prisoner, grew up among the Wyandotts, and, according to Heckewelder, became a war chief among them, and signed the treaty at Big Beaver in 1785; and Adam Brown himself signed the treaties of 1805 and 1808, and doubtless would have signed later ones had he not sided with the British Wyandotts, and retired to Canada, near Malden, where he died.

[1] It is highly probable that this foray took place in 1763. During this year, as features of the Pontiac uprising, bloody forays were made on the more advanced settlements on Jackson, Greenbrier, and Calf Pasture rivers, and several severe contests ensued between whites and Indians. Captains Moffett and Phillips, with sixty rangers, were ambuscaded with the loss of fifteen men. Col. Charles Lewis pursued the savages with 150 volunteers raised in a single night, and on October 3rd surprised them at the head of the South Fork of the Potomac, killing twenty-one, with no white losses. The spoils of this victory, beside the "five horses with all their trappings," sold for £250. This was the most notable of the several skirmishes which took place on the Virginia frontier, that year.—R. G. T.

7

to Catawba, and committed some depredations and murders there. They were discovered about midnight, encamped on the north bank of New river, opposite an island at the mouth of Indian creek. Excepting some few who were watching three prisoners, (whom they had taken on Catawba, and who were sitting in the midst of them,) they were lying around a small fire, wrapped in skins and blankets. Paul's men not knowing that there were captives among them, fired in the midst, killed three Indians, and wounded several others, one of whom drowned himself to preserve his scalp—the rest of the party fled hastily down the river and escaped.

In an instant after the firing, Capt. Paul and his men rushed forward to secure the wounded and prevent further escapes. One of the foremost of his party seeing, as he supposed, a squaw sitting composedly awaiting the result, raised his tomahawk and just as it was descending, Capt. Paul threw himself between the assailant and his victim; and receiving the blow on his arm, exclaimed, "It is a shame to hurt a woman, even a squaw." Recognising the voice of Paul, the woman named him. She was Mrs. Catharine Gunn, an English lady, who had come to the country some years before; and who, previously to her marriage, had lived in the family of Capt. Paul's father-in-law, where she became acquainted with that gentleman— She had been taken captive by the Indians, on the Catawba, a few days before, when her husband and two only children were killed by them. When questioned why she had not cried out, or otherwise made known that she was a white prisoner, she replied, "I had as soon be killed as not —my husband is murdered—my children are slain—my parents are dead. I have not a relation in America—every thing dear to me here is gone—I have no wishes—no hopes —no fears—I would not have risen to my feet to save my life."

[74] When Capt. Paul came on the enemy's camp, he silently posted his men in an advantageous situation for doing execution, and made arrangements for a simultaneous fire. To render this the more deadly and efficient, they dropped on one knee, and were preparing to take de-

liberate aim, when one of them (John M'Collum) called to his comrades, "Pull steady and send them all to hell." This ill timed expression of anxious caution, gave the enemy a moment's warning of their danger; and is the reason why greater execution was not done.

The Indians had left all their guns, blankets and plunder—these together with the three white captives, were taken by Capt. Paul to Fort Dinwiddie.[1]

---

[1] Perhaps this affair is that related by Capt. William Christian, in a letter dated Roanoke, Oct. 19th, 1763, as published in the gazettes of that day—there are, at least, some suggestive similarities: "Being joined by Capt. Hickenbotham, with twenty-five of the Amherst militia, we marched on Tuesday last, to Winston's Meadows, where our scouts informed us, that they had discovered a party of Indians about three miles off. Night coming on, prevented our meeting them; and next day, being rainy, made it difficult to follow their tracks. As they were on their return, Capt. Hickenbotham marched to join Capt. Ingles down New River. I, with nineteen men and my ensign, took a different route in quest of them. We marched next day on their tracks until two hours before sunset, when we heard some guns, and soon afterwards discovered three large fires, which appeared to be on the bank of Turkey Creek, where it empties into New river. Upon this we immediately advanced, and found they were on an island. Being within gun-shot, we fired on them, and loading again, forded the creek. The Indians, after killing Jacob Kimberlain, a prisoner they had with them, made but a slight resistance, and ran off. We found one Indian killed on the spot, and, at a little distance, four blankets shot through, and very bloody. We took all their bundles, four guns, eight tomahawks, and two mares. They had several other horses, which being frightened by the firing, ran off and were lost. The party consisted of upwards of twenty Indians. By the tracks of blood, we imagined several of them were wounded." This affair occurred Oct. 12th.—L. C. D.

[75] CHAPTER IV.

During the continuance of the French war, and of that with the Indians which immediately succeeded it, the entire frontier from New York to Georgia was exposed to the merciless fury of the savages.   In no instance were the measures of defence adopted by the different colonies, adequate to their object.—From some unaccountable fatuity in those who had the direction of this matter, a defensive war, which alone could have checked aggression and prevented the effusion of blood, was delayed 'till the whole population, of the country west of the Blue ridge, had retired east of those mountains; or were cooped up in forts.

The chief means of defence employed, were the militia of the adjoining counties, and the establishment of a line of forts and block-houses, dispersed along a considerable extent of country, and occupied by detachments of British colonial troops, or by militiamen.   All these were utterly incompetent to effect security; partly from the circumstances of the case, and somewhat from the entire want of discipline, and the absence of that subordination which is absolutely necessary to render an army effective.

So great and apparent were the insubordination and remissness of duty, on the part of the various garrisons, that Gen. Washington, declared them " utterly inefficient and useless;" and the inhabitants themselves, could place no reliance whatever on them, for protection.   In a particular instance, such were the inattention and carelessness of the garrison that several children playing under the walls of the fort, were run down and caught by the Indians, who were not discovered 'till they arrived at the very gate.[1]

In Virginia the error of confiding on the militia, soon

---

[1] At Dickenson's fort in 1755.

became apparent.[1] Upon the earnest remonstrance and entreaty of General Washington, the colonial legislature substituted a force of regulars,[2] [76] which at once effected the partial security of her frontier, and gave confidence to the inhabitants.

In Pennsylvania, from the pacific disposition of her rulers and their abhorrence of war of any kind, her border settlements suffered most severely. The whole extent of her frontier was desolated by the Indians, and irruptions were frequently made by them into the interior. The establishments, which had been made in the Conocochcague valley, were altogether broken up and scenes of the greatest barbarity, on one side, and of the utmost suffering on the other, were constantly exhibiting. A few instances of this suffering and of that barbarity, may not be improperly adduced here. They will serve to illustrate the condition of those who were within reach of the savage enemy; and perhaps, to palliate the enormities practiced on the christian Indians.

In the fall of 1754 about forty or fifty Indians entered that province, and dividing themselves into two parties, sought the unprotected settlements, for purposes of murder and devastation: the smaller party went about the forks of Delaware—the other directing their steps along the Susquehanna. On the 2nd of October, twelve of the former appeared before the house of Peter Williamson, (a Scotchman, with no family but his wife,) who had made considerable improvement near the Delaware river. Mrs. Williamson being from home, he sat up later than usual, and about 11 o'clock was astounded at the savage war whoop, resounding from various directions, near to the house. Going to the window, he perceived several Indians standing in the yard, one of whom, in broken English, promised that if he would come out and surrender he

---

[1] When the Indians were most troublesome, and threatening even the destruction of Winchester, Lord Fairfax who was commandant of the militia of Frederick and Hampshire, ordered them out. Three days active exertion on his part, brought only 20 in the field.

[2] Rather rangers, who seem to have been enlisted to serve a year, and were re-engaged when necessary.—L. C. D.

should not be killed; threatening at the same time that if he did not, they would burn him up in his house. Unable to offer an effectual resistance, and preferring the chance of safety by surrendering, to the certainty of a horrid death if he attempted an opposition, he yielded himself up a prisoner.

So soon as he was in their power they plundered the house of such articles as they could conveniently take with them, and set fire to it, and to the barn, in which was a quantity of wheat, some horses and other cattle. After inflicting some severe tortures on Williamson, and forcing him to carry a heavy weight of the plunder, which they had taken from him, they went to a neighboring house, occupied by Jacob Snyder, his wife, five children and a servant. The piercing cries, and [77] agonizing shrieks of these poor creatures, made no impression on the savages. The father, mother, and children were tomahawked and scalped, and their bodies consumed by fire together with the house. The servant was spared that he might aid in carrying their plunder; but manifesting deep distress at his situation as prisoner, he was tomahawked before they proceeded far.

Before they could accomplish farther mischief a fall of snow, making them apprehensive that they would be pursued by the united force of the settlement, induced them to return to Alamingo—taking Williamson with them.

On their way back, they met with the party of Indians, which had separated from them, as they approached the settlements. These had been lower down on the Susquehanna, and had succeeded in making greater havoc, and committing more depredations, than it had fallen to the lot of those who had taken Williamson, to commit. They had with them three prisoners and twenty scalps. According to the account of their transactions as detailed by the prisoners, they had on one day killed and scalped John Lewis, his wife and three children, and in a few days after had murdered, with almost every circumstance of cruelty, Jacob Miller, his wife and six children, and George Folke, his wife and nine children, cutting up the bodies of the latter family and giving them piece-meal to the hogs in the pen. Wherever they had been, destruction marked their course. In every instance the houses, barns and grain stacks were consumed by fire; and the stock killed.

The three prisoners who had been brought in by the last party, endeavored soon after to effect an escape; but their ignorance of the country, and the persevering activity and vigilance of the Indians, prevented the accomplishment of their attempt. They were overtaken, and brought back; and then commenced a series of cruelties, tortures and death, sufficient to shock the sensibilities of the most obdurate heart, if unaccustomed to the perpetration of such enormities.

Two of them were tied to trees, around which large fires were kindled, and they suffered to remain for some time, in the gradual but horrible state of being scorched to death. After the Indians had enjoyed awhile the writhings of agony and the tears of anguish, which were drawn from these suffering victims, one, stepping within the circle, ripped open their bodies and threw their bowels into the flames. Others, to emulate [78] this most shocking deed, approached, and with knives, burning sticks, and heated irons, continued to lacerate, pierce and tear the flesh from their breasts, arms and legs, 'till death closed the scene of horrors and rendered its victims insensible to its pains.

The third was reserved a few hours, that he might be sacrificed under circumstances of peculiar enormity. A hole being dug in the ground of a depth sufficient to enable him to stand upright, with his head only exposed, his arms were pinioned to his body, he placed in it, and the loose earth thrown in and rammed closely around him. He was then scalped and permitted to remain in that situation for several hours. A fire was next kindled near his head. In vain did the poor suffering victim of hellish barbarity exclaim, that his brains were boiling in his head; and entreat the mercy of instant death. Deaf to his cries, and inexorable to his entreaties, they continued the fire 'till his eye balls burst and gushed from their sockets, and death put a period to his sufferings.

Of all these horrid spectacles, Williamson was an unwilling spectator; and supposing that he was reserved for some still more cruel and barbarous fate, determined on escaping. This he was soon enabled to do; and returned to the settlements.[1]

The frequent infliction of such enormities as these upon the helpless and unoffending women and children, as well as upon those who were more able to resist and better qualified to endure them; together with the desolation of herds, the devastation of crops, and the conflagration of houses which invariably characterized those incursions, engendered a general feeling of resentment, that sought in some instances, to wreak itself on those who were guiltless of any participation in those bloody deeds. That vindictive spirit led to the perpetration of offences against humanity, not less atrocious than those which they were intended to requite; and which obliterated every discriminative feature between the perpetrators of them, and their savage enemies.

The Canestoga Indians, to the number of forty, lived in a village, in the vicinity of Lancaster; they were in amity with the whites, and had been in peace and quiet for a considerable length of time. An association of men, denominated the "Paxton boys," broke into their little town and murdered all who were found at home—fourteen men, women and children fell a prey to the savage brutality of those sons of civilization [79]. The safety of the others was sought to be effected, by confining them in the jail at Lancaster. It was in vain. The walls of a prison could afford no protection, from the relentless fury of these exasperated men. The jail doors were broken

---

[1] Peter Williamson had singular adventures. When a boy he was kidnapped at Aberdeen, and sent to America, for which he afterwards recovered damages. It is said that he passed a considerable period among the Cherokees. He instituted the first penny post at Edinburgh, for which, when the government assumed it, he received a pension. His *Memoirs*, and *French and Indian Cruelty Examplified*, were works of interest. He died in Edinburgh in 1799.—L. C. D.

open, and its wretched inmates cruelly murdered.—And, as if their deaths could not satiate their infuriate murderers, their bodies were brutally mangled, the hands and feet lopped off, and scalps torn from the bleeding heads of innocent infants.

A similar fate impended the christian Indians of Nequetank and Nain; and was only averted, by the timely interposition of the government of Pennsylvania. They were removed to Philadelphia, where they remained from November 1763 'till after the close of the war in December 1764; during which time the Paxton boys twice assembled in the neighborhood of the city, for the purpose of assaulting the barracks and murdering the Indians, but were deterred by the military preparations made to oppose them; and ultimately, but reluctantly, desisted.

Had the feelings excited in the minds of these misguided men, by the cruelties of the Indians, been properly directed, it would have produced a quite different result. If, instead of avenging the outrages of others, upon those who were no otherwise guilty than in the complexion of their skin, they had directed their exertions to the repressing of invasion, and the punishment of its authors, much good might have been achieved; and they, instead of being stigmatized as murderers of the innocent, would have been hailed as benefactors of the border settlements. Associations of this kind were formed in that province, and contributed no little to lessen the frequency of Indian massacres, and to prevent the effusion of blood, and the destruction of property. At the time the Paxton boys were meditating and endeavoring to effect the destruction of the peaceable christian Indians, another company, formed by voluntary league, was actively engaged in checking the intrusions, of those who were enemies, and in punishing their aggressions. A company of riflemen, called the Black boys (from the fact of their painting themselves red and black, after the Indian fashion,) under the command of Capt. James Smith, contributed to preserve the Conococheague valley, during the years 1763 and 1764, from the devastation [80] which had overspread it early after the commencement of Braddock's war.

Capt. Smith had been captured by the Indians in the spring of 1755, and remained with them until the spring of 1759, when he left them at Montreal, and after some time arrived at home in Pennsylvania. He was in Fort du Quesne, when the Indians and French went out to surprise Gen. Braddock; and witnessed the burnings and other dreadful tortures inflicted upon those who were so unfortunate as to have been made prisoners; and the orgies and demoniacal revels with which the victory was celebrated. He was subsequently adopted into a family, by which he was kindly treated; and became well acquainted with their manner of warfare, and the various arts practised by them, to ensure success in their predatory incursions, and afterwards to elude pursuit. He became satisfied from observation, that to combat Indians successfully, they must be encountered in their own way; and he accordingly instructed his men in the Indian mode of warfare, dressed them after the Indian fashion, and fought after the Indian manner.[1]

An instance of the good effect resulting from practicing the arts and stratagems of the Indians, occurred during this war; and to its success the garrison of Fort Pitt were indebted for their preservation.

After the ratification of the treaty of peace which had been concluded between England and France, war con-

---

[1] Col. James Smith was born in Franklin county, Pa., in 1737; was captured by Indians in 1755, remaining in captivity until his escape in 1759. He served as ensign in 1763, and lieutenant under Bouquet in 1764; he was a leader, for several years, of the Black Boys—a sort of regulators of the traders who, the Black Boys thought, supplied the Indians with the munitions of war. As the troubles with the mother country began, Smith was selected for frontier service, and held civil and military positions—captain in the Pennsylvania line; then in 1777 as major under Washington; in 1778, he was promoted to the rank of colonel of militia, and led an expedition against the Indian town on French Creek. In 1788, he removed to Kentucky; served in the early Kentucky conventions, preparatory to State organization, and also in the legislature. He did missionary work in Kentucky and Tennessee, and preached among the Indians. He wrote a valuable account of his Indian captivity, republished a few years since by Robert Clarke & Co., Cincinnati, and a treatise on Indian warfare, besides two controversial pamphlets against the Shakers. He died in Washington county, Ky., in 1812, aged about seventy-five years.—L. C. D.

tinued to be waged by the Indians on the whole western frontier. A large body of them had collected and marched to Fort Pitt, with a view to its reduction by famine. It had been invested for some time and the garrison being too weak to sally out and give battle to the besiegers, Capt. Ecuyer dispatched messengers with the intelligence of his situation and a request for aid and provisions: these were either compelled to return or be killed, as the country for some distance east of Fort Pitt was in the possession of the savages.[1]

At length a quantity of provisions were ordered by Gov. Amherst for the relief of the fort, and forwarded under a strong guard commanded by Colonel Boquet. The Indians were soon apprized of this and determined on intercepting the provisions, and if practicable, to prevent their reaching the place of their destination. With this object in view, a considerable force was detached, to watch the motions of Col. Boquet and [81] upon a favorable opportunity to give him battle. In a narrow defile on Turtle creek an attack was made by the Indians, and a severe engagement ensued. Both armies fought with the most obstinate bravery, from one o'clock 'till night, and in the morning it was resumed, and continued with unabated fury for several hours. At length Col. Boquet, having placed four companies of infantry and grenadiers in ambush, ordered a retreat. So soon as this was commenced, the Indians, confident of victory, pressed forward with considerable impetuosity, and fell into the ambuscade. This decided the contest—the Indians were repulsed with great slaughter and dispersed.

The loss of the British, in killed and wounded, exceeded one hundred. That they were not entirely cut off, was attributable to the stratagem of the retreat (a favorite one of the Indians:) the success of which not only saved

[1] Captain Simeon Ecuyer, like Bouquet, was a native of Switzerland; he did good service on the frontiers, especially in the gallant defense of Fort Pitt in 1763. He became disgusted with the bad conduct of his soldiers, especially the grenadiers, and begged leave to resign. "For God's sake," he implored Bouquet, "let me go, and raise cabbages."—L. C. D.

the detachment under Col. Boquet, but likewise preserved Fort Pitt, from falling into the hands of the savage foe.

The loss sustained by the enemy, must have equaled that of the British; several of their most distinguished chiefs and warriors, were of the number of the slain: and so decisive was the victory obtained over them, that in the succeeding campaign against the Indians on the Muskingum, Boquet found not much difficulty in bringing them to terms. A cessation of hostilities was agreed to, upon condition that they would give up all the whites then detained by them in captivity. Upwards of three hundred prisoners were then redeemed; but the season being far advanced and the others scattered in different parts of the country, it was stipulated, that they should be brought into Fort Pitt early in the ensuing spring; and as a security that they would comply with this condition of the armistice, six of their chiefs were delivered up as hostages—these however succeeded in making their escape before the army arrived at Fort Pitt.[1]

The ill success which had attended the combined operations of the Indians, during this war, the difficulty of procuring ammunition to support it, and the fact that it had begun to be carried into their own country, disposed them to make peace. A treaty was accordingly concluded with them by Sir William Johnson in 1765. Previous to this however, some few depredations were committed by

---

[1] Henry Bouquet was born at Rolle, in the canton of Berne, Switzerland, in 1721, and at the age of seventeen he entered into the service of the states general of Holland; subsequently engaged under the banner of Sardinia, and distinguished himself at the battle of Cony. In 1748, he was a lieutenant-colonel in the Swiss guards, in the service of Holland. At length, in 1756, he entered the English army, serving in the Royal Americans, and co-operated with Gen. Forbes on the campaign against Fort Du Quesne, repulsing an attack of French and Indians on Loyal Hanna. He afterwards served in Canada, and was sent for the relief of Fort Pitt, when beleagured in 1763. While marching on this service, he signally defeated the Indians at Bushy Run, after a two days' engagement, in August of that year, and relieved Fort Pitt. In 1764, he led an expedition against the Ohio Indians, compelling them to sue for peace. He died at Pensacola, September 2, 1765, of a prevailing fever, in the prime of life, at the age of forty-four years. He had attained the rank of general.—L. C. D.

the Indians, in contravention of the agreement made with them by Col. Boquet; and which induced a belief that the want of clothes and ammunition, [82] was the real cause of their partial forbearance. It was therefore of great consequence, to prevent their obtaining a supply of these necessaries, until there could be some stronger assurance, than had been given, of their pacific disposition.

Notwithstanding the prevalence of this impression, and the fact, that a royal proclamation had been issued, forbidding any person trading with the Indians, yet in March 1765 a number of wagons, laden with goods and warlike stores for the Indians, was sent from Philadelphia to Henry Pollens of Conocochcague, to be thence transported on pack horses to Fort Pitt. This very much alarmed the country; and many individuals remonstrated against the propriety of supplying the Indians at that particular juncture; alleging the well known fact, that they were then destitute of ammunition and clothing, and that to furnish them with those articles, would be to aid in bringing on another frontier war, and to lend themselves to the commission of those horrid murders, by which those wars were always distinguished. Remonstrance was fruitless. The gainful traffick which could be then carried on with the Indians, banished every other consideration; and seventy horses, packed with goods, were directed on to Fort Pitt.

In this situation of things, Capt. James Smith, (who had been with Boquet during the campaign of 1764, and was well convinced that a supply at that time of clothing and ammunition, would be the signal for the recommencement of hostilities) collected ten of his "Black boys," painted and dressed as Indians; and waylaid the caravan, near a place called the "Side long Hill." He disposed his men in pairs, behind trees along the road, at intervals of about 60 yards, with orders for the second not to fire 'till the first had reloaded, so that a regular, slow fire might be maintained at once, from front to rear.

As soon as the cavalcade approached, the firing commenced, and the pack horses beginning to fall by the side of their conductors, excited the fear of the latter, and induced them to cry out " Gentlemen what would you have us to do." Captain Smith replied, " collect all your loads to the front, deposit them in one place; take your private property and retire." These things were accordingly done; and the goods left (consisting of blankets, shirts, beads, vermillion, powder, lead, tomahawks, scalping knives, &c.) were immediately burned or otherwise destroyed.

[83] The traders then went to Fort Loudon, and obtaining of the commanding officer a party of Higland soldiers, proceeded in quest of the *Robbers* (as they termed them;) some of whom were taken and carried into the Fort. Capt. Smith then raised about 300 riflemen, and marching to Fort Loudon, occupied a position on an eminence near it. He had not been long there before he had more than twice as many of the garrison, prisoners in his camp, as there were of his men in the guard house. Under a flag of truce proceeding from the Fort, a convention for the exchange of prisoners was entered into between Capt. Grant, the commander of the garrison, and Capt. Smith, and the latter with his men, immediately returned to their homes.[1]

----

[1] The following song was soon after composed by Mr. George Campbell (an Irish gentleman who had been educated in Dublin,) and was frequently sung in the neighborhood to the tune of the *Black Joke.*

> Ye patriot souls who love to sing,
> What serves your country and your king,
>   In wealth, peace, and royal estate;
> Attention give whilst I rehearse,
> A modern fact, in jingling verse,
> How party interest strove what it cou'd,
> To profit itself by public blood,
>   But justly met its merited fate.
>
> Let all those Indian traders claim,
> Their just reward, in glorious fame,
>   For vile, base and treacherous ends,
> To Pollins in the spring they sent
> Much warlike stores, with an intent,
> To carry them to our barbarous foes,
> Expecting that nobody dare oppose
>   A present to their Indian friends.
>
> Astonished at the wild design
> Frontier inhabitants combin'd,

Occurrences such as this, were afterwards of too frequent [84] recurrence. The people had been taught by experience, that the fort afforded very little, if any protection to those who were not confined within its walls—they were jealous of the easy, and yet secure life led by the garrison, and apprehensive of the worst consequences

With brave souls to stop their career,
Although some men apostatized
Who first the grand attempt advis'd,
The bold frontiers they bravely stood,
To act for their king, and their country's good
    In joint league, and strangers to fear.

On March the fifth, in sixty-five,
Their Indian presents did arrive,
    In long pomp and cavalcade,
Near Sidelong-hill, where in disguise,
Some patriots did their train surprise,
And quick as lightning tumbled their loads
And kindled them bonfires in the woods;
    And mostly burnt their whole brigade.

At Loudon when they heard the news,
They scarcely knew which way to choose,
    For blind rage and discontent;
At length some soldiers they sent out,
With guides for to conduct the route,
And seized some men that were travelling there
And hurried them into London, where
    They laid them fast with one consent.

But men of resolution thought
Too much to see their neighbors caught
    For no crime but false surmise;
Forthwith they join'd a warlike band,
And march'd to Loudon out of hand,
And kept the jailors pris'ners there,
Until our friends enlarged were,
    Without fraud or any disguise.

Let mankind censure or commend,
This rash performance in the end,
    Then both sides will find their account.
'Tis true no law can justify
To burn our neighbors property,
But when this property is design'd
To serve the enemies of mankind,
    Its high treason in the amount.

from the intercourse of traders with the Indians. Under those feelings, they did not scruple to intercept the pussage of goods to the trading posts, and commit similar outrages to those above described, if there were any interference on the part of the neighboring forts. On one occasion, Capt. Grant was himself taken prisoner, and [85] detained 'till restitution was made the inhabitants of some guns, which had been taken from them, by soldiers from the garrison; and in 1769, a quantity of powder, lead and other articles was taken from some traders passing through Bedford county, and destroyed. Several persons, supposed to have been of the party who committed this outrage, were apprehended, and laid in irons in the guard house at Fort Bedford.

Capt. Smith, although in no wise engaged in this transaction, nor yet approving it, was nevertheless so indignant that an offence against the civil authorities, should be attempted to be punished by a military tribunal, that he resolved on effecting their release. To accomplish this, he collected eighteen of his " Black boys," in whom he knew he could confide; and marched along the main road in the direction of Fort Bedford. On his way to that place, he did not attempt to conceal his object, but freely told to every one who enquired, that he was going to take Fort Bedford. On the evening of the second day of their march, they arrived at the crossings of Juniata, (14 miles from Bedford) and erected tents as if they intended encamping there all night.

Previous to this, Capt. Smith had communicated his intention to Mr. William Thompson (who lived in Bedford and on whom he could rely,) and prevailed on him to obtain what information he could as to the effect produced in the garrison by the preparations which he was making for its attack; and acquaint him with it. That he might be enabled to do this with greater certainty, a place and hour were appointed at which Capt. Smith would meet him.

About 11 o'clock at night the march was resumed, and moving briskly they arrived near to Bedford, where they met Thompson; who communicated to them the fact, that the garrison had been apprized of their object that in

consequence of having heard from them on the preceding
evening, at the Crossings of Juniata, it was not expected
they would arrive before mid-day, that their number
was known, and the enterprise ridiculed. Thompson then
returned to Bedford, and the party moved silently under
covert of the banks of the river, 'till they approached near
to the Fort, where they lay concealed, awaiting the opening of the gate. About day light Thompson apprised them
that the guard had thrown open the gate, and were taking
their morning's dram; that the arms were stacked not far
from the entrace into the Fort, and three centinels on the
wall.

Upon hearing these things, Capt. Smith with his men
rushed rapidly to the Fort, and the morning being misty,
were not discovered 'till they had reached the gate. At
that instant the centinels fired their guns and gave the
alarm; but Capt. Smith and his men took possession of the
arms, and raised a loud shout, before the soldiers of the
garrison could learn the cause of the alarm, or get to the
scene of action.

[86] Having thus obtained possession of the Fort,
Capt. Smith had the prisoners released from the guard-
house, and compelling a blacksmith to knock off their
irons, left the Fort with them and returned to Conoco-
cheaque. "This, Capt. Smith says, was the first British
fort in America, taken by what they called American
rebels."

Some time after this, an attempt was made to apprehend Capt. Smith, as he was proceeding to survey and locate land on the Youghogany river. In the encounter which
succeeded, a man (by the name of Johnson) was killed;
and the murder being charged on Smith, he was confined
for a time in Bedford jail; but fearing a release, the civil
authority sent him privately through the wilderness to Carlisle, to await a trial for the alledged offence. On hearing
this, upwards of three hundred persons (among whom
were his old " Black boys,") proceeded to Carlisle to effect
a rescue; and were only prevented the accomplishment of
their object, by the solicitation of Smith himself. He

8

knew his innocence, and preferred awaiting a trial; and
how willing soever he might have been to oppose any
encroachments of the military, he held in just abhorrence,
an opposition to the civil authority of his country. He
was put on his trial and acquitted.[1]

[1] The following extract from the *Pennsylvania Gazette* of November
2d, 1769, details the circumstances of this transaction.

"James Smith, his brother and brother in law, were going out to
survey and improve their land, on the waters of the Youghogany.—Expecting to be gone some time, they took with them their arms, and
horses loaded with necessaries; and as Smith's brother in law was an
artist in surveying, he had also with him the instruments for that business. Travelling on their way and within nine miles of Bedford, they
overtook and joined in company with one Johnson and Moorhead, who
had likewise horses packed with liquor and seed wheat—their intentions being also to make improvements on their lands. Arrived at the
parting of the road near Bedford, they separated, one party going
through town for the purpose of having a horse shod; these were apprehended and put under confinement.—James Smith, Johnson and
Moorhead taking the other road, met John Holmes of Bedford, to whom
Smith spoke in a friendly manner but received no answer. Smith and
his companions proceeded to where the two roads again united; and
waited there the arrival of the others.

"At this time a number of men came riding up, and asked Smith his
name. On his telling them who he was, they immediately presented
their pistols, and commanded him to surrender or he was a dead man.
Smith stepped back and asking if they were highwaymen, charged them
to keep off; when immediately Robert George (one of the assailants)
snapped a pistol at Smith's head; and that (as George acknowledged
under oath) before Smith had offered to [87] shoot. Smith then presented
his gun at another of the assailants, who was holding Johnson with one
hand, while with the other he held a pistol, which he was preparing to
discharge. Two shots were fired, one by Smith's gun, the other by the
pistol, so quick as to be just distinguishable, and Johnson fell. Smith
was then taken and carried to Bedford, where John Holmes (who had
met him on the road, and hastened to Bedford with the intelligence)
held an inquest over the dead body of Johnson. One of the assailants
being the only witness examined, it was found that "Johnson had
been murdered by Smith," who was thereupon committed for trial.
But jealousy arising in the breasts of many, that the inquest was not so
fair as it should have been, William Deny, (the coroner of Bedford
county) thought proper to re-examine the matter; and summoning a
jury of unexceptionable men, out of three townships—men whose can-
dour, probity, and honesty are unquestionable, and having raised the
corpse, held a solemn inquest over it for three days.

"In the course of their scrutiny, they found the shirt of Johnson,
around the bullet hole, blackened by the powder of the charge with

[87] Events such as those which have been narrated, serve to shew the state of things which existed at that day; and to point out the evils necessarily resulting, from an absence of municipal regulations. Man, in every station and condition of life, requires the controlling hand of civil power, to confine him in his proper sphere, and to check every advance of invasion, on the rights of others. Unrestrained liberty speedily degenerates into licentiousness. Without the necessary curbs and restraints of law, men would relapse into a state of nature; [88] and although the obligations of justice (the basis of society) be natural obligations; yet such are the depravity and corruption of human nature, that without some superintending and coercive power, they would be wholly disregarded; and hu-

which he had been killed. One of the assailants being examined, swore to the respective spots of ground on which they stood at the time of firing, which being measured, was found to be 23 feet distance from each other. The experiment was then made of shooting at the shirt an equal distance both with and against the wind, to ascertain if the powder produced the stain; but it did not. Upon the whole the jury, after the most accurate examination and mature deliberation, brought in their verdict that one of the assailants must necessarily have done the murder."

Captain Smith was a brave and enterprising man. In 1766, he, in company with Joshua Horton, Uriah Stone, William Baker and James Smith, by the way of Holstein, explored the country south of Kentucky at a time when it was entirely uninhabited; and the country between the Cumberland and Tennessee rivers, to their entrance into the Ohio. Stone's river, a branch of the Cumberland and emptying into it not far above Nashville, was named by them in this expedition.

After his acquittal from the charge of having murdered Johnson, he was elected and served as one of the board of commissioners, for regulating taxes and laying the county levy, in the county of Bedford. [88] He was for several years a delegate from the county of Westmoreland, to the General Assembly of Pennsylvania; and in the war of the revolution was an officer of merit and distinction. In 1781 he removed to Kentucky and settled in Bourbon county not far from Paris; was a member of the convention which set at Danville, to confer about a separation from the state of Virginia, in 1788, from which time until 1799, with the exception of two years, he was either a delegate of the convention or of the General Assembly of Kentucky.

Comment by L. C. D.—It would seem from Col. Smith's own statement, that his removal to, and settlement in, Bourbon county, Ky., was in 1788.

man society, would become the field of oppression and outrage—instead of a theatre for the interchange of good offices. Civil institutions and judicial establishments; the comminations of punishment and the denunciations of law, are barely sufficient to repress the evil propensities of man. Left to themselves, they spurn all natural restrictions, and riot in the unrestrained indulgence of every passion.

[89] CHAPTER V.

The comparative security and quiet, which succeeded the treaty of 1765, contributed to advance the prosperity of the Virginia frontiers. The necessity of congregating in forts and blockhouses, no longer existing, each family enjoyed the felicities of its own fireside, undisturbed by fearful apprehensions of danger from the prowling savage, and free from the bustle and confusion consequent on being crowded together. No longer forced to cultivate their little fields in common, and by the united exertions of a whole neighborhood, with tomahawks suspended from their belts and rifles attached to their plow beams, their original spirit of enterprise was revived: and while a certainty of reaping in unmolested safety, the harvest for which they had toiled, gave to industry, a stimulus which increased their prosperity, it also excited others to come and reside among them—a considerable addition to their population, and a rapid extension of settlements, were the necessary consequence.

It was during the continuation of this exemption from Indian aggression, that several establishments were made on the Monongahela and its branches, and on the Ohio river. These were nearly cotemporaneous; the first however, in order of time, was that made on the Buchannon—a fork of the Tygart's valley river, and was induced by a flattering account of the country as given by two brothers: who had spent some years in various parts of it, under rather unpleasant circumstances.

Among the soldiers who garrisoned Fort Pitt, were William Childers, John and Samuel Pringle and Joseph Linsey. In 1761, these four men deserted from the fort, and ascended the Monongahela as far as to the mouth of George's creek (the site afterwards selected by Albert Gallatin, for the town of Geneva.) Here they remained awhile; but not liking the [90] situation crossed over to the head of the Youghogany; and encamping in the glades, continued there about twelve months.

In one of their hunting rambles, Samuel Pringle came on a path, which he supposed would lead to the inhabited part of Virginia. On his return he mentioned the discovery and his supposition, to his comrades, and they resolved on tracing it. This they accordingly did, and it conducted them to Loony's creek, then the most remote western settlement. While among the inhabitants on Loony's creek, they were recognized and some of the party apprehended as deserters. John and Samuel Pringle succeeded in making an escape to their camp in the glades, where they remained 'till some time in the year 1764.

During this year, and while in the employ of John Simpson (a trapper, who had come there in quest of furs,) they determined on removing farther west. Simpson was induced to this, by the prospect of enjoying the woods free from the intrusion of other hunters (the glades having begun to be a common hunting ground for the inhabitants of the South Branch;) while a regard for their personal safety, caused the Pringles to avoid a situation, in which they might be exposed to the observation of other men.

In journeying through the wilderness, and after having crossed Cheat river at the Horse shoe, a quarrel arose between Simpson and one of the Pringles; and notwithstanding that peace and harmony were so necessary to their mutual safety and comfort; yet each so far indulged the angry passions which had been excited, as at length to produce a separation.

Simpson crossed over the Valley river, near the mouth of Pleasant creek, and passing on to the head of another water course, gave to it the name of Simpson's creek. Thence he went westwardly, and fell over on a stream which he called Elk: at the mouth of this he erected a camp, and continued to reside for more than twelve months. During this time he neither saw the Pringles nor any other human being; and at the expiration of it went to the South Branch, where he disposed of his furs and skins and then returned to, and continued at, his encampment at the mouth of Elk, until permanent settlements were made in its vicinity.

The Pringles kept up the Valley river 'till they observed a large right hand fork, (now Buchannon),[1] which they ascended [91] some miles; and at the mouth of a small branch (afterward called Turkey run) they took up their abode in the cavity of a large Sycamore tree.[2] The stump of this is still to be seen, and is an object of no little veneration with the immediate descendants of the first settlers.

The situation of these men, during a residence here of several years, although rendered somewhat necessary by their previous conduct, could not have been very enviable. Deserters from the army, a constant fear of discovery filled their minds with inquietude.—In the vicinity of a savage foe, the tomahawk and scalping knife were ever present to their imaginations.—Remote from civilized man, their solitude was hourly interrupted by the frightful shrieks of the panther, or the hideous howlings of the wolf.—And though the herds of Buffalo, Elk and Deer, which gamboled sportively around, enabled them easily to supply their larder; yet the want of salt, of bread, and of every species of kitchen vegetable, must have abated their

---

[1] Now spelled Buckhannon.—R. G. T.

[2] Sycamores, which attain gigantic proportions, are given to rotting in the lower portions of the trunk, and chambers eight feet in diameter are not uncommon. In the course of a canoe voyage down the Ohio, in the summer of 1894, I frequently saw such cavities, with the openings stopped by pickets or rails, utilized by small bottom farmers as hog-pens, chicken-coops, and calf stalls.

L. V. McWhorter, of Berlin, W. Va., who has kindly sent me several MS. notes on Withers's *Chronicles* (all of which will be duly credited where used in this edition), writes: "The aged sycamore now (1894) occupying the site, is the third generation—the grand-child—of that which housed the Pringles. It stands on the farm of Webster Dix, who assures me that it shall not be destroyed. A tradition held by his descendants has it, that when John Pringle went back to the South Branch for ammunition, Charity, the wife of Samuel, who was left behind, started immediately for the wilderness home of her husband, and found him by the path which John had blazed for his own return."—R. G. T.

relish for the, otherwise, delicious loin of the one, and
hauch of the others. The low state of their little magazine too, while it limited their hunting, to the bare pro-
curation of articles of subsistence, caused them, from a
fear of discovery, to shrink at the idea of being driven to
the settlements, for a supply of ammunition. And not
until they were actually reduced to two loads of powder,
could they be induced to venture again into the vicinity of
their fellow men. In the latter part of the year 1767,
John left his brother, and intending to make for a trading post on the Shenandoah, appointed the period of his
return.

Samuel Pringle, in the absence of John, suffered a
good deal. The stock of provisions left him became entirely exhausted—one of his loads of powder, was ex-
pended in a fruitless attempt to shoot a buck—his brother
had already delayed his return several days longer than
was intended, and he was apprehensive that he had been
recognized, taken to Fort Pitt and would probably never
get back. With his remaining load of powder, however
he was fortunate enough to kill a fine buffalo ; and John
soon after returned with the news of peace, both with the
Indians and French. The two brothers agreed to leave
their retirement.

Their wilderness habitation was not left without some
regret. Every object around, had become more or less endeared to them. The tree, in whose hollow they had been
so [92] frequently sheltered from storm and tempest, was
regarded by them with so great reverence, that they resolved, so soon as they could prevail on a few others to
accompany them, again to return to this asylum of their
exile.

In a population such as then composed the chief part
of the South Branch settlement, this was no difficult matter. All of them were used to the frontier manner of living ; the most of them had gone thither to acquire land ;
many had failed entirely in this object, while others were
obliged to occupy poor and broken situations off the river ;
the fertile bottoms having been previously located. Add
to this the passion for hunting (which was a ruling one

with many,) and the comparative scarcity of game in their neighborhood, and it need not excite surprise that the proposition of the Pringles to form a settlement, in such a country as they represented that on Buchannon to be, was eagerly embraced by many.

In the fall of the ensuing year (1768) Samuel Pringle, and several others who wished first to examine for themselves, visited the country which had been so long occupied by the Pringles alone. Being pleased with it, they, in the following spring, with a few others, repaired thither, with the view of cultivating as much corn, as would serve their families the first year after their emigration. And having examined the country, for the purpose of selecting the most desirable situations; some of them proceeded to improve the spots of their choice. John Jackson (who was accompanied by his sons, George and Edward) settled at the mouth of Turkey run, where his daughter, Mrs. Davis, now lives—John Hacker[1] higher up on the Buchannon river, where Bush's fort was afterwards established, and Nicholas Heavener now lives—Alexander and Thomas Sleeth, near to Jackson's, on what is now known as the Forenash plantation. The others of the party (William Hacker, Thomas and Jesse Hughes, John and William Radcliff and John Brown) appear to have employed their time exclusively in hunting; neither of them making any improvement of land for his own benefit. Yet were they of very considerable service to the new settlement. Those who had commenced clearing land, were supplied by them with abundance of meat, while in their hunting excursions through the country, a better knowledge of it was obtained, than could have been acquired, had they been engaged in making improvements.

[93] In one of these expeditions they discovered, and gave name to Stone coal creek; which flowing westwardly, induced the supposition that it discharged itself directly into the Ohio. Descending this creek, to ascertain the

---

[1] This early and meritorious pioneer was born near Winchester, Va., Jan. 1, 1743, figured prominently in the Indian wars of his region, and served on Col. G. R. Clark's Illinois campaign of 1778; he died at his home on Hacker's Creek, April 20, 1821, in his 82d year.—L. C. D.

fact, they came to its confluence with a river, which they
then called, and has since been known as, the West Fork.
After having gone some distance down the river, they returned by a different route to the settlement, better pleased
with the land on it and some of its tributaries, than with
that on Buchannon.

Soon after this, other emigrants arrived under the
guidance of Samuel Pringle. Among them were, John
and Benjamin Cutright, who settled on Buchannon, where
John Cutright the younger, now lives; and Henry Rule
who improved just above the mouth of Fink's run. Before the arrival of Samuel Pringle, John Hacker had begun to improve the spot which Pringle had chosen for
himself. To prevent any unpleasant result, Hacker agreed
that if Pringle would clear as much land, on a creek which
had been recently discovered by the hunters, as he had on
Buchannon, they could then exchange places. Complying
with this condition Pringle took possession of the farm on
Buchannon, and Hacker of the land improved by Pringle
on the creek, which was hence called Hacker's creek.[1]
John and William Radcliff, then likewise settled on this
stream—the former on the farm, where the Rev. John
Mitchel now lives; the latter at the place now owned by
William Powers Esq.—These comprise all the improve-
ments which were made on the upper branches of the
Monongahela in the years 1769 and 1770.

At the close of the working season of 1769 some of
these adventurers, went to their families on the South
Branch; and when they returned to gather their crops in
the fall, found them entirely destroyed. In their absence
the buffaloes, no longer awed by the presence of man, had
trespassed on their enclosures, and eaten their corn to the
ground—this delayed the removal of their families 'till the
winter of 1770.

Soon after the happening of this event, other settlements were made on the upper branches of the Monongahela river. Capt. James Booth and John Thomas established themselves on what has been since called Booth's

[1] Its Indian name signified " Muddy Water."—R. G. T.

creek—The former at the place now owned by Jesse Martin; and the latter where William Martin at present resides, and which is perhaps the [94] most valuable landed estate in North Western Virginia, off the Ohio river.

Previous however to the actual settlement of the country above the forks of the Monongahela, some few families (in 1767) had established themselves in the vicinity of Fort Redstone, now Brownsville, in Pennsylvania.[1] At the head of these were Abraham Tegard, James Crawford, John Province, and John Harden. The latter of these gentlemen afterwards removed to Kentucky and became distinguished in the early history of that state, as well for the many excellencies of his private and public life, as for the untimely and perfidious manner of his death.

In the succeeding year Jacob Vanmeter, John Swan, Thomas Hughes and some others settled on the west side of the Monongahela, near the mouth of Muddy creek, where Carmichaelstown now stands.[2]

In this year too, the place which had been occupied for a while by Thomas Decker and his unfortunate associates, and where Morgantown is now situated, was settled by a party of emigrants; one of which was David Morgan, who became so conspicuous for personal prowess, and for the daring, yet deliberate courage displayed by him, during the subsequent hostilities with the Indians.

---

[1] We have already seen (p. 74, *note*), that Gist settled at Mount Braddock, Fayette county, in 1753, and that eleven families joined him in January, 1754. There is a tradition that settlers were in the district even before Gist. It has been shown that the Gist settlements, and others in the lower Monongahela, were burned by the French in July, 1754. The English borderers fled upon the outbreak of disturbances, and did not return until about 1760-61, when confidence had been restored.—R. G. T.

[2] Both Van Meter and Swan afterwards served under Col. G. R. Clark—at least, on the Kaskaskia campaign; Swan commanded a company on Clark's Shawnee campaign of 1780, and Van Meter on that of 1782. The latter moved to Kentucky in 1780; settled in Hardin county, Ky., Nov. 16th, 1798, in his seventy-sixth year.—L. C. D.

Comment by R. G. T.—This note, written by Dr. Draper a few days before his death (Aug. 26, 1891), was probably his last stroke of literary work.

In 1769, Col. Ebenezer Zane, his brothers Silas and
Jonathan, with some others from the south Branch, visited
the Ohio river for the purpose of commencing improvements; [1] [95] and severally proceeded to select positions
for their future residence. Col. Zane chose for his, an
eminence above the mouth of Wheeling creek, near
to the Ohio, and opposite a beautiful and considerable
island in that river. The spot thus selected by him, is
now occupied by his son Noah Zane, Esq. and is nearly
the centre of the present flourishing town of Wheeling.
Silas Zane commenced improving on Wheeling creek
where Col. Moses Shephard now lives, and Jonathan resided with his brother Ebenezer. Several of those who

---

[1] These gentlemen were descendants of a Mr. Zane who accompanied
William Penn, to his province of Pennsylvania, and from whom, one of
the principal streets in Philadelphia, derived its name. Their father
was possessed of a bold and daring spirit of adventure, which was displayed on many occasions, in the earlier part of his life. Having rendered himself obnoxious to the Society of Friends (of which he was a
member,) by marrying without the pale of that society, he moved to
Virginia and settled on the South Branch, where the town of Moorfield
has been since erected. One of his sons (Isaac) was taken by the Indians, when he was only nine years old, and carried in captivity, to
Mad river, in Ohio. Here he continued 'till habit reconciled him to his
situation, when he married a squaw, became a chief and spent the remainder of his life with them. He was never known to wage war
against the whites; but was, on several occasions, of infinite service,
by apprising them of meditated attacks of the Indians. His descendants still reside in Ohio.

The brothers, Ebenezer, Silas and Jonathan, who settled Wheeling,
[95] were also men of enterprise, tempered with prudence, and directed
by sound judgment. Ready at all times, to resist and punish the aggression of the Indians, they were scrupulously careful not to provoke them
by acts of wanton outrage, such as were then, too frequently committed
along the frontier. Col. Ebenezer Zane had been among the first, to
explore the country from the South Branch, through the Alleghany
glades, and west of them. He was accompanied in that excursion by
Isaac Williams, two gentlemen of the name of Robinson and some
others; but setting off rather late in the season, and the weather being
very severe, they were compelled to return, without having penetrated
to the Ohio river. On their way home, such was the extremity of cold,
that one of the Robinsons died of its effects. Williams was much frost
bitten, and the whole patrty suffered exceedingly. To the bravery and
good conduct of those three brothers, the Wheeling settlement was
mainly indebted for its security and preservation, during the war of the
revolution.

accompanied the adventurers, likewise remained with Colonel Zane, in the capacity of laborers.

After having made those preparations which were immediately requisite for the reception of their respective families, they returned to their former homes. In the ensuing year they finally left the South Branch, and accompanied by Col. David Shephard, (the father of Col. Moses Shepherd,) John Wetzel (the father of Lewis) and the McCulloughs—men whose names are identified with the early history of that country—repaired again to the wilderness, and took up their permanent abode in it.

Soon after this, other settlements were made at different points, both above and below Wheeling; and the country on Buffalo, Short, and Grave creeks,[1] and on the Ohio river, became the abode of civilized man. Among those who were first to occupy above Wheeling, were George Lefler, John Doddridge, Benjamin Biggs, Daniel Greathouse, Joshua Baker and Andrew Swearingen.[2]

[96] The settlement thus made constituting a kind of advance *guard*, through which an Indian enemy would have to penetrate, before they could reach the interior, others were less reluctant to occupy the country between them and the Alleghany mountains. Accordingly various establishments were soon made in it by adventurers from different parts of Maryland, Pennsylvania and Virginia; and those places in which settlements had been previously effected, received considerable accessions to their population.

In 1772, that comparatively beautiful region of country, lying on the east fork of the Monongahela river, be-

---

[1] Joseph Tomlinson surveyed a claim at the mouth of Grave Creek, about 1770, but did not settle there until 1772. His cabin was the nucleus of the present Moundsville, W. Va.—R. G. T.

[2] John Doddridge settled in Washington county, Pa., on the Ohio River a few miles east of the Pennsylvania-Virginia state line, in 1773; his son, Joseph Doddridge, was the author of *Notes on the Settlements and Indian Wars of the Western Parts of Virginia and Pennsylvania*, 1763-83, a valuable antiquarian work. The names of Greathouse and Baker became execrable through their connection with the massacre of Chief Logan's family, in 1774. Leffler and Biggs attained prominence in border warfare.—R. G. T.

tween the Alleghany mountains, on its south eastern, and the Laurel Hill, or as it is there called the Rich mountain, on its north western side, and which had received the denomination of Tygart's valley, again attracted the attention of emigrants.—In the course of that year, the greater part of this valley was located, by persons said to have been enticed thither by the description given of it, by some hunters from Greenbrier who had previously explored it. Game, though a principal, was not however their sole object. They possessed themselves at once of nearly all the level land lying between those mountains— a plain of 25 or 30 miles in length and varying from three fourths to two miles in width, and of fine soil. Among those who were first to occupy that section of country, we find the names of Hadden, Connelly, Whiteman, Warwick, Nelson, Stalnaker, Riffle and Westfall: the latter of these found and interred the bones of Files' family, which had lain, bleeching in the sun, after their murder by the Indians, in 1754.

Cheat river too, on which no attempt at settlement had been made, but by the unfortunate Eckarly's, became an object of attention, The Horse Shoe bottom was located by Capt. James Parsons, of the South Branch; and in his neighborhood settled Robert Cunningham, Henry Fink, John Goff and John Minear. Robert Butler, William Morgan and some others settled on the Dunkard bottom.

In this year too, settlements were made on Simpson's creek, the West Fork river and on Elk creek. Those who made the former, were John Powers, who purchased Simpson's right (a tomahawk improvement)[1] to the land on which Benjamin [97] Stout now resides; and James Anderson and Jonas Webb who located themselves farther up the creek.

---

[1] "At an early period of our settlements, there was an inferior kind of land title, denominated a tomahawk right. This was made by [97] deadening a few trees near a spring, and marking on one or more of them, the initials of the name of the person, by whom the improvement was made. Rights, acquired in this way, were frequently bought and sold." —*Doddridge's Notes on Western Virginia.*

On Elk, and in the vicinity of Clarksburg there settled Thomas Nutter, near to the Forge-mills—Samuel Cottrial, on the east side of the creek and nearly opposite to Clarksburg—Sotha Hickman, on the west side of the same creek, and above Cottrial—Samuel Beard at the mouth of Nanny's run—Andrew Cottrial above Beard, and at the farm now owned by John W. Patton—Daniel Davisson, where Clarksburg is now situated, and Obadiah Davisson and John Nutter on the West Fork; the former near to the old Salt works, and the latter at the place now owned by Adam Hickman, jr.

There was likewise, at this time, a considerable accession to the settlements on Buchannon and Hacker's creek. So great was the increase of population in this latter neighborhood, that the crops of the preceding season did not afford more than one third of the breadstuff, which would be ordinarily consumed in the same time, by an equal number of persons. Such indeed was the state of suffering among the inhabitants, consequent on this scarcity, that the year 1773 is called in the traditionary legends of that day, the *starving year;* and such were the exertions of William Lowther to mitigate that suffering, and so great the success with which they were crowned, that his name has been transmitted to their descendants, hallowed by the blessings of those, whose wants he contributed so largely to relieve.[1]

---

[1] William Lowther was the son of Robert, and came with his father to the Hacker creek settlement in 1772. He soon became one of the most conspicuous men in that section of country; while his private virtues and public actions endeared him to every individual of the community. During the war of 1774 and subsequently, he was the most active and efficient defender of that vicinity, against the insidious attacks of the savage foe; and there were very few if any scouting parties proceeding from thence, by which the Indians were killed or otherwise much annoyed, but those which were commanded by him.

He was the first justice of the peace in the district of West Augusta—the first sheriff in the county of Harrison and Wood, and [98] once a delegate to the General Assembly of the States. His military merits carried him through the subordinate grades to the rank of Colonel. Despising the pomp and pageantry of office, he accepted it for the good of the community, and was truly an effective man. Esteemed, beloved by all, he might have exerted his influence, over others, to the advancement

[98] These were the principal settlements begun in North Western Virginia, prior to the year 1774. Few and scattered as they were, no sooner was it known that they were commenced, than hundreds flocked to them from different parts; and sought there the gratifications of their respective predilections. That spirit of adventurous emigration, which has since peopled, with such unprecedented rapidity, the south western and western states, and which was then beginning to develope itself, overcame the fond attachments of youth, and impelled its possessors, to the dreary wilderness. Former homes, encircled by the comforts of civilization, endeared by the grateful recollections of by-gone days, and not unfrequently, consecrated as the spots where their tenants had first inhaled the vital fluid, were readily exchanged for " the variety of untried being, the new scenes and changes," which were to be passed, before the trees of the forest could be supplanted, by the fruits of the field, or society be reared in the solitude of the desert. With a capability to sustain fatigue, not to be subdued by toil; and with a cheerfulness, not easily to be depressed; a patience which could mock at suffering and a daring which nothing could daunt, every difficulty which intervened, every obstacle which was interposed between them and the accomplishment of the objects of their pursuit, was surmounted or removed; and in a comparatively brief space of time, they rose to the enjoyment of many of those gratifications, which are experienced in earlier and more populous settlements. That their morals should, for a while, have suffered deterioration, and their manners and habits, instead of [99] approximating those of refined society, should have become perhaps, more barbarous and uncouth, was the inevitable consequence of their situation,

---

of his individual interest; but he sought the advancement of the general weal, not a personal or family aggrandizement. His example might teach others, that offices were created for the public good, not for private emolument. If aspirants for office at the present day, were to regard its perquisites less, and their fitness for the discharge of its duties more, the country would enjoy a greater portion of happiness and prosperity, and a sure foundation for the permanence of these be laid, in the more disinterested character of her counsellors, and their consequently, increased devotion to her interests:

and the certain result of circumstances, which they could not control. When that situation was changed, and these circumstances ceased to exist, a rapid progress was made in the advancement of many sections of the country, to the refinements of civilized society.

The infantile state of all countries exhibits, in a greater or less degree, a prevalence of barbarism. The planting of colonies, or the formation of establishments in new countries, is ever attended with circumstances unpropitious to refinement. The force with which these circumstances act, will be increased or diminished in proportion to the remoteness or proximity of those new establishments, to older societies, in which the arts and sciences are cultivated; and to the facility of communication between them. Man is, at all times, the creature of circumstances. Cut off from an intercourse with his fellow men, and divested of the conveniences of life, he will readily relapse into a state of nature.—Placed in contiguity with the barbarous and the vicious; his manners will become rude, his morals perverted.—Brought into collision with the sanguinary and revengeful; and his own conduct will eventually be distinguished, by bloody and vindictive deeds.

Such was really the situation of those who made the first establishments in North Western Virginia. And when it is considered, that they were, mostly, men from the humble walks of life; comparatively illiterate and unrefined; without civil or religious institutions, and with a love of liberty, bordering on its extreme; their more enlightened descendants can not but feel surprise, that their dereliction from propriety had not been greater; their virtue less.

The objects, for the attainment of which they voluntarily placed themselves in this situation, and tempted the dangers inseparable from a residence in the contiguity of Indians, jealous of territorial encroachment, were almost as various as their individual character. Generally speaking, they were men in indigent circumstances, unable to purchase land in the neigborhoods from which they came,

9

and unwilling longer to remain the tenants of others. These were induced to [100] emigrate, with the laudable ambition of acquiring homes, from which they would not be liable to expulsion, at the whim and caprice of some haughty lordling. Upon the attainment of this object, they were generally content; and made but feeble exertions to acquire more land, than that to which they obtained title, by virtue of their settlements. Some few, however, availed themselves of the right of pre-emption, and becoming possessed of the more desirable portions of the country, added considerably to their individual wealth.

Those who settled on the Ohio, were of a more enterprising and ambitious spirit, and looked more to the advancement of their condition in a pecuniary point of view. The fertile bottoms of that river, and the facility with which, by means of it, their surplus produce might be transported to a ready market,[1] were considerations which influenced many. Others, again, looking forward to the time when the Indians would be divested of the country north west of the Ohio river, and it be open to location in the same manner its south eastern shores were, selected this as a situation, from which they might more readily obtain possession of the fertile

---

[1] The Spaniards at New Orleans, from the first settlement of the country west of the Alleghany Mountains, sought to attach it to the province of Louisiana. Knowing the powerful efficacy of gold, in producing such results, they dispensed it with a liberal hand, to such as made New Orleans their market. The attachment of the first settlers, to the free institutions of our country, baffled every attempt to detach them from it.

Comment by R. G. T.—The Spanish conspiracy was, in the main, " baffled " by the prompt action of our general government. George Rogers Clark and several other leading Kentuckians were quite willing to be " detached," for a consideration. The fact is, that at first the sense of national patriotism was weak, west of the Alleghanies; the eighteenth century had closed before efforts at separation from the East were commonly regarded as treason. The interests of the Western people apparently were centered in the south-flowing Mississippi; they seemed to have at the time little in common with the East. So long as Spain held the mouth of the river, many Western leaders thought it not improper that the West should ally itself with that power ; when our government finally purchased the Spanish claim, the Western men had no further complaint. See Roosevelt's treatment of the Spanish conspiracy, in his *Winning of the West*, III., ch. iii.—R. G. T.

land, with which its ample plains were known to abound. In anticipation of this period, there were some who embraced every opportunity, afforded by intervals of peace with the Indians, to explore that country and select in it what they deemed, its most valuable parts. Around these they would generally mark trees, or otherwise define boundaries, by which they could be afterwards identified. The cession by Virginia to the United States, of the North Western Territory, and the manner in which its lands were subsequently brought into market, prevented the realization of those flattering, and apparently, well founded expectations.

There were also, in every settlement, individuals, who had been drawn to them solely by their love of hunting, and an attachment to the wild, unshackled scenes of a wilderness life. These were perhaps, totally regardless of all the inconveniencies, [101] resulting from their new situation; except that of being occasionally pent up in forts; and thus debarred the enjoyment of their favorite pastimes.

Although hunting was not the object of most of the old settlers, yet it was for a good part of the year, the chief employment of their time. And of all those, who thus made their abode in the dense forest, and tempted aggression from the neighboring Indians, none were so well qualified to resist this aggression, and to retaliate upon its authors, as those who were mostly engaged in this pursuit. Of all their avocations, this " mimickry of war" best fitted them to thwart the savages in their purpose, and to mitigate the horrors of their peculiar mode of warfare. Those arts which enabled them, unperceived to approach the watchful deer in his lair, enabled them likewise to circumvent the Indian in his ambush; and if not always punish, yet frequently defeat him in his object. Add to this the perfect knowledge which they acquired of the woods, and the ease and certainty with which they consequently, when occasion required, could make their way to any point of the settlements and apprize the inhabitants of approaching danger; and it will be readily admitted that the more expert and successful the huntsman, the more skillful and effective the warrior.

But various soever, as may have been their objects in emigrating, no sooner had they come together, than there existed in each settlement, a perfect unison of feeling. Similitude of situation and community of danger, operating as a magic charm, stifled in their birth those little bickerings, which are so apt to disturb the quiet of society. Ambition of preferment and the pride of place, too often lets and hindrances to social intercourse, were unknown among them. Equality of condition rendered them strangers alike, to the baneful distinctions created by wealth and other adventitious circumstances ; and to envy, which gives additional virus to their venom. A sense of mutual dependence for their common security linked them in amity; and conducting their several purposes in harmonious concert, together they toiled and together suffered.

Not all the " pomp and pride and pageantry " of life, could vie with the Arcadian scenes which encircled the rude cottages of those men. Their humble dwellings were the abode of virtues, rarely found in the " cloud capt towers and [102] gorgeous palaces" of splendid ambition. And when peace reigned around them, neither the gaudy trappings of wealth, nor the insignia of office, nor the slaked thirst for distinction, could have added to the happiness which they enjoyed.

In their intercourse with others they were kind, beneficent and disinterested; extending to all, the most generous hospitality which their circumstances could afford. That selfishness, which prompts to liberality for the sake of remuneration, and proffers the civilities of life with an eye to individual interest, was unknown to them. They were kind for kindness sake; and sought no other recompense, than the never failing concomitant of good deeds—the reward of an approving conscience.

It is usual for men in the decline of life, to contrast the scenes which are then being exhibited, with those through which they passed in the days of youth; and not unfrequently, to moralize on the decay of those virtues, which enhance the enjoyment of life and give to pleasure its highest relish. The mind is then apt to revert to

earlier times, and to dwell with satisfaction on the manners and customs which prevailed in the hey-day of youth.
Every change which may have been wrought in them is
deemed a deteriorating innovation, and the sentence of
their condemnation unhesitatingly pronounced. This is
not always, the result of impartial and discriminating
judgment. It is perhaps, more frequently founded in
prepossession; and based on the prejudices of education
and habit.

On the other hand those who are just entering on the
vestibule of life, are prone to give preference to the habits
of the present generation; viewing, too often, with con-
temptuous derision, those of the past. Mankind certainly
advance in intelligence and refinement; but virtue and
happiness do not at all times keep pace with this progress.
"To inform the understanding," is not always "to correct
and enlarge the heart;" nor do the blandishments of life
invariably add to the sum of moral excellence; they are
often "as dead sea fruit that tempts the eye, but turns to
ashes on the lips."—While a rough exterior as frequently
covers a temper of the utmost benignity, happy in itself
and giving happiness to all around.

Such were the pioneers of this country; and the
greater part of mankind might now derive advantage from
the [103] contemplation of "their humble virtues, hospita-
ble homes and spirits patient, noble, proud and free—their
self respect, grafted on innocent thoughts; their days of
health and nights of sleep—their toils, by danger dignified, yet guiltless—their hopes of cheerful old age and
a quiet grave, with cross and garland over its green turf,
and their grand children's love for epitaph."

[104] CHAPTER VI.

In the year 1774, the peace, which had subsisted with but little violation since the treaty of 1765, received an interruption, which checked for a while the emigration to the North Western frontier; and involved its infant settlements in a war with the Indians. This result has been attributed to various causes. Some have asserted that it had its origin in the murder of some Indians on the Ohio river both above and below Wheeling, in the spring of that year. Others suppose it to have been produced by the instigation of British emissaries, and the influence of Canadian traders.

That it was not caused by the murders at Captina, and opposite the mouth of Yellow creek,[1] is fairly inferrible from the fact, that several Indians had been previously murdered by the whites in a period of the most profound tranquillity, without having led to a similar is-

---

[1] Mr. Jefferson, in his Notes on Virginia, represents this as happening at Grave creek, which empties into the Ohio from the south eastern, or Virginia side of this river, twelve miles below Wheeling. Those who lived near at the time and are supposed to have had the best opportunity of ascertaining the fact, say that it happened near the mouth of Captina, a creek sixteen miles below Wheeling, and on the Ohio side.

Comment by R. G. T.—What is called the "Captina affair" happened April 27th, at Pipe Creek, emptying into the Ohio from the west, fourteen miles below Wheeling, and six above Captina Creek. Two friendly Shawnees were killed here by a party commanded by Michael Cresap, of Redstone, who at the time was in the neighborhood of Wheeling, surveying and clearing farms for new settlers. Cresap and his men, among whom was George Rogers Clark, then a young surveyor who had a claim at the mouth of Fish Creek, thereupon started out to destroy Chief Logan's camp, at Baker's Bottom, opposite the mouth of Yellow Creek, fifty-three miles up the Ohio, and forty miles west of Pittsburg by land; but as Logan was a well-known friend of the whites, they became ashamed of their project, and marched on across country to Fort Redstone. Meanwhile, as will be seen in due course, others were preparing to destroy Logan's band, and on April 30th occurred that infamous massacre which Logan wrongly believed to be Cresap's work.

suc; or even given rise to any act of retaliation, on the part of the friends or countrymen of those, who had been thus murdered.

At different periods of time, between the peace of 1765, and the renewal of hostilities in 1774, three Indians were unprovokedly killed by John Ryan, on the Ohio, Monongahela and Cheat rivers. The first who suffered from the unrestrained licentiousness of this man, was an Indian of distinction in his tribe, and known by the name of Capt. Peter; the other two were private warriors. And but that Governor Dunmore, from the representations made to him, was induced [105] to offer a reward for his apprehension, which caused him to leave the country, Ryan would probably have continued to murder every Indian, with whom he should chance to meet, wandering through the settlements.

Several Indians were likewise killed on the South Branch, while on a friendly visit to that country, in the interval of peace. This deed is said to have been done by Henry Judah, Nicholas Harpold and their associates; and when Judah was arrested for the offence, so great was the excitement among those who had suffered from savage enmity, that he was rescued from confinement by upwards of two hundred men, collected for that especial purpose.

The Bald Eagle was an Indian of notoriety, not only among his own nation, but also with the inhabitants of the North Western frontier; with whom he was in the habit of associating and hunting. In one of his visits among them, he was discovered alone, by Jacob Scott, William Hacker and Elijah Runner, who, reckless of the consequences, murdered him, solely to gratify a most wanton thirst for Indian blood. After the commission of this most outrageous enormity, they seated him in the stern of a canoe, and with a piece of journey-cake thrust into his mouth, set him afloat in the Monongahela. In this situation he was seen descending the river, by several, who supposed him to be as usual, returning from a friendly hunt with the whites in the upper settlements, and who expressed some astonishment that he did not stop to see them. The canoe floating near to the shore, below the mouth of George's creek, was observed by a Mrs. Province, who had it brought to the bank, and the friendly, but unfortunate old Indian decently buried.

Not long after the murder of the Bald Eagle, another outrage of a similar nature was committed on a peaceable Indian, by William White; and for which he was apprehended and taken to Winchester for trial. But the fury of the populace did not suffer him to remain there awaiting that event.—The prison doors were forced, the irons knocked off him and he again set at liberty.

But a still more atrocious act is said to have been soon after perpetrated. Until then the murders committed, were only on such as were found within the limits of white settlements, and on men & warriors. In 1772, there is every reason to believe, that women and children likewise became victims to the exasperated feelings of our [106] own citizens; and this too, while quietly enjoying the comforts of their own huts, in their own village.

There was at that time an Indian town on the Little Kenhawa, (called Bulltown) inhabited by five families, who were in habits of social and friendly intercourse with the whites on Buchannon and on Hacker's creek; frequently visiting and hunting with them.[1] There was likewise residing on Gauley river, the family of a German by the name of Stroud.[2] In the summer of that year, Mr. Stroud

---

[1] Capt. Bull was a Delaware chief whose original village of Oghkwaga was on Unadilla River, an eastern branch of the Susquehanna, in what is now Boone county, N. Y. He had been the prime mover in an attempt to interest the Delawares in Pontiac's conspiracy (1763). In March, 1764, a strong party of whites and friendly Indians were sent out to capture him, by Sir William Johnson, English Indian superintendent in New York. After a sharp struggle, Bull and a number of his adherents were captured and conveyed in irons to New York City, where they were imprisoned for a time, but finally discharged. The Delaware towns on the Unadilla having been burned, Bull and five families of his relatives settled what the whites called Bulltown, on the Little Kanawha. This was at a salt spring about a mile and a quarter below the present Bulltown P. O., Braxton county, Va. Capt. Bull and his people were inoffensive, and very friendly to their white neighbors, as our author says.—R. G. T.

[2] Adam Stroud lived on Elk River, a few miles south of Indian

being from home, his family were all murdered, his house plundered, and his cattle driven off. The trail made by these leading in the direction of Bulltown, induced the supposition that the Indians of that village had been the authors of the outrage, and caused several to resolve on avenging it upon them.

A party of five men, (two of whom were William White and William Hacker,[1] who had been concerned in previous murders) expressed a determination to proceed immediately to Bulltown. The remonstrance of the settlement generally, could not operate to effect a change in that determination. They went; and on their return, circumstances justified the belief that the pre-apprehension of those who knew the temper and feelings of White and Hacker, had been well founded; and that there had been some fighting between them and the Indians. And notwithstanding that they denied ever having seen an Indian in their absence, yet it was the prevailing opinion, that they had destroyed all the men, women and children at Bulltown, and threw their bodies into the river. Indeed,

---

Bulltown. The massacre of his family—his wife and seven children—occurred in June, 1772. Shawnees were the murderers, and not Bull's people.—R. G. T.

[1] Mr. McWhorter writes me that two others were Jesse Hughes and John Cutright (corruption of Cartwright?), both of them settlers on Hacker's Creek. Hughes was a noted border scout, but a man of fierce, unbridled passions, and so confirmed an Indian hater that no tribesman, however peaceful his record, was safe in his presence. Some of the most cruel acts on the frontier are by tradition attributed to this man. The massacre of the Bulltown Indians was accompanied by atrocities as repulsive as any reported by captives in Indian camps; of these there had long been traditions, but details were not fully known until revealed by Cutright upon his death-bed in 1852, when he had reached the age of 105 years. Want of space alone prevents me from giving Mr. McWhorter's narrative of Hughes's long and bloody career. "Hughes died," he says, "in Jackson county, W. Va., at a date unknown to me, but in very old age. While he was a great scout and Indian trader, he never headed an expedition of note. This no doubt was because of his fierce temperament, and bad reputation among his own countrymen." In studying the annals of the border, we must not fail to note that here and there were many savage-hearted men among the white settlers, whose deeds were quite as atrocious as any attributed to the red-skins. Current histories of Indian warfare seldom recognize this fact.—R. G. T.

one of the party is said to have, inadvertently, used expressions, confirmatory of this opinion ; and to have then
justified the deed, by saying that the clothes and other
things known to have belonged to Stroud's family, were
found in the possession of the Indians. The village was
soon after visited, and found to be entirely desolated, and
nothing being ever after heard of its former inhabitants,
there can remain no doubt but that the murder of Stroud's
family, was requited on them.

Here then was a fit time for the Indians to commence
a system of retaliation and war, if they were disposed to
engage in hostilities, for offences of this kind alone. Yet
no such event was the consequence of the killing of the
Bulltown Indians, or of those other murders which preceded that outrage; and it may be hence rationally concluded, that the murders on the Ohio river did not lead to
such an event. If however, a doubt should still remain,
that doubt is surely removed by the declaration of Logan
himself. It was his family that was killed opposite Yellow creek, about the last of April; and in the following
July (after the expedition against the Wappatomica towns,
under Col. McDonald) he says, "the Indiens are not angry
on account of those murders, but only myself." The fact
is, that hostilities had commenced before the happening
of the affair at Captina, or that near Yellow creek; and
these, instead of having produced that event, were the
consequence of the previous hostile movements of the Indians.

[107] Those who lived more immediately in the neighborhood of the scene of action at that time, were generally
of opinion, that the Indians were urged to war by the instigation of emissaries from Great Britain, and of the
Canadian traders; and, independently of any knowledge
which they may have had of the conduct of these, circumstances of a general nature would seem to justify that
opinion.

The relative situation of the American colonies and
the mother country, is matter of general history, and too
well known to require being repeated here. It is equally
well known too, that from the first establishment of a

colony in Canada, the Canadians obtained an influence over the Natives, greater than the Anglo-Americans were ever able to acquire; and that this influence was frequently exercised by them, to the great annoyance, and manifest injury of the latter. France and England have been long considered as natural enemies; and the inhabitants of their respective plantations in America, entertained strong feelings of jealousy towards each other. When by the treaty of Paris, the French possessions in North America (which had not been ceded to Spain,) were transferred to Great Britain, those feelings were not subdued. The Canadians still regarded themselves as a different people. Their national prejudices were too great to be extinguished by an union under the same prince. Under the influence of these prejudices, and the apprehension, that the lucrative commerce of the natives might, by the competition of the English traders, be diverted from its accustomed channels, they may have exerted themselves to excite the Indians to war; but that alone would hardly have produced this result. There is in man an inherent partiality for self, which leads him to search for the causes of any evil, elsewhere than in his own conduct; and under the operation of this propensity to assign the burden of wrong to be borne by others, the Jesuits from Canada and Louisiana were censured for the continuation of the war on the part of the Indians, after it had been terminated with their allies by the treaty of 1763. Yet that event was, no doubt, justly attributable to the erection of forts, and the location of land, in the district of country claimed by the natives, in the province of Pennsylvania. And in like manner, the origin of the war of 1774 may fairly be charged to the encroachments which were then being made on the Indian territory. To be convinced of this, it is necessary to advert to the promptitude of resistance on the part of the Natives, by which those encroachments were invariably met; and to recur to events happening in other sections of the country.—Events, perhaps no otherwise connected with the history of North Western Virginia, than as they are believed to have been the proximate causes of an hostility, eventuating in the effusion of much of its blood;

and pregnant with other circumstances, having an important bearing on its prosperity and advancement.

In the whole history of America, from the time when it first [108] became apparent that the occupancy of the country was the object of the whites, up to the present period, is there perhaps to be found a solitary instance, in which an attempt, made by the English to effect a settlement in a wilderness claimed by the Natives, was not succeeded by immediate acts of hostility on the part of the latter. Every advance of the kind was regarded by them, as tending to effect their expulsion from a country, which they had long considered as their own, and as leading, most probably, to their entire extinction as a people. This excited in them feelings of the most dire resentment; stimulating to deeds of cruelty and murder, at once to repel the encroachment and to punish its authors. Experience of the utter futility of those means to accomplish these purposes, has never availed to repress their use, or to produce an acquiesence in the wrong. Even attempts to extend jurisdiction over a country, the right of soil in which was never denied them, have ever given rise to the most lively apprehensions of their fatal consequences, and prompted to the employment of means to thwart that aim. An Indian sees no difference between the right of empire and the right of domain; and just as little can he discriminate between the right of property, acquired by the actual cultivation of the earth, and that which arises from its appropriation to other uses.

Among themselves they have lines of demarkation, which distinguish the territory of one nation from that of another; and these are of such binding authority, that a transgression of them by neighboring Indians, leads invariably to war. In treaties of purchase, and other conventional arrangements, made with them by the whites, the validity of their rights to land, have been repeatedly recognized; and an infraction of those rights by the Anglo-Americans, encounters opposition at its threshold. The history of every attempt to settle a wilderness, to which the Indian title was not previously extinguished, has consequently been a history of plunder, conflagration and massacre.

That the extension of white settlements into the Indian country, was the cause of the war of 1774, will be abundantly manifested by a recurrence to the early history of Kentucky; and a brief review of the circumstances connected with the first attempts to explore and make establishments in it. For several reasons, these circumstances merit a passing notice in this place. Redstone and Fort Pitt (now Brownsville and Pittsburgh) were for some time, the principal points of embarkation for emigrants to that country; many of whom were from the establishments which had been then not long made, on the Monongahela. The Indians, regarding the settlements in North Western Virginia as the line from which swarmed the adventurers to Kentucky, directed their operations to prevent the success of these adventurers, as well against the inhabitants of the upper country, as against them. While at the same time, in the efforts which were made to compel the Indians to desist from farther opposition, the North Western Virginians frequently combined [109] their forces, and acted in conjunction, the more certainly to accomplish that object. In truth the war, which was then commenced, and carried on with but little intermission up to the treaty of Fort Greenville in 1795 was a war in which they were equally interested, having for its aim the indiscriminate destruction of the inhabitants of both, those sections of country, as the means of preventing the farther extension of settlements by the whites.[1]

---

[1] Lord Dunmore's War (1774) was a natural outgrowth of the strained relations which had long existed between the savages and the white colonists in their midst. As our author has made clear, minor hostilities had broken out here and there ever since the Pontiac uprising, but there had been no general campaign since Bouquet's treaty in 1764. Affairs had come to that pass by the early spring of 1774, that diplomacy was no longer possible, and an Indian war was inevitable. It was merely a question of detail, as to how and when. The immediate cause of precipitation—not the cause of the war, for that lay deeper—was the territorial dispute over the Ft. Pitt region, between Virginia and Pennsylvania. Dunmore, as royal governor of Virginia, had several reasons for bringing matters to a head—he was largely interested

When Kentucky was first begun to be explored, it is said not to have been claimed in individual property by any nation of Indians. Its extensive forests, grassy plains and thick cane brakes, abounding with every variety of game common to such latitudes, were used as common hunting grounds, and considered by them, as open for all who chose to resort to them. The Cherokees, the Chickasaws, the Cataubas, and the Chicamaugas, from the south east; and the Illinois, the Peorias, the Delawares, the Mingoes and Shawanees from the west, claimed and exercised equal rights and privileges within its limits. When the tribes of those different nations would however meet there, frequent collisions would arise between them; and so deadly were the conflicts ensuing upon these, that, in conjunction with the gloom of its dense forests, they acquired for it the impressive appellation of "the dark and bloody ground." But frequent and deadly as may have been those conflicts, they sprang from some other cause, than a claim to exclusive property in it.

In the summer of 1769, Daniel Boone, in company with John Finley (who had previously hunted through the country) and a few other men, entered Kentucky, and travelled over much of its surface, without meeting with

---

in land speculations under Virginia patents that would be vitiated if Pennsylvania, now becoming aggressive, should succeed in planting her official machinery at Ft. Pitt, which was garrisoned by Virginia; again, his colonists were in a revolutionary frame of mind, and he favored a distraction in the shape of a popular Indian war; finally, it seemed as though a successful raid by Virginia militia would clinch Virginia's hold on the country and the treaty of peace that must follow would widen the area of provincial lands and encourage Western settlements. April 25, 1774, he issued a proclamation in which, after reference to Pennsylvania's claims, it was asserted that Ft. Pitt was "in danger of some annoyance from the Indians," and he called on his local military commandant, the fire-eating Dr. John Connolly, "to embody a sufficient number of men to repel any insult." Connolly, evidently as part of a preconcerted plan, at once (April 26) issued a circular letter to the excited borderers, which was well calculated to arouse them, being in effect a declaration of war against the Indians. The very next day occurred the Pipe Creek affair, then came the Logan tragedy at Baker's Bottom, three days later, and at once the war was on at full-head.— R. G. T.

an Indian, until the December following.[1]   At this time
Boone and John Steward (one of his companions,) while
on a hunting excursion, were discovered by a party of
Indians, who succeeded in making them prisoners.   After

---

[1] Of John Findlay (so he signed his name), "the precursor and
pilot of Daniel Boone to Kentucky," but little is known and less has
been published.   Apparently he was a native of the north of Ireland.
In early life he emigrated to the neighborhood of Carlisle, Cumberland
county, Pa., a district almost wholly settled by Scotch-Irish Protestants.
In February, 1752, we find him a trader among the Shawnees; the
following year, he was robbed and driven off.   It is probable that he
served in the Pennsylvania frontier militia from the opening of the
French and Indian War (1754).   Boone met him on the Braddock campaign (1755), and they became fast friends.   Findlay had already (1752)
been in Kentucky as far as the Falls of the Ohio, in the course of his ramb-
lings as a trader, and inspired Boone with an intense desire to seek this El
Dorado of the West. It was in 1767, when settled near the head of the Yadkin River, that Boone first tried to reach Kentucky by way of the Sandy,
but failed.   In the winter of 1768–69, Findlay, now a peddler, with a horse
to carry his traps, appeared at Boone's cabin on the Yadkin, and the
two old comrades had a happy time rehearsing their various adventures
during the thirteen years of separation.   An expedition to Kentucky
was agreed upon, and the party set out from Boone's cabin, May 1, 1769;
it was composed of Findlay, now advanced in years, Daniel Boone, the
latter's brother-in-law, John Stuart, and three Yadkin neighbors, Joseph Holden, James Mooney, and William Cooley.   The story of their
expedition through Cumberland Gap, and their long hunt, is now familiar to readers of Western history.   Their principal camp was probably on
Red Lick Fork of Station Camp Creek.   In December, Stuart and Boone
were captured by Indians, but escaped early in January (1770), and on rejoining their comrades on Rockcastle River found that Daniel's brother,
Squire, had arrived with fresh horses and traps from the North Carolina
home; and with him was Alexander Neely, whom Squire had found on
New (Great Kanawha) River.   Findlay, Holden, Mooney, and Cooley
now elected to return home, leaving the others to spend a longer period
in Kentucky; Findlay took the left-hand road through the West Virginia settlements, to Pennsylvania, and the others, turning to the right,
wended their way to North Carolina through Cumberland Gap.   Not
long after this, Stuart was killed by Indians, while alone in the woods,
and Neely, discouraged by his fate, returned home.   The story, often
copied from Withers, that Neely was killed by a wolf, is erroneous.   As
for Findlay, he appears to have again become an Indian trader in Western Pennsylvania; for late in 1771 he is reported to have been robbed
of $500 worth of goods, by a Seneca war party raiding the Youghiogheny
district.   There is a tradition that not long after this he " was lost in the
wilds of the West."   Holden and Cooley spent the rest of their days on
the Upper Yadkin.   Mooney was killed at the battle of Point Pleasant
(1774).—R. G. T.

a detention of but few days, these men effected their escape; & returning to their old camp, found that it had
been plundered, and their associates, either killed or taken
into captivity. They were shortly after joined by a brother
of Daniel Boone and another man, from North Carolina,
who were so fortunate in wandering through the wilderness, as to discover the only, though temporary residence
of civilized man within several hundred miles. But the
Indians had become alarmed for the possession of that
country; and fearing that if Boone and Steward should be
suffered to escape to the settlements, they might induce
others to attempt its permanent occupancy, they sought
with vigilance to discover and murder them. They succeeded in killing Steward; but Daniel Boone and his
brother, then the only persons left (the man who came out
with the younger Boone having been killed by a wolf,) escaped from them, and soon after returned to North Carolina.

The Indians were not disappointed in their expectations. The description given of the country by the
Boones, soon led others to attempt its settlement; and in
1773, six families and about forty men, all under the
guidance of Daniel Boone, commenced their journey [110]
to Kentucky with a view of remaining there. Before
they proceeded far, they were attacked in the rear by a
party of Indians, who had been observing their movements; and who in the first fire killed six of the emigrants and dispersed their cattle. Notwithstanding that,
in the engagement which ensued upon this attack, the
assailants were repulsed, yet the adventurers were so
afflicted at the loss of their friends, and dispirited by such
serious and early opposition, that they abandoned their
purpose for a time, and returned to the inhabited parts of
Tennessee.[1]

---

[1] The Boones and five other families set out from their homes on the
Yadkin, Sept. 25, 1773. In Powell's Valley they were joined by forty
people under Boone's brother-in-law, William Bryan. While the main
party were slowly advancing through the valley, a small squad, under
Boone's oldest son, James, went on a side expedition for flour, cattle,
and other supplies. With these they had nearly caught up to the advance,

The Indians elated with their success in defeating this first attempt at the settlement of Kentucky, and supposing that the route pursued by the party which they had driven back, would be the pass for future adventurers, determined on guarding it closely, and checking, if possible, every similar enterprise. But while their attention was directed to this point, others found their way into the country by a different route and from a different direction.

The Virginia troops, who had served in the Canadian war, had been promised a bounty in Western lands. Many of them being anxious to ascertain their value, and deeming this a favorable period for the making of surveys, collected at Fort Pitt in the fall of 1773; and descending the Ohio river to its falls, at Louisville, proceeded from thence to explore the country preparatory to a perfection of their grants.[1]

---

when, not knowing they were so near, they camped on the evening of October 9 a few miles in the rear. Early in the morning of the 10th, a small band of Shawnees and Cherokees, who were nominally at peace with the whites, fell upon and, after cruel tortures, slaughtered them. In Dunmore's speech at Fort Pitt, this tragedy in Powell's Valley was alluded to as one of the chief causes of the Indian war of 1774. At the Camp Charlotte treaty (October, 1774), some of the plunder from this massacre was delivered up by the savages. After the tragedy, the greater part of the Kentucky caravan returned to their homes, but the Boones spent the winter of 1773-74 at a settlement some forty miles distant, on Clinch River. During the Dunmore War, Boone was active as an Indian fighter.—R. G. T.

[1] The leader of this party was Capt. Thomas Bullitt. He was born in Fauquier county, Va., in 1730; was one of Washington's captains at the Great Meadows (1754), and fought gallantly with Braddock (1755) and Forbes (1758); in 1763, was made adjutant-general of Virginia; during the early part of the Revolution he held the same office in the Southern Department of the United States, but resigned in 1776 because not promoted; he died in Fauquier county, in 1778. The project of Franklin, Walpole, and others to found the Colony of Pittsylvania, with its seat at the mouth of the Great Kanawha, greatly stimulated Western land speculation, and there was a rush of those holding military land warrants to locate claims. Lord Dunmore's agent at Fort Pitt, Dr. John Connolly—with whom his lordship was doubtless in partnership—had large interests of this character, and Bullitt went to the Falls of the Ohio (1773) to survey lands for him. Bullitt had a surveyor's commission from Williams and Mary College, but Col. William Preston, county sur-

About the same time too, General Thompson of Pennsylvania, commenced an extensive course of surveys, of the rich land on the North Fork of Licking; and other individuals following his example, in the ensuing winter the country swarmed with land adventurers and surveyors. So sensible were they all, that these attempts to appropriate those lands to their own use, would produce acts of hostility, that they went prepared to resist those acts; and the first party who took up their abode in Kentucky, no sooner selected a situation for their residence, than they proceeded to erect a fort for their security.[1] The conduct of the Indians soon convinced them that their apprehensions were not ill founded; and many of them, in consequence of the hostile movements which were being made, and the robberies which were committed, ascended the Ohio river to Wheeling.

It is not known that any murders were done previously to this, and subsequently to the attack and repulse of the emigrants who were led on by Boone in 1773. This event happened on the tenth day of October; and it was in April the ensuing year, that the land adventurers retired to Wheeling. In this interval of time, nothing could, perhaps, be done by the Indians, but make preparation [111] for hostilities in the spring. Indeed it very rarely happens, that the Indians engage in active war dur-

veyor for Fincastle county—in which Kentucky was then included—declined to recognize any but his own deputies. Preston carried his point, and the lands were re-surveyed the following year (1774) by his deputies. Bullitt had laid off a town on this Connolly survey; but the Revolution soon broke out, Bullitt was otherwise engaged, Dunmore was deposed, Connolly was imprisoned, and the scheme fell through. In 1778, George Rogers Clark camped at the Falls on his way to the Illinois, and the garrison he established there grew into the town of Louisville. With Bullitt's surveying party in 1773, were James Douglas, James Harrod, James Sodousky, Isaac Hite, Abraham Haptonstall, Ebenezer Severns, John Fitzpatrick, John Cowan,—prominent names in later Kentucky history,—and possibly others. George Rogers Clark was probably with the party during a part of its canoe voyage down the Ohio, but seems to have gone no farther than Big Bone Creek.—R. G. T.

[1] This was done by a party of men from the Monongahela, under the guidance of James Harrod; by whom was built the first cabin for human habitancy ever erected in Kentucky. This was on the present site of Harrodsburg.

ing the winter; and there is, moreover, a strong presumption, that they were for some time ignorant of the fact that there were adventurers in the country; and consequently, they knew of no object there, on which their hostile intentions could operate.—Be this as it may, it is certain that, from the movements of the Indians at the close of the winter, the belief was general, that they were assuming a warlike attitude, and meditating a continuance of hostilities. War was certainly begun on their part, when Boone and his associates, were attacked and driven back to the settlement; and if it abated for a season, that abatement was attributable to other causes, than a disposition to remain quiet and peaceable, while the country was being occupied by the whites.

If other evidence were wanting, to prove the fact that the war of 1774 had its origin in a determination of the Indians to repress the extension of white settlements, it could be found in the circumstance, that although it was terminated by the treaty with Lord Dunmore, yet it revived as soon as attempts were again made to occupy Kentucky, and was continued with increased ardour, 'till the victory obtained over them by General Wayne. For, notwithstanding that in the struggle for American liberty, those Indians became the allies of Great Britain, yet when independence was acknowledged, and the English forces withdrawn from the colonies, hostilities were still carried on by them; and, as was then well understood, because of the continued operation of those causes, which produced the war of 1774. That the Canadian traders and British emissaries, prompted the Indians to aggression, and extended to them every aid which they could, to render that aggression more effectually oppressive and overwhelming, is readily admitted. Yet this would not have led to a war, but for the encroachments which have been mentioned. French influence, united to the known jealousy of the Natives, would have been unavailingly exerted to array the Indians against Virginia, at the commencement of Braddock's war, but for the proceedings of the Ohio company, and the fact that the Pennsylvania traders represented the object of that association to be purely territorial. And equally fruitless would have been their endeavor to involve them in a contest [112] with Virginians at a later period, but for a like manifestation of an intention to encroach on their domain.

In the latter end of April 1774, a party of land adventurers, who had fled from the dangers which threatened them below, came in collision with some Indians, near the mouth of Captina, sixteen miles below Wheeling. A slight skirmish ensued, which terminated in the discomfiture of the whites, notwithstanding they had only one man wounded, and one or two of the enemy were killed. About the same time, happened the affair opposite the mouth of Yellow creek; a stream emptying into the Ohio river from the northwest, nearly midway between Pittsburg and Wheeling.[1]

In consequence of advices received of the menacing conduct of the Indians, Joshua Baker (who lived at this place) was preparing, together with his neighbors, to retire for safety, into some of the nearer forts, or to go to the older and more populous settlements, remote from danger. There was at that time a large party of Indians, encamped on both sides of Yellow creek, at its entrance into the river; and although in their intercourse at Baker's, they had not manifested an intention of speedily commencing depredations, yet he deemed his situation in the immediate contiguity of them, as being far from secure, and was on the eve of abandoning it, when a party of whites, who had just collected at his house, fired upon and killed some Indians, who were likewise there.—Among them were the brother and daughter of the celebrated chief, Logan.[2]

---

[1] These are the Pipe Creek and Baker's Bottom affairs, respectively mentioned on pp. 134, 149, *notes.* Yellow Creek, opposite Baker's Bottom, empties into the Ohio 51 miles below Pittsburg; Wheeling is 91 miles below Pittsburg, and Pipe Creek 104.—R. G. T.

[2] There is some difficulty in fixing on the precise time when these occurrences happened. Col. Ebenezer Zane says that they took place in the latter part of April, and that the affair at Captina preceded the one at Yellow creek a few days. John Sappington, who was of the party at Baker's, and is said to be the one who killed Logan's brother, says, the murders at that place occurred on the 24th of May, and that the

In justification of this conduct it has been said, that on the preceding evening a squaw came over from the encampment and informed Mrs. Baker that the Indians meditated the murder of her family on the next day; and that before the firing [113] at Baker's, two canoes, con-

---

skirmish at Captina was on the day before (23rd May.) Col. Andrew Swearingen, a presbyterian gentleman of much respectability, one of the early settlers near the Ohio above Wheeling, and afterwards intimate with those engaged at both places, says that the disturbance opposite Yellow creek preceded the engagement [113] at Captina, and that the latter, as was then generally understood, was caused by the conduct of the Indians, who had been at Yellow creek and were descending the river, exasperated at the murder of their friends at Baker's. Mr. Benjamin Tomlinson, who was the brother-in-law of Baker and living with him at the time, says that this circumstance happened in May, but is silent as to the one at Captina. These gentlemen all agree in the fact that Logan's people were murdered at Baker's. Indeed Logan himself charges it as having been done there. The statement of Sappington, that the murders were caused by the abusive epithets of Logan's brother and his taking the hat and coat of Baker's brother in law is confirmed by Col. Swearingen and others; who also say that for some days previous, the neighborhood generally had been engaged in preparing to leave the country, in consequence of the menacing conduct of the Indians.

Comment by R. G. T.—The date is now well established—April 30. Withers is altogether too lenient, in his treatment of the whites engaged in this wretched massacre. Logan, encamped at the mouth of Yellow River, on the Ohio side, was a peaceful, inoffensive Indian, against whom no man harbored a suspicion; he was made a victim of race hatred, in a time of great popular excitement. Joshua Baker, who was settled opposite him on Baker's Bottom, in Virginia, kept a low grog-shop tavern, and had recently been warned not to sell more liquor to Indians. Daniel Greathouse lived in the vicinity—a cruel, bloodthirsty fellow, who served Connolly as a local agent in fomenting hatred of Indians. It will be remembered (p. 134, *note*) that Cresap's party were intending to strike the camp of Logan, but that they abandoned the project. In the meantime, probably without knowledge of Cresap's intent, Greathouse had collected a party of 32 borderers to accomplish the same end. Logan's camp seemed too strong for them to attack openly; so they secreted themselves in Baker's house, and when Logan's family, men and women, came over to get their daily grog, and were quite drunk, set upon them and slew and tomahawked nine or ten. The chief, standing on the Ohio bank, heard the uproar and witnessed the massacre; he naturally supposed that the murderers were led by Cresap. From a friend of the whites, Logan became their implacable enemy, and during the ensuing war his forays were the bloodiest on the border. We shall hear of him and his famous speech. later on.

taining Indians painted and armed for war, were seen to leave the opposite shore. Under these circumstances, an apparently slight provocation, and one, which would not perhaps have been, otherwise heeded, produced the fatal result. As the canoes approached the shore, the party from Baker's commenced firing on them, and notwithstanding the opposition made by the Indians, forced them to retire.

An interval of quiet succeeded the happening of these events; but it was as the solemn stillness which precedes the eruption of an earthquake, when a volcanic explosion has given notice of its approach;—rendered more awful by the uncertainty where its desolating influence would be felt. It was however, a stillness of but short duration. The gathering storm soon burst over the devoted heads of those, who had neglected to seek a shelter from its wrath. The traders in the Indian country were the first victims sacrificed on the altar of savage ferocity; and a general massacre of all the whites found among them, quickly followed. A young man, discovered near the falls of Muskingum and within sight of White Eyes town, was murdered, scalped; literally cut to pieces, and the mangled members of his body, hung up on trees. White Eyes, a chief of the friendly Delawares, hearing the scalp halloo, went out with a party of his men; and seeing what had been done, collected the scattered limbs of the young man, and buried them. On the next day, they were torn from the ground, severed into smaller pieces, and thrown dispersedly at greater distances from each other.

[114] Apprized of impending danger, many of the inhabitants on the frontiers of North Western Virginia, retired into the interior, before any depredations were committed, in the upper country; some took refuge in forts which had been previously built; while others, collecting together at particular houses, converted them into temporary fortresses, answering well the purposes of protection, to those who sought shelter in them. Fort Redstone, which had been erected after the successful expedition of General Forbes; and Fort Pitt, at the confluence of the Alleghany and Monongahela rivers, afforded an asylum

to many. Several private forts were likewise established in various parts of the country ;[1] and every thing which individual exertion could effect, to ensure protection to the border inhabitants, was done.

Nor did the colonial government of Virginia neglect the security of her frontier citizens. When intelligence of the hostile disposition of the Natives, reached Williamsburg, the house of Burgesses was in session ; and measures were immediately adopted, to prevent massacres, and to restore tranquillity. That these objects might be the more certainly accomplished, it was proposed by General Andrew Lewis (then a delegate from Bottetourt,) to organize a force, sufficient to overcome all intermediate opposition, and to carry the war into the enemy's country. In accordance to this proposition, orders were issued by Governor Dunmore for raising the requisite number of troops, and for making other necessary preparations for the contemplated campaign; the plan of which was concerted by the Governor, Gen. Lewis and Colonel Charles Lewis (then a delegate from Augusta.) But as some time must necessarily have elapsed before the consummation of the preparations which were being made; and as much individual suffering might result from the delays unavoidably incident to the raising, equipping and [115] organizing a large body of troops, it was deemed advisable to take some previous and immediate step to prevent the invasion of exposed and defenceless portions of the country.—The best plan for the accomplishment of this object was believed to be, the sending of an advance army into the Indian country, of sufficient strength to act offensively, before a confederacy could be formed of the different tribes, and their combined forces be brought into the field. A sense

---

[1] It was then that Westfall's and Casinoe's forts were erected in Tygart's valley,—Pricket's, on Pricket's creek,—Jackson's on Ten Mile, and Shepherd's on Wheeling creek, a few miles above its mouth. There were also others established in various parts of the country and on the Monongahela and Ohio rivers. Nutter's fort, near to Clarksburg, afforded protection to the inhabitants on the West Fork, from its source, to its confluence with the Valley river; and to those who lived on Buchannon and on Hacker's creek, as well as to the residents of its immediate vicinity.

of the exposed situation of their towns in the presence of
an hostile army, requiring the entire strength of every
village for its defence, would, it was supposed, call home
those straggling parties of warriors, by which destruction
is so certainly dealt to the helpless and unprotected.   In
conformity with this part of the plan of operations, four
hundred men, to be detailed from the militia west of the
mountains, were ordered to assemble at Wheeling as soon
as practicable.   And in the mean time, lest the surveyors
and land adventurers, who were then in Kentucky, might
be discovered and fall a prey to the savages, Daniel Boone
was sent by the Governor to the falls of Ohio, to conduct
them home from thence, through the wilderness; the only
practicable road to safety, the Ohio river being so effectually guarded as to preclude the hope of escaping up it.[1]

---

[1] June 20, Col. William Preston, having charge of the defenses of
Fincastle county, authorized Capt. William Russell to employ two faithful woodsmen to go to Kentucky and inform the several surveying parties
at work there, of their danger.   June 26, Russell replied, "I have engaged to start immediately on the occasion, two of the best hands I
could think of—Daniel Boone and Michael Stoner; who have engaged
to reach the country as low as the Falls, and to return by way of Gas-
per's Lick on Cumberland, and through Cumberland Gap; so that, by
the assiduity of these men, if it is not too late, I hope the gentlemen
will be apprized of the imminent danger they are daily in."

Boone and Stoner journeyed overland to Harrodsburg, where Col.
James Harrod and thirty men were making improvements and laying
out the town.   The thrifty Boone secured a good lot, hastily built a
claim cabin, and proceeded on his tour.   At Fontaine Blue, three miles
below Harrodsburg, the two scouts found another party of surveyors,
whom they warned; and in going down the Kentucky River came across
Capt. John Floyd's surveying party,—eight men, who had left Preston's
house for Kentucky, April 9,—who agreed to meet them farther down
the river.   But circumstances prevented a reunion, and Floyd's band
penetrated through the wilderness on their own account, and had a
painful journey of sixteen days' duration before reaching Russell's Fort
on Clinch River.   Meanwhile, Boone and Stoner descended to the mouth
of the Kentucky, and thence to the Falls of the Ohio, and found more
surveyors at Mann's Lick, four miles southeast.   Indians were making
bloody forays through the district, and the scouts had frequent thrilling
adventures.   Finally, after having been absent sixty-one days and travelled 800 miles, they reached Russell's on the Clinch, in safety.   Russell
was absent on the Point Pleasant campaign, and Boone set out with a
party of recruits to reinforce him, but was ordered back to defend the
Clinch settlements.   He was busy at this task until the close of the war.

Early in June, the troops destined to make an incursion into the Indian country, assembled at Wheeling, and being placed under the command of Colonel Angus McDonald, descended the Ohio to the mouth of Captina. Debarking, at this place, from their boats and canoes, they took up their march to Wappatomica, an Indian town on the Muskingum. The country through which the army had to pass, was one unbroken forest, presenting many obstacles to its speedy advance, not the least of which was the difficulty of proceeding directly to the point proposed.[1] To obviate this, however, they were accompanied by three persons in the capacity of guides;[2] whose knowledge of the woods, and familiarity with those natural indices, which so unerringly mark the direction of the principal points, enabled them to pursue the direct course.—When they had approached within six miles of the town, the [116] army encountered an opposition from a party of fifty or sixty Indians lying in ambush; and before these could be dislodged, two whites were killed, and eight or ten wounded;—one Indian was killed, and several wounded. They then proceeded to Wappatomica without further molestation.[3]

When the army arrived at the town, it was found to be entirely deserted. Supposing that it would cross the river, the Indians had retreated to the opposite bank, and concealing themselves behind trees and fallen timber, were awaiting that movement in joyful anticipation of a suc-

He was present at the Watauga treaty, March 17, 1775; later that year, he led another band to Kentucky, and early in April built Fort Boone, on Kentucky River, "a little below Big Lick," the nucleus of the Henderson colony.—R. G. T.

[1] The party numbered about four hundred men. The line of march was about ninety miles in length, as estimated by the zig-zag course pursued.—R. G. T.

[2] They were Jonathan Zane, Thomas Nicholson and Tady Kelly. A better woodsman than the first named of these three, perhaps never lived.

[3] Doddridge locates Wapatomica "about sixteen miles below the present Coshocton." Butterfield (*History of the Girtys*) places it "just below the present Zanesville, in Logan county, Ohio, not a great distance from Mac-a-cheek." For localities of Indian towns on the Muskingum, see map in St. John de Creve Cœur's *Lettres d'un Cultivateur Américain* (Paris, 1787), III., p. 413.—R. G. T.

cessful surprise.—Their own anxiety and the prudence of the commanding officer, however, frustrated that expectation. Several were discovered peeping from their covert, watching the motion of the army; and Colonel McDonald, suspecting their object, and apprehensive that they would recross the river and attack him in the rear, stationed videttes above and below, to detect any such purpose, and to apprise him of the first movement towards effecting it. Foiled by these prudent and precautionary measures and seeing their town in possession of the enemy, with no prospect of wresting it from them, 'till destruction would have done its work, the Indians sued for peace; and the commander of the expedition consenting to negotiate with them, if he could be assured of their sincerity, five chiefs were sent over as hostages, and the army then crossed the river, with these in front.

When a negotiation was begun, the Indians asked, that one of the hostages might be permitted to go and convoke the other chiefs, whose presence, it was alleged, would be necessary to the ratification of a peace. One was accordingly released; and not returning at the time specified, another was then sent, who in like manner failed to return. Colonel McDonald, suspecting some treachery, marched forward to the next town, above Wappatomica, where another slight engagement took place, in which one Indian was killed and one white man wounded. It was then ascertained, that the time which should have been spent in collecting the other chiefs, preparatory to negotiation, had been employed in removing their old men, their women and children, together with what property could be readily taken off, and for making preparations for a combined attack on the Virginia troops. To punish this duplicity and to render peace really desirable, Col. McDonald burned their towns and destroyed their crops; [117] and being then in want of provisions, retraced his steps to Wheeling, taking with him the three remaining hostages, who were then sent on to Williamsburg.[1]

---

[1] John Hargus, a private in Capt. Cresap's company, while stationed as a vidette below the main army, observed an Indian several times raising his head above his blind, and looking over the river. Charging

The inconvenience of supplying provisions to an army in the wilderness, was a serious obstacle to the success of expeditions undertaken against the Indians. The want of roads, at that early period, which would admit of transportation in wagons, rendered it necessary to resort to pack horses; and such was at times the difficulty of procuring these, that, not unfrequently, each soldier had to be the bearer of his entire stock of subsistence for the whole campaign. When this was exhausted, a degree of suffering ensued, often attended with consequences fatal to individuals, and destructive to the objects of the expedition. In the present case, the army being without provisions before they left the Indian towns, their only sustenance consisted of weeds, an ear of corn each day, and occasionally, a small quantity of venison: it being impracticable to hunt game in small parties, because of the vigilance and success of the Indians, in watching and cutting off detachments of this kind, before they could accomplish their purpose and regain the main army.

No sooner had the troops retired from the Indian country, than the savages, in small parties, invaded the settlements in different directions, seeking opportunities of gratifying their insatiable thirst for blood. And although the precautions which had been taken, lessened the frequency of their success, yet they did not always prevent it. Persons leaving the forts on any occasion, were almost always either murdered or carried into captivity,—a lot sometimes worse than death itself.

Perhaps the first of these incursions into North Western Virginia, after the destruction of the towns on the Muskingum, was that made by a party of eight Indians, at the head of which was the Cayuga chief Logan.[1] This

---

his rifle with a second ball, he fired, and both bullets passed through the neck of the Indian, who was found next day and scalped by Hargus.

[1] Logan was the son of Shikellemus, a celebrated chief of the Cayuga nation, who dwelt at Shamokin, and always attached to the [118] English, was of much service to them on many occasions. After the close of Dunmore's war, Logan became gloomy and melancholy, drank freely and manifested symptoms of mental derangement. He remained some time at Detroit, and while there, his conduct and expressions evinced a

very celebrated [118] Indian is represented as having hitherto, observed towards the whites, a course of conduct by no means in accordance with the malignity and steadfast implacability which influenced his red brethren generally; but was, on the contrary, distinguished by a sense of humanity, and a just abhorrence of those cruelties so frequently inflicted on the innocent and unoffending, as well as upon those who were really obnoxious to savage enmity. Such indeed were the acts of beneficence which characterized him, and so great his partiality for the English, that the finger of his brethren would point to his cabin as the residence of Logan, "the friend of white men." "In the course of the French war, he remained at home, idle and inactive;" opposed to the interference of his nation, "an advocate for peace." When his family fell before the fury of exasperated men, he felt himself impelled to avenge their deaths; and exchanging the pipe of peace, for the tomahawk of war, became active in seeking opportunities to glut his vengeance.[1] With this object in view, at the head of the party which has been mentioned, he traversed the county from the Ohio to the West Fork, before an opportunity was presented him of achieving any mischief. Their distance from what was supposed would be the theatre of war, had rendered the inhabitants of that section of country, comparatively inattentive to their safety. Relying on the expectation that the first blow would be struck on the Ohio, and that they would have sufficient notice of this to prepare for their own security, before danger could reach them, many had continued to perform the ordinary business of their farms.

On the 12th day of July, as William Robinson, Thomas Hellen and Coleman Brown were pulling flax in a field opposite the mouth of Simpson's creek, Logan and his party approached unperceived and fired at them. Brown fell

---

weariness of the world. Life he said had become a burden to him, he knew no more what pleasure was, and thought it had been better if he had never existed. In this disponding and disconsolate condition he left Detroit, and on his way between that place and Miami, is said to have been murdered.

[1] See p. 149, *note*, for account of the massacre.—R. G. T.

instantly; his body perforated by several balls; and Hellen
and Robinson [119] unscathed, sought safety in flight.
Hellen being then an old man, was soon overtaken and
made captive; but Robinson, with the elasticity of youth,
ran a considerable distance before he was taken; and but
for an untoward accident might have effected an escape.
Believing that he was outstripping his pursuers, and
anxious to ascertain the fact, he looked over his shoulder,
but before he discovered the Indian giving chase, he ran
with such violence against a tree, that he fell, stunned by
the shock and lay powerless and insensible. In this situation he was secured with a cord; and when he revived,
was taken back to the place where the Indians had Hellen
in confinement, and where lay the lifeless body of Brown.
They then set off to their towns, taking with them a horse
which belonged to Hellen.

When they had approached near enough to be distinctly heard, Logan (as is usual with them after a successful scout,) gave the scalp halloo, and several warriors
came out to meet them, and conducted the prisoners into
the village. Here they passed through the accustomed
ceremony of running the guantlet; but with far different
fortunes. Robinson, having been previously instructed by
Logan (who from the time he made him his prisoner, manifested a kindly feeling towards him,) made his way, with
but little interruption, to the council house; but poor Hellen, from the decrepitude of age, and his ignorance of
the fact that it was a place of refuge, was sadly beaten
before he arrived at it; and when he at length came near
enough, he was knocked down with a war club, before he
could enter. After he had fallen, they continued to beat
and strike him with such unmerciful severity, that he
would assuredly have fallen a victim to their barbarous
usage, but that Robinson (at some peril for the interference)
reached forth his hand and drew him within the sanctuary.
When he had however, recovered from the effects of the
violent beating which he had received, he was relieved
from the apprehension of farther suffering, by being
adopted into an Indian family.

A council was next convoked to resolve on the fate

of Robinson; and then arose in his breast, feelings of the most anxious inquietude. Logan assured him, that he should not be killed; but the council appeared determined that he should die, and he was tied to the stake. Logan then addressed them, and with much vehemence, insisted that Robinson too should be spared; and had the eloquence displayed on that occasion been less than Logan is believed to have possessed, [120] it is by no means wonderful that he appeared to Robinson (as he afterwards said) the most powerful orator he ever heard. But commanding as his eloquence might have been, it seems not to have prevailed with the council; for Logan had to interpose otherwise than by argument or entreaty, to succeed in the attainment of his object. Enraged at the pertinacity with which the life of Robinson was sought to be taken, and reckless of the consequences, he drew the tomahawk from his belt, and severing the cords which bound the devoted victim to the stake, led him in triumph, to the cabin of an old squaw, by whom he was immediately adopted.

After this, so long as Logan remained in the town where Robinson was, he was kind and attentive to him; and when preparing to go again to war, got him to write the letter which was afterwards found on Holstein at the house of a Mr. Robertson, whose family were all murdered by the Indians. Robinson remained with his adopted mother, until he was redeemed under the treaty concluded at the close of the Dunmore campaign.

[121] CHAPTER VII.

When information of the hostile deportment of the Indians was carried to Williamsburg, Col. Charles Lewis sent a messenger with the intelligence to Capt. John Stuart, and requesting of him, to apprize the inhabitants on the Greenbrier river that an immediate war was anticipated, and to send out scouts to watch the warrior's paths beyond the settlements. The vigilance and activity of Capt. Stuart, were exerted with some success, to prevent the re-exhibition of those scenes which had been previously witnessed on Muddy creek and in the Big Levels: but they could not avail to repress them altogether.

In the course of the preceding spring, some few individuals had begun to make improvements on the Kenhawa river below the Great Falls; and some land adventurers, to examine and survey portions of the adjoining country. To these men Capt. Stuart despatched an express, to inform them that apprehensions were entertained of immediate irruptions being made upon the frontiers by the Indians, and advising them to remove from the position which they then occupied; as from its exposed situation, without great vigilance and alertness, they must necessarily fall a prey to the savages.

When the express arrived at the cabin of Walter Kelly, twelve miles below the falls, Capt. John Field of Culpepper (who had been in active service during the French war, and was then engaged in making surveys,) was there with a young Scotchman and a negro woman. Kelly with great prudence, directly sent his family to Greenbrier, under the care of a younger brother. But Capt. Field, considering the apprehension as groundless, determined on remaining with Kelly, who from prudential motives did not wish to subject himself to observation by mingling with others.[1] Left with no persons but the Scotchman and negro, they were not long permitted to doubt the reality of those dangers, of which they had been forewarned by Capt Stuart.

[122] Very soon after Kelly's family had left the cabin, and while yet within hearing of it, a party of Indians approached, unperceived, near to Kelly and Field, who were engaged in drawing leather from a tan trough in the yard. The first intimation which Field had of their approach was the discharge of several guns and the fall of Kelly. He then ran briskly towards the house to get possession of a gun, but recollecting that it was unloaded, he changed his course, and sprang into a cornfield which screened him from the observation of the Indians; who, supposing that he had taken shelter in the cabin, rushed immediately into it. Here they found the Scotchman and the negro woman, the latter of whom they killed; and making prisoner of the young man, returned and scalped Kelly.

When Kelly's family reached the Greenbrier settlement, they mentioned their fears for the fate of those whom they had left on the Kenhawa, not doubting but that the guns which they heard soon after leaving the house, had been dischaaged at them by Indians. Capt. Stuart, with a promptitude which must ever command admiration, exerted himself effectually to raise a volunteer corps, and proceed to the scene of action, with the view of ascertaining whether the Indians had been there; and if they had, and he could meet with them, to endeavor to punish them for the outrage, and thus prevent the repetition of similar deeds of violence.

They had not however gone far, before they were met by Capt. Field, whose appearance of itself fully told the tale of woe. He had ran upwards of eighty miles, naked except his shirt, and without food; his body nearly exhausted by fatigue, anxiety and hunger, and his limbs greviously lacerated with briers and brush. Captain

---

[1] He is said to have committed some offence, in the upper part of South Carolina, which rendered him obnoxious to the laws of that colony, and to evade the punishment for which, he had fled to the wilderness and taken up his abode in it.

Stuart, fearing lest the success of the Indians might induce them to push immediately for the settlements, thought proper to return and prepare for that event.

In a few weeks after this another party of Indians came to the settlement on Muddy creek, and as if a certain fatality attended the Kelly's, they alone fell victims to the incursion. As the daughter of Walter Kelly was walking with her uncle (who had conducted the family from the Kenhawa) some distance from the house, which had been converted into a temporary fort, and in which they lived, they were discovered and fired upon; the latter was killed and scalped, and the former being overtaken in her flight, was carried into captivity.

After the murder of Brown, and the taking of Hellen and Robinson, the inhabitants on the Monongahela and its upper branches, alarmed for their safety, retired into forts. But in the ensuing September, as Josiah Pricket and Mrs. Susan Ox, who had left Pricket's fort for the purpose of driving up their cows, were returning in the evening they were way laid by a party of Indians, who had been drawn to the path by the tinkling of the cowbell. Pricket was killed and scalped, and Mrs. Ox taken prisoner.

[123] It was in the course of this season, that Lewis Wetsel[1] first gave promise of that daring and discretion, which were so fully developed in his maturer years, and which rendered him among the most fortunate and successful of Indian combatants. When about fourteen years old, he and his brother Jacob, (still younger) were discov-

---

[1] Lewis Wetzel, the son of a German settler on Wheeling Creek, some fourteen miles above its mouth, was born about 1764. He and his brothers Martin, Jacob, John, and George became famous in border warfare after the close of the Revolution; the annals of the frontier abound in tales of their hardy achievements. Martin and Lewis were the heroes of most remarkable escapes from Indian captivity; John was also famous as an Indian fighter; and Jacob's name will ever be connected with the exploits of that other great border scout, Simon Kenton. But of all the brothers, Lewis achieved the widest celebrity, and two biographies of him have been published: by Cecil B. Hartley (Phila., 1860), and by R. C. V. Meyers (Phila., 1883).—R. G. T.

11

ered some distance from the house, by a party of Indians, who had been prowling through the settlements on the Ohio river, with the expectation of fortunately meeting with some opportunity of taking scalps or making prisoners. As the boys were at some distance from them, and in a situation too open to admit of their being approached without perceiving those who should advance towards them, the Indians determined on shooting the larger one, lest his greater activity might enable him to escape. A shot was accordingly discharged at him, which, partially taking effect and removing a portion of his breast bone, so far deprived him of his wonted powers, that he was easily overtaken; and both he and his brother were made prisoners. The Indians immediately directed their steps towards their towns, and having travelled about twenty miles beyond the Ohio river, encamped at the Big Lick, on the waters of McMahon's creek, on the second night after they had set off. When they had finished eating, the Indians laid down, without confining the boys as on the preceding night, and soon fell to sleep. After making some little movements to test the soundness of their repose, Lewis whispered to his brother that he must get up and go home with him; and after some hesitation on the part of Jacob, they arose and set off. Upon getting about 100 yards from the camp, Lewis stopped, and telling his brother to await there, returned to the camp and brought from thence a pair of mocasons for each of them. He then observed, that he would again go back and get his father's gun; this he soon effected, and they then commenced their journey home. The moon shining brightly, they were easily able to distinguish the trail which they had made in going out; but had not however pursued it far, before they heard the Indians coming in pursuit of them. So soon as Lewis perceived by the sound of their voices that they were approaching tolerably near to them, he led his brother aside from the path, and squatting down, concealed themselves 'till their pursuers had passed them; when they again commenced travelling and in the rear of the Indians. Not overtaking the boys as soon as was expected, those who had been sent after them, began to retrace their steps.

Expecting this, the boys were watchful of every noise or object before them, and when they heard the Indians returning, again secreted themselves in the bushes, and escaped observation. They were then followed by two, of the party who had made them prisoners, on horseback; but by practising the same stratagem, they eluded them also; and on the next day reached the Ohio river opposite to Wheeling. Apprehensive that it would be dangerous to apprize those on the opposite side of the river of their situation, by hallooing, Lewis set himself to work as silently, and yet as expeditiously [124] as possible, and with the aid of his little brother, soon completed a raft on which they safely crossed the Ohio; and made their way home.

That persons, should, by going out from the forts, when the Indians were so generally watching around them, expose themselves to captivity or death, may at first appear strange and astonishing. But when the mind reflects on the tedious and irksome confinement, which they were compelled to undergo; the absence of the comforts, and frequently, of the necessaries of life, coupled with an overweening attachment to the enjoyment of forest scenes and forest pastimes, it will perhaps be matter of greater astonishment that they did not more frequently forego the security of a fortress, for the uncertain enjoyment of those comforts and necessaries, and the doubtful gratification of this attachment. Accustomed as they had been "free to come and free to go," they could not brook the restraint under which they were placed; and rather than chafe and pine in unwilling confinement, would put themselves at hazard, that they might revel at large and wanton in the wilderness. Deriving their sustenance chiefly from the woods, the strong arm of necessity led many to tempt the perils which environed them; while to the more chivalric and adventurous "the danger's self were lure alone." The quiet and stillness which reigned around, even when the enemy were lurking nearest and in greater numbers, inspired many too, with the delusive hope of exemption from risk, not unfrequently the harbinger of fatal consequences. It seemed indeed, impracticable at first to realize the existence of a danger, which could not be perceived. And not until taught by reiterated suffering did they properly appreciate the perilous situation of those, who ventured beyond the walls of their forts. But this state of things was of short duration. The preparations, which were necessary to be made for the projected campaign into the Indian country, were completed; and to resist this threatened invasion, required the concentrated exertions of all their warriors.

The army destined for this expedition, was composed of volunteers and militia, chiefly from the counties west of the Blue ridge, and consisted of two divisions. The northern division, comprehending the troops, collected in Frederick, Dunmore,[1] and the adjacent counties, was to be commanded by Lord Dunmore, in person;[2] and the southern, comprising the different companies raised in Botetourt, Augusta and the adjoining counties east of the Blue ridge, was to be led on by Gen. Andrew Lewis. These two divisions, proceeding by different routes, were to form a junction at the mouth of the Big Kenhawa, and from thence penetrate the country north west of the Ohio river, as far as the season would admit of their going; and destroy all the Indian towns and villages which they could reach.

About the first of September, the troops placed under the command [125] of Gen. Lewis rendezvoused at Camp Union (now Lewisburg) and consisted of two regiments, commanded by Col. William Fleming of Botetourt and Col. Charles Lewis of Augusta, and containing about four hundred men each. At Camp Union they were joined by an independent volunteer company under Col. John Field of Culpepper; a company from Bedford under Capt. Bu-

---

[1] Now Shenandoah.

[2] The northern wing was composed of men from Frederick, Berkeley, and Dunmore (afterwards Shenandoah) counties, and Col. Adam Stephen was placed in command. With this wing went Lord Dunmore and Major John Connolly. Counting the forces already in the field under Maj. Angus McDonald and Capt. William Crawford, this levy numbered some twelve hundred men. Among them, as scouts, were George Roger Clark, Simon Kenton, and Michael Cresap.—R. G. T.

ford and two from the Holstein settlement (now Washington county) under Capts. Evan Shelby and Harbert. These three latter companies were part of the forces to be led on by Col. Christian, who was likewise to join the two main divisions of the army at Point Pleasant, so soon as the other companies of his regiment could be assembled. The force under Gen. Lewis, having been thus augmented to eleven hundred men, commenced its march for the mouth of Kenhawa on the 11th of September 1774.[1]

From Camp Union to the point proposed for the junction of the northern and southern divisions of the army, a distance of one hundred and sixty miles, the intermediate country was a trackless forest, so rugged and mountainous as to render the progress of the army, at once, tedious and laborious. Under the guidance of Capt. Matthew Arbuckle, they however, succeeded in reaching the Ohio river after a march of nineteen days; and fixed their encampment on the point of land immediately between that river and the Big Kenhawa.[2] The provisions and ammunition, transported on packhorses, and the beeves in droves, arrived soon after.

When the army was preparing to leave Camp Union, there was for a while some reluctance manifested on the

---

[1] Lewis was colonel of the militia of Botetourt county. Camp Union (so called because several bodies of troops met there) was on the Big Savannah or Great Levels of Greenbrier River; the town of Lewisburg now occupies the site.

In Dunmore's letter to Andrew Lewis, dated July 12, he directed him to raise a sufficient body of men, and proceeding to the mouth of the Great Kanawha there erect a fort; if he deemed best he was to cross the Ohio, proceed directly to the Indian towns, and destroy their crops and supplies; in any event he was to keep communication open between Fort Wheeling and Fort Dunmore (Pittsburg). It is evident that his lordship then contemplated no separate expedition of his own, for he talks of sending Major Angus McDonald's party and a new levy to Lewis's assistance. But he changed his mind, and August 30 wrote to Lewis directing that the latter meet him at the mouth of the Little Kanawha. Lewis replied through Col. William Preston that it was now too late to change his plans; he should proceed at once with the levy just summoned, to the mouth of the Great Kanawha, and there await further orders.—R. G. T.

[2] This cape was called Point Pleasant, and is now occupied by the West Virginia town of that name.—R. G. T.

part of Col. Field to submit to the command of Gen. Lewis. This proceeded from the fact, that in a former military service, he had been the senior of Gen. Lewis; and from the circumstance that the company led on by him were Independent Volunteers, not raised in pursuance of the orders of Governor Dunmore, but brought into the field by his own exertions, after his escape from the Indians at Kelly's. These circumstances induced him to separate his men from the main body of the army on its march, and to take a different way from the one pursued by it,—depending on his own knowledge of the country to lead them a practicable route to the river.[1]

While thus detached from the forces under Gen. Lewis, two of his men (Clay and Coward) who were out hunting and at some little distance from each other, came near to where two Indians were concealed. Seeing Clay only, and supposing him to be alone, one of them fired at him; and running up to scalp him as he fell, was himself shot by Coward, who was then about 100 yards off. The other Indian ran off unarmed, and made his escape. A bundle of ropes found where Clay was killed, induced the belief that it was the object of these Indians to steal horses;—it is not however improbable, that they had been observing the progress of the army, and endeavoring to ascertain its numbers. Col. Field, fearing that he might [126] encounter a party of the enemy in ambush, redoubled his vigilance 'till he again joined General Lewis; and the utmost concert and harmony then prevailed in the whole army.[2]

When the Southern division arrived at Point Pleasant, Governor Dunmore with the forces under his com-

---

[1] This is misleading. On September 6, Col. Charles Lewis, with his Augusta troops, numbering about six hundred, were detached to proceed to the mouth of the Elk, and there make canoes for transporting the supplies to the mouth of the Great Kanawha. This body had in charge a drove of 108 beef cattle, and 400 pack-horses laden with 54,000 lbs. of flour. Field's company soon followed this advance.—R. G. T.

[2] Saturday, the 10th, Clay and Coward were sent out to hunt deer for Field's company, on the banks of the Little Meadow. Then occurred the incident related by Withers. The Indian who escaped, hurried on to the Shawnee towns and gave them their first notice of the approach of

mand, had not reached there; and unable to account for
his failure to form the preconcerted junction at that place,
it was deemed advisable to await that event; as by so
doing, a better opportunity would be afforded to Col.
Christian of coming up, with that portion of the army,
which was then with him.[1] Meanwhile General Lewis, to
learn the cause of the delay of the Northern division, despatched runners by land, in the direction of Fort Pitt, to
obtain tidings of Lord Dunmore, and to communicate
them to him immediately. In their absence, however, advices were received from his Lordship, that he had determined on proceeding across the country, directly to the
Shawanee towns; and ordering General Lewis to cross the
river, march forward and form a junction with him, near
to them. These advices were received on the 9th of October, and preparations were immediately begun to be made
for the transportation of the troops over the Ohio river.[2]

the army. Alarmed at this incident, Field hurried and caught up with
the advance under Charles Lewis. The text reads as though he had
hastened back to Andrew Lewis, who had not yet left Camp Union.—
R. G. T.

[1] Col. Andrew Lewis marched out of Camp Union the 12th, with
about 450 men. These consisted of Fleming's Botetourt troops, three
companies of Fincastle men under Capts. Evan Shelby, William Herbert, and William Russell; the Bedford men under Thomas Buford, and
Dunmore men under Slaughter. They had with them 200 pack-horses
laden with flour, and the remainder of the beeves. Col. William
Christian, who arrived at Camp Union the day Andrew Lewis left, was
ordered, with the rest of the Fincastle men, to remain there, to guard
the residue of the provisions, and when the brigade of horses sent to
the mouth of the Elk had returned, to hurry every thing forward to
the mouth of the Great Kanawha. Five weeks were thus consumed
in transporting the troops and the supplies a distance of 160 miles
through the tangled forest, to Point Pleasant, where the main army,
upwards of 1,100 strong, had arrived, quite spent with exertions, on the
6th of October.

When Christian left Camp Union for the front, Anthony Bledsoe,
with a company of Fincastle men, was detailed to remain behind with
the sick, while the base of supplies at the mouth of the Elk was placed
in charge of Slaughter. As will be seen, Christian arrived too late to
engage in the battle of Point Pleasant.—R. G. T.

[2] When Lewis arrived at Point Pleasant (October 6th), he found
awaiting him in a hollow tree dispatches from Dunmore, brought by
Simon Kenton and two companions, directing him to join his lordship

Early on the morning of Monday the tenth of that month, two soldiers [1] left the camp, and proceeded up the Ohio river, in quest of deer. When they had progressed about two miles, they unexpectedly came in sight of a large number of Indians, rising from their encampment, and who discovering the two hunters fired upon them and killed one;—the other escaped unhurt, and running briskly to the camp, communicated the intelligence, "that he had seen a body of the enemy, covering four acres of ground as closely as they could stand by the side of each other." The main part of the army was immediately ordered out under Colonels Charles Lewis,[2] and William Fleming; and having formed into two lines, [127] they proceeded about four hundred yards, when they met the Indians, and the action commenced.

---

at the mouth of the Big Hockhocking, where the governor's northern wing, under Major Crawford, was building a stockade. But Lewis's men were spent, and pens had to be built for the cattle, and shelter for the stores, so no move was made. On Saturday, the 8th, came a further message from the governor, who was still at the Big Hockhocking. Lewis replied that he would join him there as soon as the troops, food supply, and powder had all reached Point Pleasant. His men were angry at Dunmore's interference, and argued with Lewis that it was sixty miles by river and over half that by land, to Dunmore's camp, whereas it was less than either to the hostile towns which they had started out to attack; and to turn aside from this purpose was to leave open for the hostiles the back-door to the frontier settlements of Virginia. The 9th was Sunday, and these sturdy Scotch-Irish Presbyterians spent the day in religious exercises, listening to a stout sermon from their chaplain. On the morrow, they were surprised by the Indians, as the sequel relates.—R. G. T.

[1] James Mooney, of Russell's company, and Joseph Hughey, of Shelby's. They were surprised at the mouth of Old Town Creek, three miles distant. Hughey was killed by a shot fired by Tavenor Ross, a white renegade in Cornstalk's party.—R. G. T.

[2] Few officers were ever more, or more deservedly, endeared to those under their command than Col. Charles Lewis. In the many skirmishes, which it was his fortune to have, with the Indians he was uncommonly successful; and in the various scenes of life, thro' which he passed, his conduct was invariably marked by the distinguishing characteristicks of a mind, of no ordinary stamp. His early fall on this bloody field, was severely felt during the whole engagement; and to it has been attributed the partial advantages gained by the Indian army near the commencement of the action. When the [127] fatal ball struck him, he fell at the root of a tree; from whence he was carried to his

At the first onset, Colonel Charles Lewis having fallen, and Colonel Fleming being wounded, both lines gave way and were retreating briskly towards the camp, when they were met by a reinforcement under Colonel Field,[1] and rallied. The engagement then became general, and was sustained with the most obstinate fury on both sides. The Indians perceiving that the "tug of war" had come, and determined on affording the Colonial army no chance of escape, if victory should declare for them, formed a line extending across the point, from the Ohio to the Kenhawa, and protected in front, by logs and fallen timber. In this situation they maintained the contest with unabated vigor, from sunrise 'till towards the close of evening; bravely and successfully resisting every charge which was made on them; and withstanding the impetuosity of every onset, with the most invincible firmness, until a fortunate movement on the part of the Virginia troops, decided the day.

Some short distance above the entrance of the Kenhawa river into Ohio, there is a stream, called Crooked creek, emptying into the former of these, from the North east,[2] whose banks are tolerably high, and were then covered with a thick and luxuriant growth of weeds. Seeing the impracticability of dislodging the Indians, by the most vigorous attack, and sensible of the great danger, which must arise to his army, if the contest were not decided before night, General Lewis detached the three companies which were commanded by Captains Isaac Shelby, George Matthews, and John Stuart, with orders to proceed up the Kenhawa river, and Crooked creek under cover of the banks and weeds, 'till they should [128] pass some distance beyond the enemy; when they were to emerge from

tent, against his wish, by Capt. Wm. Morrow and a Mr. Bailey, of Captain Paul's company, and died in a few hours afterwards. In remembrance of his great worth, the legislature named the county of Lewis after him.

[1] An active, enterprising and meritorious officer, who had been in service in Braddock's war, and profited by his experience of the Indian mode of fighting. His death checked for a time the ardor of his troops, and spread a gloom over the countenances of those, who had accompanied him on this campaign.

[2] A half-mile up the Big Kanawha.—R. G. T.

their covert, march downward towards the point and attack the Indians in their rear.[1] The manœuvre thus planned, was promptly executed, and gave a decided victory to the Colonial army. The Indians finding themselves suddenly and unexpectedly encompassed between two armies, & not doubting but that in their rear, was the looked for reinforcement under Colonel Christian, soon gave way, and about sun down, commenced a precipitate retreat across the Ohio, to their towns on the Scioto.

Some short time after the battle had ended, Colonel Christian arrived with the troops which he had collected in the settlements on the Holstein, and relieved the anxiety of many who were disposed to believe the retreat of the

---

[1] From MS. journals and letters in possession of the Wisconsin Historical Society, it appears that the conduct of the battle was as follows: Andrew Lewis, who as yet thought the enemy to be but a scouting party, and not an army equal in size to his own, had the drums beat to arms, for many of his men were asleep in their tents; and while still smoking his pipe, ordered a detachment from each of the Augusta companies, to form 150 strong under Col. Charles Lewis, with John Dickinson, Benjamin Harrison, and John Skidmore as the captains. Another party of like size was formed under Col. Fleming, with Captains Shelby, Russell, Buford, and Philip Love. Lewis's party marched to the right, near the foot of the hills skirting the east side of Crooked Creek. Fleming's party marched to the left, 200 yards apart from the other. A quarter of a mile from camp, and half a mile from the point of the cape, the right-going party met the enemy lurking behind trees and fallen logs at the base of the hill, and there Charles Lewis was mortally wounded. Fleming marched to a pond three-quarters of a mile from camp, and fifty rods inland from the Ohio—this pond being one of the sources of Crooked Creek. The hostile line was found to extend from this pond along Crooked Creek, half way to its mouth. The Indians, under Cornstalk, thought by rushes to drive the whites into the two rivers, "like so many bullocks," as the chief later explained; and indeed both lines had frequently to fall back, but they were skillfully reinforced each time, and by dusk the savages placed Old Town Creek between them and the whites. This movement was hastened, a half hour before sunset, by a movement which Withers confounds with the main tactics. Captains Matthews, Arbuckle, Shelby, and Stuart were sent with a detachment up Crooked creek under cover of the bank, with a view to securing a ridge in the rear of the enemy, from which their line could be enfiladed. They were discovered in the act, but Cornstalk supposed that this party was Christian's advance, and in alarm hurried his people to the other side of Old Town Creek. The battle was, by dark, really a drawn game; but Cornstalk had had enough, and fled during the night.—R. G. T.

Indians to be only a feint;[1] and that an attack would be again speedily made by them, strengthened and reinforced by those of the enemy who had been observed during the engagement, on the opposite side of the Ohio and Kenhawa rivers. But these had been most probably stationed there, in anticipation of victory, to prevent the Virginia troops from effecting a retreat across those rivers, (the only possible chance of escape, had they been overpowered by the enemy in their front;) and the loss sustained by the Indians was too great, and the prospect of a better fortune, too gloomy and unpromising, for them to enter again into an engagement. Dispirited by the bloody repulse with which they had met, they hastened to their towns, better disposed to purchase security from farther hostilities by negotiation, than risk another battle with an army whose strength and prowess, they had already tested; and found superior to their own. The victory indeed, was decisive, and many advantages were obtained by it; but they were not cheaply bought. The Virginia army sustained, in this engagement, a loss of seventy-five killed, and one hundred and forty wounded.—About one fifth of the entire number of the troops.

Among the slain were Colonels Lewis and Field; Captains Buford, Morrow, Wood, Cundiff, Wilson, and Robert McClannahan; and Lieutenants Allen, Goldsby and Dillon, with some other subalterns. The loss of the enemy could not be ascertained. On the morning after the action, Colonel Christian marched his men over the battle ground and found twenty-one of the Indians lying dead; and twelve others [129] were afterwards discovered, where they had been attempted to be concealed under some old logs and brush.[2]

---

[1] During the day, a messenger had been dispatched to hurry on Christian, who with 250 men was convoying cattle and powder. In the early evening, fifteen miles from Point Pleasant, this rear party was found, toiling painfully over the wilderness trail. Christian at once left his property in charge of a small party, and arrived in camp by midnight.—R. G. T.

[2] Most of the killed and wounded, on both sides, were shot in the head or breast, which indicates good marksmanship. The Indians,

From the great facility with which the Indians either carry off or conceal their dead, it is always difficult to ascertain the number of their slain; and hence arises, in some measure, the disparity between their known loss and that sustained by their opponents in battle. Other reasons for this disparity, are to be found in their peculiar mode of warfare, and in the fact, that they rarely continue a contest, when it has to be maintained with the loss of their warriors. It would not be easy otherwise to account for the circumstance, that even when signally vanquished, the list of their slain does not, frequently, appear more than half as great, as that of the victors. In this particular instance, many of the dead were certainly thrown into the river.

Nor could the number of the enemy engaged, be ever ascertained. Their army is known to have been composed of warriors from the different nations, north of the Ohio; and to have comprised the flower of the Shawanee, Delaware, Mingo, Wyandotte and Cayuga tribes; led on by men, whose names were not unknown to fame,[1] and at the head of whom was Cornstalk, Sachem of the Shawanees, and King of the Northern Confederacy.[2]

---

though skillful marksmen, did not exhibit sufficient mechanical knowledge to enable them properly to clean their guns, and thus were at some disadvantage.

The statistician was at work in those days, as now, for we learn from an old diary that at Old Town Creek were found by the white victors, 78 rafts with which the Indians had crossed the Ohio to the attack, the night of October 9-10; and on the battlefield during the 10th and 12th, were collected 23 guns, 27 tomahawks, 80 blankets, and great numbers of war-clubs, shot-pouches, powder-horns, match-coats, deer-skins, "and other articles," all of which were put up at auction by the careful commissary, and brought nearly £100 to the army chest.—R. G. T.

[1] Such were Redhawk, a Delaware chief,—Scoppathus, a Mingo,—Ellinipsico, a Shawanee, and son to Cornstalk,—Chiyawee, a Wyandotte, and Logan, a Cayuga.

[2] The first recorded foray of Cornstalk was on October 10, 1759, against the Gilmore family and others, on Carr's Creek, in what is now Rockbridge county, Va. "The Carr's Creek massacre" was long remembered on the border as one of the most daring and cruel on record. He was again heard of during the Pontiac conspiracy, in 1763, when he led a large war-party from the Scioto towns against the Virginia frontier. Both at Muddy Creek, and the Clendenning farm near Lewisburg, on the

This distinguished chief and consummate warrior, proved himself on that day, to be justly entitled to the prominent station which he occupied. His plan of alternate retreat & attack, was well conceived, and occasioned the principal loss sustained by the writes. If at any time his warriors were believed to waver, his voice could be heard above the din of arms, exclaiming in his native tongue, "Be strong! Be strong;" and when one near him, by trepidation and reluctance to proceed to the charge, evinced a dastardly disposition, fearing the example might have a pernicious influence, with one blow of the tomahawk he severed his skull. It was perhaps a solitary instance in which terror predominated. Never did men exhibit a more conclusive evidence of bravery, in making a charge, and fortitude in withstanding an onset, than did these undisciplined soldiers of the forest, in the [130] field at Point Pleasant. Such too was the good conduct of those who composed the army of Virginia, on that occasion; and such the noble bravery of many, that high ex-

---

Levels of the Greenbrier, the marauders pretended to be friendly with the settlers, and in an unguarded moment fell upon and slew them. Other massacres, in connection with the same foray, were at Carr's Creek, Keeney's Knob, and Jackson's River. The story of the captivity of Mrs. Clendenning and her children, who were taken to the Shawnee towns on the Scioto, is one of the most heartrendering in Western history. In 1764, Bouquet raided these towns, and Cornstalk was one of the hostages sent to Fort Pitt in fulfillment of the terms of the treaty, but later he effected his escape. Nothing more is heard of this warrior until 1774, when he became famous as leader of the Indians at the battle of Point Pleasant. Cornstalk's intelligence was far above that of the average Shawnee. He had, before the Dunmore War, strongly counseled his people to observe the peace, as their only salvation; but when defeated in council, he with great valor led the tribesmen to war. After the treaty of Fort Charlotte, he renewed his peace policy, and was almost alone in refusing to join the Shawnee uprising in 1777. Late in September, that year, he visited his white friends at Fort Randolph (Point Pleasant), and was retained as one of several hostages for the tribe. Infuriated at some murders in the vicinity, the private soldiers in the fort turned upon the Indian prisoners and basely killed them, Cornstalk among the number. Governor Patrick Henry and General Hand—the latter then organizing his futile expedition against the Shawnees—wished to punish the murderers; but in the prevalent state of public opinion on the border, it was easy for them to escape prosecution.— R. G. T.

pectations were entertained of their future distinction. Nor were those expectations disappointed. In the various scenes through which they subsequently passed, the pledge of after eminence then given, was fully redeemed; and the names of Shelby, Campbell, Matthews, Fleming, Moore, and others, their compatriots in arms on the memorable tenth of October, 1774, have been inscribed in brilliant characters on the roll of fame.[1]

Having buried the dead, and made every arrangement of which their situation admitted, for the comfort of the wounded, entrenchments were thrown up, and the army commenced its march to form a junction with the northern division, under Lord Dunmore. Proceeding by the way of the Salt Licks, General Lewis pressed forward with astonishing rapidity (considering that the march was through a trackless desert); but before he had gone far, an express arrived from Dunmore, with orders to return immediately to the mouth of the Big Kenhawa. Suspecting the integrity of his Lordship's motives, and urged by the advice of his officers generally, General [131] Lewis refused to obey these orders; and continued to advance 'till he was met, (at Kilkenny creek, and in sight of an Indian village, which its inhabitants had just fired and deserted,)

---

[1] The following gentlemen, with others of high reputation in private life, were officers in the battle at Point Pleasant. Gen. Isaac Shelby, the first governor of Kentucky, and afterwards, secretary of war;—Gen. William Campbell and Col. John Campbell, heroes of King's mountain and Long Island;—Gen. Evan Shelby, one of the most favored citizens of Tennessee, often honored with the confidence of that state;—Col. William Fleming, an active governor of Virginia during the revolutionary war;—Gen. Andrew Moore of Rockbridge, the only man ever elected by Virginia, from the country west of the Blue ridge, to the senate of the United States;—Col. John Stuart, of Greenbrier;—Gen. Tate, of Washington county, Virginia;—Col. William McKee, of Lincoln county, Kentucky;—Col. John Steele, since a governor of Mississippi territory; —Col. Charles Cameron, of Bath;—Gen. Bazaleel Wells, of Ohio; and Gen. George Matthews, a distinguished officer in the war of the revolution, the hero of Brandywine, Germantown, and of Guilford;—a governor of Georgia, and a senator from that state in the congress of the United States. The salvation of the American army at Germantown, is ascribed, in Johnston's life of Gen. Green, to the bravery and good conduct of two regiments, one of which was commanded by General, then Col. Matthews.

by the Governor, (accompanied by White Eyes,) who informed him, that he was negotiating a treaty of peace which would supersede the necessity of the further movement of the Southern division, and repeating the order for its retreat.

The army under General Lewis had endured many privations and suffered many hardships. They had encountered a savage enemy in great force, and purchased a victory with the blood of their friends. When arrived near to the goal of their anxious wishes, and with nothing to prevent the accomplishment of the object of the campaign; they received those orders with evident chagrin; and did not obey them without murmuring. Having, at his own request, been introduced severally to the officers of that division; complimenting them for their gallantry and good conduct in the late engagement, and assuring them of his high esteem, Lord Dunmore returned to his camp; and General Lewis commenced his retreat.[1]

---

[1] In order to get a clearer view of the situation, a few more details are essential here. For several days after the battle of Point Pleasant, Lewis was busy in burying the dead, caring for the wounded, collecting the scattered cattle, and building a store-house and small stockade fort. Early on the morning of October 13th, messengers who had been sent on to Dunmore, advising him of the battle, returned with orders to Lewis to march at once with all his available force, against the Shawnee towns, and when within twenty-five miles of Chillicothe to write to his lordship. The next day, the last rear guard, with the remaining beeves, arrived from the mouth of the Elk, and while work on the defenses at the Point was hurried, preparations were made for the march. By evening of the 17th, Lewis, with 1,150 men in good condition, had crossed the Ohio and gone into camp on the north side. Each man had ten days' supply of flour, a half pound of powder, and a pound and a half of bullets; while to each company was assigned a pack-horse for the tents. Point Pleasant was left in command of Col. Fleming,—who had been severely wounded in the battle,—Captains Dickinson, Lockridge, Herbert, and Slaughter, and 278 men, few of whom were fit for service. On the 18th, Lewis, with Captain Arbuckle as guide, advanced towards the Shawnee towns, eighty miles distant in a straight line, and probably a hundred and twenty-five by the circuitous Indian trails. The army marched about eleven miles a day, frequently seeing hostile parties but engaging none. Reaching the salt licks near the head of the south branch of Salt Creek (in the present Lick township, Jackson county, O.), they descended that valley to the Scioto, and thence to a

If before the opening of this campaign, the belief was
prevalent, that to the conduct of emissaries from Great
Britain, because of the contest then waging between her
and her American colonies, the Indian depredations of
that year, were mainly attributable; that belief had become more general, and had received strong confirmation,
from the more portentous aspect which that contest had
assumed, prior to the battle at Point Pleasant. The destruction of the tea at Boston had taken place in the
March preceding. The *Boston Port Bill*, the signal for
actual conflict between the colonies and mother country,
had been received early in May. The house of Burgesses in Virginia, being in session at the time, recommended that the first of June, the day on which that

prairie on Kinnikinnick (not Kilkenny) Creek, where was the freshly-
deserted Indian village referred to above, by Withers. This was thirteen miles south of Chillicothe (now Westfall). Here they were met,
early on the 24th, by a messenger from his lordship, ordering them to
halt, as a treaty was nearly concluded at Camp Charlotte. But Lewis's
army had been fired on that morning, and the place was untenable for
a camp in a hostile country, so he concluded to seek better ground. A
few hours later another messenger came, again peremptorily ordering a
halt, as the Shawnees had practically come to terms. Lewis now concluded to join the northern division in force, at Camp Charlotte, not
liking to have the two armies separated in the face of a treacherous
enemy; but his guide mistook the trail, and took one leading directly
to the Grenadier Squaw's Town. Lewis camped that night on the
west bank of Congo Creek, two miles above its mouth, and five and a
quarter miles from Chillicothe, with the Indian town half-way between.
The Shawnees were now greatly alarmed and angered, and Dunmore
himself, accompanied by the Delaware chief White Eyes, a trader, John
Gibson, and fifty volunteers, rode over in hot haste that evening to stop
Lewis, and reprimand him. His lordship was mollified by Lewis's explanations, but the latter's men, and indeed Dunmore's, were furious
over being stopped when within sight of their hated quarry, and tradition has it that it was necessary to treble the guards during the night
to prevent Dunmore and White Eyes from being killed. The following
morning (the 25th), his lordship met and courteously thanked Lewis's
officers for their valiant service; but said that now the Shawnees had
acceded to his wishes, the further presence of the southern division
might engender bad blood. Thus dismissed, Lewis led his army
back to Point Pleasant, which was reached on the 28th. He left there
a garrison of fifty men under Captain Russell, and then by companies
the volunteers marched through the wilderness to their respective
homes, where they disbanded early in November.—R. G. T.

bill was to go into operation, be observed throughout
the colony "as a day of fasting, humiliation and prayer,
imploring the divine interposition to avert the heavy
calamity which threatened destruction to their civil
rights, and the evils of a civil war." In consequence
of this recommendation and its accompanying resolutions,
the Governor had dissolved the Assembly. The Legislature of Massachusetts had likewise passed declaratory
resolutions, expressive of their sense of the state of public affairs and the designs of Parliament; and which led
[132] to their dissolution also. The committee of correspondence at Boston, had framed and promulgated an
agreement, which induced Governor Gage, to issue a
proclamation, denouncing it as "an unlawful, hostile and
traitorous combination, contrary to the allegiance due to
the King, destructive of the legal authority of Parliament,
and of the peace, good order, and safety of the community;" and requiring of the magistrates, to apprehend
and bring to trial, all such as should be in any wise guilty
of them. A congress, composed of delegates from the
different colonies, and convened for the purpose "of uniting and guiding the councils, and directing the efforts of
North America," had opened its session on the 4th of September. In fine, the various elements of that tempest,
which soon after overspread the thirteen united colonies,
had been already developed, and were rapidly concentrating,
before the orders for the retreat of the Southern division of
the army, were issued by Lord Dunmore. How far these
were dictated by a spirit of hostility to the cause of the
colonies, and of subservience to the interests of Great
Britain, in the approaching contest, may be inferred from
his conduct during the whole campaign; and the course
pursued by him, on his return to the seat of government.
If indeed there existed (as has been supposed,) between
the Indians and the Governor from the time of his arrival
with the Northern Division of the army at Fort Pitt, a
secret and friendly understanding, looking to the almost
certain result of the commotions which were agitating
America, then was the battle at Point Pleasant, virtually

12

the first in the series of those brilliant achievements which burst the bonds of British tyranny; and the blood of Virginia, there nobly shed, was the first blood spilled in the sacred cause of American liberty.[1]

It has been already seen that Lord Dunmore failed to form a junction with General Lewis, at the mouth of the Great Kenhawa, agreeably to the plan for the campaign, as concerted at Williamsburg by the commanding officer of each division. No reason for changing the direction of his march, appears to have been assigned by him; and others were left to infer his motives, altogether from circumstances.

While at Fort Pitt Lord Dunmore was joined by the notorious Simon Girty,[2] who accompanied him from thence 'till the close of the expedition. The subsequent conduct of this man, his attachment to the side of Great Britain, in her [133] attempts to fasten the yoke of slavery upon the necks of the American people,—his withdrawal from the garrison at Fort Pitt while commissioners were there for the purpose of concluding a treaty with the Indians, as was stipulated in the agreement made with them by Dunmore,—the exerting of his influence over them, to prevent the chiefs from attending there, and to win them to the cause of England,—his ultimate joining the savages in the war which (very much from his instigation,) they waged against the border settlements, soon after,—the horrid cruelties, and fiendish tortures inflicted on unfor-

---

[1] This is not the view of students in our own day, coolly looking at the affair from the distance of a hundred and twenty years. There now seems no room to doubt that Dunmore was thoroughly in earnest, that he prosecuted the war with vigor, and knew when to stop in order to secure the best possible terms. Our author wrote at a time when many heroes of Point Pleasant were still alive, and his neighbors; he reflected their views, and the passions of the day. That it was, in view of the events then transpiring, the best policy to turn back the southern army, after the great battle, and not insist too closely on following up the advantage gained, seems now incontrovertible.—R. G. T.

[2] Butterfield's *History of the Girtys* (Cincinnati, 1890) is a valuable contribution to Western history. Simon, James, and George Girty were notorious renegade whites, who aided the Indians against the borderers from 1778 to 1783; Simon and George were similarly active in the Indian war of 1790–95.—R. G. T.

tunate white captives by his orders and connivance;—all combined to form an exact counterpart to the subsequent conduct of Lord Dunmore when exciting the negroes to join the British standard;—plundering the property of those who were attached to the cause of liberty,—and applying the brand of conflagration to the most flourishing town in Virginia.

At Wheeling, as they were descending the river, the army delayed some days; and while proceeding from thence to form a junction with the division under general Lewis, was joined, near the mouth of the Little Kenhawa, by the noted John Connoly, of great fame as a tory.

Of this man, Lord Dunmore thence forward became an intimate associate; and while encamped at the mouth of Hock Hocking—seemed to make him his confidential adviser. It was here too, only seventy miles distant from the head quarters of General Lewis, that it was determined to leave the boats and canoes and proceed by land to the Chilicothe towns.[1]

The messengers, despatched by Lord Dunmore to apprize the lower army of this change of determination, were Indian traders; one of whom being asked, if he supposed the Indians would venture to give battle to the superior force of the whites, replied that they certainly would, and

---

[1] Upon leaving Pittsburg,—where the governor held a council with several Delaware and Mingo chiefs, to whom he recited the outrages perpetrated by the Shawnees since Bouquet's treaty of 1764—the northern division divided into two wings. One, 700 strong, under Dunmore, descended the river in boats; the other 500 went across the "pan-handle" by land, with the cattle, and both rendezvoused, September 30th, at Wheeling, 91 miles below Pittsburg. Next day, Crawford resumed his march along the south bank of the Ohio, to a point opposite the mouth of Big Hockhocking, 107 miles farther down. Here the men, the 200 bullocks, and the 50 pack-horses swam the Ohio, and just above the Big Hockhocking (the site of the present Hockingport) erected a blockhouse and stockade, which they called Fort Gower, in honor of the English earl of that name. A part of the earthwork can still (1894) be seen in the garden of a Hockingport residence. Dunmore's party, in 100 canoes and pirogues, arrived a few days later. While at Fort Gower, he was joined by the Delaware chiefs, White Eyes and John Montour, the former of whom was utilized as an agent to negotiate with the Shawnees—R. G. T.

that Lewis' division would soon see his prediction verified.[1] This was on the day previous to the engagement. On the return of these men, on the evening of the same day, they must have seen the Indian army which made the attack on the next morning; and the belief was general on the day of battle, that they had communicated to the Indians, the present strength and expected reinforcement of the southern division. It has also been said that on the evening of the 10th of October, while [134] Dunmore, Connoly and one or two others were walking together, his Lordship remarked "by this time General Lewis has warm work."[2]

The acquaintance formed by the Governor with Connoly, in the ensuing summer was further continued, and at length ripened into one of the most iniquitous conspiracies, that ever disgraced civilized man.

In July, 1775, Connoly presented himself to Lord Dunmore with proposals, well calculated to gain the favor of the exasperated Governor, and between them a plan was soon formed, which seemed to promise the most certain success. Assurances of ample rewards from Lord Dunmore, were transmitted to such officers of the militia on the frontiers of Virginia, as were believed to be friendly to the royal cause, on putting themselves under the command of Connoly; whose influence with the Indians, was

---

[1] This was William McCulloch.—R. G. T.

[2] The authority for this is Stuart's *Indian Wars*, p. 56. Abraham Thomas, in his *Sketches*, relates that the governor, placing his ear at the surface of the river, said he thought he heard the firing of guns; and Thomas, then a young militiaman, was asked to do likewise, and reported that it was the rattle of musketry. The distance across country to Point Pleasant was but twenty-eight miles, but by the river windings was sixty-six. These anecdotes have been related as proof that Dunmore desired Lewis beaten. White Eyes had notified the governor that a conflict was expected, though he had reported a much smaller Indian army than Lewis's; hence his lordship had no fear of the result. Had he known that the opposing forces were equal in number, and that the whites had been surprised, he doubtless would have sent relief. Knowing the Shawnee warriors were away from home, fighting Lewis, whom he had reason to suppose was very well able to handle them, he determined to advance inland to the deserted towns on the Scioto and destroy their houses and crops. He was upon this errand when met and stopped by the messengers of peace.—R. G. T.

to ensure their co-operation against the friends of America. To perfect this scheme, it was necessary to communicate with General Gage; and about the middle of September, Connoly, with despatches from Dunmore, set off for Boston, and in the course of a few weeks returned, with instructions from the Governor of Massachusetts, which developed their whole plan. Connoly was invested with the rank of Colonel of a regiment, (to be raised among those on the frontiers, who favored the cause of Great Britain,) with which he was to proceed forthwith to Detroit, where he was to receive a considerable reinforcement, and be supplied with cannon, muskets and ammunition. He was then to visit the different Indian nations, enlist them in the projected enterprise, and rendezvous his whole force at Fort Pitt. From thence he was to cross the Alleghany mountain, and marching through Virginia join Lord Dunmore, on the 20th of the ensuing April, at Alexandria.

This scheme, (the execution of which would at once, have laid waste a considerable portion of Virginia, and ultimately perhaps, nearly the whole state,) was frustrated by the taking of Connoly, and all the particulars of it, made known. This development, served to shew the villainous connexion existing between Dunmore and Connoly, and to corroborate the suspicion of General Lewis and many of his officers, that the conduct of the former, during the campaign of 1774, was [135] dictated by any thing else than the interest and well being of the colony of Virginia.

This suspicion was farther strengthened by the readiness with which Lord Dunmore embraced the overtures of peace, and the terms on which a treaty was concluded with them; while the encamping of his army, without entrenchments, in the heart of the Indian country, and in the immediate adjacency of the combined forces of the Indian nations of Ohio, would indicate, that there must have been a friendly understanding between him and them. To have relied solely on the bravery and good conduct of his troops, would have been the height of imprudence. His army was less than that, which had been scarcely delivered from the fury of a body of savages in-

ferior in number, to the one with which he would have
had to contend; and it would have been folly in him to
suppose, that he could achieve with a smaller force, what
required the utmost exertions of General Lewis and his
brave officers, to effect with a greater one.[1]

When the Northern division of the army resumed its
march for Chilicothe, it left the greater part of its provisions in a block house which had been erected during its
stay at the mouth of the Hockhocking, under the care of
Captain Froman with a small party of troops to garrison
it. On the third day after it left Fort Gore (the block
house at the mouth of Hockhocking) a white man by the
name of Elliott came to Governor Dunmore, with a request from the Indians that he would withdraw the army
from their country, and appoint commissioners to meet
their chiefs at Pittsburg to confer about the terms of a
treaty. To this request a reply was given, that the Governor was well inclined to make peace, and was willing
that hostilities should cease; but as he was then so near
their towns, and all the chiefs of the different nations
were at that time with the army, it would be more con-
convenient to negotiate then, than at a future period. He
then named a place at which he would encamp, and listen
to their proposals; and immediately despatched a courier
to General Lewis with orders for his return.[2]

---

[1] The two wings of the white army had about the same strength—
1100 under Dunmore, and 1150 (after leaving Point Pleasant) under
Lewis. The fighting quality was also the same, in both. It is to be remembered that in the army under Dunmore there was very little discontent at the issue, and at the close of the campaign the men heartily
thanked his lordship for his valuable services in behalf of the people.
They did this, too, at a time when they knew from Eastern news received in camp, that the Revolution was near at hand, and Dunmore
must soon be fighting against them in behalf of his royal master.
—R. G. T.

[2] Dunmore had, through White Eyes, summoned the Shawnee chiefs
to treat with him at Fort Gower (not Gore), but they had declined to
come in. He then set out, October 11th, to waste their towns on the
Scioto, as previously noted, leaving the fort in charge of Captain Kuy-
kendall (not Froman), with whom remained the disabled and the
beeves. Each man on the expedition carried flour for sixteen days.
Just after the Point Pleasant battle, Lewis had dispatched a messenger

The Indian spies reporting that General Lewis had disregarded these orders, and was still marching rapidly towards their towns, the Indians became apprehensive of the result; and one of their chiefs (the White Eyes) waited on Lord Dunmore in person, and complained that the "Long Knives" [136] were coming upon them and would destroy all their towns. Dunmore then, in company with White Eyes, visited the camp of General Lewis, and prevailed with him, as we have seen, to return across the Ohio.

In a few days after this, the Northern division of the army approached within eight miles of Chilicothe, and encamped on the plain, at the place appointed for the chiefs to meet without entrenchments or breast works, or any protection, save the vigilance of the sentinels and the bravery of the troops.[1] On the third day from the halting of the army eight chiefs, with Cornstalk at their head, came into camp; and when the interpreters made known who Cornstalk was, Lord Dunmore addressed them, and from a written memorandum, recited the various infractions, on the part of the Indians, of former treaties, and different murders, unprovokedly committed by them. To all this Cornstalk replied, mixing a good deal of recrimination with the defence of his red brethren; and when he

---

to his lordship with news of the affair; Dunmore's messenger to Lewis, with instructions to the latter to join him *en route*, crossed Lewis's express on the way. The messenger from Lewis found that his lordship had marched up the Big Hockhocking valley for the Scioto, and hurried after him. The governor was overtaken at the third camp out (west of the present Nelsonville, Athens county, O.), and the good news caused great joy among the soldiers. October 17th, Dunmore arrived at what he styled Camp Charlotte (on the northern bank of Sippo Creek, Pickaway county, eight miles east of Chillicothe, in view of Pickaway Plains), and here the treaty of peace was concluded.—R. G. T.

[1] Doddridge's *Notes* says that the camp was surrounded by a breastwork of fallen trees, and an entrenchment, and Roosevelt's *Winning of the West* follows him. But Dr. Draper was distinctly told (in 1846–51) by two survivors of the campaign, Samuel Murphy and John Grim, that Withers's account is correct; and this is confirmed in Whittlesey's *Fugitive Essays*. In the center of the field, a building of poles was erected, in which to hold the council; around this, the army encamped. A large white oak having been peeled, Dunmore wrote upon it in red chalk, "Camp Charlotte," thus honoring the then English queen.—R. G. T.

had concluded, a time was specified when the chiefs of the different nations should come in, and proceed to the negotiation of a treaty.

Before the arrival of that period, Cornstalk came alone to the camp, and acquainted the Governor that none of the Mingoes would attend; and that he was apprehensive there could not a full council be convened. Dunmore then requested that he would convoke as many chiefs of the other nations as he could, and bring them to the council fire without delay, as he was anxious to close the war at once; and that if this could not be effected peaceably, he should be forced to resume hostilities. Meantime two interpreters were despatched to Logan,[1] by Lord Dunmore, requesting his attendance;—but Logan replied, that " he was a warrior, not a councillor, and would not come."[2]

On the night after the return of the interpreters to camp [137] Charlotte (the name of Dunmore's encamp-

---

[1] Logan was the Mingo chief, the massacre of whose family at Baker's Bottom, the previous April, has already been described. He had just returned (October 21) from a foray on the Holston border, bringing several scalps and three prisoners, when the trader Gibson and the scout Simon Girty were sent to him by his lordship.—R. G. T.

[2] Colonel Benjamin Wilson, Sen. (then an officer in Dunmore's army, and whose narrative of the campaign furnished the facts which are here detailed) says that he conversed freely with one of the interpreters (Nicholson) in regard to the mission to Logan, and that neither from the interpreter, nor any other one during the campaign, did he hear of the charge preferred in Logan's speech against Captain Cresap, as being engaged in the affair at Yellow creek.—Captain Cresap was an officer in the division of the army under Lord Dunmore; and it would seem strange indeed, if Logan's speech had been made public, at camp Charlotte, and neither he, (who was so materially interested in it, and could at once have proved the falsehood of the allegation which it contained,) nor Colonel Wilson, (who was present during the whole conference between Lord Dunmore and the Indian chiefs, and at the time when the speeches were delivered sat immediately behind and close to Dunmore,) should have heard nothing of it until years after.

Comment by R. G. T.—Withers thus shortly disposes of the famous speech by Logan, which schoolboys have been reciting for nearly a hundred years as one of the best specimens extant, of Indian eloquence. The evidence in regard to the speech, which was undoubtedly recited to Gibson, and by him written out for Lord Dunmore's perusal, and later "improved" by Jefferson, is clearly stated in Roosevelt's *Winning of the West*, I., app. iii.

ment,) Major William Crawford, with three hundred men, left the main army about midnight, on an excursion against a small Mingo village, not far off. Arriving there before day, the detachment surrounded the town; and on the first coming out of the Indians from their huts, there was some little firing on the part of the whites, by which one squaw and a man were killed—the others about 20 in number were all made prisoners and taken to the camp; where they remained until the conclusion of a treaty. Every thing about the village, indicated an intention of their speedily deserting it.[1]

Shortly after Cornstalk and two other chiefs, made their appearance at camp Charlotte, and entered into a negotiation which soon terminated in an agreement to forbear all farther hostilities against each other,—to give up the prisoners then held by them, and to attend at Pittsburgh, with as many of the Indian chiefs as could be prevailed on to meet the commissioners from Virginia, in the ensuing summer, where a treaty was to be concluded and ratified—Dunmore requiring hostages, to guarantee the performance of those stipulations, on the part of the Indians.

If in the battle at Point Pleasant, Cornstalk manifested the bravery and generalship of a mighty captain; in the negotiations at camp Charlotte, he displayed the skill of a statesman, joined to powers of oratory, rarely, if ever surpassed. With the most patriotic devotion to his country, and in a strain of most commanding eloquence, he recapitulated the accumulated wrongs, which had oppressed their fathers, and which were oppressing them. Sketching in lively colours, the once happy and powerful condition of the Indians, he placed in striking

---

[1] The reason for the attack was, that the Mingoes were implacable, and Dunmore had learned that instead of coming into the treaty they purposed retreating to the Great Lakes with their prisoners and stolen horses. This Mingo village was Seekonk (sometimes called the Hill Town), 30 or 40 miles up the Scioto. Crawford left Camp Charlotte the night of the 25th, and surprised the town early in the morning of the 27th. Six were killed, several wounded, and fourteen captured; the rest escaping into the forest. Crawford burned several Mingo towns in the neighborhood.—R. G. T.

contrast, their present fallen fortunes and unhappy destiny. Exclaiming against the perfidiousness of the whites, and the dishonesty of the traders, he proposed as the basis of a treaty, that no persons should be permitted to carry on a commerce with the Natives, for individual profit; but that [138] their white brother should send them such articles as they needed, by the hands of honest men, who were to exchange them at a fair price, for their skins and furs; and that no spirit of any kind should be sent among them, as from the "fire water" of the whites, proceeded evil to the Indians.[1]

This truly great man, is said to have been opposed to the war from its commencement; and to have proposed on the eve of the battle at Point Pleasant, to send in a flag, and make overtures for peace; but this proposal was overruled by the general voice of the chiefs. When a council was first held after the defeat of the Indians, Cornstalk, reminding them of their late ill success, and that the Long Knives were still pressing on them, asked what should be then done. But no one answered. Rising again, he proposed that the women and children should be all killed; and that the warriors should go out and fight, until they too were slain. Still no one answered. Then, said he, striking his tomahawk into the council post, "I will go and make peace." This was done, and the war of 1774 concluded.

---

[1] In remarking on the appearance and manner of Cornstalk while speaking, Colonel Wilson says, "When he arose, he was in no wise confused or daunted, but spoke in a distinct, and audible voice, without stammering or repetition, and with peculiar emphasis. His looks while addressing Dunmore, were truly grand and majestic; yet graceful and attractive. I have heard the first orators in Virginia, Patrick Henry and Richard Henry Lee, but never have I heard one whose powers of delivery surpassed those of Cornstalk on that occasion."

[139] CHAPTER VIII.

Upon the close of the campaign of 1774, there succeeded a short period of perfect quiet, and of undisturbed repose from savage invasion, along the borders of North Western Virginia. The decisive battle of the 10th of October, repressed incursion for a time, and taught those implacable enemies of her citizens, their utter inability, alone and unaided, to maintain a contest of arms, against the superior power of Virginia. They saw that in any future conflict with this colony, her belligerent operations would no longer be confined to the mere purposes of defence; but that war would be waged in their own country, and their own towns become the theatre of its action. Had the leading objects of the Dunmore campaign, been fully accomplished,—had the contemplated junction of the different divisions of the army taken place:—had its combined forces extended their march into the Indian territory, and effected the proposed reduction of the Chilicothe, and other towns on the Scioto and Sandusky, it would have been long indeed, before the frontier settlements, became exposed to savage inroad. A failure to effect these things however, left the Indians comparatively at liberty, and prepared to renew invasion, and revive their cruel and bloody deeds, whenever a savage thirst for vengeance should incite them to action, and the prospect of achieving them with impunity, be open before them. In the then situation of our country, this prospect was soon presented to them.

The contest between Great Britain and her American colonies, which had been for some time carried on with increasing warmth, was ripening rapidly into war. The events of every day, more and more confirmed the belief, that the "*unconditional submission*" of the colonies, was the object of the parent state; and that to accomplish this, she was [140] prepared to desolate the country by a civil war, and imbrue her hands in the blood of its citizens. This state of things the Indians knew, would favor the consummation of their hopes. Virginia, having to apply her physical strength to the repulsion of other enemies, could not be expected to extend her protecting ægis over the remote and isolated settlements on her borders. These would have to depend on themselves alone, for resistance to ruthless irruption, and exemption from total annihilation. The Indians well knew the weakness of those settlements, and their consequent incapacity to vie in open conflict with the overwhelming force of their savage foes; and their heriditary resentment to the whites prompted them to take advantage of that weakness, to wreak this resentment, and involve them once more in hostilities.

Other circumstances too, combined in their operation, to produce this result. The plan of Lord Dunmore and others, to induce the Indians to co-operate with the English in reducing Virginia to subjection, and defeated by the detection and apprehension of Connoly, was soon after resumed on a more extensive scale. British agents were busily engaged from Canada to the Gulph of Mexico, in endeavoring by immediate presents and the promise of future reward, to excite the savages to a war upon the western frontiers. To accomplish this object, no means which were likely to be of any avail, were neglected to be used. Gratified resentment and the certainty of plunder, were held up to view as present consequences of this measure; and the expulsion of the whites, and the repossession, by the Natives, of the country from which their fathers had been ejected, as its ultimate result.—Less cogent motives might have enlisted them on the side of Great Britain. These were too strong to be resisted by them, and too powerful to be counteracted by any course of conduct, which the colonies could observe towards them ; and they became ensnared by the delusive bait, and the insidious promises which accompanied it.

There were in the colonies too, many persons, who from principle or fear, were still attached to the cause of Great Britain ; and who not only, did not sanction the opposition of their country to the supremacy of Parliament, but were willing in any wise to lend their aid to the royal cause. Some of those disaffected Americans, (as they were at first denominated) who resided on the frontiers, foreseeing the [141] attachment of the Indians to the side of Britain, and apprehensive that in their inroads, the friends as well as the enemies of that country, might, from the difficulty of discriminating, be exposed to savage fury; and at the same time, sensible that they had become obnoxious to a majority of their neighbors, who were perhaps, too much inclined to practice summary modes of punishment, sought a refuge among the Indians, from those impending evils. In some instances, these persons were under the influence of the most rancorous and vindictive passions, and when once with the savages, strove to infuse those passions into their breasts, and stimulate them to the repetition of those enormities, which had previously, so terribly annoyed the inhabitants of the different frontiers.[1] Thus wrought upon, their inculcated enmity to the Anglo-Americans generally, roused them to action, and the dissonant notes of the war song, resounded in their villages. For a while indeed, they refrained from hostilities against North Western Virginia. It was however, but to observe the progress of passing events, that they might act against the mountain borders, simultaneously with the British on the Atlantic coast; as a premature movement on their part, might, while Virginia was yet at liberty to bear down upon them with concentrated forces, bring upon their towns the destruction which had so appallingly threatened them after the battle at Point Pleasant.

But though the inhabitants on the Virginia frontiers, enjoyed a momentary respite from savage warfare; yet were the Indians not wholly unemployed in deeds of aggression. The first attempt to occupy Kentucky, had been the signal of hostilities in 1774; and the renewed endeavors to form establishments in it, in 1775, induced their

---

[1] Chief among the fomenters of disorder were the renegades Simon Girty, Matthew Elliott, and Alexander McKee. The dastardly deeds of this trio are fully set forth in Butterfield's *History of the Girtys,* an important work to all students of the annals of the West during the Revolutionary War.—R. G. T.

continuance, and brought on those who were engaged in effecting them, all the horrors of savage warfare.

Upon the close of the campaign under Lord Dunmore, Kentucky became more generally known. James Harrod, with those who had associated themselves with him in making a settlement in that country and aided in the erection of the fort at Harrodsburg, joined the army of General Lewis at Point Pleasant; and when, after the treaty of Camp Charlotte, the army was disbanded, many of the soldiers and some of the officers, enticed by the description given of it by Harrod, returned to south Western Virginia, through that country.[1] The result of their

---

[1] James Harrod's father emigrated from England to Virginia, about 1734, and was one of the first settlers on the Shenandoah, in the Valley of Virginia. One of his sons, Samuel, accompanied Michael Stoner on his famous Western hunting and exploring trip, in 1767; another, William, born at the new family seat, at Big Cove, in what is now Bedford County, Pa., served with distinction under George Rogers Clark. James, born in 1742, was twelve years old when his father died, leaving a large family on an exposed frontier, at the opening of the French and Indian War. In November, 1755, a raid was made on the Big Cove settlement, by the Delaware chief Shingiss (p. 45, *note*), but the Harrods were among the few families who escaped unharmed to Fort Littleton. When James was sixteen years of age he served with his brother William on Forbes's campaign, and very likely saw further service during that war. In 1772, when he had attained wide celebrity on the border as an adept in woodcraft, he helped William settle on Ten Mile Creek, a tributary of the Monongahela; and in 1773 he and several other explored Kentucky, returning home by way of Greenbrier River. We have seen (p. 152, *note*) that he was surveying the site of Harrodsburg in 1774, when warned by Boone and Stoner. Retiring with his men to the Holston, he and they joined Col. Christian's regiment, but arrived at Point Pleasant a few hours after the battle of October 10. Returning to his abandoned Kentucky settlement March 18, 1775, a fortnight before Boonesborough was founded, he was chosen a delegate to the Transylvania convention, and became a man of great prominence in the Kentucky colony. In 1779 he commanded a company on Bowman's campaign, and the year following was a captain on Clark's Indian campaign; declining a majorship, he served as a private on Clark's campaign of 1782. He was a member of the Kentucky convention (at Danville) of December, 1784, and at one time represented Kentucky in the Virginia legislature. In February, 1792, having made his will, he set out from Washington, Ky., with two men, in search of a silver mine reported to be at the Three Forks of the Kentucky. No more was heard of him or his companions, and it is still the belief of the family

examination of it, induced many to migrate thither immediately; and in 1775, families began to take up their residence in it.

At that time, the only white persons residing in Kentucky, were those at Harrod's fort; and for a while, emigrants to that country [142] established themselves in its immediate vicinity, that they might derive protection from its walls, from the marauding irruptions of Indians. Two other establishments were, however, soon made, and became, as well as Harrod's, rallying points for land adventurers, and for many of those, whose enterprising spirits led them, to make their home in that wilderness. The first of these was that at Boonesborough, and which was made, under the superintendence of Daniel Boone.

The prospect of amassing great wealth, by the purchase of a large body of land from the Indians, for a comparatively trifling consideration, induced some gentlemen in North Carolina, to form a company, and endeavor by negotiation to effect such purpose. This association was known under the title of Henderson and company; and its object was, the acquisition of a considerable portion of Kentucky.[1] The first step, necessary towards the

---

that the latter murdered him. He was survived by his wife and a daughter, and left a large landed estate. Harrod, although unlettered, was a man of fine presence and many sterling qualities, and made a strong impress on his generation. He is still remembered in Kentucky as one of the worthiest pioneers of that state.—R. G. T.

[1] The company—successively called The Louisa Company, Henderson & Co., and The Transylvania Company—was composed of Col. Richard Henderson, Col. John Williams, Thomas Hart, Col. David Hart, Capt. Nathaniel Hart, Col. John Luttrell, James Hogg, William Johnston, and Leonard Henley Bullock.

Henderson's paternal great-grandfather was a Scottish immigrant, and one of his grandmothers was Welsh. The family settled in Hanover County, Va., where Richard, son of Samuel Henderson, was born April 20, 1735. Samuel moved with his family to North Carolina, in 1745, and became sheriff of Granville County. Richard had the education of a rural youth of good station, and became a lawyer. In 1767 he was appointed one of the two associate justices of the superior court of the colony, and served with great credit for six years, when the court was abolished. During professional visits to Salisbury, Henderson heard frequently—chiefly through the brothers Hart—of the exploits of Boone, and the latter's glowing reports of the beauty and fertility of Kentucky.

accomplishment of this object, was, to convene a council
of the Indians; and as the territory sought to be acquired,
did not belong, in individual property to any one nation

Relying implicitly on Boone's statements, these four men energetically
resolved to settle the country. In the autumn of 1774, Henderson and
Nathaniel Hart visited the Cherokees to ascertain if they would sell
their claims to Kentucky, and receiving a favorable reply agreed to
meet the Indians in treaty council at the Sycamore Shoals, on Watauga
River. On their return home, they were accompanied by a wise old
Indian (Little Carpenter), and a young buck and his squaw, delegates
to see that proper goods were purchased for the proposed barter. These
goods were bought in December at Cross Creek, now Fayetteville, N. C.,
and forwarded by wagons to Watauga.

Boone was then sent out to collect the Indians, and when the council opened (March 14, 1775) had twelve hundred assembled at the Sycamore Shoals—half of them warriors. The council proceeded slowly,
with much characteristic vacillating on the part of the Indians; but on
the third day (March 17) the deed of sale was signed to what came to
be known as "the great grant:" The tract from the mouth of the Kentucky (or Louisa) River to the head spring of its most northerly fork;
thence northeasterly to the top of Powell's Mountain; thence westerly
and then northwesterly to the head spring of the most southerly
branch of the Cumberland; thence down that stream, including all its
waters, to the Ohio, and thence up the Ohio to the mouth of the Kentucky. The Indians were conscious that they had sold what did not
belong to them; and Dragging Canoe and other chiefs were outspoken in
their opinion that the whites would have difficulty in settling the tract.
The Indians were much dissatisfied with the division of the goods.
These "filled a house" and cost £10,000 sterling, yet when distributed
among so many greedy savages each had but a small share. One warrior, who received but a shirt for his portion, said he "could have shot
more game in one day on the land ceded, than would pay for so slight
a garment."

Governors Martin, of North Carolina, and Dunmore, of Virginia,
issued proclamations against the purchase, as contrary to the royal
proclamation of 1763. But those who were present at the treaty—
among them such prominent borderers as Daniel Boone, James Robertson, John Sevier, Isaac Shelby, Felix Walker, the Bledsoes, Richard
Callaway, William Twitty, William Cocke, and Nathaniel Henderson—
were heedless of such proclamations, and eager to become settlers under the company's liberal offer made to them on the spot: for each man
who assisted in the first settlement, and went out and raised a crop of
corn that year, a grant of 500 acres for £5 sterling, clear of all charges.

Boone, as the company's agent, started out at once (March 10) with
twenty men, soon reinforced to thirty; with their hatchets they blazed
a bridle path over Cumberland Gap, and across Cumberland, Laurel,
and Rockcastle rivers, to the banks of the Kentucky, where, after a
running fight with the Indians, they arrived April 1, and founded

of them, it was deemed advisable to convoke the chiefs of the different nations south of the Ohio river. A time was then appointed at which these were to assemble; and it became necessary to engage an agent, possessing the requisite qualifications, to attend the council, on behalf of Henderson and company, and to transact the business for them. The fame of Daniel Boone which had reached them, recommended him, as one eminently qualified to discharge the duties devolving on an agent; and he was employed in that capacity. At the appointed period, the council was held, and a negotiation commenced, which resulted in the transfer, to Henderson and company, of the title of the southern Indians to the land lying south of the Kentucky river, and north of the Tennessee.[1]

Boonesborough. Henderson, at the head of thirty men conveying the wagons and supplies, arrived at Boonesborough April 20; with him were Luttsell and Nathaniel Hart. May 23, there met at Boonesborough the Legislature of Transylvania, in which sat eighteen delegates from the little group of four frontier forts, all established at about this time—Harrodsburg, Boiling Springs, and St. Asaph's (or Logan's Station), lying some thirty or more miles southwest of Boonesborough, the capital of this little western colony. Withers does not mention this first legislative assembly held in the Mississippi Valley. It is an interesting and suggestive episode in American commonwealth-building, and deserves careful study. Roosevelt gives it admirable treatment, in his *Winning of the West*. The journal of the convention is given at length in the appendix to the second edition of Butler's *Kentucky;* Hall's *Sketches of the West*, i., pp. 264, 265; Louisville *Literary News-Letter*, June 6, 1840; and Hazard's *U. S. Register*, iii., pp. 25–28. Henderson's MS. Journal is in the possession of the Wisconsin Historical Society, and has never yet been published.

Virginia and North Carolina did not favor an independent government in Kentucky, and annulled the title of the Henderson company—but Virginia (1795) granted the proprietors in recompense 200,-000 acres on Powell's and Clinch rivers.

We hear little more of Richard Henderson, in pioneer history. In 1779, he was one of the North Carolina commissioners to extend the western boundary between that State and Virginia. During the winter of 1789–90 he was at the French Lick on Cumberland, where he opened a land office. His last public service was in 1781, when a member of the North Carolina house of commons. He died at his country seat in Granville County, N. C., January 30, 1785, in his fiftieth year. Two of his sons, Archibald and Leonard, attained eminence at the bar of their native State.—R. G. T.

[1] Among Dr. Draper's manuscripts I find this succinct review of the

13

Boone was then placed at the head of a party of enterprising men, sent to open a road from the Holstein settlement, through the wilderness, to the Kentucky river,

---

aboriginal claims to Kentucky: "There is some reason to suppose that the Catawbas may once have dwelt upon the Kentucky River; that stream, on some of the ancient maps published a hundred years ago, was called the 'Cuttawa or Cawtaba River.' But that tribe of Indians, so far as we know, never laid any claim to the territory.

"It would appear from the historical evidences extant, that the Shawanoes were the earliest occupants of Kentucky of whom we have any certain knowledge. Colden, the primitive historian of the Iroquois Confederacy, informs us, that when the French commenced the first settlement of Canada in 1603, the Five Nations, who then resided near the present locality of Montreal, were at war with the powerful Adirondacks, who at that time lived three hundred miles above the Three Rivers, in Canada. The Iroquois found it difficult to withstand the vigorous attacks of their enemies, whose superior hardihood was to be attributed to their constant devotion to the chase, while the Iroquois had been chiefly engaged in the more peaceful occupation of planting corn. Compelled to give way before their haughty foes, the confederates had recourse to the exercise of arms, in order, if possible, to retrieve their martial character and prowess. To raise the spirits of their people, the Iroquois leaders turned their warriors against the Satanas or Shawanoes, 'who then,' says Colden, 'lived on the banks of the lakes,'—or, as other historians assert, in Western New York, and south of Lake Erie,—and soon subdued and drove them out of the country. The Shawanoes then retired to the Ohio, along which and its tributaries they planted numerous settlements. Some of them, however, when driven from Western New York, seem to have located somewhere on the Delaware, for De Laet, in 1624, speaks of *Sawanoos* residing on that river.

"The *Jesuit Relations* of 1661–62, allude to their residence in the West under the name of Ontouagannha or Chaoüanons; they seem to have been the same as were called Tongorias, Erighecks, Eriechonons, Eries, or Cats, by the early missionaries and historians; and the same, moreover, known in the traditions of the Senecas as Gah-kwahs, who resided on Eighteen Mile Creek, a few miles southwest of Buffalo, in Western New York, which the Senecas still call Gah-kwah-gig-a-ah Creek, which means *the place where the Gah-kwahs lived.* In 1672, the Shawanoes and their confederates in the Ohio Valley met with a disastrous overthrow by the Five Nations at Sandy Island, just below the Falls of Ohio, where large numbers of human bones were still to be seen at the first settlement of the country. The surviving Shawanoes must then have retired still farther down the Ohio, and settled probably in the western part of Kentucky; and Marquette, in 1673, speaks of their having twenty-three villages in one district, and fifteen in another, all lying quite near each other. At length the Shawanoes departed from Kentucky, and seem to have gone to the upper part of the Caro-

and to take possession of the company's purchase. When within fifteen miles of the termination of their journey, they were attacked by a body of northern Indians, who killed two of Boone's comrades, and wounded two others.

---

linas, and to the coast of Florida, and ever after proved a migratory people. They were evidently 'subdued,' as Colden, Evans, and Pownall inform us, and the decisive battle was fought at Sandy Island, where a vital blow was given to the balance of power on the Ohio, which decided finally the fall of Kentucky with its ancient inhabitants.

"It was this conquest that gave to the powerful Iroquois all the title they ever acquired to Kentucky. At the peace of Ryswick, in 1697, their right to their western conquests was fully acknowledged; and at the treaty of Lancaster, in Pennsylvania, in 1744, they ceded to Virginia all their lands west of that colony. In 1752, the Shawanoes and other western tribes, at Logstown on the Ohio, confirmed the Lancaster treaty, and sold their claim to the country south of the Ohio; and, at the treaty of Fort Stanwix, in 1768, the Six Nations made a new cession of their claim to Kentucky as low as the Cherokee or Tennessee River. Up to this period, the Cherokees never so much as thought of contesting with the Iroquois their claim to the Kentucky country; for some of the visiting Cherokees, while on their route to attend the Fort Stanwix treaty, killed game for their subsistence, and on their arrival at Fort Stanwix, tendered the skins to the Six Nations, saying, 'They are yours, we killed them after passing the Big River,' the name by which they had always designated the Tennessee. But probably discovering that other Indian nations were driving a good business by disposing of their distant land rights, the Cherokees managed to hatch up some sort of claim, which they, in part, relinquished to Virginia, at the treaty of Lochaber in 1770; and when Col. Donelson ran the line the following year, the boundary was fixed, at the suggestion of the Cherokee deputies, on the Kentucky River as the south-western line, as they delighted, they said, in natural landmarks. This considerably enlarged the cession, for which they received an additional compensation.

"In 1772, the Shawanoes made no claim to Kentucky; and at the treaty of Camp Charlotte, in October, 1774, they tacitly confirmed their old sale of that country in 1752, by agreeing not even to hunt south of the Ohio. Thus, then, we see that the Iroquois had twice ceded their right to Kentucky as low as the Tennessee River, and twice received their pay; the Shawanoes had disposed of their claim, such as it was, and received for it a valuable consideration; and the Cherokees, finding it profitable to lay claim to some valuable unoccupied region, sold their newly assumed right to the country south and east of Kentucky River. Their claim, if indeed it rises to the dignity of a claim, south and west of the Kentucky, was fairly purchased by Henderson and Company, and thus with the subsequent purchase by treaty, of the Chickasaws, of the strip between the Tennessee and Mississippi, the Indian title to the whole Kentucky country was fully and fairly extinguished."—R. G. T.

Two days after, they were again attacked by them, and had two more of their party killed and three wounded.[1] From this time they experienced no farther molestation until they had arrived within the limits of the purchase, and erected a fort, at a lick near the southern bank of the Kentucky river—the site of the present town of Boonesborough. Enfeebled by the loss sustained in the attacks made on them by the Indians; and worn down by the continued labor of opening a road through an almost impervious wilderness, it was some time before they could so far complete the fort, so as to render it secure against anticipated assaults of the savages, and justify a detachment being sent from the garrison, to escort the family of Boone to his new situation. When it was thus far completed, an office [143] was opened for the sale of the company's land;[2] and Boone and some others returned to Holstein, and from thence, guarded the family of Boone, through the wilderness, to the newly erected fort. Mrs. Boone and her daughter, are believed to be the first white females who ever stood on the banks of the Kentucky river.[3]

---

[1] The first attack occurred the morning of March 25, when the party were encamped near the head of Taylor's Fork of Silver Creek. Capt. Twitty and Felix Walker were severely wounded, and a negro servant killed; Twitty subsequently died from his wound. The other attack was on an outlying company, probably on Tate's Creek; this occurred the 27th, and "Thomas McDowell and Jeremiah McFeeters were," Boone wrote to Henderson, "killed and sculped."—R. G. T.

[143] [2] The purchase of Henderson and company, was subsequently declared by the legislature of Virginia, to be null and void, so far as the purchasers were concerned; but effectual as to the extinguishment of the Indian title, to the territory thus bought of them. To indemnify the purchasers for any advancement of money or other things which they had made to the Indians, the assembly granted to them 200,000 acres of land, lying at the mouth of Green river, and known generally as Henderson's grant.

[3] Boone set out from Boonesborough, June 13, 1775. He left the settlement in a state approaching anarchy; there were several good men in the district, but the majority were shiftless wanderers who would brook no exercise of authority. The buffalo were fast moving westward, and all game was now getting scarce—"hunt or starve" was the motto of the hour. A diarist (Capt. Floyd) estimated that there were then a total of 300 people in all the Kentucky settlements—not reckoning "a great many land-jobbers from towards Pittsburg, who go about on the north side of Kentucky, in companies, and build forty or fifty cabins a piece on lands

In 1775 Benjamin Logan, who had been with Lord Dunmore at Camp Charlotte, visited Kentucky and selected a spot for his future residence, near to the present village of Stamford, erected thereon a fort; and in the following year moved his family thither.

These were the only settlements then begun to be made within the limits of the now state of Kentucky. As the tide of emigration flowed into the country, those three forts afforded an asylum, from the Indian hostility to which the whites were incessantly subjected; and never perhaps lived three men better qualified by nature and habit, to resist that hostility, and preserve the settlers from captivity and death, than James Harrod, Daniel Boone, and Benjamin Logan. Reared in the lap of danger, and early inured to the hardships and sufferings of a wilderness life, they were habitually acquainted with those arts which were necessary to detect and defeat the one, and to lessen and alleviate the others. Intrepid and fearless, yet cautious and prudent, there was united in each of them, the sly, circumventive powers of the Indian, with the bold defiance, and open daring of the whites. Quick, almost to intuition, in the perception of impending dangers, instant in determining, and prompt in action; to see, to resolve, and to execute, were with them the work of the same moment. Rife in expedients, the most perplexing difficulties rarely found them at a loss. Possessed of these qualities, they were placed at the head of the little colonies planted around them; not by ambition, but by the universal voice of the people; from a deep and thorough conviction, that they only were adequate to the exigencies of their situa-

where no surveying has yet been done." Among the best of the numerous arrivals, were George Rogers Clark, Simon Kenton, Benjamin Logan, and Whitley, who came to be very prominent characters in Kentucky history. Boone, with his wife and daughters, and twenty-one men, arrived at Boonesborough September 6 or 7. "My wife and daughters,' writes Boone, " were the first women that ever stood on the banks of Kentucky river." Mrs. McGary, Mrs. Hogan, and Mrs. Denton arrived at Harrodsburg the 8th of September, and were the first white women in that settlement. With the arrival of these families, and fresh fighting men, the Kentucky colony began to take on a permanent air, and thenceforward there was better order.—R. G. T.

tion. The conviction was not ill founded. Their intellectual and physical resources were powerfully and constantly exerted for the preservation and security of the settlements; and frequently, with astonishing success, under the most inauspicious circumstances. Had they indeed, by nature, been supine and passive, their isolated situation, and the constantly repeated attempts of the Indians, at their extermination, would have aroused them, as it did others, to activity and energy, and brought their every [144] nerve into action. For them, there were no " weak, piping times of peace,"—no respite from danger. The indefatigable vigilance and persevering hostility of an unrelenting foe, required countervailing exertions on their part; and kept alive the life, which they delighted to live.

From the instant those establishments were made, and emigrants placed themselves in their vicinity, the Savages commenced their usual mode of warfare; and marauding parties were ever in readiness, to seize upon, those, whose misfortune it was to become exposed to their vigilance. In the prosecution of these hostilities, incidents of the most lively and harrowing interest, though limited in their consequences, were constantly recurring; before a systematic course of operations, was undertaken for the destruction of the settlers.

The Indians, seeing that they had to contend with persons, as well skilled in their peculiar mode of warfare, as themselves, and as likely to detect them, while lying in wait for an opportunity to strike the deadly blow, as they were to strike it with impunity, they entirely changed their plans of annoyance. Instead of longer endeavoring to cut off the whites in detail, they brought into the country a force, sufficiently numerous and powerful to act simultaneously against all the settlements. The consequence of this was, much individual suffering and several horrid massacres. Husbandmen, toiling to secure the product of the summer's labor, for their sustenance another season, were frequently attacked, and murdered.—Hunters, engaged in procuring meat for immediate and pressing use, were obliged to practise the utmost wariness to evade the ambushed Indian, and make sure their return to the fort. Springs and other watering places, and the paths leading to them, were constantly guarded by the savages; who would lie near them day and night, until forced to leave their covert, in quest of food to satisfy their extreme hunger; and who, when this end was attained, would return to their hiding places, with renovated strength, and increased watchfulness. The cattle belonging to the garrisons were either driven off, or killed, so that no supplies could be derived from them. This state of things continued, without intermission, 'till the severity of winter forced the Indians to depart for their towns; and then succeeded, of necessity, a truce, which had become extremely desirable to the different settlements.

When we reflect on the dangers, the difficulties, the complicated distresses, to which the inhabitants were then exposed, it is really matter of astonishment that they did not abandon the country, and seek elsewhere an exemption from those evils. How women, with all the feminine weakness of the sex, could be prevailed upon to remain during the winter, and encounter with the returning spring, the returning horrors of savage warfare, is truly surprising. The frequent recurrence of danger, does indeed, produce a comparative insensibility and indifference to it; but it is difficult to conceive, [145] that familiarity with the tragic scenes which were daily exhibited there, could reconcile persons to a life of constant exposure to them. Yet such was the fact; and not only did the few, who were first to venture on them, continue in the country, but others, equally adventurous, moved to it; encountering many hardships and braving every danger, to aid in maintaining possession of the modern Canaan, and to obtain a home in that land of milk and honey. If for a while, they flattered themselves with the hope, that the ravages which had been checked by winter, would not be repeated on the return of spring, they were sadly disappointed. Hostilities were resumed, as soon as the abatement of cold, suffered the Indians to take the field; and were carried on with renovated ardor, and on an enlarged scale.[1]

Feeling the hopelessness of extirpating the settlements, so long as the forts remained to afford a safe retreat to the inhabitants; and having learned, by the experience of the preceding season, that the whites were but little, if at all, inferior to them in their own arts, and were competent to combat them, in their own mode of warfare, the Indians resolved on bringing into the country a larger force, and to direct their united energies to the demolition of the different forts. To prevent any aid being afforded by the other garrisons, while operations were leveled against one, they resolved on detaching from their main body, such a number of men as was deemed sufficient to keep watch around the other forts, and awe their inmates from attempting to leave them, on any occasion. This was a course of excellent policy. It was calculated not only to prevent the marching of any auxiliary forces from one to the other of the fortresses, but at the same time by preventing hunting parties from ranging the woods, cut off the principal source, from which their supplies were derived; and thus tended to render their fall, the more certain and easy.

Accordingly in March 1777, they entered Kentucky with a force of upwards of two hundred warriors; and sending some of their most expert and active men to watch around Boone's and Logan's forts, marched with

---

[1] In the winter of 1776–77, McClelland's Station and Logan's Station, (indifferently styled Fort or Station) were abandoned because of Indian attacks, and the settlers huddled into Boonesborough and Harrodsburg—although possibly Price's settlement, on the Cumberland, maintained a separate existence throughout the winter. There were at this time not to exceed a hundred and fifty white men in the country, available for active militia duty. As during January and February, 1777, the Indians were quiet, confidence was restored in some degree, and during the latter month, Logan, with his own and some half dozen other families, left Harrodsburg and re-occupied Logan's Station. Thus far, each settlement had chosen its own military leader, and discipline was practically unknown. March 5, under order and commissions from Virginia, the militia of Kentucky county were assembled and organized at Boonesborough, Harrodsburg, and Logan's Station, with George Rogers Clark as major, and Daniel Boone, James Harrod, John Todd, and Benjamin Logan as captains.—R. G. T.

the chief part of their army to attack Harrodsburg. On the 14th of March three persons (who were engaged in clearing some land) not far from Harrod's fort, discovered the Indians proceeding through the woods, and sought to escape observation and convey the intelligence to the garrison. But they too, were discovered and pursued; and one of them was killed, another taken prisoner, and the third (James, afterwards Gen. Ray, then a mere youth) reached Harrodsburg alone in safety.[1] Aware that the place had become alarmed, and that they had then no chance of operating on it, by surprise, they encamped near to it on that evening; and early on the morning of the 15th commenced a furious and animated attack.

Apprized of the near approach of the enemy, the garrison had made every preparation for defense, of which their situation admitted; and when the assailants rushed to the assault, not intimidated by their horrible and unnatural yells, nor yet dispirited by the [146] presence of a force so far superior to their own, they received them with a fire so steady and well directed, as forced them to recoil; leaving one of their slain on the field of attack. This alone, argued a great discomfiture of the Indians; as it is well known to be their invariable custom, to remove, if practicable, those of their warriors who fall in battle. Their subsequent movements, satisfied the inmates of the fort, that there had been indeed a discomfiture; and that they had but little to apprehend from a renewed assault on their little fortress. After reconnoitering for a while, at a prudent distance from the garrison, the Indians kindled their fires for the night; and in the following day, leaving a small party for the purpose of annoyance, decamped with the main body of their army, and marched

---

[1] This foray took place March 6—not the 14th, as in the text—at Shawnee Springs, four miles north-east of Harrodsburg. The whites—James Ray, William Ray, Thomas Shores, and William Coomes—were sugar-making, when attacked by about seventy Shawnees, under Black Fish. William Ray was killed, and Shores taken prisoner. James Ray outran his pursuers and gave the alarm. The unsuccessful attack on the incomplete fort of Harrodsburg occurred early the following morning, the 7th. Other brief attacks on Harrodsburg, were on March 18 and 28.—R. G. T.

towards Boonesborough.[1] In consequence however, of a severe spell of March weather, they were forced to remain inactive for a time; and did not make their appearance there, until the middle of April.

In the assault on Boone's fort, the Indians soon became satisfied that it was impregnable against them; and although their repulse was not as signal here, as it had been at Harrodsburg, yet they soon withdrew from the contest, and marched towards Logan's fort,—having killed one and wounded four, of the whites.[2]

Several causes combined to render an attack on the fort at Logan's station, an event of most fearful consequence.[3] Its inmates had been but a short time in the country, and were not provided with an ample supply either of provisions or ammunition. They were few in number; and though of determined spirit and undaunted fortitude, yet such was the disparity between thirteen and two hundred—the force of the garrison and the force of the assailants, joined to their otherwise destitute situation, that hope itself, could scarcely live in so perilous a situation. Had this been the first point, against which the enemy levelled their operations when they arrived in the country, it must have fallen before them. But by deferring the attack on it, 'till they had been repulsed at the two other forts, the garrison was allowed time; and availing themselves of it, to fortify their position more strongly, the issue was truly, most fortunate, though unexpected.

On the night preceding the commencement of the attack on the fort, the Indians had approached near to it unperceived, and secreted themselves in a cane brake, which had been suffered to remain around the cabins.

---

[1] A small detachment from Black Fish's party made a dash on workers in the Boonesborough fields, the day after the Harrodsburg fight—killing a negro, and wounding several whites.—R. G. T.

[2] This assault on Boonesborough occurred the morning of Thursday, April 24. The Indians numbered about one hundred. Boone was wounded, and very nearly lost his life, in a sortie. The story of the fight abounds with instances of heroism on the part of both women and men.—R. G. T.

[3] It occurred throughout Friday, May 30. The Indians are reported to have numbered fifty-seven.—R. G. T.

Early in the morning the women, went out to milk, guarded by most of the garrison; and before they were aware of impending danger, the concealed Indians opened a general fire, which killed three of the men, and drove the others, hastily within the fort.[1] A most affecting spectacle was then presented to view, well calculated to excite the sympathies of human nature, and arouse to action a man possessed of the generous sensibility and noble daring, which animated the bosom of Logan.

One of the men who had fallen on the first fire of the Indians and had been supposed by his comrades to be dead, was in truth though [147] badly wounded, yet still alive; and was observed feebly struggling to crawl towards the fort. The fear of laceration and mangling from the horrid scalping knife, and of tortures from more barbarous instruments, seemed to abate his exertions in draging his wounded body along, lest he should be discovered and borne off by some infuriated and unfeeling savage. It was doubtful too, whether his strength would endure long enough to enable him to reach the gate, even if unmolested by any apprehension of danger. The magnanimous and intrepid Logan resolved on making an effort to save him. He endeavored to raise volunteers, to accompany him without the fort, and bring in their poor wounded companion. It seemed as if courting the quick embrace of death, and even his adventurous associates for an instant, shrunk from the danger. At length a man

---

[1] Those who went out early in the morning to milk the cows, were Mrs. Ann Logan, Mrs. Whitley, and a negro woman. They were guarded only by William Hudson, Burr Harrison, John Kennedy, and James Craig. The women and Craig escaped into the fort unharmed; Kennedy, with four balls in his body, contrived also to escape; Hudson was killed outright, and Harrison fell wounded. He was supposed by friend and foe to have been killed. The story of his final rescue by Logan, is related by Withers below. As told to Dr. Draper, by Capt. Benjamin Biggs, and as recorded in Whitley's MS. Narrative, in possession of the Wisconsin Historical Society, the story in Withers is substantially correct. It is said that Logan rolled a bag of wool before him, and thus approached Harrison under cover; then making a rush towards the latter, he picked him up in his arms and dashed successfully into the fort. These accounts make no mention of Martin's intervention. Harrison died of his wounds, June 13.—R. G. T.

by the name of Martin, who plumed himself on rash and daring deeds, consented to aid in the enterprise; and the two proceeded towards the gate. Here the spirit of Martin forsook him, and he recoiled from the hazardous adventure. Logan was then alone. He beheld the feeble, but wary exertions of his unfortunate comrade, entirely subside; and he could not hesitate. He rushed quickly through the gate, caught the unhappy victim in his arms, and bore him triumphantly into the fort, amid a shower of bullets aimed at him; and some of which buried themselves in the pallisades close by his head. A most noble and disinterested achievement, and worthy of all commendation.[1]

[148] The siege being maintained by the Indians, the animation of the garrison was nearly exhausted, in repelling the frequent assaults made on the fort; and it was apparent, that the enemy did not intend speedily to withdraw their forces. Parties of Indians were frequently detached from the main body, as well to obtain a supply of provisions by hunting, as to intercept and cut off any

[147] [1] Benjamin Logan was by birth a Virginian; and at the age of fourteen was left by the death of his father, to provide for his mother and her other children, and with the other cares of a family upon his infant hands. He discharged the duties thus devolving on him, with the utmost fidelity; and having provided amply for the support of his mother, and placed the other members of her household in eligible situations, he removed to the Holstein, married, purchased land, and commenced making improvements. From thence he went to Kentucky, where he spent the balance of his life, in the discharge of every social and relative duty, with credit to himself and advantage to the community. He was a delegate to the Virginia legislature from the county of Kentucky in 1780; was soon after commissioned county Lieutenant, (then the highest military title in the militia of a county) and in the various battles, as well as in the many skirmishes, which he fought with the Indians, his conduct and bearing were such, as fully established for him the reputation of a brave, skilful, prudent and meritorious officer. In private life, and in his intercourse with his fellow men, his whole course was distinguished by the most uncompromising honor, and expanded philanthrophy. The heroic adventure, by which he saved his wounded comrade, from the tomahawk, the scalping knife, and from fire, was but one of many such exploits, whereby he achieved good to others, at the most imminent hazard of his own life.

aid, which might be sent to St. Asaph's[1] from the other forts. In this posture of affairs, it was impossible that the garrison could long hold out, unless its military stores could be replenished; and to effect this, under existing circumstances, appeared to be almost impossible. Harrodsburg and Boonesborough were not themselves amply provided with stores; and had it been otherwise, so closely was the intermediate country between them and St. Asaph's, guarded by the savages, that no communication could be carried from one to the other of them. The settlement on the Holstein was the nearest point, from which it could be practicable to derive a supply of ammunition, and the distance to that neighborhood, was considerable.

Logan knew the danger which must result to the garrison, from being weakened as much as it must be, by sending a portion of it on this hazardous enterprise; but he also knew, that the fort could not be preserved from falling, unless its magazine was soon replenished. Preferring the doubtful prospect of succeeding in its relief, by adopting the plan of sending to Holstein, he proposed the measure to his companions, and they eagerly embraced it. It remained then to select the party, which was to venture on this high enterprise. Important as the presence of Logan, was known to be, in the fort, yet as the lives of all within, depended on the success of the expedition and as to effect this, required the exercise of qualities rarely possessed in so great degree by any other individual, he was unanimously chosen to conduct the enterprise.

Accompanied by four of the garrison, Logan, as slyly as possible, slipped from the fort, and commenced his tedious journey.[2] To lessen the chance of coming in contact

[148] [1] This was the name given to the station of Logan.

[2] Whitley's MS. Narrative and Cowan's MS. Diary, in the Wisconsin Historical Society's library, say that Logan left alone during the night of June 6. Logan returned to his fort on the 23d, having travelled almost incessantly, and brought news that relief would soon come. Soon after Logan's expedition to the Holston, other messengers were sent to the East, clamoring for help—McGary and Hoggin to Fort Pitt, and Smith to the Yadkin; and twice Harrod vainly went forth to meet expected troops. But the Continental army was hard pressed in those days, and despite the rumor on the coast that Kentucky was in a sad way, it was long before relief could be sent.—R. G. T.

with straggling bands of Indians, he avoided the pack road which had been opened by Boone; and pursuing an untrodden route, reached the settlement in safety. The requisite supplies were soon engaged; and while they were being prepared for transportation, Logan was actively engaged in endeavoring to prevail on the inhabitants, to form a company as expeditiously as possible and march to their relief. With a faint promise of assistance, and with the assurance that their situation should be immediately made known to the executive authority of the state, he set off on his return. Confiding the ammunition which he had obtained, to the care of his companions, and prudently advising and instructing them in the course best to be pursued, he left them, and hastened to make his way alone, back to St. Asaph. In ten days after his departure from the fort, he returned to it again; and his [149] presence contributed much to revive and encourage the garrison; 'till then in almost utter despair of obtaining relief. In a few days after, the party arrived with the ammunition, and succeeded in entering the fort unperceived; though it was still surrounded by the Indians. With so much secrecy and caution had the enterprise been conducted, that the enemy never knew it had been undertaken, until it was happily accomplished.

For some time after this the garrison continued in high expectation of seeing the besiegers depart, despairing of making any impression on the fort. But they were mistaken in this expectation. Each returning day shewed the continued investiture of the fort, and exhibited the Indians as pertinaciously intent on its reduction by assault or famine, as they were on the day of their arrival before it. Weeks elapsed, and there was no appearance of the succours which had been promised to Logan, when in the settlement on Hoistein. And although the besieged were still successful in repelling every assault on the garrison, yet their stock of provisions was almost entirely exhausted; and there was no chance of obtaining a farther supply, but from the woods around them. To depend on the success of hunting parties, to relieve their necessities and prevent their actual starvation or surrender, seemed indeed, but a slender reed on which to rely; and the gloom of despondency overshadowed their hitherto sanguine countenances. But as they were resigning themselves to despair, and yielding up the last hope of being able to escape from savage fury and savage vengeance, Colonel Bowman arrived to their relief, and forced the Indians to raise the siege. It was not however, without some loss on his part. A detachment of his men, which had preceded the advance of the main army, was unfortunately unable to reach the fort, undiscovered by the besiegers; who attacked and killed them before they could enter the garrison. On the body of one of these men, was left a proclamation, issued by the Governor of Detroit promising protection and reward to those who would renounce the cause of the American colonies, and espouse that of Great Britain; and denouncing those who would not. When this proclamation was carried to Logan, he carefully kept secret its contents, lest it might produce an unfavorable effect on the minds of some of his men; worn down, exhausted, and discouraged as they then were.[1]

[150] After the arrival of Colonel Bowman in the country, there was for a time, a good deal of skirmishing between his forces, aided by individuals from the different forts, and those Indians. In all of them, the superiority of the whites in the use of the rifle, became apparent to the savages; and as the feat of Captain Gibson with the sword, had previously acquired for the Virginians, the appellation of the Long Knives,[2] the fatal certainty, with which Bowman's men and the inhabitants of the various settlements in Kentucky, then aimed their shots, might have added to that title, the forcible epithet of sharp-

---

[1] Bowman arrived at Boonesborough the first of August, with two companies from Virginia, under Capts. Henry Pauling and John Dunkin—the latter being soon succeeded by Isaac Ruddell. The force numbered 100 men. August 25, while six of Bowman's men were on their way to Logan's, they were attacked by Indians, two being killed and one wounded. Before escaping, the Indians left on the body of one of the men, several copies of a proclamation addressed to Clark and Logan in person, by Lieut.-Gov. Henry Hamilton, at the head of the British forces at Detroit, offering immunity to repentant rebels.—R. G. T.

[2] See pp. 79, 80, *note*, for origin of the term " Long Knives."—R. G. T.

shooters. They were as skilful and successful, too, in the practice of those arts, by which one is enabled to steal unaware upon his enemy, as the Natives themselves; and were equally as sure to execute the purposes, for which those arts were put in requisition, as these were. The consequence was, that the Indians were not only more shy in approaching the garrison, than they had been; but they likewise became, more cautious and circumspect, in their woods operations, than formerly.

The frequent success of Colonel Bowman's men, in scouring the surrounding country, gave to the inhabitants of all the settlements, an opportunity of cultivating their little fields, and of laying in such a stock of provisions and military stores, as would suffice in the hour of need; when that force should be withdrawn from the country, and the Indians consequently be again enabled to overrun it. All that the inhabitants, by reason of the paucity of their numbers, could yet do, was to shut themselves in forts, and preserve these from falling into the hands of the enemy. When the term of those, who had so opportunely came to their relief, expired, and they returned to their homes, there were at Boonsborough only twenty-two, at Harrodsburg sixty-five, and at St. Asaph's fifteen men. Emigrants however, flocked to the country during the ensuing season, in great numbers; and their united strength enabled them the better to resist aggression, and conduct the various operations of husbandry and hunting—then the only occupations of the men.

While these things were transacting in Kentucky, North Western Virginia enjoyed a repose undisturbed, save by the conviction of the moral certainty, that it would be again involved in all the horrors of savage warfare; and that too, at no distant period. The machinations of British agents, to [151] produce this result, were well known to be gaining advocates daily, among the savages; and the hereditary resentments of these, were known to be too deeply seated, for the victory of Point Pleasant to have produced their eradication, and to have created in their stead, a void, to become the future receptacle of kindlier feelings, towards their Virginia neighbors. A coalition of the many tribes north west of the Ohio river, had been some time forming, and the assent of the Shawanees, alone, was wanting to its perfection. The distinguished Sachem at the head of that nation, was opposed to an alliance with the British, and anxious to preserve a friendly intercourse with the colonists. All his influence, with all his energy, was exerted, to prevent his brethren from again involving themselves, in a war with the whites. But it was likely to be in vain. Many of his warriors had fallen at the mouth of the Kenhawa, and his people had suffered severely during the continuance of that war; they were therefore, too intent on retaliation, to listen to the sage counsel of their chief. In this posture of affairs, Cornstalk, in the spring of 1777, visited the fort, which had been erected at Point Pleasant after the campaign of 1774, in company with the Red Hawk, and another Indian. Captain Matthew Arbuckle was then commandant of the garrison; and when Cornstalk communicated to him the hostile preparations of the Indians,—that the Shawanees alone were wanting to render a confederacy complete,—that, as the " current set so strongly against the colonies, even they would float with the stream in despite of his endeavors to stem it," and that hostilities would commence immediately, he deemed it prudent to detain him and his companions as hostages, for the peace and neutrality of the different tribes of Indians in Ohio. He at the same time acquainted the newly organized government of Virginia, with the information which he had received from Cornstalk, and the course which he had taken with that chief, and the others who accompanied him to the garrison.

Upon the receipt of this intelligence, it was resolved, if volunteers could be had for this purpose, to march an army into the Indian country and effectually accomplish the objects, which had been proposed to be achieved in the campaign of Lord Dunmore in 1774. The volunteers in Augusta and Bottetourt, were to rendezvous as early as possible, at the mouth of the Big Kenhawa, where they would be joined by [152] other troops under General

14

Hand,[1] who would then assume the command of the whole expedition.

In pursuance of this resolve, three or four companies only, were raised in the counties of Bottetourt and Augusta; and these immediately commenced their march, to the place of general rendezvous, under the command of Colonel George Skillern. In the Greenbrier country, great exertions were made by the militia officers there, to obtain volunteers, but with little effect. One company only was formed, consisting of thirty men, and the officers, laying aside all distinctions of rank, placed themselves in the line as common soldiers, and proceeded to Point Pleasant with the troops led on by Colonel Skillern. Upon their arrival at that place, nothing had been heard of General Hand, or of the forces which it was expected would accompany him from Fort Pitt; and the volunteers halted, to await some intelligence from him.

---

[1] Edward Hand was born in Ireland. He came to America in 1774 as a surgeon's mate in the Eighth (Royal Irish) Regiment, and soon settled in Pennsylvania as a physician. When the Revolution broke out he joined a Pennsylvania regiment as lieutenant colonel, and served in the siege of Boston. In April, 1777, he was appointed brigadier-general in the Continental army, and the first of June assumed command of Fort Pitt. Lieut.-Gov. Henry Hamilton, of Detroit, under orders from London, was actively engaged in stirring up the Northwest Indians to forays on the Virginia and Pennsylvania borders, thus harrying the Americans in the rear. Hand, in whose charge was the frontier from Kittanning to the Great Kanawha, determined on an aggressive policy, and in February, 1778, undertook a campaign against the savages. An open winter, with heavy rains, prevented the force of about 500 men—chiefly from Westmoreland county—making satisfactory headway. Finally, the expedition was abandoned when it had proceeded no farther than Mahoning Creek. From the fact that this first American movement against the savages, during the Revolution, resulted only in the capture of non-combatants, in the almost deserted villages, it was long known as "the squaw campaign." Hand was a competent officer, but was much pestered, at Fort Pitt, with the machinations of tories, who were numerous among the borderers. Succeeded at Fort Pitt in 1778, by Brig.-Gen. Lachlan McIntosh, Hand in turn succeeded Stark in command at Albany. We find him, in 1779, actively engaged on Sullivan's campaign against the New York Indians, and in 1780 he became adjutant general. A member of congress in 1784–85, he was in 1790 a member of the constitutional convention of Pennsylvania, and died at Rockford, Lancaster County, Pa., September 3, 1802—R. G. T.

The provisions, for the support of the army in its projected invasion of the Indian country, were expected to be brought down the river, from Fort Pitt; and the troops under Colonel Skillern had only taken with them, what was deemed sufficient for their subsistence on their march to the place of rendezvous. This stock was nearly exhaused, and the garrison was too illy supplied, to admit of their drawing on its stores.—While thus situated, and anxiously awaiting the arrival of General Hand with his army and provisions, the officers held frequent conversations with Cornstalk, who seemed to take pleasure in acquainting them with the geography of the country west of the Ohio river generally, and more particularly with that section of it lying between the Mississippi and Missouri rivers. One afternoon while he was engaged in delineating on the floor a map of that territory, with the various water courses emptying into those two mighty streams, and describing the face of the country, its soil and climate, a voice was heard hallooing from the opposite shore of the Ohio, which he immediately recognised to be that of his son Ellinipsico, and who coming over at the instance of Cornstalk, embraced him most affectionately. Uneasy at the long absence of his father, and fearing that some unforseen evil might have befallen him, he had come to learn some tidings of him here; knowing that it was the place, to go to which he had left the nation. His visit was prompted by feelings [153] which do honor to human nature—anxious solicitude for a father,—but it was closed by a most terrible catastrophe.

On the day after the arrival of Ellinipsico, and while he was yet in the garrison, two men, from Captain Hall's company of Rockbridge volunteers, crossed the Kenhawa river on a hunting excursion. As they were returning to the canoe for the purpose of recrossing to the Fort, after the termination of the hunt, Gilmore was espied by two Indians, concealed near the bank, who fired at, killed and scalped him. At that instant, Captains Arbuckle and Stuart (the latter having accompanied the Greenbrier volunteers as a private soldier) were standing on the point opposite to where lay the canoe in which Hamilton and

Gilmore had crossed the river; and expressed some astonishment that the men should be so indiscreet as to be
shooting near to the encampment, contrary to commands.
They had scarcely time to express their disapprobation at
the supposed violation of orders, when Hamilton was seen
running down the bank of the river, and heard to exclaim,
that Gilmore was killed.   A party of Captain Hall's men
immediately sprang into a canoe and went over to relieve
Hamilton from danger, and to bring the body of Gilmore
to the encampment.   Before they relanded with the bloody
corpse of Gilmore, a cry arose, "let us go and kill the Indians in the fort;" and pale with rage they ascended the
bank, with captain Hall at their head, to execute their
horrid purpose.   It was vain to remonstrate.   To the interference of Captains Arbuckle and Stuart to prevent the
fulfilling of this determination, they responded, by cocking
their guns, and threatening instant death to any one who
should dare to oppose them.

   The interpreter's wife, (who had lately returned from
Indian captivity, and seemed to entertain a feeling of affection for Cornstalk and his companions) seeing their danger,
ran to their cabin to apprise them of it, and told them that
Ellinipsico was charged with having brought with him the
Indians who had killed Gilmore.   This however he positively denied, averring that he came alone, and with the
sole object of learning something of his father.   In this
time Captain Hall and his men had arrived within hearing,
and Ellinipsico appeared much agitated.   Cornstalk however, encouraged him to meet his fate composedly, saying,
"my son, the Great Spirit has seen fit that we should die
together, and has sent you here to that [154] end.   It is
his will and let us submit;—it is all for the best;" and
turning to meet his murderers at the door, received seven
bullets in his body and fell without a groan.

   Thus perished the mighty Cornstalk, Sachem of the
Shawanees, and king of the northern confederacy in 1774:
A chief remarkable for many great and good qualities.
He was disposed to be at all times the friend of white men;
as he ever was, the advocate of honorable peace.   But
when his country's wrongs "called aloud to battle," he be-

came the thunderbolt of war; and made her oppressors feel
the weight of his uplifted arm. He sought not to pluck
the scalp from the head of the innocent, nor to war against
the unprotected and defenceless; choosing rather to encounter his enemies, girded for battle, and in open conflict.
His noble bearing,—his generous and disinterested attachment to the colonies, when the thunder of British cannon
was reverberating through the land—his anxiety to preserve the frontier of Virginia from desolation and death,
(the object of his visit to Point Pleasant)—all conspired to
win for him the esteem and respect of others; while the
untimely, and perfidious manner of his death, caused a
deep and lasting regret to pervade the bosoms, even of
those who were enemies to his nation; and excited the
just indignation of all, towards his inhuman and barbarous
murderers.

When the father fell, Ellinipsico continued still and
passive; not even raising himself from the seat, which he
had occupied before they received notice, that some infuriated whites were loudly demanding their immolation. He
met death in that position, with the utmost composure
and calmness. The trepidation which first seized upon
him, was of but momentary duration, and was succeeded
by a most dignified sedateness and stoical apathy. It was
not so with the young Red Hawk. He endeavored to
conceal himself up the chimney of the cabin, in which
they were; but without success. He was soon discovered
and killed. The remaining Indian was murdered by
piece-meal; and with almost all those circumstances of
cruelty and horror, which characterize the savage, in
wreaking vengeance upon an enemy.

Cornstalk is said to have had a presentiment of his
approaching fate. On the day preceding his death, a
council of officers was convoked, in consequence of the
continued absence of General Hand, and their entire ignorance of his [155] force or movements, to consult and
determine on what would be the course for them to pursue under existing circumstances. Cornstalk was admitted to the council; and in the course of some remarks,
with which he addressed it, said, "When I was young and

went to war, I often thought, each might be my last adventure, and I should return no more. I still lived. Now I am in the midst of you, and if you choose, may kill me. I can die but once. It is alike to me, whether now or hereafter." Little did those who were listening with delight to the eloquence of his address, and deriving knowledge from his instruction, think to see him so quickly and inhumanly, driven from the theatre of life. It was a fearful deed; and dearly was it expiated by others. The Shawanees were a warlike people, and became henceforward the most deadly foe, to the inhabitants on the frontiers.

In a few days after the perpetration of this diabolical outrage upon all propriety, General Hand arrived from Pittsburg without an army, and without provisions for those who had been awaiting his coming. It was then determined to abandon the expedition; and the volunteers returned to their homes.[1]

---

[1] See p. 172, *note* 2, for sketch of life and death of Cornstalk.— R. G. T.

[156] CHAPTER IX.

While Cornstalk was detained at Point Pleasant, as surety for the peace and neutrality of the Shawanees, Indians, of the tribes already attached to the side of Great Britain, were invading the more defenceless and unprotected settlements. Emerging, as Virginia then was, from a state of vassalage and subjection, to independence and self-government — contending in fearful inferiority of strength and the munitions of war with a mighty and warlike nation — limited in resources, and wanting in means, essential for supporting the unequal conflict, she could not be expected to afford protection and security from savage inroad, to a frontier so extensive as hers; and still less was she able to spare from the contest which she was waging with that colossal power, a force sufficient to maintain a war in the Indian country and awe the savages into quiet. It had not entered into the policy of this state to enlist the tomahawk and scalping knife in her behalf; or to make allies of savages, in a war with Christians and civilized men. She sought by the force of reason and the conviction of propriety, to prevail on them to observe neutrality—not to become her auxiliaries. "To send forth the merciless cannibal, thirsting for blood, against protestant brethren," was a refinement in war to which she had not attained. That the enemy, with whom she was struggling for liberty and life as a nation, with all the lights of religion and philosophy to illumine her course, should have made of them allies, and "let loose those horrible hell-hounds of war against their countrymen in America, endeared to them by every tie which should sanctify human nature," was a most lamentable circumstance—in its consequences, blighting and desolating the fairest portions of the country, and covering the face of [157] its border settlements, with the gloomy mantle of sorrow and woe.

There is in the Indian bosom an hereditary sense of injury, which naturally enough prompts to deeds of revengeful cruelty towards the whites, without the aid of adventitious stimulants. When these are superadded, they become indeed, the most ruthless and infuriated enemy—"thirsting for blood," and causing it literally to flow, alike from the hearts of helpless infancy and hoary age—from the timorous breast of weak woman, and the undaunted bosom of the stout warrior. Leagued with Great Britain, the Indians were enabled more fully and effectually, to glut their vengeance on our citizens, and gratify their entailed resentment towards them.

In the commencement of Indian depredations on North Western Virginia, during this war, the only places of refuge for the inhabitants, besides private forts and block-houses, were at Pittsburg, Redstone, Wheeling and Point Pleasant. Garrisons had been maintained at Fort Pitt and Redstone, ever after their establishment; and fortresses were erected at the two latter places in 1774. They all seemed to afford an asylum to many, when the Indians were known to be in the country; but none of them had garrisons, strong enough to admit of detachments being sent, to act offensively against the invaders. All that they could effect, was the repulsion of assaults made on them, and the expulsion from their immediate neighborhoods, of small marauding parties of the savage enemy. When Captain Arbuckle communicated to the Governor the information derived from Cornstalk, that extensive preparations were making by the Indians, for war, and the probability of its early commencement, such measures were immediately adopted, to prevent its success, as the then situation of the country would justify. A proclamation was issued, advising the inhabitants of the frontier, to retire into the interior as soon as practicable; and that they might be enabled the better to protect themselves from savage fury, some ammunition was forwarded to settlements on the Ohio river, remote from the state forts, and more immediately exposed to danger from incursion. General Hand too, then stationed at Fort Pitt, sent an express to the different settlements, recommending that they should be immediately abandoned, and the individuals composing them, should forthwith seek shelter in some contiguous fortress, or retire east of the [158] mountain. All were apprized of the impending danger, and that it was impracticable in the pressing condition of affairs, for the newly organized government to extend to them any effective protection.

Thus situated, the greater part of those who had taken up their abode on the western waters, continued to reside in the country. Others, deeming the means of defence inadequate to security, and unwilling to encounter the horrors of an Indian war, no better provided than they were, pursued the advice of government, and withdrew from the presence of danger. Those who remained, sensible of dependence on their individual resources, commenced making preparations for the approaching crisis. The positions which had been selected as places of security and defence in the war of 1774, were fortified anew, and other block-houses and forts were erected by their unaided exertion, into which they would retire on the approach of danger. Nor was it long before this state of things was brought about.

In June 1777,[1] a party of Indians came to the house of Charles Grigsby on Booting creek, a branch of the West Fork, and in the county of Harrison. Mr. Grigsby being from home, the Indians plundered the house of every thing considered valuable by them, and which they could readily carry with them; and destroying many other articles, departed, taking with them Mrs. Grigsby and her two children as prisoners. Returning home soon after, seeing the desolation which had been done in his short absence, and unable to find his wife and children, Mr. Grigsby collected some of his neighbors and set out in pursuit of those, by whom the mischief had been effected,—hoping that he might overtake and reclaim from them the partner of his bosom, and the pledges of her affection. His hopes were of but momentary existence.

---

[1] This "year of the three sevens," as it was called, was long known as "the bloody year" of border history.—R. G. T.

Following in the trail of the fugitives, when they had arrived near to Loss creek, a distance of but six miles, they found the body of Mrs. Grigsby and of her younger child, where they had recently been killed and scalped. The situation of this unfortunate woman (being near the hour of confinement,) and the entire helplessness of the child, were hindrances to a rapid retreat; and fearing pursuit, the Indians thus inhumanly rid themselves of those incumbrances to their flight and left them to accidental discovery, or to become food for the beasts of the forest.

[159] Stimulated to more ardent exertions by the distressing scene just witnessed, the pursuers pushed forward, with increased expectation of speedily overtaking and punishing, the authors of this bloody deed; leaving two of their party to perform the sepulture of the unfortunate mother, and her murdered infant. But before the whites were aware of their nearness to the Indians, these had become apprized of their approach, and separated, so as to leave no trail by which they could be farther traced. They had of course to give over the pursuit; and returned home, to provide more effectually against the perpetration of similar acts of atrocity and darkness.

A short time after this, two Indians came on the West Fork, and concealed themselves near to Coon's fort, awaiting an opportunity of effecting some mischief. While thus lying in ambush, a daughter of Mr. Coon came out for the purpose of lifting some hemp in a field near to the fort, and by the side of the road. Being engaged in performing this business, Thomas Cunningham and Enoch James passing along, and seeing her, entered into conversation with her, and after a while proceeded on their road. But before they had gone far, alarmed by the report of a gun, they looked back and saw an Indian run up to the girl, tomahawk and scalp her. The people of the fort were quickly apprised of what had been done, and immediately turned out in pursuit; but could not trace the course taken by the savages. It afterwards appeared that the Indians had been for some time waiting for the girl to come near enough for them to catch and make her prisoner, before she could alarm the fort, or get within reach of its guns; but when one of them crossed the fence for this purpose, she espied him and ran directly towards the fort.—Fearing that he would not be able to overtake her, without approaching the fort so as to involve himself in some danger, he shot her as she ran; and going up to her he tomahawked and scalped her. In endeavoring then to secure himself by flight, he was shot at by James, but at so great distance as to prevent the doing of execution.

In the neighborhood of Wheeling, some mischief of this kind was done about the same time, and by Indians who acted so warily, as to avoid being discovered and punished. A man by the name of Thomas Ryan was killed in a field some distance from the house, and a negro fellow at work with him, [160] taken prisoner and carried off. No invasion however, of that country, had been as yet, of sufficient importance to induce the people to forsake their homes and go into the forts.—Scouting parties were constantly traversing the woods in every direction, and so successfully did they observe every avenue to the settlements, that the approach of Indians was generally discovered and made known, before any evil resulted from it. But in August the whole country bordering on the Ohio, from Fort Pitt to Wheeling, became justly alarmed for its fate; and the most serious apprehensions for the safety of its inhabitants, were excited in the bosoms of all. Intelligence was conveyed to General Hand at Fort Pitt,[1] by some friendly Indians from the Moravian towns, that a large army of the north western confederacy, had come as far as those villages, and might soon be expected to strike an awful blow on some part of the Ohio settlements. The Indian force was represented as being so great, as to preclude all idea of purchasing safety, by open conflict;

---

[1] General Hand was commandant, and George Morgan Indian agent, at Fort Pitt. Runners from the Moravian towns on the Tuscarawas and Muskingum rivers, in Ohio, frequently came into the fort during the summer, with dispatches for either of these officials. The Delawares, as a nation, were friendly throughout the year. The hostiles were chiefly composed of Wyandots and Mingoes, but with them were a few Shawnees and Delawares.—R. G. T.

and the inhabitants along the river, generally retired into forts, as soon as they received information of their danger, and made every preparation to repel an assault on them. They did not however, remain long in suspense, as to the point against which the enemy would direct its operations.

Wheeling Fort, although it had been erected by the proper authorities of the government, and was supplied with arms and ammunition from the public arsenal, was not at this time garrisoned, as were the other state forts on the Ohio, by a regular soldiery; but was left to be defended solely by the heroism and bravery of those, who might seek shelter within its walls.[1] The settlement around it was flourishing, and had grown with a rapidity truly astonishing, when its situation, and the circumstances of the border country generally, are taken into consideration. A little village, of twenty-five or thirty houses, had sprung up, where but a few years before, the foot of civilized man had never trod; and where the beasts of the forest had lately ranged undisturbedly, were to be seen lowing herds and bleating flocks, at once, the means of sustenance, and the promise of future wealth to their owners.—In the enjoyment of this, comparatively, prosperous condition of things, the inhabitants little dreamed, how quickly those smiling prospects were to be blighted, their future hopes blasted, and they deprived of almost every necessary of life. They [161] were not insensible to the danger which in time of war was ever impending over

---

[1] The first fort at Wheeling was built in the summer of 1774, by order of Lord Dunmore, under direction of Majors William Crawford and Angus McDonald. It stood upon the Ohio bank about a quarter of a mile above the entrance of Wheeling Creek. Standing in open ground, it was a parallelogram of square pickets pointed at top, with bastions and sentry boxes at the angles, and enclosed over half an acre. It ranked in strength and importance, next to Fort Pitt. Within the fort were log barracks, an officers' house, a storehouse, a well, and cabins for families. A steep hill rises not far inland; between the fort and the base of this hill the forest had been leveled, and a few log cabins were nestled in the open. Such was Wheeling in 1777. At first the fort had been called Fincastle, for the Ohio Valley settlements were then in Fincastle County, Va.; but upon the opening of the Revolution the post, now in Ohio County, was named Fort Henry, in honor of the first state governor of Virginia.—R. G. T.

them; but relying on the vigilance of their scouts, to ascertain and apprize them of its approach, and on the proximity of a fort into which they could retire upon a minute's warning, they did not shut themselves up within its walls, until advised of the immediate necessity of doing so, from the actual presence of the enemy.

On the night of the first of September, Captain Ogal, who with a party of twelve men, had been for some days engaged in watching the paths to the settlement and endeavoring to ascertain the approach of danger,[1] came into Wheeling with the assurance that the enemy were not at hand. In the course of that night, however, the Indian army, consisting of three hundred and eighty-nine warriors,[2] came near to the village, and believing from the lights in the fort, that the inhabitants were on their guard, and that more might be effected by an ambuscade in the morning, than by an immediate and direct attack, posted themselves advantageously for that purpose. Two lines were formed, at some distance from each, extending from the river across the point to the creek, with a cornfield to afford them concealment. In the centre between these lines, near a road leading through the field to the fort, and in a situation easily exposing them to observation, six Indians were stationed, for the purpose of decoy-

---

[1] News came to Fort Pitt, early in August, that an Indian attack in force, on Wheeling, might be expected at any time. Says the Shane MSS., "White Eyes came to Fort Pitt and told them the Indians were going to take Wheeling home." August 2d, Gen. Hand wrote to David Shepherd, lieutenant of Ohio County, warning him of the perilous situation, and ordering him to leave his own fort, six miles from Fort Henry, and to rally at the latter all the militia between the Ohio and Monongahela,—the "pan-handle." Shepherd did this, and by the close of the month Fort Henry was, as he said, "Indian proof." But the non-arrival of the foe caused a relaxation of vigilance. Nine companies were allowed to go home, and by the last day of August only two companies remained in the fort, those of Capts. Joseph Ogle and Samuel Mason.—R. G. T.

[2] Shepherd to Hand, Sept. 15, 1777: "By the best judges here . . . it is thought their numbers must have been not less than between two and three hundred." The Shepherd, Hand, Shane, and Doddridge MSS., in the library of the Wisconsin Historical Society, throw much light on this episode.—R. G. T.

ing within the lines, any force which might discover, and come out to molest them.

Early in the morning of the second, two men, going to a field for horses, passed the first line, and came near to the Indians in the centre, before they were aware of danger.[1]—Perceiving the six savages near them, they endeavored to escape by flight. A single shot brought one of them to the ground : the other was permitted to escape that he might give the alarm. Captain Mason (who, with Captain Ogal and his party, and a few other men had occupied the fort the preceding night) hearing that there were but six of the enemy, marched with fourteen men, to the place where they had been seen. He had not proceeded far from the fort, before he came in view of them ; and leading his men briskly towards where they were, soon found themselves enclosed by a body of Indians, who 'till then had remained concealed.—Seeing the impossibility of maintaining a conflict with them, he endeavored to retreat with his men, to the fort; but in [162] vain. They were intercepted by the Indians, and nearly all literally, cut to pieces.[2] Captain Mason however, and his sergeant succeeded in passing the front line, but being observed by some of the enemy, were pursued, and fired at, as they began to rise the hill. The sergeant was so wounded by the ball aimed at him, that he fell, unable again to get up ; but seeing his Captain pass near without a gun and so crippled that he moved but slowly in advance

---

[1] The Indians made their appearance on the night of August 31st—not September 1st, as in the text. The incident here related occurred at about sunrise of September 1st. Andrew Zane, young John Boyd, Samuel Tomlinson, and a negro, set out to hunt for the horses of Dr. James McMechen, because the latter wished that day to return to the older settlements, either on the Monongahela, or east of the mountains. Boyd was killed, but his companions escaped—Zane, by leaping from a cliff, the height of which local tradition places at seventy feet.—R. G. T.

[2] De Hass, in his *History of the Early Settlement and Indian Wars of West Virginia*,—a conscientious work, which depends, however, too closely on traditions,--says (p. 225), "out of the fourteen. but two escaped."—R. G. T.

of his pursuers, he handed him his, and calmly surrendered himself to his fate.

Captain Mason had been twice wounded, and was then so enfeebled by the loss of blood, and faint from fatigue that he almost despaired of ever reaching the fort; yet he pressed forward with all his powers. He was sensible that the Indian was near him, and expecting every instant, that the tomahawk would sever his skull, he for a while forgot that his gun was yet charged. The recollection of this, inspiring him with fresh hopes, he wheeled to fire at his pursuer, but found him so close that he could not bring his gun to bear on him. Having greatly the advantage of ground, he thrust him back with his hand. The uplifted tomahawk descended to the earth with force; and before the Indian could so far regain his footing as to hurl the fatal weapon from his grasp, or rush forward to close in deadly struggle with his antagonist, the ball from Captain Mason's gun had done its errand, and the savage fell lifeless to the earth. Captain Mason was able to proceed only a few paces farther; but concealing himself by the side of a large fallen tree, he remained unobserved while the Indians continued about the fort.

The shrieks of Captain Mason's men, and the discharge of the guns, induced Capt. Ogal to advance with his twelve scouts, to their relief. Being some distance in the rear of his men, the Indians, in closing round them, fortunately left him without the circle, and he concealed himself amid some briers in the corner of the fence; where he lay until the next day. The same fate awaited his men, which had befallen Capt. Mason's. Of the twenty six who were led out by these two officers, only three escaped death, and two of these were badly wounded: a striking evidence of the fact, that the ambuscade was judiciously planned, and the expectations of its success, well founded.[1]

While these things were doing, the inhabitants of the village were busily employed in removing to the fort and

---

[1] Among the survivors was Ogle who, like Mason, hid himself in the bushes until nightfall enabled him to return to the fort.—R. G. T.

preparing for its defense. A single glance at the situation
of the parties led on by Mason and Ogal, convinced them
of the overwhelming force of the [163] Indians, and the
impossibility of maintaining an open contest with them.
And so quick had been the happening of the events which
have been narrated, that the gates of the fort were scarcely
closed, before the Indian army appeared under its walls,
with a view to its reduction by storm.[1] But before the assault was begun to be made, the attention of the garrison
was directed to a summons for its surrender, made by that
infamous renegado, Simon Girty.[2]

This worse than savage wretch, appeared at the end
window of a house not far from the fort, and told them,
that he had come with a large army to escort to Detroit,
such of the Inhabitants along the frontier, as were willing
to accept the terms offered by Governor Hamilton, to
those who would renounce the cause of the colonies and
attach themselves to the interest of Great Britain; calling
upon them to remember their fealty to their sovereign;
assuring them of protection, if they would join his standard, and denouncing upon them, all the woes which spring
from the uncurbed indulgence of savage vengeance, if
they dared to resist, or fire one gun to the annoyance of

---

[1] As a matter of fact, the Indians made no attack on the fort at this
time, being content with the success of their ambuscade. After throwing
up some rude earth-works and blinds, scalping the dead whites, killing
all the live stock within reach, and setting fire to the outlying cabins,
they retired across the Ohio in the night, and dispersed. Their loss was
one killed and nine wounded; the whites lost fifteen killed and five
wounded. The next day (September 2), the whites buried their dead,
and unavailingly scoured the country for Indians.

Tradition has made sad havoc with the records, in regard to this
first "siege" of Wheeling. Some of the deeds of heroism related below,
by Withers, were incidents of the second siege—September 11, 1782,
seven years later; but most of them are purely mythical, or belong
to other localities. Perhaps no events in Western history have been
so badly mutilated by tradition, as these two sieges.—R. G. T.

[2] This statement of Withers, that Simon Girty was at the siege of
Wheeling, was long accepted as fact by Western historians. But it is
now established beyond doubt, that neither Simon nor his brothers
were present at that affair, being at the time in the employ of Indian
Agent Morgan, at Fort Pitt. For details of the evidence, consult Butterfield's *History of the Girtys, passim.*—R. G. T.

his men. He then read to them, Gov. Hamilton's proclamation; and told them, he could allow only fifteen minutes to consider of his proposition. It was enough. In love with liberty, attached to their country, and without faith in his proffered protection, they required but little time to "deliberate, which of the two to choose, slavery or death." Col. Zane replied to him, "that they had consulted their wives and children, and that all were resolved to perish, sooner than place themselves under the protection of a savage army with him at its head, or abjure the cause of liberty and of the colonies." Girty then represented to them the great force of the Indians,—the impossibility that the fort could withstand the assault,—the certainty of protection if they acceded to his propositions, and the difficulty of restraining the assailants, if enraged and roused to vengeance by opposition and resistance. A shot discharged at him from the fort, caused him to withdraw from the window and the Indians commenced the assault.

There were then in the fort but thirty-three men, to defend it against the attack of upwards of three hundred and eighty Indians; and bravely did they maintain their situation against the superior force of the enemy, and all that art and fury could effect to accomplish their destruction. For twenty-three hours, all was life, and energy, and activity within the walls. Every individual had particular duties to perform; and promptly and faithfully were they discharged. The more expert of the women, took stations by the side of the men; and handling their guns with soldier like readiness, aided in the repulse, with fearless intrepidity.[1] Some were engaged in moulding bullets; others in loading and supplying the [164] men with guns already charged; while the less ro-

[1] [163] The notes furnished the compiler, mention particularly a Mrs. Glum and Betsy Wheat, as performing all the duties of soldiers with firmness and alacrity.

Comment by R. G. T.—Withers derived his information from traditional notes in the possession of Noah Zane, son of Ebenezer.

15

bust were employed in cooking, and in furnishing to the combatants, provisions and water, during the continuance of the attack. It seemed indeed, as if each individual were sensible, that the safety of all depended on his lone exertions; and that the slightest relaxation of these, would involve them all in one common ruin.

Finding that they could make no impression on the fort, and fearing to remain longer before it, lest their retreat might be cut off, by reinforcements from the surrounding country, the assailants fired all the houses without the walls; killed all the stock, which could be found; and destroying every thing on which they could lay their hands, retired about day light, and left the garrison in possession of the fortress, but deprived of almost every thing else. The alarm of the presence of Indians having been given after day light, and the attack on the fort commencing before sun rise, but little time was afforded them, for securing their moveable property. The greater part had taken with them nothing but their clothes, while some had left their homes with their night apparel only. Few were left the enjoyment of a bed, or the humble gratification of the coarse repast of bread and milk. Their distress was consequently great; and their situation for some time, not much more enviable, than when pent within the fort, and straining every nerve to repel its savage assailants.

Before this, the Governor had sent to Col. Andrew Swearingen, a quantity of ammunition for the defence of those who remained in the country above Wheeling. By his exertions, and under his superintendence, Bolling's and Holliday's old forts were repaired, and the latter made strong enough to serve as a magazine. In it was collected, all the inhabitants from its neighborhood; and it was generally regarded, as a strong position, and able, occasionally, to detach part of its garrison, for the aid of other portions of the country. Soon after the attack was begun to be made on Wheeling, the alarm reached Shepherd's fort, and a runner was despatched from thence to Holliday's fort with the intelligence, and the apprehension that if speedy relief were not afforded, the garrison at Wheeling must fall. No expectation, of being able to collect a force sufficient to cope with the assailants, was entertained. All that was expected was, to throw succours into the fort, and thus enable the garrison the more successfully to repel assaults, and preserve it from the violence of the Indian onsets. For this purpose, Col. Swearingen left Holliday's with fourteen men, who nobly volunteered to accompany him in this hazardous enterprise, to the regret of those who remained, from an apprehension that thus weakened, if Holliday's fort were attacked it must fall easily into the hands of the enemy. These men got into a large *continental canoe*, and plied their paddles industriously, to arrive in time to be of service to the besieged. But the night being dark, and a dense fog hanging over the river, they toiled to great disadvantage, frequently coming in contact with the banks; until [165] at length it was thought advisable to cease rowing and float with the current, lest they might, unknowingly, pass Wheeling, and at the appearance of day be obliged to contend with the force of the stream, to regain that point. Floating slowly, they at length descried the light which proceeded from the burning of the houses at Wheeling, and with all their exertion could not then attain their destination before the return of day. Could they have realized their expectation of arriving before day, they might from the river bank, in the darkness of the night, have gained admission into the fort; but being frustrated in this, they landed some of the men near above Wheeling, to reconnoiter and ascertain the situation of things: it being doubtful to them, from the smoke and fog, whether the fort and all, were not a heap of ruins. Col. Swearingen, Cap. Bilderbock and William Boshears, volunteered for this service, and proceeding cautiously soon reached the fort.

When arrived there, it was still questionable whether the Indians had abandoned the attack, or were only lying concealed in the cornfield, in order to fall on any, who might come out from the fort, under the impression that danger was removed from them. Fearing that the latter was the case, it was thought prudent, not to give the pre-

concerted signal for the remainder of Col. Swearingen's
party to come on, lest it might excite the Indians to
greater vigilance and they intercept the men on their way
to the fort. To obviate the difficulty arising from this apprehension, Col. Swearingen, Capt. Bilderbock and William
Boshears, taking a circuitous route to avoid passing near the
cornfield, returned to their companions, and escorted them
to Wheeling. It then remained to ascertain whether the
Indians had really withdrawn, or were only lying in ambush. A council, consisting of Col. Zane, Col. Shepherd,
Doctor McMahon and Col. Swearingen, being requested
to devise some expedient by which to be assured of the
fact, recommended that two of their most active and vigilant men, should go out openly from the fort, and carelessly, but surely, examine the cornfield near to the
palisade. Upon their return, twenty others, under the
guidance of Col. Zane, marched round at some distance
from the field, and approaching it more nearly on their return, became assured that the Indians had indeed despaired
of success, and were withdrawn from the field. About
this time Major M'Cullough arrived with forty-five men,
and they all proceeded to view the battle ground.

Here was indeed a pitiable sight. Twenty-three of the
men who had accompanied Capts. Mason and Ogal in the
preceding morning, were lying dead; few of them had
been shot, but the greater part, most inhumanly and bar-
barously butchered with the tomahawk and scalping
knife. Upwards of three hundred head of cattle, horses,
and hogs, wantonly killed by the savages, were seen lying
about the field, and all the houses, with every thing which
they contained, and which could not be conveniently
taken off by the enemy, were but heaps of ashes. It was
long indeed, before the [166] inhabitants of that neighborhood regained the comforts, of which that night's desolation had deprived them.

Soon after the happening of these events a company
of militia under the command of Capt. Foreman, arrived
from east of the Alleghany, to afford protection to the
settlements around Wheeling, and occupy the fort at this
place. While stationed in it, it was known that parties of

Indians were still lurking about, seeking opportunities of doing mischief, and to prevent which, detachments were frequently sent on scouting expeditions. On the 26th of September, Capt. Foreman with forty five men, went about twelve miles below Wheeling and encamped for the night. He was ignorant of the practices of the Indians, and seemed rather indisposed to take council of those, who were conversant with them. After building fires for the night, he remained with his men close around them, contrary to the advice of one of the settlers, by the name of Lynn, who had accompanied him as a spy. Lynn however, would not consent to remain there himself, but taking with him those of the frontiers men who were in company, retired some distance from the fires, and spent the night. Before it was yet light, Lynn, being awake, thought he heard such a noise, as would be probably produced by the launching of rafts on the river, above the position occupied by Capt. Foreman. In the morning he communicated his suspicion that an Indian force was near them, and advised the Captain to return to Wheeling along the hill sides and avoid the bottoms. His advice was rejected; but Lynn, with the caution of one used to such a condition of things, prudently kept on the hill side with four others, while they, who belonged to the command of Capt. Foreman, continued along the level at the base of the hill.

In marching along the Grave creek narrows, one of the soldiers saw a parcel of Indian ornaments lying in the path; and picking them up, soon drew around him the greater part of the company. While thus crowded together inspecting the trinkets, a galling fire was opened on them by a party of Indians who lay in ambush, and which threw them into great confusion. The fire was continued with deadly effect, for some minutes; and must eventually have caused the loss of the whole party, but that Lynn, with his few comrades rushed from the hill discharging their guns, and shouting so boisterously, as induced the Indians to believe that a reinforcement was at hand, and they precipitately retreated.

In this fatal ambuscade there were twenty-one of Captain Foreman's party killed, and several much wounded; among the slain were the Captain and his two sons.

It appeared that the Indians had dropped their ornaments, purposely to attract the attention of the whites; while they themselves were lying concealed in two parties; the one to the right of the path, in a sink-hole on the bottom, and the other to the left, under covert of the river bank. From these advantageous positions, they [167] fired securely on our men; while they were altogether exempt from danger 'till the party in the sink hole was descried by Lynn. His firing was not known to have taken effect; but to his good conduct is justly attributable the saving of the remnant of the detachment. The Indian force was never ascertained. It was supposed to have been small; not exceeding twenty warriors.

On the ensuing day, the inhabitants of the neighborhood of Wheeling under the direction and guidance of Colonel Zane, proceeded to Grave Creek and buried those who had fallen.[1]

---

[1] After the affair at Wheeling, September 1, the Indians returned home. But soon thereafter, Half King, head chief of the Wyandots, set out with forty of that tribe to again harry the Wheeling country. On the morning of the 26th, Capts. William Foreman with twenty-four men, Ogle with ten men, and William Linn with nine, started from Fort Henry on a scout. Linn was ranking officer, although there was little discipline. Foreman was a new arrival from Hampshire County, enlisted to go on Hand's intended expedition. They intended crossing the Ohio at Grave Creek, 12 miles below, and proceeding 8 miles farther down to Captina. At Grave, however, they found that the Tomlinson settlement (nucleus of the present Mound City, W. Va.) had been abandoned, and sacked by Indians, and no canoes were to be had. They camped for the night, and the next morning (the 27th) started to return along the river bank, to Wheeling. Linn, apprehensive of Indians, marched along the hill crest, but Ogle and Foreman kept to the trail along the bottom. At a point where the bottom narrows because of the close approach of the hills to the river—a defile then known as Mc-Mechen's (or McMahon's) Narrows—they were set upon by Half King's party, awaiting them in ambush. Foreman and twenty others were killed, and one captured. The story about Linn's gallant attack on the Indians from his vantage point on the hilltop, is without foundation. His party helped to secrete a wounded man who escaped in the melee, and then put off in hot haste for home. It was not until four days later, when reinforcements had arrived from Fort Pitt, that Colonel Shepherd ventured from the fort to bury the dead. In 1835, an inscribed stone was set up at the Narrows, to commemorate the slain. R. G. T.

At the time of the happening of those occurrences the belief was general, that the army which had been led to Wheeling by Girty, had been ordered on, for the purpose of conducting the tories from the settlements to Detroit; and that detachments from that army continued to hover about the frontiers for some time, to effect that object. There was then, unfortunately for the repose and tranquility of many neighborhoods, a considerable number of those misguided and deluded wretches, who, disaffected to the cause of the colonies, were willing to advance the interest of Britain, by the sacrifice of every social relation, and the abandonment of every consideration, save that of loyalty to the king. So far did their opposition, to those who espoused the cause of American liberty, blunt every finer and more noble feeling, that many of them were willing to imbrue their hands in the blood of their neighbors, in the most sly and secret manner, and in the hour of midnight darkness, for no offence but attachment to the independence of the colonies. A conspiracy for the murder of the whigs and for accepting the terms, offered by the Governor of Canada to those who would renounce their allegiance to the United States and repair to Detroit, by the relenting of one individual, was prevented being carried into effect; and many were consequently saved from horrors, equalling, if not transcending in enormity, the outrages of the savages themselves. Scenes of licentiousness and fury, followed upon the discovery of the plot.—Exasperated at its heinousness, and under the influence of resentful feelings, the whigs retaliated upon the tories, some of the evils which these had conspired to inflict upon them. In the then infuriated state of their minds, and the little restraint at that time imposed on the passions by the operation of the laws, it is really matter of admiration that they did not proceed farther, and requite upon those deluded wretches, the full measure of their premeditated wrongs. The head only of this fiendish league, lost his life; but many depredations were committed, on the property of its members.

A court, for the trial of the conspirants, was held at Redstone Fort; and many of them were arraigned at its bar. But as their object had been defeated by its discovery, and as no farther danger was apprehended from them, they were released, after having been required to take the oath of allegiance to the United States and to bear with the injuries which had [168] been done their property. Those who were suspected for the murder of the chief conspirator, were likewise arraigned for that offence, but were acquitted.

Hitherto the inhabitants of Tygart's Valley had escaped the ill effects of savage enmity; Indian hostility not having prompted an incursion into that country, since its permanent settlement was effected previous to the war of 1774. This however had not the effect to lull them into confident security. Ascribing their fortunate exemption from irruptions of the enemy, to other causes than a willingness on the part of the Indians, to leave them in quiet and repose, they exercised the utmost vigilance to discover their approach, and used every precaution to ensure them safety, if the enemy should appear among them. Spies were regularly employed in watching the warriors paths beyond the settlements, to detect their advance and to apprize the inhabitants of it.

In September of this year (1777) Leonard Petro and Wm. White, being engaged in watching the path leading up the Little Kenhawa, killed an Elk late in the evening; and taking part of it with them, withdrew a short distance for the purpose of eating their suppers and spending the night. About midnight, White, awaking from sleep, discovered by the light of the moon, that there were several Indians near, who had been drawn in quest of them by the report of the gun in the evening. He saw at a glance, the impossibility of escaping by flight; and preferring captivity to death, he whispered to Petro to lie still, lest any movement of his, might lead to this result. In a few minutes the Indians sprang on them; and White raising himself as one lay hold on him, aimed a furious blow, with his tomahawk, hoping to wound the Indian by whom he was beset, and then make his escape. Missing his aim he affected to have been ignorant of the fact that he was encountered by Indians, professed great joy at meeting with them, and declared that he was then on his way to their towns. They were not deceived by the artifice; for although he assumed an air of pleasantness and gaity, calculated to win upon their confidence, yet the woful countenance and rueful expression of poor Petro, convinced them that White's conduct was feigned, that he might lull them into inattention, and they be enabled to effect an escape. They were both tied for the night; and in the morning White being painted red, and Petro black, they were forced to proceed to the Indian towns. When approaching a [169] village, the whoop of success brought several to meet them; and on their arrival at it, they found that every preparation was made for their running the gauntlet; in going through which ceremony both were much bruised. White did not however remain long in captivity. Eluding their vigilance, he took one of their guns and began his flight homeward.—Before he had travelled far, he met an Indian on horseback, whom he succeeded in shooting; and mounting the horse from which he fell, his return to the Valley was much facilitated. Petro was never heard of afterwards. The painting of him black, had indicated their intention of killing him; and the escape of White probably hastened his doom.

During this time, and after the return of White among them, the inhabitants of Tygart's Valley practiced their accustomed watchfulness 'till about the twentieth of November; when there was a considerable fall of snow. This circumstance induced them to believe, that the savages would not attempt an irruption among them until the return of spring; and they became consequently, inattentive to their safety.

Generally, the settlements enjoyed perfect quiet from the first appearance of winter, until the return of spring. In this interval of time, the Indians are usually deterred from penetrating into them, as well because of their great exposure to discovery and observation in consequence of the nakedness of the woods and the increased facility of pursuing their trail in the snows which then usually covered the earth, as of the suffering produced by their lying in wait and travelling, in their partially unclothed condition, in this season of intense cold. Instances of their being troublesome during the winter were rare indeed; and never occurred, but under very peculiar circumstances: the inhabitants, were therefore, not culpably remiss, when they relaxed in their vigilance, and became exposed to savage inroad.

A party of twenty Indians, designing to commit some depredations during the fall, had nearly reached the upper end of Tygart's Valley, when the snow, which had inspired the inhabitants with confidence in their security, commenced falling. Fearful of laying themselves open to detection, if they ventured to proceed farther at that time, and anxious to effect some mischief before they returned home, they remained concealed about ten miles from the settlements, until the snow disappeared. On the 15th of December, they came to the [170] house of Darby Connoly, at the upper extremity of the Valley, and killed him, his wife and several of the children, and took three others prisoners. Proceeding to the next house, killed John Stewart, his wife and child, and took Miss Hamilton (sister-in-law to Stewart) into captivity. They then immediately changed their direction, and with great dispatch, entered upon their journey home; with the captives and plunder, taken at those two places.

In the course of the evening after these outrages were committed, John Hadden passing by the House of Connoly saw a tame elk belonging there, lying dead in the yard. This, and the death-like silence which reigned around, excited his fears that all was not right; and entering into the house, he saw the awful desolation which had been committed. Seeing that the work of blood had been but recently done, he hastened to alarm the neighborhood, and sent an express to Capt. Benjamin Wilson, living about twenty miles lower in the Valley, with the melancholy intelligence. With great promptitude, Capt. Wilson went through the settlement, exerting himself to procure as many volunteers, as would justify going in pursuit of the aggressors; and so indefatigable was he in accomplishing his purpose, that, on the day after the murders were perpetrated, he appeared on the theatre of their exhibition with thirty men, prepared to take the trail and push forward in pursuit of the savages. For five days they followed through cold and wet, without perceiving that they had gained upon them. At this time many of the men expressed a determination to return. They had suffered much, travelled far, and yet saw no prospect of overtaking the enemy. It is not wonderful that they became dispirited. In order to expedite their progress, the numerous water courses which lay across their path, swollen to an unusual height and width, were passed without any preparation to avoid getting wet; the consequence was that after wading one of them, they would have to travel with icicles hanging from their clothes the greater part of a day, before an opportunity could be allowed of drying them. They suffered much too for the want of provisions. The short time afforded for preparation, had not admitted of their taking with them as much as they expected would be required, as they had already been on the chase longer than was anticipated. Under these circumstances it was with great difficulty, Captain Wilson could prevail [171] on them to continue the pursuit one day longer; hoping the Indians would have to halt, in order to hunt for food. Not yet being sensible that they gained upon them, the men positively refused going farther; and they returned to their several homes.

This was the last outrage committed by the savages on North Western Virginia, in this year. And although there was not as much mischief effected by them in this season, as had been in others, yet the year 1777, has become memorable in the annals of Border Warfare. The murder of Cornstalk and his companions,—the attack on Wheeling Fort,—the loss of lives and destruction of property which then took place, together with the fatal ambuscade at Grave Creek Narrows, all conspired to render it a period of much interest, and to impress its incidents deeply on the minds of those who were actors in these scenes.

[172] CHAPTER X.

After the winter became so severe as to prevent the
Indians from penetrating the country and committing farther aggression, the inhabitants became assured of safety,
and devoted much of their time to the erection of new
forts, the strengthening of those which had been formerly
established, and the making of other preparations, deemed
necessary to prevent the repetition of those distressing occurrences, which had spread gloom and sorrow over almost
every part of North Western Virginia. That the savages
would early renew their exertions to destroy the frontier
settlements, and harrass their citizens, could not for an
instant be doubted.—Revenge for the murder of Cornstalk,
and the other chiefs killed in the fort by the whites, had
operated to unite the warlike nation of the Shawanees in
a league with the other Indians, against them; and every
circumstance seemed to promise increased exertions on
their part, to accomplish their purposes of blood and
devastation.

Notwithstanding all which had been suffered during
the preceding season; and all, which it was confidently
anticipated, would have to be undergone after the return
of spring, yet did the whole frontier increase in population, and in capacity to defend itself against the encroachments of a savage enemy, aided by British emissaries, and
led on by American tories. The accession to its strength,
caused by the number of emigrants, who came into the
different settlements, was indeed considerable; yet it was
insufficient, to enable the inhabitants to purchase by offensive operations, exemption from [173] invasion, or security
from the tomahawk and scalping knife. Assured of this,
Virginia extended to them farther assistance; and a small
body of regular troops, under the command of General
McIntosh, was appropriated to their defence.

In the spring of 1778, General McIntosh,[1] with the regulars and some militiamen, attached to his command, descended the Ohio river from Fort Pitt, to the mouth of Big Beaver—a creek discharging itself into that river from the north-west.[2] This was a favorable position, at which to station his troops to effect the partial security of the frontier, by intercepting parties of Indians on their way to the settlements on the opposite side of the river, and by pursuing and punishing them while engaged, either in committing havoc, or in retreating to their towns, after the consummation of their horrid purposes. Fort McIntosh was accordingly erected here, and garrisoned; a six pounder mounted for its defence.

From Wheeling to Point Pleasant, a distance of one hundred and eighty-six miles,[3] there was then no obstacle whatever, presented to the advance of Indian war parties, into the settlements on the East and West Forks of the Monongahela, and their branches. The consequences of this exposure had been always severely felt; and never more so than after the establishment of Fort McIntosh. Every impediment to their invasion of one part of the country, caused more frequent irruptions into others, where no difficulties were interposed to check their progress, and brought heavier woes on them.—This had been already experienced, in the settlements on the upper branches of the Monongahela, and as they were the last

---

[1] Lachlan McIntosh was born near Inverness, Scotland, March 17, 1725. With his father, and 100 others of the Clan McIntosh, he emigrated to Georgia in 1736, in the train of Oglethorpe. The party founded New Inverness, in McIntosh County. Lachlan entered the Colonial army at the opening of the Revolution, and rose to be brigadier-general. In a duel with Button Gwinnett, a signer of the Declaration of Independence, he killed the latter. General McIntosh was at the siege of Savannah in 1779, was a prisoner of war in 1780, a member congress in 1784, and in 1785 a commissioner to treat with the Southern Indians. He died at Savannah, February 20, 1806.—R. G. T.

[2] The distance below Pittsburg is 26 miles. See p. 45, *note*, for notice of Shingiss Old Town, at this point.—R. G. T.

[3] The distance, according to the shore meanderings of the U. S. Corps of Engineers, is 263 miles; the mileage of the channel would be somewhat greater.—R. G. T.

to feel the effects of savage enmity in 1777, so were they first to become sacrificed to its fury in 1778.

Anticipating the commencement of hostilities at an earlier period of the season, than usual, several families retired into Harbert's block-house, on Ten Mile (a branch of the West Fork,) in the month of February. And notwithstanding the prudent caution manifested by them in the step thus taken; yet, the state of the weather lulling them into false security, they did not afterwards exercise the vigilance and provident care, which were necessary to ensure their future safety. On the third of March, some children, playing with a crippled crow, at a short distance from the yard, espied a number of Indians proceeding towards them; and running briskly to the house, told "that a number of *red men* were close by."—[174] John Murphey stepped to the door to see if danger had really approached, when one of the Indians, turning the corner of the house, fired at him. The ball took effect, and Murphey fell back into the house. The Indian springing directly in, was grappled by Harbert, and thrown on the floor. A shot from without, wounded Harbert, yet he continued to maintain his advantage over the prostrate savage, striking him as effectually as he could with his tomahawk, when another gun was fired at him from without the house. The ball passed through his head, and he fell lifeless. His antagonist then slipped out at the door, sorely wounded in the encounter.

Just after the first Indian had entered, an active young warrior, holding in his hand a tomahawk with a long spike at the end, also came in. Edward Cunningham instantly drew up his gun to shoot him; but it flashed, and they closed in doubtful strife. Both were active and athletic; and sensible of the high prize for which they were contending, each put forth his utmost strength, and strained his every nerve, to gain the ascendency. For a while, the issue seemed doubtful. At length, by great exertion, Cunningham wrenched the tomahawk from the hand of the Indian, and buried the spike end to the handle, in his back. Mrs. Cunningham closed the contest. Seeing her husband struggling closely with the

savage, she struck at him with an axe. The edge wounding his face severely, he loosened his hold, and made his
way out of the house.

The third Indian, which had entered before the door
was closed, presented an appearance almost as frightful as
the object which he had in view. He wore a cap made
of the unshorn front of a buffalo, with the ears and horns
still attached to it, and which hanging loosely about his
head, gave to him a most hideous aspect. On entering
the room, this infernal monster, aimed a blow with his
tomahawk at a Miss Reece, which alighting on her head,
wounded her severely. The mother of this girl, seeing
the uplifted arm about to descend on her daughter, seized
the monster by the horns; but his false head coming readily off, she did not succeed in changing the direction of
the weapon. The father then caught hold of him; but
far inferior in strength and agility, he was soon thrown
on the floor, and must have been killed, but for the timely
interference of Cunningham. Having [175] succeeded in
ridding the room of one Indian, he wheeled, and sunk a
tomahawk into the head of the other.

During all this time the door was kept by the women,
tho' not without great exertion. The Indians from without endeavored several times to force it open and gain
admittance; and would at one time have succeeded, but
that, as it was yielding to their effort to open it, the Indian, who had been wounded by Cunningham and his
wife, squeezing out at the aperture which had been made,
caused a momentary relaxation of the exertions of those
without, and enabled the women again to close it, and
prevent the entrance of others.—These were not however,
unemployed. They were engaged in securing such of the
children in the yard, as were capable of being carried
away as prisoners, and in killing and scalping the others;
and when they had effected this, despairing of being able
to do farther mischief, they retreated to their towns.

Of the whites in the house, one only was killed and
four were wounded; and seven or eight children in the
yard, were killed or taken prisoners. One Indian was
killed, and two badly wounded. Had Reece engaged

sooner in the conflict, the other two who had entered the
house, would no doubt have been likewise killed; but being a quaker, he looked on, without participating in the
conflict, until his daughter was wounded. Having then
to contend singly, with superior prowess, he was indebted
for the preservation of his life, to the assistance of those
whom he refused to aid in pressing need.

On the eleventh of April, some Indians visited the
house of Wm. Morgan, at the Dunkard bottom of Cheat
river. They there killed a young man by the name of
Brain, Mrs. Morgan, (the mother of William) and her
grand daughter, and Mrs. Dillon and her two children;
and took Mrs. Morgan (the wife) and her child prisoners.
When, on their way home, they came near to Pricket's
fort, they bound Mrs. Morgan to a bush, and went in
quest of a horse for her to ride, leaving her child with
her. She succeeded in untying with her teeth, the bands
which confined her, and wandered the balance of that day
and part of the next before she came in sight of the fort.
Here she was kindly treated and in a few days sent home.
Some men going out from Pricket's fort some short time
after, found at the spot where Mrs. Morgan had [176] been
left by the Indians, a fine mare stabbed to the heart.—Exasperated at the escape of Mrs. Morgan, they had no doubt
vented their rage on the animal which they had destined
to bear her weight.

In the last of April, a party of about twenty Indians
came to the neighborhoods of Hacker's creek and the
West Fork. At this time the inhabitants of those neighborhoods had removed to West's fort, on the creek, and to
Richards' fort on the river; and leaving the women and
children in them during the day, under the protection of a
few men, the others were in the habit of performing the
usual labors of their farms in companies, so as to preserve
them from attacks of the Indians. A company of men,
being thus engaged, the first week of May, in a field, now
owned by Minter Bailey, on Hacker's creek, and being a
good deal dispersed in various occupations, some fencing,
others clearing, and a few ploughing, they were unexpectedly fired upon by the Indians, and Thomas Hughes and

Jonathan Lowther shot down: the others being incautiously without arms fled for safety. Two of the company, having the Indians rather between them and West's fort, ran directly to Richards', as well for their own security as to give the alarm there. But they had been already apprized that the enemy was at hand. Isaac Washburn, who had been to mill on Hacker's creek the day before, on his return to Richards' fort and near to where Clement's mill now stands, was shot from his horse, tomahawked and scalped. The finding of his body, thus cruelly mangled, had given them the alarm, and they were already on their guard, before the two men from Hacker's creek arrived with the intelligence of what had been done there. The Indians then left the neighborhood without effecting more havoc: and the whites were too weak to go in pursuit, and molest them.

The determination of the Shawanees to revenge the death of their Sachem, had hitherto been productive of no very serious consequences. A while after his murder, a small band of them made their appearance near the fort at Point Pleasant; and Lieutenant Moore was dispatched from the garrison, with some men, to drive them off. Upon his advance, they commenced retreating; and the officer commanding the detachment, fearing they would escape, ordered a quick pursuit. He did not proceed far before he fell into an ambuscade. He and three of his men were killed at the first [177] fire;—the rest of the party saved themselves by a precipitate flight to the fort.

In the May following this transaction, a few Indians again came in sight of the fort. But as the garrison had been very much reduced by the removal of Captain Arbuckle's company, and the experience of the last season had taught them prudence, Captain McKee forbore to detach any of his men in pursuit of them. Disappointed, in their expectations of enticing others to destruction, as they had Lieutenant Moore in the winter, the Indians suddenly rose from their covert, and presented an unbroken line, extending from the Ohio to the Kanawha river in front of the fort. A demand for the surrender of the gar-

16

rison, was then made; and Captain McKee asked 'till the next morning to consider of it. In the course of the night, the men were busily employed in bringing water from the river, expecting that the Indians would continue before the fort for some time.

In the morning, Captain McKee sent his answer by the grenadier squaw, (sister to Cornstalk, and who, notwithstanding the murder of her brother and nephew, was still attached to the whites, and was remaining at the fort in the capacity of interpreter)[1] that he could not comply with their demand.—The Indians immediately began the attack, and for one week kept the garrison closely besieged. Finding however, that they made no impression on the fort, they collected the cattle about it and instead of returning towards their own country with the plunder, proceeded up the Kanawha river towards the Greenbrier settlement.

Believing their object to be the destruction of that settlement, and knowing from their great force that they would certainly accomplish it, if the inhabitants were unadvised of their approach, Captain McKee despatched two men to Col. Andrew Donnelly's, (then the frontier house,) with the intelligence. These men soon came in view of the Indians; but finding that they were advancing in detached groups, and dispersed in hunting parties, through the woods, they despaired of being able to pass them, and returned to the fort. Captain McKee then made an appeal to the chivalry of the garrison, and asked, " who would risk his life to save the people of Greenbrier." John Pryor and Philip Hammond, at once stepped forward, and replied " WE WILL." They were then habited after the Indian manner, and painted in Indian style by the Grenadier Squaw, and departed on their hazardous, but noble and generous undertaking. Travelling, night and day, with great rapidity, they [178] passed the Indians at Meadow river, and arrived, about sunset of that day at Donnelly's fort, twenty miles farther on.

---

[1] See p. 176, *note*, for notice of Grenadier Squaw's Town, near Chillicothe.—R. G. T.

As soon as the intelligence of the approach of the Indians, was communicated by these men, Col. Donnelly had the neighbors all advised of it; and in the course of the night, they collected at his house. He also dispatched a messenger to Capt. John Stuart, to acquaint him with the fact; and made every preparation to resist attack and ensure their safety, of which his situation admitted. Pryor and Hammond told them how, by the precaution of Captain McKee, the garrison at Point Pleasant had been saved from suffering by the want of water; and advised them to lay in a plentiful supply, of that necessary article. A hogshead was accordingly filled and rolled behind the door of the kitchen, which adjoined the dwelling house.

Early next morning, John Pritchet (a servant to Col. Donnelly) went out for some firewood, and while thus engaged, was fired at and killed. The Indians then ran into the yard, and endeavored to force open the kitchen door; but Hammond and Dick Pointer (a negro belonging to Col. Donnelly) who were the only persons within, aided by the hogshead of water, prevented their accomplishing this object. They next proceeded to cut it in pieces, with their tomahawks. Hammond seeing that they would soon succeed in this way, with the assistance of Dick, rolled the hogshead to one side, and letting the door suddenly fly open, killed the Indian at the threshold, and the others who were near gave way. Dick then fired among them, with a musket heavily charged with swan shot, and no doubt with effect, as the yard was crowded with the enemy; a war club with a swan shot in it, was afterwards picked up near the door.

The men in the house, who were asleep at the commencement of the attack, being awakened at the firing of Hammond and Dick, now opened a galling fire upon the Indians. Being chiefly up stairs they were enabled to do greater execution, and fired with such effect that, about one o'clock, the enemy retired a small distance from the house. Before they retired however, some of them succeeded in getting under the floor, when they were aided by the whites below in raising some of the puncheons of which it was made. It was to their advantage to do this;

and well did they profit by it. Several of the Indians were killed in this attempt to gain admittance, while only one of the whites received a wound, which but slightly injured his hand.

When intelligence was conveyed to Capt. Stuart of the approach of so large a body of savages, Col. Samuel Lewis was with him; and they both exerted themselves to save the settlement from destruction, by collecting the inhabitants at a fort where Lewisburg now stands. Having succeeded in this, they sent two men to Donnelly's to learn whether the Indians had advanced that far. As they approached, the firing became distinctly audible, and they returned [179] with the tidings. Capt. Stuart and Col. Lewis proposed marching to the relief of Donnelly's fort, with as many men as were willing to accompany them; and in a brief space of time, commenced their march at the head of sixty-six men. Pursuing the most direct route without regarding the road, they approached the house on the back side; and thus escaped an ambuscade of Indians placed near the road to intercept and cut off any assistance which might be sent from the upper settlements.

Adjoining the yard, there was a field of well grown rye, into which the relief from Lewisburg, entered about two o'clock; but as the Indians had withdrawn to a distance from the house, there was no firing heard. They soon however, discovered the savages in the field, looking intently towards Donnoly's; and it was resolved to pass them. Capt. Stuart and Charles Gatliff fired at them, and the whole party rushed forward into the yard, amid a heavy discharge of balls from the savage forces. The people in the fort hearing the firing in the rear of the house, soon presented themselves at the port holes, to resist, what they supposed, was a fresh attack on them; but quickly discovering the real cause, they opened the gates, and all the party led on by Stuart and Lewis, safely entered.

The Indians then resumed the attack, and maintained a constant fire at the house, until near dark, when one of them approached, and in broken English called out, "we want peace." He was told to come in and he should have it; but he declined the invitation to enter, and they all retreated, dragging off those of their slain, who lay not too near the fort.

Of the whites, four only were killed by the enemy. Pritchet, before the attack commenced,—James Burns and Alexander Ochiltree, as they were coming to the house early in the morning,—and James Graham while in the fort. It was impossible to ascertain the entire loss of the Indians. Seventeen lay dead in the yard; and they were known to carry off others of their slain. Perhaps the disparity of the killed, equalled, if it did not exceed the disparity of the number engaged. There were twenty-one men at Donnoly's fort, before the arrival of the reinforcement under Stuart and Lewis; and the brunt of the battle was over before they came. The Indian force exceeded two hundred men.

It was believed, that the invasion of the Greenbrier country had been projected, some time before it actually was made. During the preceding season, an Indian calling himself John Hollis, had been very much through the settlement; and was known to take particular notice of the different forts, which he entered under the garb of friendship. He was with the Indians in the attack on Donnoly's fort; and was recognized as one of those who were left dead in the yard.

On the morning after the Indians departed, Capt. Hamilton went in pursuit of them with seventy men : but following two days, without [180] perceiving that he gained on them, he abandoned the chase and returned.

About the middle of June, three women went out from West's fort, to gather greens in a field adjoining ; and while thus engaged were attacked by four Indians, lying in wait. One gun only was fired, and the ball from it, passed through the bonnet of Mrs. Hacker, who screamed aloud and ran with the others towards the fort. An Indian, having in his hand a long staff, with a spear in one end, pursuing closely after them, thrust it at Mrs. Freeman with such violence that, entering her back just below the shoulder, it came out at her left breast. With his tomahawk, he cleft the upper part of her head, and carried it off to save the scalp.

The screams of the women alarmed the men in the fort; and seizing their guns, they ran out, just as Mrs. Freeman fell. Several guns were fired at the Indian while he was getting her scalp, but with no effect. They served however, to warn the men who went out, that danger was at hand; and they quickly came in.

Jesse Hughs[1] and John Schoolcraft (who were out) in making their way to the fort, came very near two Indians standing by the fence looking towards the men at West's, so intently, that they did not perceive any one near them. They however, were observed by Hughs and Schoolcraft, who, avoiding them, made their way in, safely, Hughs immediately took up his gun, and learning the fate of Mrs. Freeman, went with some others to bring in the corpse. While there, he proposed to go and shew them, how near he had approached the Indians after the alarm had been given, before he saw them. Charles and Alexander West, Chas. Hughs, James Brown and John Steeth, went with him. Before they had arrived at the place, one of the Indians was heard to howl like a wolf; and the men with Hughs moved on in the direction from which the sound proceeded. Supposing that they were then near the spot, Jesse Hughs howled in like manner, and being instantly answered, they ran to a point of the hill and looking over it, saw two Indians coming towards them. Hughs fired and one of them fell. The other took to flight. Being pursued by the whites, he sought shelter in a thicket of brush; and while they were proceeding to intercept him at his coming out, he returned by the way he had entered, and made his escape. The wounded Indian likewise got off. When the whites were in pursuit of the one who took to flight, they passed near to him who had fallen, and one of the men was for stopping and finishing him; but Hughs called to him, "he is safe—let us have the other," and they all pressed forward. On their return, however, he was gone; and although his free bleeding enabled them to pursue his track readily for a while, yet a heavy shower of rain soon falling, all trace of him was quickly lost and could not be afterwards regained.

On the 16th of June as Capt. James Booth and Nathaniel Cochran, were at work in a field on Booth's creek, they were fired at by [181] the Indians. Booth fell, but Cochran, being very slightly wounded, took to flight. He was however, overtaken, and carried into captivity to their towns. From thence he was taken to Detroit, where he remained some time; and endeavoring to escape from that place, unfortunately took a path which led him immediately to the Maumee old towns. Here he was detained a while, & then sent back to Detroit, where he was exchanged, and from whence he made his way home, after having had to endure much suffering and many hardships. The loss of Booth was severely felt by the inhabitants in that settlement. He was not only an active and enterprising man, but was endowed with superior talents, and a better education than most of those who had settled in the country; and on these accounts was very much missed.

In a few days after this transaction, Benjamin Shinn, Wm. Grundy, and Benjamin Washburn, returning from a lick on the head of Booth's creek, were fired on by the Indians, when near to Baxter's run. Washburn and Shinn escaped unhurt, but Grundy was killed: he was brother to Felix Grundy of Tennessee, whose father was then residing at Simpson's creek, at a farm afterwards owned by Colonel Benjamin Wilson, senior.

This party of Indians continued for some days, to prowl about the neighborhood, seeking opportunities of committing murder on the inhabitants; fortunately however, with but little success. James Owens, a youth of sixteen years of age, was the only one whom they succeeded in killing after the murder of Grundy. Going from Powers' fort on Simpson's creek, to Booth's creek, his saddle girth gave way, and while he was down mending it, a ball was discharged at him, which killed both him and the horse.

Seeing that the whites, in that neighborhood, had all retired to the fort; and being too weak, openly to attack it, they crossed over to Bartlett's run, and came to the house of Gilbert Hustead, who was then alone, and engaged in fixing his gun lock. Hearing a noise in the yard, for which he was unable to account, he slipped to the door, to ascertain from whence it proceeded. The Indians were immediately round it, and there was no chance for his escape. Walking out with an air of the utmost pleasantry, he held forth his hand to the one nearest him, and asked them all to walk in. While in the house he affected great cheerfulness, and by his tale [182] won their confidence and friendship. He told them that he was a King's man and unwilling to live among the rebels; for which reason, when others retired into the fort, he preferred staying at his own house, anxiously hoping for the arrival of some of the British Indians, to afford him an opportunity of getting among English friends. Learning upon enquiry, that they would be glad to have something to eat, he asked one of them to shoot a fat hog which was in the yard, that they might regale on it that night, and have some on which to subsist while travelling to their towns. In the morning, still farther to maintain the deception he was practising, he broke his furniture to pieces, saying "the rebels shall never have the good of you." He then accompanied them to their towns, acting in the same, apparently, contented and cheerful manner, 'till his sincerity was believed by all, and he obtained leave to return for his family. He succeeded in making his way home, where he remained, sore at the destruction of his property, but exulting in the success of his artifice.

While this party of Indians were thus engaged, on Booth's creek and in the circumjacent country, a more numerous body had invaded the settlements lower down, and were employed in the work of destruction there. They penetrated to Coburn's creek unperceived, and were making their way (as was generally supposed) to a fort not far from Morgantown, when they fell in with a party of whites, returning from the labors of the cornfield, and then about a mile from Coburn's fort. The Indians had placed themselves on each side of the road leading to the fort, and from their covert fired on the whites, before they

were aware of danger. John Woodfin being on horseback, had his thigh broken by a ball; which killed his
horse and enabled them to catch him easily.—Jacob Miller was shot through the abdomen, and soon overtaken,
tomahawked and scalped.—The others escaped to the fort.

Woodfin was afterwards found on a considerable eminence overlooking the fort, tomahawked and scalped.
The Indians had, most probably, taken him there, that he
might point out to them the least impregnable part of the
fortress, and in other respects give them such information, as would tend to ensure success to their meditated
attack on it; but when they heard its strength and the
force with which it was garrisoned, despairing of being
able to reduce it, in a fit of disappointed fury, they murdered him on the spot.

[183] They next made their appearance on Dunkard
creek, and near to Stradler's fort. Here, as on Coburn's
creek, they lay in ambush on the road side, awaiting the
return of the men who were engaged at work, in some of
the neighboring fields. Towards evening the men came
on, carrying with them some hogs which they had killed
for the use of the fort people, and on approaching where
the Indians lay concealed, were fired on and several fell.
Those who escaped injury from the first fire, returned the
shot, and a severe action ensued. But so many of the
whites had been killed before the savages exposed themselves to view, that the remainder were unable long to
sustain the unequal contest. Overpowered by numbers,
the few, who were still unhurt, fled precipitately to the
fort, leaving eighteen of their companions dead in the
road. These were scalped and mangled by the Indians in
a most shocking manner, and lay some time, before the
men in the fort, assured of the departure of the enemy,
went out and buried them.

Weakened by the severe loss sustained in this bloody
skirmish, had the Indians pushed forward to attack the
fort, in all human probability, it would have fallen before
them. There were at that day very few settlements which
could have maintained possession of a garrison for any
length of time, after having suffered so great a diminu-

tion of the number of their inhabitants, against the onsets of one hundred savages, exercising their wonted
energy: and still less would they be able to leave their
strong holds, and cope with such superior force, in open
battle. Nor were the settlements, as yet, sufficiently contiguous to each other, to admit of their acting in concert,
and combining their strength, to operate effectively against
their invaders. When alarmed by the approach of the
foe, all that they could generally do, was, retire to a fort,
and endeavor to defend it from assault. If the savages,
coming in numbers, succeeded in committing any outrage,
it usually went unpunished. Sensible of their want of
strength, the inhabitants rarely ventured in pursuit, to
harrass or molest the retiring foe. When, however, they
would hazard to hang on their retreat, the many precautions which they were compelled to exercise, to prevent
falling into ambuscades and to escape the entangling artifices of their wily enemies, frequently rendered their enterprises abortive, and their exertions inefficient.

[184] The frequent visits paid by the Indians to the
country on the West Fork, and the mischief which they
would effect at these times, led several of the inhabitants
to resolve on leaving a place so full of dangers, as soon as
they could make the necessary preparations. A family
of Washburns particularly, having several times very narrowly escaped destruction, commenced making arrangements and fitting up for their departure. But while two
of them were engaged in procuring pine knots, from which
to make wax for shoemaking, they were discovered, and
shot at by the Indians. Stephen fell dead, and James was
taken prisoner and carried to their towns.—He was there
forced to undergo repeated and intense suffering before
death closed the scene of his miseries.

According to the account given by Nathaniel Cochran
on his return from captivity, Washburn was most severely
beaten, on the first evening of his arrival at their village,
while running the gauntlet; and although he succeeded in
getting into the council house, where Cochran was, yet
he was so disfigured and mutilated, that he could not be
recognised by his old acquaintance; and so stunned and

stupified, that he remained nearly all night in a state of insensibility. Being somewhat revived in the morning, he walked to where Cochran sat by the fire, and being asked if he were not James Washburn, replied with a smile—as if a period had been put to his sufferings by the sympathetic tone in which the question was proposed—that he was. The gleam of hope which flashed over his countenance, was transient and momentary. In a few minutes he was again led forth, that the barbarities which had been suspended by the interposition of night, might be revived; and he made to endure a repetition of their cruelties. He was now feeble and too much exhausted to save himself from the clubs and sticks, even of the aged of both sexes. The old men and the old women, who followed him, had strength and activity enough to keep pace with his fleetest progress, and inflict on him their severest blows. Frequently he was beaten to the ground, and as frequently, as if invigorated by the extremity of anguish, he rose to his feet. Hobbling before his tormentors, with no hope but in death, an old savage passed a knife across his ham, which cutting the tendons, disabled him from proceeding farther. Still they repeated their unmerciful blows with all their energy. He was next scalped, though alive, and struggling to regain his feet. [185] Even this did not operate to suppress their cruelty. They continued to beat him, until in the height of suffering he again exhibited symptoms of life and exerted himself to move. His head was then severed from his shoulders, attached to a pole, and placed in the most public situation in the village.

After the attack on the Washburns, there were but two other outrages committed in the upper country during that season. The cessation on the part of the savages, of hostile incursions, induced an abandonment of the forts, and the people returned to their several homes, and respective occupations. But aggression was only suspended for a time. In October, two Indians appeared near the house of Conrad Richards, and finding in the yard a little girl at play, with an infant in her arms, they scalped her and rushed to the door. For some time they endeavored to force it open; but it was so securely fastened within, that Richards was at liberty to use his gun for its defence. A fortunate aim wounded one of the assailants severely, and the other retreated, helping off his companion. The girl who had been scalped in the yard, as soon as she observed the Indians going away, ran, with the infant still in her arms and uninjured, and entered the house—a spectacle of most heart-rending wretchedness.

Soon after, David Edwards, returning from Winchester with salt, was shot near the Valley river, tomahawked and scalped; in which situation he lay for some time before he was discovered. He was the last person who fell a victim to savage vengeance, in North Western Virginia in the year 1778.

The repeated irruptions of the Indians during the summer of the year;[1] and the frequent murders and great devastation committed by them, induced Government to undertake two expeditions into the Indian country. One thousand men were placed under the command of General McIntosh, some time in the fall, and he received orders to proceed forthwith against the Sandusky towns. Between two and three hundred soldiers were likewise placed under Colonel Clarke, to operate against the Canadian settlements in Illinois. It was well known that the Governor of those settlements was an indefatigable agent of British cruelty, stimulating the savages to aggression, and paying them well for scalps, torn alike from the heads of the aged matron and the helpless infant.[2] [186] The settlements in Kentucky, were constantly the theatre of outrage and murder; and to preserve these from entire destruction, it was necessary that a blow should be aimed, at the

---

[1] These war parties largely emanated from the Detroit region. Lieutenant-Governor Hamilton, the British commander at Detroit, writing to his superior, General Haldimand, September 16, 1778, mentions incidentally that he sent out small parties of Miamis and Chippewas, August 5, and September 5 and 9; these were but three of dozens of such forays which he incited against the Virginia and Pennsylvania borders, during that year.—R. G. T.

[2] This reference is to Lieut.-Governor Hamilton, whom George Rogers Clark called "the hair-buying general."—R. G. T.

hives from which the savages swarmed, and if possible, that those holds, into which they would retire to reap the rewards of their cruelties and receive the price of blood, should be utterly broken up. The success of those two expeditions could not fail to check savage encroachments, and give quiet and security to the frontier; and although the armies destined to achieve it, were not altogether adequate to the service required, yet the known activity and enterprize of the commanding officers, joined to their prudence and good conduct, and the bravery and indefatigable perseverance and hardiness of the troops, gave promise of a happy result.

The success of the expedition under Colonel Clarke,[1]

---

[1] Gen. George Rogers Clark was born November 19, 1752, near Monticello, Albemarle County, Va. At the age of twenty he was practicing his profession as a surveyor on the upper Ohio, and took up a claim at the mouth of Fish Creek. In 1774, he participated as a captain in Dunmore's campaign against the Shawnees and Mingoes. Early in 1775, Clark went as a surveyor to Kentucky, where he acquired marked popularity, and in 1776 was elected as "a delegate to the Virginia convention, to urge upon the state authorities the claims of the colony for government and defense." He secured the formation of the new county of Kentucky, and a supply of ammunition for the defense of the border. In 1777, Clark, now a major of militia, repelled the Indian attacks on Harrodsburg, and proceeded on foot to Virginia to lay before the state authorities his plan for capturing the Illinois country and repressing the Indian forays from that quarter. His scheme being approved, he was made a lieutenant-colonel, and at once set out to raise for the expedition a small force of hardy frontiersmen. He rendezvoused and drilled his little army of a hundred and fifty on Corn Island in the Ohio river, at the head of the Falls (or rapids), opposite the present city of Louisville. June 24, 1778, he started in boats down the Ohio, and landed near the deserted Fort Massac, which was on the north bank, ten miles below the mouth of the Tennessee; thence marching across country, much pressed for food, he reached Kaskaskia in six days. The inhabitants there were surprised and coerced during the night of July 4–5, without the firing of a gun. Cahokia and Vincennes soon quietly succumbed to his influence. Lieut.-Governor Hamilton, on hearing of this loss of the Illinois country and the partial defection to the Americans of the tribes west and southwest of Lake Michigan, at once set out to organize an army, chiefly composed of Indians, to retake the Illinois. He proceeded via the Wabash and Maumee, with eight hundred men, and recaptured Vincennes, December 17.

The intelligence of this movement of Hamilton was not long in reaching Clark at Kaskaskia, and he at once set out for Vincennes to fully realized the most sanguine expectations of those, who were acquainted with the adventurous and enterprising spirit of its commander; and was productive of essential benefit to the state, as well as of comparative security to the border settlements. Descending the Ohio river, from Fort Pitt to the Falls, he there landed his troops, and concealing his boats, marched directly towards Kaskaskias. Their provisions, which were carried on their backs, were soon exhausted; and for two days, the army subsisted entirely on roots. This was the only circumstance, which

recapture it. The march thither was one of the most heroic in American military annals. Hamilton surrendered to him, February 25, and was forwarded to Virginia as a prisoner. Early in 1780 he established Fort Jefferson, just below the mouth of the Ohio, and later in the season aided in repelling a body of British and Indians who had come to regain the Illinois country and attack the Spaniards at St. Louis. Leaving Colonel Montgomery to pursue the enemy up the Mississippi, Clark, with what force could be spared, hastened to Kentucky, where he quickly raised a thousand men, and invaded and laid waste the Shawnee villages, in retaliation for Capt. Henry Bird's invasion (see p. 262, *note*).

Later, he was engaged in some minor forays, and was appointed a brigadier-general; but his favorite scheme of an expedition to conquer Detroit miscarried, owing to the poverty of Virginia and the activity of the enemy under Brant, McKee, Girty, and other border leaders. In 1782 Clark led a thousand men in a successful campaign against the Indians on the Great Miami. This was his last important service, his subsequent expeditions proving failures. His later years were spent in poverty and seclusion, and his social habits became none of the best. In 1793 he imprudently accepted a commission as major-general from Genet, the French diplomatic agent, and essayed to raise a French revolutionary legion in the West to overcome the Spanish settlements on the Mississippi; upon Genet's recall, Clark's commission was canceled. Later, he sought to secure employment under the Spanish (see p. 130, *note*.) He died February 18, 1818, at Locust Grove, near Louisville, and lies buried at Cave Hill, in the Louisville suburbs. In his article on Clark, in Appleton's *Cyclop. of Amer. Biog.*, i., pp. 626, 627, Dr. Draper says: "Clark was tall and commanding, brave and full of resources, possessing the affection and confidence of his men. All that rich domain northwest of the Ohio was secured to the republic, at the peace of 1783, in consequence of his prowess." Cf. William F. Poole, in Winsor's *Narr. and Crit. Hist. Amer.*, vi., pp. 710–742. While due credit should be given to Clark for his daring and successful undertaking, we must not forget that England's jealousy of Spain, and shrewd diplomacy on the part of America's peace plenipotentiaries, were factors even more potent in winning the Northwest for the United States.—R. G. T.

occurred during their march, calculated to damp the ardor of the troops. No band of savage warriors, had interposed to check their progress,—no straggling Indian, had discovered their approach. These fortunate omens inspired them with flattering hopes; and they pushed forward, with augmented energy. Arriving before Kaskaskias in the night, they entered it, unseen and unheard, and took possession of the town and fort, without opposition. Relying on the thick and wide extended forests which interposed between them and the American settlements, the inhabitants had been lulled to repose by fancied security, and were unconscious of danger until it had become too late to be avoided. Not a single individual escaped, to spread the alarm in the adjacent settlements.

But there still remained other towns, higher up the Mississippi, which, if unconquered, would still afford shelter to the savages and furnish them the means of annoyance and of ravage. Against these, Colonel Clarke immediately directed [187] operations. Mounting a detachment of men, on horses found at Kaskaskias, and sending them forward, three other towns were reduced with equal success. The obnoxious governor at Kaskaskias was sent directly to Virginia, with the written instructions which he had received from Quebec, Detroit and Michillimacinac, for exciting the Indians to war, and remunerating them for the blood which they might shed.

Although the country within which Colonel Clarke had so successfully carried on operations, was considered to be within the limits of Virginia; yet as it was occupied by savages and those who were but little, if any, less hostile than they; and being so remote from her settlements, Virginia had as yet exercised no act of jurisdiction over it. But as it now belonged to her, by conquest as well as charter, the General Assembly created it into a distinct county, to be called Illinois; a temporary government was likewise established in it, and a regiment of infantry and a troop of cavalry, ordered to be enlisted for its defence, and placed under the command of its intrepid and enterprising conqueror.

The expedition directed under General McIntosh, was

not equally successful. The difficulty of raising, equipping, and organizing, so large a force as was placed under
his command, at so great a distance from the populous
district of the state, caused the consumption of so much
time, that the season for carrying on effective operations
had well nigh passed before he was prepared to commence
his march. Anxious however, to achieve as much as could
then be effected for the security of the frontier, he penetrated the enemy's country, as far as Tuscarawa, when it
was resolved to build and garrison a fort, and delay farther
operations 'till the ensuing spring. Fort Laurens was accordingly erected on the banks of the Tuscarawa, a garrison of one hundred and fifty men, under the command of
Colonel John Gibson, left for its preservation, and the main
army returned to Fort Pitt.

[188] CHAPTER XI.

No sooner had the adventurous advance of Col. Clarke, and the success with which it was crowned, become known at Detroit, than preparations were made to expel him from Kaskaskias, or capture his little army, and thus rid the country of this obstacle to the unmolested passage of the savages, to the frontier of Virginia. An army of six hundred men, principally Indians, led on by Hamilton, the governor of Detroit—a man at once bold and active, yet blood-thirsty and cruel, and well known as a chief instigator of the savages to war, and as a stay and prop of tories—left Detroit and proceeded towards the theatre of Clarke's renown. With this force, he calculated on being able to effect his purpose as regarded Col. Clarke and his little band of bold and daring adventurers, and to spread devastation and death along the frontier, from Kentucky to Pennsylvania. Arriving at Fort St. Vincent,[1] on the Wabash, about the middle of December, and deeming it too late to advance towards Kaskaskias, he repaired its battlements and converting it into a repository for war-like implements of every description, he detached the greater part of his force in marauding parties to operate against the settlements on the Ohio river, reserving for the security of his head quarters only one company of men.

While these alarming preparations were being made, Col. Clarke was actively engaged in acquiring an ascendency over the neighboring tribes of Indians; and in endeavors to attach them to the cause of the United States, from principle or fear. The aid which had been voted him, fell far short of [189] the contemplated assistance, and had not yet arrived; but his genius and activity amply compensated for the deficiency. In the heart of an

---

[1] Called by the English, Fort Sackville.—R. G. T.

17

Indian country,—remote from every succour,—and in the vicinity of powerful and hostile tribes, he yet not only maintained his conquest and averted injury, but carried terror and dismay into the very strongholds of the savages.   Intelligence of the movement of Hamilton at length reached him, and hostile parties of Indians soon hovered around Kaskaskias.   Undismayed by the tempest which was gathering over him, he concentrated his forces, withdrawing garrisons from the other towns to strengthen this, and made every preparation to enable him to endure a siege, and withstand the assault of a powerful army. The idea of abandoning the country never occurred to him.   He did not despair of being able to maintain his position, and he and his gallant band resolved that they would do it, or perish in the attempt.   In this fearful juncture, all was activity and industry, when the arrival of a Spanish merchant who had been at St. Vincents brought information of the reduced state of Hamilton's army.[1]   Convinced that a crisis had now arrived, Clarke resolved by one bold stroke to change the aspect of affairs, and instead of farther preparing to resist attack, himself to become the assailant.   For this purpose, a galley, mounting two four pounders and four swivels, and having on board a company of men, was despatched, with orders to the commanding officer, to ascend the Wabash and station himself a few miles below St. Vincents, allowing no one to pass him until the arrival of the main army.   Garrisoning Kaskaskias, with militia, and embodying the inhabitants for the protection of the other towns, Colonel Clarke set forward on his march across the country, on the 7th of February, 1779, at the head of one hundred and thirty brave and intrepid men.[2]

---

[1] From Clark's Journal: "January 29.—M. Vigo, a Spanish subject who had been at Post St. Vincents on his lawful business, arrived and gave us intelligence that Governor Hamilton, with thirty regulars and fifty volunteers and about 400 Indians, had arrived in November and taken that post with Capt. Helms and such other Americans who were there with arms, and disarmed the settlers and inhabitants."— R. G. T.

[2] Forty-six men, under Lieut. John Rogers, went with the artillery

Such was the inclemency of the weather, and so many and great the obstacles which interposed, that in despite of the ardor, perseverance and energy of the troops, they could yet advance very slowly towards the point of destination. They were five days in crossing the drowned lands of the Wabash, and for five miles had to wade through water and ice, frequently up to their breasts. They overcame every difficulty and arrived before St. Vincents on the evening of the twenty-third of February and almost simultaneously with the galley.

Thus far fortune seemed to favor the expedition. The army had not been discovered on its march, and the garrison was totally ignorant of its approach. Much however yet remained to be done. They had arrived within view of the enemy, but the battle was yet to be fought.

Sensible of the advantage to be derived from commencing the attack, while the enemy was ignorant of his approach, at seven o'clock he marched to the assault. The inhabitants instead of offering opposition, received the troops with gladness, and surrendering [190] the town, engaged with alacrity in the siege of the fort. For eighteen hours the garrison resisted the repeated onsets of the assailants; but during the night succeeding the commencement of the attack, Colonel Clarke had an entrenchment thrown up within rifle shot of the enemy's strongest battery, and in the morning, from this position, poured upon it such a well-directed shower of balls, that in fifteen minutes he silenced two pieces of cannon without sustaining any loss whatever. The advantages thus gained, induced Hamilton to demand a parley, intimating an intention of surrendering. The terms were soon arranged. The governor and garrison became prisoners of war, and a considerable quantity of military stores fell into the hands of the conqueror.[1]

---

and stores, in a large galley or batteau, called the "Willing." The distance to Vincennes by land, was a hundred and fifty miles.—R. G. T.

[1] The originals of the correspondence between Clark and Hamilton are, with much other MS. material relative to the movements of Clark, in possession of the Wisconsin Historical Society. Hamilton's letter, in a neat, scholarly hand, ran:

"Lieutenant Governor Hamilton proposes to Colonel Clark a Truce

During the continuance of the siege, Colonel Clarke received information that a party of Indians which had been detached by Hamilton to harrass the frontiers, was returning and then near to St. Vincents with two prisoners. He immediately ordered a detachment of his men to march out and give them battle—nine Indians were taken and the two prisoners released.

History records but few enterprises, which display as strikingly the prominent features of military greatness, and evince so much of the genius and daring which are necessary to their successful termination, as this; while the motives which led to its delineation, were such, as must excite universal admiration. Bold and daring, yet generous and disinterested, Colonel Clarke sought not his individual advancement in the projection or execution of this campaign. It was not to gratify the longings of ambition, or an inordinate love of fame, that prompted him to penetrate the Indian country to the Kaskaskias, nor that tempted him forth from thence, to war with the garrison at St. Vincent. He was not one of

---

· for three days, during which time he promises, there shall not be any defensive work carried on in the Garrison, on Condition Colo! Clark shall observe on his part a like cessation from any offensive Work—

"He further proposes that whatever may pass between them two and any persons (mutually agreed upon to be) present, shall remain secret, till matters be finally concluded—

" As he wishes that whatever the result of their conference may be the honor and credit of each party may be considered, so he wishes to confer with Colo! Clark as soon as may be—

" As Colo! Clark makes a difficulty of coming into the Garrison, L! G. Hamilton will speak with him before the Gate—

HENRY HAMILTON.

" Feb! 24ᵗʰ 1779—Fort Sackville—"

Clark's gruff reply, in rugged, but not unclerical chirography, was as follows:

"Colonel Clark's Compliments to M! Hamilton and begs leave to inform him that Co! Clark will not agree to any Other Terms than that of M! Hamilton's Surrendering himself and Garrison, Prisoners at Discretion—

" If M! Hamilton is Desirous of a Conferance with Co! Clark he will meet him at the Church with Capt? Helms—

" Feb! 24ᵗʰ, 1779.   G. R. CLARK."—R. G. T.

"Those worshippers of glory,
    Who bathe the earth in blood,
And launch proud names for an after age,
    Upon the crimson flood."

The distress and sufferings of the frontier of Virginia required that a period should speedily be put to them, to preserve the country from ravage and its inhabitants from butchery. Clarke had seen and participated in that distress and those sufferings, and put in requisition every faculty of his mind and all the energies of his body, to alleviate and prevent them. Providence smiled on his undertaking, and his exertions were crowned with complete success. The plan which had been concerted for the ensuing campaign against the frontier of Virginia, threatening to involve the whole country west of the Alleghany mountains in destruction and death, was thus happily frustrated; and he, who had been mainly instrumental in impelling the savages to war, and in permitting, if not instigating them to the commission of the most atrocious barbarities, was a prisoner in the hands of the enemy. So justly obnoxious had he [191] rendered himself by his conduct, that a more than ordinary rigor was practised upon him; and by the orders of the governor of Virginia, the governor of Detroit was manacled with irons, and confined in jail.[1]

Far different was the termination of the enterprise entrusted to the conduct of General McIntosh. It has been already seen that the approach of winter forced the main army to retire to the settlements into winter quarters, before they were able to accomplish any thing, but the erection of Fort Laurens.[2] Colonel Gibson, the commandant of the garrison, though a brave and enterprising officer, was so situated, that the preservation of the fort,

---

[1] Hamilton, in a letter of July 6, 1781, contained in the Haldimand Papers, in the British Museum, gives what he calls "a brief account" of his ill-starred expedition. See Roosevelt's *Winning of the West, passim.*—R. G. T.

[2] On the Tuscarawas River, about ten miles north of the present New Philadelphia, O., and a mile south of what is now Bolivar, Tuscarawas County. At the time Withers alludes to, it was garrisoned by 150 men under Col. John Gibson.—R. G. T.

was all which he could accomplish; and this was no little hazard of failure, from the very superior force of the enemy, and the scarcity of provisions for the subsistance of the garrison. So soon as the Indians became acquainted with the existence of a fort so far in their country, they put in practice those arts which enable them, so successfully to annoy their enemies.

Early in January, a considerable body of savages approached Fort Laurens unperceived and before the garrison was apprised that an Indian knew of its erection.[1] In the course of the night they succeeded in catching the horses outside of the fort; and taking off their bells, carried them into the woods, some distance off. They then concealed themselves in the prairie grass, along a path leading from the fort, and in the morning commenced rattling the bells, at the farther extremity of the line of ambushment, so as to induce the belief that the horses was there to be found. The stratagem succeeded. Sixteen men were sent out to bring in the horses. Allured by the sound of the bells, they kept the path, along which the Indians lay concealed, until they found themselves unexpectedly in the presence of an enemy, who opened upon them a destructive fire from front and rear. Fourteen were killed on the spot, and the remaining two were taken prisoners.

---

[1] Simon Girty and seventeen Indians, mostly Mingoes. Withers confounds this raid with the more formidable siege in February and March. In the January assault, Girty's band ambushed Capt. John Clark, a sergeant, and fourteen men, returning to Fort Pitt from convoying provisions to Fort Laurens. Two whites were killed, four wounded, and one taken prisoner. In February, came an attacking party of a hundred and twenty Indians (mostly Wyandots and Mingoes), led by Capt. Henry Bird, of the Eighth (or King's) Regiment; with him were Simon Girty and ten soldiers. The enemy arrived February 22, but remained in hiding. The next day Gibson sent out a guard of eighteen men, despite warnings of the enemy's presence, to assist the wagoner in collecting the horses of the fort. All the party were killed and scalped, within sight of the fort, save two, who were made prisoners. The fort was then openly invested until March 20, when the besiegers withdrew, torn with dissensions and short of supplies. See Butterfield's *Washington-Irvine Correspondence* for further details.—R. G. T.

On the evening of the day on which this unfortunate surprise took place, the Indian army, consisting of eight hundred and forty-seven warriors, painted and equipped for war, marched in single file through a prairie near the fort and in full view of the garrison, and encamped on an adjacent elevation on the opposite side of the river. From this situation, frequent conversations were held by them with the whites, in which they deprecated the longer continuance of hostilities, but yet protested against the encroachment made upon their territory by the whites, the erection of a fort and the garrisoning soldiers within their country, not only unpermitted by them, but for some time before they knew any thing of it. For these infringements on their rights, they were determined on prosecuting the war, and continued the investure of the fort, for six weeks. In this time they became straitened for provisions, and aware that without a fresh supply of them, they would be forced to abandon the siege, they sent word to the commander of the garrison, by a Delaware [192] Indian, calling himself John Thompson, (who, though with the whites in the fort, was permitted by both parties to go in and out, as he choose) that they were desirous of peace, and were willing to enter into a negotiation, if he would send them a barrel of flour and some tobacco. Scarce as these articles had actually become in the garrison, yet Col. Gibson complied with their request, hoping that they might be induced to make peace, or withdraw from the fort, and hopeless of timely succours from the settlements. Upon the receipt of those presents, the Indians raised the siege and marched their army off, much to the relief of the garrison, although they did not fulfil their promise of entering into a treaty.

During the time the Indians remained about the fort, there was much sickness in the garrison; and when they were believed to have retired, the commandant detached Col. Clarke, of the Pennsylvania line,[1] with a party of fifteen men, to escort the invalids to Fort McIntosh. They proceeded but a small distance from the gate, where they

---

[1] Not to be confounded with George Rogers Clark, of Kentucky.— R. G. T.

were attacked by some Indians, who had been left concealed near the fort, for the purpose of effecting farther mischief. A skirmish ensued; but overpowered by numbers and much galled by the first fire, Col. Clarke could not maintain the conflict. With much difficulty, he and three others reached the fort in safety: the rest of the party were all killed.

Col. Gibson immediately marched out at the head of the greater part of the garrison, but the Indians had retreated as soon as they succeeded in cutting off the detachment under Col. Clarke, and prudence forbade to proceed in pursuit of them, as the main army was believed to be yet in the neighborhood. The dead were however brought in, and buried with the honors of war, in front of the fort gate.

In a few days after this, Gen. McIntosh arrived with a considerable body of troops and a supply of provisions for the garrison. While the savages were continuing the siege, a friendly Indian, had been despatched by Col. Gibson to acquaint Gen. McIntosh with the situation at Fort Laurens, and that without the speedy arrival of a reinforcement of men and an accession to their stock of provisions, the garrison would have to surrender; or seek a doubtful safety, by evacuating the fort and endeavoring to regain the Ohio river, in the presence of an overwhelming body of the enemy. With great promptitude the settlers flocked to the standard of Gen. McIntosh, and loading pack horses, with abundance of provisions for the supply of the garrison at Fort Laurens, commenced a rapid march to their relief. Before their arrival, they had been relieved from the most pressing danger, by the withdrawal of the Indian army; and were only suffering from the want of flour and meat. A manifestation of the great joy felt upon the arrival of Gen. McIntosh, had well nigh deprived them of the benefit to be derived from the provisions brought for them. When the relief army approached the fort, a salute was fired by the garrison, which, alarming the pack horses, caused them [193] to break loose and scatter the greater part of the flour in every direction through the woods, so that it was impossible to be again collected.

The remains of those, who had unfortunately fallen into the ambuscade in January, and which had lain out until then, were gathered together and buried;[1] and a fresh detachment, under Major Vernon, being left to garrison the fort, in the room of that which had been stationed there during winter, Gen. McIntosh, withdrew from the country and returned to Fort McIntosh. In the ensuing fall, Fort Laurens was entirely evacuated; the garrison having been almost reduced to starvation, and it being found very difficult to supply them with provisions at so great a distance from the settlements and in the heart of the Indian country.

During the year 1778, Kentucky was the theatre of many outrages. In January, a party of thirty men, among whom was Daniel Boone, repaired to the "Lower Blue Licks" for the purpose of making salt; and on the 7th of February, while Boone was alone in the woods, on a hunt to supply the salt makers with meat, he was encountered by a party of one hundred and two Indians and two Canadians, and made prisoner. The savages advanced to the Licks, and made prisoners of twenty-seven of those engaged in making salt.[2] Their object in this incursion, was

---

[193] [1] The bodies of these men were found to have been much devoured by the wolves, and bearing the appearance of having been recently torn by them. With a view of taking revenge on these animals for devouring their companions, the fatigue party sent to bury their remains, after digging a grave sufficiently capacious to contain all, and having deposited them in it, they covered the pit with slender sticks, bark and rotten wood, too weak to bear the weight of a wolf, and placed a piece of meat on the top and near the center of this covering, as a bait. In the morning seven wolves were found in the pit, and killed and the grave then filled up.

[2] Boone had left Boonesborough January 8, in charge of thirty men, to make salt at the Lower Blue Licks, on Licking River. They carried with them, on horses, several large boiling pans, given to the settlement by the government of Virginia. So weak was the water there, that 840 gallons were necessary to make a bushel of salt, against ninety at the Kanawha salines, and forty at Onondaga. While the salt-makers were at work, two or three others of the party served as scouts and hunters; generally, Boone was one of these. This day (Saturday, February 7) Boone started out alone with his pack-horse for a supply of game, which

the destruction of Boonesborough; and had they continued their march thither, there is no doubt but that
place, weakened as it was by the loss of so many of its
men and not expecting an attack at that inclement season,
would have fallen into their hands; but elated with their
success, the Indians marched directly back with their
prisoners to Chillicothe. The extreme suffering of the

usually was plenty in the neighborhood of the salt licks; Thomas
Brooks and Flanders Callaway, his fellow scouts, were taking another
circuit. Having killed a buffalo, Boone was on his way home in the
afternoon, with the choicest of the meat packed upon his horse. Snow
was falling fast, and he was ten miles from camp, when discovered by
four Indians, outlying members of a large party of Shawnees under
Munseka and Black Fish, who had taken the war-path to avenge the murder of Cornstalk (see p. 172, *note*. 2). Benumbed by cold, and unable
easily to untie or cut the frozen thongs which bound on the pack, Boone
could not unload and mount the horse, and after a sharp skirmish
was captured, and led to the main Indian encampment, a few miles
away. Boone induced his fellow salt-makers to surrender peaceably the
following day (February 8); the number of prisoners was, including
Boone, twenty-seven—two scouts and two salt-packers being absent.
After a ten days' "uncomfortable journey, in very severe weather,"
says Boone, in which they "received as good treatment as prisoners
could expect from savages," the party arrived at Little Chillicothe, on
Little Miami—so called in contradistinction to Old Chillicothe, on the
Scioto. Boone's strong, compact build caused the Indians to call him
Big Turtle, and under that name he was adopted as the son of Black
Fish, who took a fancy to him; sixteen of his companions were also
adopted by other warriors. The ten who were not adopted were, with
Boone, taken on a trip to Detroit (starting March 10), guarded by forty
Indians under Black Fish. The ten were sold to Lieut. Governor Hamilton and citizens of Detroit, for £20 each, the usual price for American
prisoners. Boone remained in Detroit until April 10, during which he
was treated with great courtesy by Hamilton, who offered Black Fish
£100 for him, but the latter declined and took the great pioneer home
with him; but Boone himself was given by Hamilton a horse and trappings, with silver trinkets to give to the Indians. At Little Chillicothe,
Boone was kindly treated by Black Fish, and little by little his liberty
was extended. June 16, while the family were making salt on the
Scioto, preparatory to another expedition against Boonesborough, Boone
escaped on the horse given him by Hamilton. After many curious
adventures, in the course of which he swam the Ohio, he safely reached
Boonesborough, June 20, having traveled, he estimated, a hundred and
sixty miles in four days. Boone's wife and family, supposing him dead,
had returned to their old home in North Carolina, but Boone himself
remained to assist in the defense of Boonesborough against the impending attack, of which he had brought intelligence.—R. G. T.

prisoners, during this march, inspired the savages with pity, and induced them to exercise an unusual lenity towards their captives. In March, Boone was carried to Detroit, where the Indians refused to liberate him, though an hundred pounds were offered for his ransom, and from which place he accompanied them back to Chillicothe in the latter part of April. In the first of June, he went with them to the Scioto salt springs, and on his return found one hundred and fifty choice warriors of the Shawanee nation, painting, arming, and otherwise equipping themselves to proceed again to the attack of Boonesborough.

[194] Hitherto Boone had enjoyed as much satisfaction, as was consistent with his situation, and more than would have been experienced by the most of men, in captivity to the Indians; but when he found such great preparations making for an attack on the place which contained all that he held most dear, his love of family, his attachment to the village reared under his superintending hand, and to its inhabitants protected by his fostering care, determined him to attempt an immediate escape. Early on the morning of the 16th of June, he went forth as usual to hunt. He had secreted as much food as would serve him for one meal, and with· this scanty supply, he resolved on finding his way home. On the 20th, having travelled a distance of one hundred and sixty miles, crossed the Ohio and other rivers, and with no sustenance, save what he had taken with him from Chillicothe, he arrived at Boonesborough. The fort was quickly repaired, and every preparation made to enable it to withstand a siege.

In a few days after, another, of those who had been taken prisoners at the Blue Licks, escaped, and brought intelligence that in consequence of the flight of Boone, the Indians had agreed to postpone their meditated irruption, for three weeks.[1] This intelligence determined Boone

---

[1] This was William Hancock, who had, like Boone, been adopted into an Indian family. Not so expert a woodsman as Boone, he had consumed twelve days in the journey from Chillicothe to Boonesborough, and suffered great hardships. He arrived at the fort July 17. In consequence of Boone's escape, he reported, the Indians had postponed

to invade the Indian country, and at the head of only ten men he went forth on an expedition against Paint creek town. Near to this place, he met with a party of Indians going to join the main army, then on its march to Boonesborough, whom he attacked and dispersed without sustaining any loss on his part. The enemy had one killed and two severely wounded in this skirmish; and lost their horses and baggage. On their return, they passed the Indian army on the 6th of August, and on the next day entered Boonesborough.[1]

On the 8th of August, the Indian army, consisting of four hundred and fifty men, and commanded by Capt. Du Quesne, eleven other Frenchmen, and their own chiefs, appeared before the Fort and demanded its surrender.[2] In order to gain time, Boone requested two days' consideration, and at the expiration of that period, returned for answer, that the garrison had resolved on defending it, while one individual remained alive within its walls.

Capt. Du Quesne then made known, that he was charged by Gov. Hamilton, to make prisoners of the gar-

---

their intended attack for three weeks. The next day (July 18), Boone wrote to Arthur Campbell, lieutenant of Washington County, Va. (the Holston settlements, 200 miles away), that he expected the enemy in twelve days, and that the fort was prepared for a siege of three or four weeks; but relief would then be of infinite service.—R. G. T.

[1] At the close of six weeks after Hancock's arrival, Boone had become weary of waiting for the enemy, hence his expedition with nineteen men—not ten, as in the text—against the Shawnee town on Paint Creek, during the last week of August. It was the 5th of September when, undiscovered, he passed the Indian force encamped at Lower Blue Licks, and the next day arrived at Boonesborough.—R. G. T.

[2] About 10 A. M. of Monday, September 7,—Withers places it a month, less a day, too early,—the hostiles crossed the Kentucky a mile and a half above Boonesborough, at a point since known as Black Fish's Ford, and soon made their appearance marching single file, some of them mounted, along the ridge south of the fort. They numbered about 400, and displayed English and French flags. The strength of the force has been variously estimated, from 330 Indians and 8 Frenchmen (Col. John Bowman), to 444 Indians and 12 Frenchmen (Boone's Narrative, by Filson). The English Indian department was represented by Capt. Isidore Chêne, who had with him several other French-Canadians; there was also a negro named Pompey, who had long lived with the Indians, and served them as interpreter; the principal chiefs were, Black Fish, Moluntha, Black Hoof, and Black Beard.—R. G. T.

rison, but not to treat them harshly; and that if nine of their principal men would come out, and negotiate a treaty, based on a renunciation of allegiance to the United States, and on a renewal of their fealty to the king, the Indian army should be instantly withdrawn. Boone did not confide in the sincerity of the Frenchman, but he determined to gain the advantage of farther preparation for resistance, by delaying the attack. He consented to negotiate on the terms proposed; but suspecting treachery, insisted that the conference should be held near the fort walls. The garrison were on the alert, while the negotiation continued, and did not fail to remark that many of the Indians, not [195] concerned in making the treaty, were stalking about, under very suspicious circumstances. The terms on which the savage army was to retire were at length agreed upon, and the articles signed, when the whites were told that it was an Indian custom, in ratification of compacts, that two of their chiefs should shake hands with one white man. Boone and his associates, consenting to conform to this custom, not without suspicion of a sinister design, were endeavored to be dragged off as prisoners by the savages; but strong and active, they bounded from their grasp, and entered the gate, amid a heavy shower of balls—one only of the nine, was slightly wounded. The Indians then commenced a furious assault on the fort, but were repulsed with some loss on their part; and every renewed attempt to carry it by storm, was in like manner, frustrated by the intrepidity and gallantry of its inmates.[1]

Disappointed in their expectation of succeeding in this way, the savages next attempted to undermine the fort, commencing at the water mark of the Kentucky river, only sixty yards from the walls. This course was no doubt dictated to them by their French commanders, as they are ignorant of the practice of war, farther than

---

[1] The garrison numbered, old and young, white and black, sixty persons capable of bearing arms; only forty, however, were really effective. Women and children, dressed and armed as men, frequently appeared upon the walls, to give an appearance of greater strength.— R. G. T.

depends on the use of the gun, and tomahawk, and the exercise of stratagem and cunning. The vigilance of the besieged however, soon led to a discovery of the attempt— the water below, was colored by the clay thrown out from the excavation, while above it retained its usual transparency; and here again they were foiled by the active exertion of the garrison. A countermine was begun by them, the earth from which being thrown over the wall, manifested the nature of their operations, and led the enemy to raise the siege, and retire from the country.[1]

In the various assaults made on the fort by this savage army, two only, of the garrison, were killed, and four wounded. The loss of the enemy, as usual, could not be properly ascertained: thirty-seven were left dead on the field, and many, were no doubt wounded.[2]

So signally was the savage army repulsed, in their repeated attacks on Boonesborough, that they never afterwards made any great effort to effect its reduction. The heroism and intrepidity of Boone and his assistants rendered it impregnable to their combined exertions to demolish it; while the vigilance and caution of the inhabitants, convinced them, that it would be fruitless and unavailing to devise plans for gaining admission into the fort, by stratagem or wile. Still however, they kept up a war of ravage and murder, against such as were unfortunately found defenceless and unprotected; and levelled combined operations against other and weaker positions.

[196] The success of the expedition under Col. Clarke, though productive of many and great advantages to the

---

[1] This ruse of the Indians was discovered on Friday, the 11th. The garrison commenced its countermine immediately, and prosecuted the work for several days. The rival parties could hear each other at work underground. When the Indians had proceeded about forty yards, two-thirds of the distance from the river bank, successive rainstorms had so saturated the earth that sections of their tunnel caved in, and this it was that frustrated their scheme.—R. G. T.

[195] [2] When the Indians retired from before Boonesboro, one hundred and twenty-five pounds weight of bullets were picked up by the garrison, besides many that stuck in the logs of the fort. A conclusive proof that the Indians were not idle, during the continuance of the siege.

frontier inhabitants, did not achieve for them, an unmolested security. Their property was still liable to plunder, and families newly arrived among them, to be murdered or taken prisoners. Combined efforts were required, to put a period to savage aggression; and a meeting of the settlers was held at Harrodsburg, to concert measures to effect that object. Their consultation resulted in a determination, to carry the war into the enemy's country; and as the Shawanees had been most efficient in waging hostilities, it was resolved to commence operations, against their most considerable town. Two hundred volunteers were accordingly raised, and when rendezvoused at Harrodsburg, were placed under the command of Col. Bowman, and proceeded against Chillicothe.[1]

The expedition thus fitted out, arrived, by forced marches, near to Chillicothe in the evening towards the latter end of July, 1779; and on deliberation, it was agreed to defer the attack 'till next morning. Before dawn the army was drawn up and arranged in order of battle. The right wing led on by Col. Bowman, was to assume a posi-

---

[1] John Bowman, of Harrodsburgh, was lieutenant of Kentucky County, and colonel of its militia. During the spring of 1779, there was a general desire to raid the unsuspecting Shawnees, in retaliation for their invasions of Kentucky, and Bowman decided to command in person this "first regular enterprise to attack, in force, the Indians beyond the Ohio, ever planned in Kentucky." The company of volunteers of the interior rendezvoused in May at Harrodsburgh, and under Capts. Benjamin Logan and Silas Harlan marched to Lexington, where they met the Boonesborough company under Capt. John Holder, and another party under Capt. Levi Todd. At the mouth of the Licking (site of Covington, Ky.), the general rendezvous agreed on, they found a company from the Falls of the Ohio (site of Louisville), under Capt. William Harrod. Also in the little army, which finally mustered 297 men, including officers, were frontiersmen from Redstone Old Fort, and other settlements in the valleys of the Ohio and Monongahela. The Redstone men were on their way home, when they heard of the expedition, and joined it at the Licking; they had been on a visit to Big Bone Lick, and had a canoe-load of relics therefrom, which they were transporting up river. The force crossed the Ohio, May 28, just below the mouth of the Licking; 32 men remained behind in charge of the boats, leaving 265 to set out for the Shawnee town of Little Chillicothe, on the Little Miami, distant about sixty-five miles northeast. George Clark and William Whitley were pilots, and George M. Bedinger adjutant and quartermaster.—R. G. T.

tion on one side of the town, and the left, under Capt. Logan, was to occupy the ground on the opposite side; and at a given signal, both were to develope to the right and left, so as to encircle and attack it in concert.[1] The party, led on by Logan, repaired to the point assigned, and was waiting in anxious, but vain expectation for the signal of attack to be given, when the attention of the Indians was directed towards him by the barking of their dogs. At this instant a gun was discharged by one of Bowman's men, and the whole village alarmed. The squaws and children were hurried into the woods, along a path not yet occupied by the assailants, and the warriors collected in a strong cabin.[2] Logan, being near enough to perceive every movement of the enemy, ordered his men quietly to occupy the deserted huts, as a momentary shelter from the Indian fires, until Col. Bowman should march forward. It was now light; and the savages began a regular discharge of shot at his men, as they advanced to the deserted cabins. This determined him to move directly to the attack of the cabin, in which the warriors were assembled; and ordering his men to tear off the doors and hold them in front, as a shield, while advancing to the assault, he was already marching on the foe, when he was overtaken by an order from Col. Bowman, to retreat.

Confounded by this command, Capt. Logan was for a time reluctant to obey it; a retreat was however, directed; and each individual, sensible of his great exposure while retiring from the towns, sought to escape from danger, in the manner directed by his own judgment; and fled to the woods at his utmost speed. There they rallied, and resumed

---

[1] Without having seen an Indian, the expedition arrived in sight of Little Chillicothe, at dusk of May 29—Withers places the date two months ahead of the actual time. Capt. Logan had charge of the left wing, Harrod of the right, and Holder of the center. The white force now numbered 263—two men having returned to the boats, disabled; the Indians numbered about 100 warriors and 200 squaws and children. Black Fish was the principal village chief, and subordinate to him were Black Hoof and Black Beard.—R. G. T.

[2] This was the council house, which was so stoutly defended that the white assailants were glad to take refuge in a neighboring hut, from which they escaped with difficulty.—R. G. T.

more of order, though still too much terrified to stand a
contest, when the Indians sallied out to give battle. Intimidated by the apprehension of danger, which they had
not seen, [197] but supposed to be great from the retreating order of Col. Bowman, they continued to fly before
the savages, led on by their chief, the Black Fish. At
length they were brought to a halt, and opened a brisk,
though inefficient fire, upon their pursuers. Protected by
bushes, the Indians maintained their ground, 'till Capts.
Logan and Harrod, with some of the men under their
immediate command, mounted on pack horses, charged
them with great spirit, and dislodged them from their
covert. Exposed in turn to the fire of the whites, and seeing their chief fall, the savages took to flight, and Col.
Bowman continued his retreat homeward, free from farther
interruption.[1]

In this illy conducted expedition, Col. Bowman had
nine of his men killed and one wounded. The Indian loss
was no doubt less: only two or three were known to be
killed. Had the commanding officer, instead of ordering
a retreat when Logan's men were rushing bravely to the
conflict, marched with the right wing of the army to their
aid, far different would have been the result. The enemy,
only thirty strong, could not long have held out, against

---

[1] The chief cause of alarm, and the consequent disorder, was a false
report started among the whites, that Simon Girty and a hundred Shawnees from the Indian village of Piqua, twelve miles distant, were marching to the relief of Black Fish. Order was soon restored, and when,
fourteen miles out upon the homeward trail, Indians were discovered
upon their rear, the enemy were met with vigor, and thereafter the retreat was unhampered. The force reached the Ohio, just above the
mouth of the Little Miami, early on June 1. The "pack-horses" alluded
to by Withers, were 163 Indian ponies captured in the Chillicothe
woods; the other plunder was considerable, being chiefly silver ornaments and clothing. After crossing the Ohio in boats—the horses swimming—there was an auction of the booty, which was appraised at
£32,000, continental money, each man getting goods or horses to the value
of about £110. The Indian loss was five killed at the town, and many
wounded; the whites had seven men killed. Little Chillicothe had
been for the most part destroyed by fire, and its crops destroyed. The
newspapers of the day regarded the expedition as an undoubted success.—R. G. T.

18

the bravery and impetuosity of two hundred backwoods-
men, stimulated to exertion by repeated suffering, and
nerved by the reflection, that they were requiting it upon
its principal authors.   Col. Bowman doubtless believed
that he was pursuing a proper course.   The gallantry and
intrepidity, displayed by him on many occasions, forbid
the supposition that he was under the influence of any un-
military feeling, and prompted to that course by a disposition to shrink from ordinary dangers.   His motives were
certainly pure, and his subsequent exertions to rally his
men and bring them to face the foe, were as great as could
have been made by any one; but disheartened by the fear
of unreal danger, and in the trepidation of a flight, deemed
to be absolutely necessary for their safety, they could not
be readily brought to bear the brunt of battle.   The efforts
of a few cool and collected individuals, drove back the
pursuers, and thus prevented an harrassed retreat.

   Notwithstanding the frequent irruptions of the Indians, and the constant exposure of the settlers to suffering and danger, Kentucky increased rapidly in population.
From the influx of emigrants during the fall and winter
months, the number of its inhabitants were annually
doubled for some years; and new establishments were
made in various parts of the country.   In April 1779, a
block house was erected on the present site of Lexington,[1]
and several stations were selected in its vicinity, and in the
neighborhood of the present town of Danville.   Settlements were also made, in that year, on the waters of Bear
Grass, Green and Licking rivers, and parts of the country
began to be distinguished by their interior and frontier
situation.

---

   [1] George W. Ranck: "April 1. Robert Patterson, at the head of
twenty-five men, commenced a block house where Lexington now
stands."—R. G. T.

In North Western Virginia, the frequent inroads of small parties of savages in 1778, led to greater preparations for security, from renewed hostilities after the winter should have passed away; and many settlements received a considerable accession to their strength, from the number of persons emigrating to them. In some neighborhoods, the sufferings of the preceding season and the inability of the inhabitants, from the paucity of their numbers, to protect themselves from invasion, led to a total abandonment of their homes. The settlement on Hacker's creek was entirely broken up in the spring of 1779,—some of its inhabitants forsaking the country and retiring east of the mountains; while the others went to the fort on Buchannon, and to Nutter's fort, near Clarksburg, to aid in resisting the foe and in maintaining possession of the country. When the campaign of that year opened, the whole frontier was better prepared to protect itself from invasion and to shield its occupants from the wrath of the savage enemy, than it had ever been, since it became the abode of white men. There were forts in every settlement, into which the people could retire when danger threatened, and which were capable of withstanding the assaults of savages, however furious they might be, if having to depend for success, on the use of small arms only. It was fortunate for the country, that this was their dependence. A few well directed shots even from small cannon, would have demolished [199] their strongest fortress, and left them no hope from death, but captivity.

In the neighborhood of Pricket's fort, the inhabitants were early alarmed, by circumstances which induced a belief that the Indians were near, and they accordingly entered that garrison. It was soon evident that their fears were groundless, but as the season was fast approaching, when the savages might be expected to commence depredations, they determined on remaining in the fort, of a night, and yet prosecute the business of their farms as usual during the day. Among those who were at this time in the fort, was David Morgan, (a relation of General Daniel Morgan,) then upwards of sixty years of age. Early in April, being himself unwell, he sent his two children—Stephen, a youth of sixteen, and Sarah, a girl of fourteen—to feed the cattle at his farm, about a mile off. The children, thinking to remain all day and spend the time in preparing ground for water melons, unknown to their father took with them some bread and meat. Having fed the stock, Stephen set himself to work, and while he was engaged in grubbing, his sister would remove the brush, and otherwise aid him in the labor of clearing the ground; occasionally going to the house to wet some linen which she had spread out to bleach. Morgan, after the children had been gone some time, betook himself to bed, and soon falling asleep, dreamed that he saw Stephen and Sarah walking about the fort yard, scalped. Aroused from slumber by the harrowing spectacle presented to his sleeping view, he enquired if the children had returned, and upon learning they had not, he set out to see what detained them, taking with him his gun. As he approached the house, still impressed with the horrible fear that he should find his dream realized, he ascended an eminence, from which he could distinctly see over his plantation, and descrying from thence the objects of his anxious solicitude, he proceeded directly to them, and seated himself on an old log, near at hand. He had been here but a few minutes, before he saw two Indians come out from the house and make toward the children. Fearing to alarm them too much, and thus deprive them of the power of exerting themselves ably to make an escape, he apprized them in a careless manner, of their danger, and told them to run towards the fort—himself still maintaining his seat on the log. The Indians then raised a hideous yell and ran in pursuit; but the old [200] gentleman shewing himself at that instant, caused them to forbear the chase, and shelter themselves behind trees. He then endeavored to effect an escape, by flight, and the Indians followed after him. Age and consequent infirmity, rendered him unable long to continue out of their reach; and aware that they were gaining considerably on him, he wheeled to shoot. Both instantly sprang behind trees, and Morgan seeking shelter in the same manner, got behind a sugar, which was so small as to leave part of his body exposed. Looking round, he saw a large oak about twenty yards farther, and he made to it. Just as he reached it, the foremost Indian sought security behind the sugar sapling, which he had found insufficient for his protection. The Indian, sensible that it would not shelter him, threw himself down by the side of a log which lay at the root of the sapling. But this did not afford him sufficient cover, and Morgan, seeing him exposed to a shot, fired at him. The ball took effect, and the savage, rolling over on his back, stabbed himself twice in the breast.

Having thus succeeded in killing one of his pursuers, Morgan again took to flight, and the remaining Indian after him. It was now that trees could afford him no security—His gun was unloaded, and his pursuer could approach him safely.—The unequal race was continued about sixty yards, when looking over his shoulder, he saw the savage within a few paces of him, and with his gun raised. Morgan sprang to one side, and the ball whizzed harmlessly by him. The odds was now not great, and both advanced to closer combat, sensible of the prize for which they had to contend, and each determined, to deal death to his adversary. Morgan aimed a blow with his gun; but the Indian hurled a tomahawk at him, which cutting the little finger of his left hand entirely off, and injuring the one next it very much, knocked the gun out of his grasp, and they closed. Being a good wrestler, Morgan succeeded in throwing the Indian; but soon found himself overturned, and the savage upon him, feeling for his knife and sending forth a most horrifick yell, as is their custom when they consider victory as secure. A woman's apron, which he had taken from the house and fastened round him above his knife, so hindered him in getting at it quickly, that Morgan, getting one of his fingers in his

mouth, deprived him of the use of that hand, and discon-
certed him very much by continuing to grind it between
his teeth. At length the [201] Indian got hold of his
knife, but so far towards the blade, that Morgan too got a
small hold on the extremity of the handle; and as the Indian drew it from the scabbard, Morgan, biting his finger
with all his might, and thus causing him somewhat to relax his grasp, drew it through his hand, gashing it most
severely.

By this time both had gained their feet, and the Indian, sensible of the great advantage gained over him,
endeavored to disengage himself; but Morgan held fast to
the finger, until he succeeded in giving him a fatal stab,
and felt the almost lifeless body sinking in his arms. He
then loosened his hold and departed for the fort.

On his way he met with his daughter, who not being
able to keep pace with her brother, had followed his footsteps to the river bank where he had plunged in, and was
then making her way to the canoe. Assured thus far of
the safety of his children, he accompanied his daughter to
the fort, and then, in company with a party of the men,
returned to his farm, to see if there were any appearance
of other Indians being about there. On arriving at the
spot where the desperate struggle had been, the wounded
Indian was not to be seen; but trailing him by the blood
which flowed profusely from his side, they found him concealed in the branches of a fallen tree.—He had taken the
knife from his body, bound up the wound with the apron,
and on their approaching him, accosted them familiarly,
with the salutation " How do do broder, how do broder."
Alas! poor fellow! their brotherhood extended no farther
than to the gratification of a vengeful feeling. He was
tomahawked and scalped; and, as if this would not fill
the measure of their vindictive passions, both he and his
companion were flayed, their skins tanned and converted
into saddle seats, shot pouches and belts—A striking instance of the barbarities, which a revengeful spirit will
lead its possessors to perpetrate.[1]

<hr>

[1] L. V. McWhorter, of Berlin, W. Va., writes me: "A few years
ago, the descendants of David Morgan erected a monument on the spot

The alarm which had caused the people in the neighborhood of Pricket's fort, to move into it for safety, induced two or three families on Dunkard creek to collect at the house of Mr. Bozarth, thinking they would be more exempt from danger when together, than if remaining at their several homes. About the first of April, when only Mr. Bozarth and two men were in the house, the children, who had been out at play, came running into the yard, exclaiming that there were [202] *"ugly red men coming."* Upon hearing this, one of the two men in the house, going to the door to see if Indians really were approaching, received a glancing shot on his breast, which caused him to fall back. The Indian who had shot him, sprang in immediately after, and grappling with the other white man, was quickly thrown on the bed. His antagonist having no weapon with which to do him any injury called to Mrs. Bozarth for a knife. Not finding one at hand, she siezed an axe, and at one blow, let out the brains of the prostrate savage. At that instant a second Indian entering the door, shot dead the man engaged with his companion on the bed. Mrs. Bozarth turned on him, and with a well directed blow, let out his entrails and caused him to bawl out for help. Upon this, others of his party, who had been engaged with the children in the yard, came to his relief. The first who thrust his head in at the door, had it cleft by the axe of Mrs. Bozarth and fell lifeless on the ground. Another, catching hold of his wounded, bawling companion, drew him out of the house, when Mrs. Bozarth, with the aid of the white man who had been first shot and was then somewhat recovered, succeeded in closing and making fast the door. The children in the yard were all killed, but the heroism and exertions of Mrs. Bozarth and the wounded white man, enabled them to resist the re-

---

where fell one of the Indians. On the day of the unveiling of the monument, there was on exhibition at the spot, a shot-pouch and saddle skirt made from the skins of the Indians. Greenwood S. Morgan, a great-grandson of the Indian slayer, informs me that the shot-pouch is now in the possession of a distant relative, living in Wetzel County, W. Va. The knife with which the Indian was killed, is owned by Morgan's descendants in Marion County, W. Va."—R. G. T.

peated attempts of the Indians, to force open the door, and to maintain possession of the house, until they were relieved by a party from the neighboring settlement.— The time occupied in this bloody affair, from the first alarm by the children to the shutting of the door, did not exceed three minutes. And in this brief space, Mrs. Bozarth, with infinite self possession, coolness and intrepidity, succeeded in killing three Indians.

On the eleventh of the same month, five Indians came to a house on Snowy creek, (in the, now, county of Preston,) in which lived James Brain and Richard Powell, and remained in ambush during the night, close around it. In the morning early, the appearance of some ten or twelve men, issuing from the house with guns, for the purpose of amusing themselves in shooting at a mark, deterred the Indians from making their meditated attack. The men seen by them, were travellers, who had associated for mutual security, and who, after partaking of a morning's repast, resumed their journey, unknown to the savages; when Mr. Brain and the sons of Mr. Powell [203] went to their day's work. Being engaged in carrying clap-boards for covering a cabin, at some distance from the house, they were soon heard by the Indians, who, despairing of succeeding in an attack on the house, changed their position, & concealed themselves by the side of the path, along which those engaged at work had to go. Mr. Brain and one of his sons being at a little distance in front of them, they fired and Brain fell. He was then tomahawked and scalped, while another of the party followed and caught the son as he was attempting to escape by flight.

Three other boys were then some distance behind and out of sight, and hearing the report of the gun which killed Brain, for an instant supposed that it proceeded from the rifle of some hunter in quest of deer. They were soon satisfied that this supposition was unfounded. Three Indians came running towards them, bearing their guns in one hand, and tomahawks in the other. One of the boys stupefied by terror,—and unable to stir from the spot, was immediately made prisoner. Another, the son of Powell, was also soon caught; but the third, finding himself out

of sight of his pursuer, ran to one side and concealed him
self in a bunch of alders, where he remained until the Indian passed the spot where he lay, when he arose, and
taking a different direction, ran with all his speed, and effected an escape. The little prisoners were then brought
together; and one of Mr. Powell's sons, being discovered
to have but one eye, was stripped naked, had a tomahawk
sunk into his head, a spear ran through his body, and the
scalp then removed from from his bleeding head.

The little Powell who had escaped from the savages,
being forced to go a direction opposite to the house, proceeded to a station about eight miles off, & communicated
intelligence of what had been done at Brain's. A party
of men equipped themselves and went immediately to the
scene of action; but the Indians had hastened homeward,
as soon as they perpetrated their horrid cruelties. One
of their little captives, (Benjamin Brain) being asked by
them, "how many men were at the house," replied
"twelve." To the question, "how far from thence was
the nearest fort," he answered "two miles." Yet he well
knew that there was no fort, nearer than eight miles, and
that there was not a man at the house,—Mr. Powell being
from home, and the twelve travellers having departed, before his father and he had gone out to [204] work. His
object was to save his mother and the other women and
children, from captivity or death, by inducing them to
believe that it would be extremely dangerous to venture
near the house. He succeeded in the attainment of his
object. Deterred by the prospect of being discovered, and
perhaps defeated by the superior force of the white men,
represented to be at Mr. Brain's, they departed in the
greatest hurry, taking with them their two little prisoners,
Benjamin and Isaac Brain.

So stilly had the whole affair been conducted (the report of a gun being too commonly heard to excite any suspicion of what was doing,) and so expeditiously had the
little boy who escaped, and the men who accompanied
him back, moved in their course, that the first intimation
given Mrs. Brain of the fate of her husband, was given by
the men who came in pursuit.

Soon after the happening of this affair, a party of Indians came into the Buchannon settlement, and made prisoner Leonard Schoolcraft, a youth of about sixteen, who had been sent from the fort on some business.—When arrived at their towns and arrangements being made for his running the gauntlet, he was told that he might defend himself against the blows of the young Indians who were to pursue him to the council house. Being active and athletic, he availed himself of this privilege, so as to save himself from the beating which he would otherwise have received, and laying about him with well timed blows, frequently knocked down those who came near to him— much to the amusement of the warriors, according to the account given by others, who were then prisoners and present. This was the last certain information which was ever had concerning him. He was believed however, to have been afterwards in his old neighborhood in the capacity of guide to the Indians, and aiding them, by his knowledge of the country, in making successful incursions into it.

In the month of June, at Martin's fort on Crooked Run, another murderous scene was exhibited by the savages. The greater part of the men having gone forth early to their farms, and those who remained, being unapprehensive of immediate danger, and consequently supine and careless, the fort was necessarily, easily accessible, and the vigilance of the savages who were lying hid around it, discovering its exposed and [205] weakened situation, seized the favorable moment to attack those who were without. The women were engaged in milking the cows outside the gate, and the men who had been left behind were loitering around. The Indians rushed forward, and killed and made prisoners of ten of them. James Stuart, James Smally and Peter Crouse, were the only persons who fell, and John Shiver and his wife, two sons of Stuart, two sons of Smally and a son of Crouse, were carried into captivity. According to their statement upon their return, there were thirteen Indians in the party which surprised them, and emboldened by success, instead of retreating with their prisoners, remained at a little distance from the fort 'till night, when they put the captives in a waste house near, under custody of two of the savages, while the remaining eleven, went to see if they could not succeed in forcing an entrance at the gate. But the disaster of the morning had taught the inhabitants the necessity of greater watchfulness. The dogs were shut out at night, and the approach of the Indians exciting them to bark freely, gave notice of impending danger, in time for them to avert it. The attempt to take the fort being thus frustrated, the savages returned to the house in which the prisoners were confined, and moved off with them to their towns.

In August, two daughters of Captain David Scott living at the mouth of Pike run, going to the meadow with dinner for the mowers, were taken by some Indians who were watching the path. The younger was killed on the spot; but the latter being taken some distance farther, and every search for her proving unavailing, her father fondly hoped that she had been carried into captivity, and that he might redeem her. For this purpose he visited Pittsburg and engaged the service of a friendly Indian to ascertain where she was and endeavour to prevail on them to ransom her. Before his return from Fort Pitt, some of his neighbors directed to the spot by the buzzards hovering over it, found her half eaten and mutilated body.

In September, Nathaniel Davisson and his brother, being on a hunting expedition up Ten Mile, left their camp early on the morning of the day on which they intended to return home; and naming an hour at which they would be back, proceeded through the woods in different directions. At the appointed time, Josiah went to the camp, and after waiting there in vain for the arrival of his brother, and becoming uneasy lest [206] some unlucky accident had befallen him, he set out in search of him. Unable to see or hear anything of him he returned home, and prevailed on several of his neighbors to aid in endeavouring to ascertain his fate. Their search was likewise unavailing; but in the following March, he was found by John Read, while hunting in that neighborhood. He had been shot and scalped; and notwithstanding he had lain out nearly six months, yet he was but little torn by wild beasts, and was easily recognized.

During this year too, Tygarts Valley, which had escaped being visited by the Indians in 1778 again heard their harrowing yells ; and although but little mischief was done by them while there, yet its inhabitants were awhile, kept in fearful apprehension that greater ills would betide them. In October of this year, a party of them lying in ambush near the road, fired several shots at Lieut. John White, riding by, but with no other effect than by wounding the horse to cause him to throw his rider. This was fatal to White. Being left on foot and on open ground, he was soon shot, tomahawked and scalped.

As soon as this event was made known, Capt. Benjamin Wilson, with his wonted promptitude and energy, raised a company of volunteers, and proceeding by forced marches to the Indian crossing at the mouth of the Sandy fork of Little Kenhawa, he remained there nearly three days with a view to intercept the retreat of the savages. They however, returned by another way and his scheme, of cutting them off while crossing the river, consequently failed.

Some time after this several families in the Buchannon settlement, left the fort and returned to their homes, under the belief that the season had advanced too far, for the Indians again to come among them. But they were sorely disappointed. The men being all assembled at the fort for the purpose of electing a Captain, some Indians fell upon the family of John Schoolcraft, and killed the women and eight children,—two little boys only were taken prisoners. A small girl, who had been scalped and tomahawked 'till a portion of her brains was forced from her head, was found the next day yet alive, and continued to live for several days, the brains still oozing from the fracture of her skull.

The last mischief that was done this fall, was perpetrated at the house of Samuel Cottrail near to the present town of Clarksburg.—During the night considerable fear was excited, both at Cottrial's and at Sotha Hickman's on the opposite side of Elk creek, by the continued barking

of the dogs, that Indians were lurking near, and in consequence of this apprehension Cottrial, on going to bed, secured well the doors and directed that no one should stir
out in the morning until it was ascertained that there was
no danger threatening. A while before day, Cottrial being fast asleep, Moses Coleman, who lived with him, got
up, shelled some corn, and giving a few ears to Cottrial's
nephew with directions to feed the pigs around [207] the
yard, went to the hand mill in an out house, and commenced grinding. The little boy, being squatted down
shelling the corn to the pigs, found himself suddenly
drawn on his back and an Indian standing over him, ordering him to lie there. The savage then turned toward the
house in which Coleman was, fired, and as Coleman fell
ran up to scalp him. Thinking this a favorable time for
him to reach the dwelling house, the little boy sprang to
his feet, and running to the door, it was opened and he
admitted. Scarcely was it closed after him, when one of
the Indians with his tomahawk endeavored to break it
open. Cottrail fired through the door at him, and he went
off. In order to see if others were about, and to have a
better opportunity of shooting with effect, Cottrail ascended the loft, and looking through a crevice saw them
hastening away through the field and at too great distance
for him to shoot with the expectation of injuring them.
Yet he continued to fire and halloo; to give notice of
danger to those who lived near him.

The severity of the following winter put a momentary
stop to savage inroad, and gave to the inhabitants on the
frontier an interval of quiet and repose extremely desirable to them, after the dangers and confinement of the
preceding season. Hostilities were however, resumed upon
the first appearance of spring, and acts of murder and devastation, which had, of necessity, been suspended for a
time, were begun to be committed, with a firm determination on the part of the savages, utterly to exterminate the
inhabitants of the western country. To effect this object,
an expedition was concerted between the British commandant at Detroit and the Indian Chiefs north west of
the Ohio to be carried on by their united forces against

Kentucky, while an Indian army alone, was to penetrate North Western Virginia, and spread desolation over its surface. No means which could avail to ensure success and which lay within their reach, were left unemployed. The army destined to operate against Kentucky, was to consist of six hundred Indians and Canadians, to be commanded by Col. Byrd (a British officer) and furnished with every implement of destruction, from the war club of the savages, to the cannon of their allies.[1] Happily for North Western Virginia, its situation exempted its inhabitants from having to contend against these instruments of war; the want of roads prevented the transportation of cannon through the intermediate forests, and the difficulty and labor of propelling them up the Ohio river, forbade the attempt in that way.

While the troops were collecting for these expeditions, and other preparations were making for carrying them on, the settlements of North Western Virginia were not free from invasion. Small parties of Indians would enter them at unguarded moments, and kill and plunder, whenever opportunities occurred of their being done with impunity, and then retreat to their villages. Early in March (1780) Thomas Lackey discovered some mocason tracks near the upper extremity of Tygarts Valley, and thought he heard a voice saying in [208] an under tone, "*let him alone, he will go and bring more.*" Alarmed by these circumstances, he proceeded to Hadden's fort and told there what he had seen, and what he believed, he had heard. Being so early in the season and the weather yet far from mild, none heeded his tale, and but few believed it. On the next day however, as Jacob Warwick, William Warwick and some others from Greenbrier were about leaving the fort on their return home, it was agreed that a company of men should accompany them some distance on the road. Unapprehensive of danger, in spite of the warning of Lackey, they were proceeding carelessly on their way, when they were suddenly attacked by some Indians lying in ambush,

---

[1] See p. 262, *note*, for account of Capt. Henry Bird's attack on Fort Laurens.—R. G. T.

near to the place, where the mocason tracks had been seen
on the preceding day. The men on horse back, all got
safely off; but those on foot were less fortunate. The Indians having occupied the pass both above and below, the
footmen had no chance of escape but in crossing the river
and ascending a steep bluff, on its opposite side. In attempting this several lost their lives. John McLain was
killed about thirty yards from the brow of the hill.—
James Ralston, when a little farther up it, and James
Crouch was wounded after having nearly reached its summit, yet he got safely off and returned to the fort on the
next day. John Nelson, after crossing over, endeavored
to escape down the river; but being there met by a stout
warrior, he too was killed, after a severe struggle. His
shattered gun breech, the uptorn earth, and the locks of
Indian hair in his yet clenched hands, showed that the
victory over him had not been easily won.

Soon after this, the family of John Gibson were surprised at their sugar camp, on a branch of the Valley
river, and made prisoners. Mrs. Gibson, being incapable
of supporting the fatigue of walking so far and fast, was
tomahawked and scalped in the presence of her children.

West's fort on Hacker's creek, was also visited by the
savages, early in this year.[1] The frequent incursions of

---

[1] Mr. McWhorter says that this fort stood on an eminence, where is
now the residence of Minor C. Hall. Upon the fort being abandoned by
the settlers, the Indians burned it. When the whites again returned to
their clearings, a new fort was erected, locally called Beech Fort, "because built entirely of beech logs—beech trees standing very thick in
this locality." Beech Fort was not over 500 yards from the old West
Fort; it was "in a marshy flat, some 75 yards east of the house built by
the pioneer Henry McWhorter, and still extant as the residence of Ned
J. Jackson." In the same field where Beech Fort was, "Alexander West
discovered an Indian one evening; he fired and wounded him in the
shoulder. The Indian made off, and fearing an ambuscade West would
not venture in pursuit. Two weeks later, he ventured to hunt for the
red man. Two miles distant, on what is now known as Life's Run, a
branch of Hacker's Creek, the dead savage was found in a cleft of rocks,
into which he had crawled and miserably perished. His shoulder was
badly crushed by West's bullet."

Henry McWhorter, born in Orange County, N. Y., November 13,
1760, was a soldier in the Revolution, from 1777 to the close. In 1784,
he settled about two miles from West's Fort; three years later, he

the Indians into this settlement, in the year **1778**, had caused the inhabitants to desert their homes the next year, and shelter themselves in places of greater security; but being unwilling to give up the improvements which they had already made and commence anew in the woods, some few families returned to it during the winter, & on the approach of spring, moved into the fort. They had not been long here, before the savages made their appearance, and continued to invest the fort for some time. Too weak to sally out and give them battle, and not knowing when to expect relief, the inhabitants were almost reduced to despair, when Jesse Hughs resolved at his own hazard, to try to obtain assistance to drive off the enemy. Leaving the fort at night, he broke by their sentinels and ran with speed to the Buchannon fort. Here he prevailed on a party of the men to accompany him to West's, and relieve those who had been so long confined there. They arrived before day, and it was thought advisable to abandon the place once more, and remove to Buchannon. On their way, the [209] Indians used every artifice to separate the party, so as to gain an advantageous opportunity of attacking them; but in vain. They exercised so much caution, and kept so well together, that every stratagem was frustrated, and they all reached the fort in safety.

Two days after this, as Jeremiah Curl, Henry Fink and Edmund West, who were old men, and Alexander West,[1] Peter Cutright, and Simon Schoolcraft, were returning to the fort with some of their neighbor's property, they were fired at by the Indians who were

moved nearer to the fort, and there built the house of hewn logs, mentioned above, which "is to-day in a good state of preservation." McWhorter died February 4, 1848.—R. G. T.

[1] Alexander West was prominent as a frontier scout. Rev. J. M. McWhorter, who saw him frequently, gives this description of him: "A tall, spare-built man, very erect, strong, lithe, and active; dark-skinned, prominent Roman nose, black hair, very keen eyes; not handsome, rather raw-boned, but with an air and mien that commanded the attention and respect of those with whom he associated. Never aggressive, he lifted his arm against the Indians only in time of war." West died in 1834. His house of hewed logs is, with its large barn, still standing and occupied by his relatives, about a mile east of the site of West's Fort.—R. G. T.

lying concealed along a run bank. Curl was slightly wounded under the chin, but disdaining to fly without making a stand he called to his companions, "*stand your ground, for we are able to whip them.*" At this instant a lusty warrior drew a tomahawk from his belt and rushed towards him. Nothing daunted by the danger which seemed to threaten him, Curl raised his gun; but the powder being damped by the blood from his wound, it did not fire. He instantly picked up West's gun (which he had been carrying to relieve West of part of his burden) and discharging it at his assailant, brought him to the ground.

The whites being by this time rid of their encumbrances, the Indians retreated in two parties and pursued different routes, not however without being pursued. Alexander West being swift of foot, soon came near enough to fire, and brought down a second, but having only wounded him, and seeing the Indians spring behind trees, he could not advance to finish him; nor could he again shoot at him, the flint having fallen out when he first fired. Jackson (who was hunting sheep not far off) hearing the report of the guns, ran towards the spot, and being in sight of the Indian when West shot, saw him fall and afterwards recover and hobble off. Simon Schoolcraft, following after West, came to him just after Jackson, with his gun cocked; and asking where the Indians were, was advised by Jackson to get behind a tree, or they would soon let him know where they were. Instantly the report of a gun was heard, and Schoolcraft let fall his arm. The ball had passed through it, and striking a steel tobacco box in his waistcoat pocket, did him no farther injury. Cutright, when West fired at one of the Indians, saw another of them drop behind a log, and changing his position, espied him, where the log was a little raised from the earth. With steady nerves, he drew upon him. The moaning cry of the savage, as he sprang from the ground and moved haltingly away, convinced them that the shot had taken effect. The rest of the Indians continued behind trees, until they observed a reinforcement coming up to the aid of the whites, and they

19

fled with the utmost precipitancy. Night soon coming on, those who followed them, had to give over the pursuit.

A company of fifteen men went early next morning to the battle ground, and taking the trail of the Indians and pursuing it some distance, came to where they had some horses (which they had stolen after the skirmish) hobbled out on a fork of Hacker's creek. They [210] then found the plunder which the savages had taken from neighboring houses, and supposing that their wounded warriors were near, the whites commenced looking for them, when a gun was fired at them by an Indian concealed in a laurel thicket, which wounded John Cutright.[1] The whites then caught the stolen horses and returned with them and the plunder to the fort.

For some time after this, there was nothing occurring to indicate the presence of Indians in the Buchannon settlement, and some of those who were in the fort, hoping that they should not be again visited by them this season, determined on returning to their homes. Austin Schoolcraft was one of these, and being engaged in removing some of his property from the fort, as he and his niece were passing through a swamp in their way to his house, they were shot at by some Indians. Mr. Schoolcraft was killed and his niece taken prisoner.

In June, John Owens, John Juggins and Owen Owens, were attacked by some Indians, as they were going to their cornfield on Booth's creek; and the two former were killed and scalped. Owen Owens being some distance behind them, made his escape to the fort. John Owens the younger, who had been to the pasture field for the plough horses, heard the guns, but not suspecting any danger to be near, rode forward towards the cornfield. As he was proceeding along the path by a fence side, riding one and leading another horse, he was fired at by several Indians, some of whom afterwards rushed forward and caught at the bridle reins; yet he escaped unhurt from them all.

---

[1] L. V. McWhorter says: "The branch of Hacker's creek on which John Cutright was wounded, is now known as Laurel Lick, near Berlin, W. Va." For notice of Cutright, see p. 137, *note.* - R. G. T.

The savages likewise visited Cheat river, during the spring, and coming to the house of John Sims, were discovered by a negro woman, who ran immediately to the door and alarmed the family.—Bernard Sims (just recovering from the small pox) taking down his gun, and going to the door, was shot. The Indians, perceiving that he was affected with a disease, of all others the most terrifying to them, not only did not perform the accustomed operation of scalping, but retreated with as much rapidity, as if they had been pursued by an overwhelming force of armed men,—exclaiming as they ran "*small pox, small pox.*"

After the attack on Donnelly's fort in May 1778, the Indians made no attempt to effect farther mischiefs in the Greenbrier country, until this year. The fort at Point Pleasant guarded the principal pass to the settlements on the Kenhawa, in the Levels, and on Greenbrier river, and the reception with which they had met at Col. Donnelly's, convinced them that not much was to be gained by incursions into that section of the frontiers. But as they were now making great preparations for effectual operations against the whole border country, a party of them was despatched to this portion of it, at once for the purpose of rapine and murder, and to ascertain the state of the country and its capacity to resist invasion.

The party then sent into Greenbrier consisted of twenty-two [211] warriors, and committed their first act of atrocity near the house of Lawrence Drinnan, a few miles above the Little Levels. Henry Baker and Richard Hill, who were then staying there, going early in the morning to the river to wash, were shot at by them: Baker was killed, but Hill escaped back to the house. When the Indians fired at Baker, he was near a fence between the river and Drinnan's and within gunshot of the latter place. Fearing to cross the fence for the purpose of scalping him, they prized it up, and with a pole fastening a noose around his neck, drew him down the river bank & scalped and left him there.

Apprehensive of an attack on the house, Mr. Drinnan made such preparations as were in his power to repel them, and despatched a servant to the Little Levels, with the intelligence and to procure assistance. He presently returned with twenty men, who remained there during the night, but in the morning, seeing nothing to contradict the belief that the Indians had departed, they buried Baker, and set out on their return to the Levels, taking with them all who were at Drinnan's and the most of his property. Arrived at the fork of the road, a question arose whether they should take the main route, leading through a gap which was deemed a favorable situation for an ambuscade, or continue on the farther but more open and secure way. A majority preferred the latter; but two young men, by the name of Bridger, separated from the others, and travelling on the nearer path, were both killed at the place, where it was feared danger might be lurking.

The Indians next proceeded to the house of Hugh McIver, where they succeeded in killing its owner, and in making prisoner his wife; and in going from thence, met with John Prior, who with his wife and infant were on their way to the country on the south side of the Big Kenawha. Prior was shot through the breast, but anxious for the fate of his wife and child, stood still, 'till one of the Indians came up and laid hold on him. Notwithstanding the severe wound which he had received, Prior proved too strong for his opponent, and the other Indians not interfering, forced him at length to disengage himself from the struggle. Prior, then seeing that no violence was offered to Mrs. Prior or the infant, walked off without any attempt being made to stop, or otherwise molest him: the Indians no doubt suffering him to depart under the expectation that he would obtain assistance and endeavor to regain his wife and child, and that an opportunity of waylaying any party coming with this view, would be [212] then afforded them. Prior returned to the settlement, related the above incidents and died that night. His wife and child were never after heard of, and it is highly probable they were murdered on their way, as being unable to travel as expeditiously as the Indians wished.

They next went to a house, occupied by Thomas

Drinnon and a Mr. Smith with their families, where they made prisoners of Mrs. Smith, Mrs. Drinnon and a child; and going then towards their towns, killed, on their way, an old gentleman by the name of Monday and his wife. This was the last outrage committed by the Indians in the Greenbrier settlements. And although the war was carried on by them against the frontier settlements, with energy for years after, yet did they not again attempt an incursion into it. Its earlier days had been days of tribulation and wo, and those who were foremost in occupying and forming settlements in it, had to endure all that savage fury could inflict. Their term of probation, was indeed of comparatively short duration, but their sufferings for a time, were many and great. The scenes of murder and blood, exhibited on Muddy creek and the Big Levels in 1776, will not soon be effaced from the memory; and the lively interest excited in the bosoms of many, for the fate of those who there treacherously perished, unabated by time, still gleams in the countenance, when tradition recounts the tale of their unhappy lot.

[213] CHAPTER XIII.

Early in June 1780, every necessary preparation having been previously made, the Indian and Canadian forces destined to invade Kentucky, moved from their place of rendezvous, to fulfil the objects of the expedition. In their general plan of the campaign, Louisville was the point against which operations were first to be directed. The hero of Kaskaskias and St. Vincent had been for some time stationed there, with a small body of troops, to intercept the passage of war parties into the interior, and the force thus placed under his command, having been considerably augmented by the arrival of one hundred and fifty Virginia soldiers under Colonel Slaughter, that place had assumed the appearence of a regular fortification, capable of withstanding a severe shock;[1] while detachments from it gave promise of security to the settlements remote from the river, as well by detecting and checking every attempt at invasion, as by acting offensively against the main Indian towns, from which hostile parties would sally, spreading desolation along their path. The reduction of this establishment, would at once give wider scope to savage hostilities and gratify the wounded pride of the Canadians. Stung by the boldness and success of Colonel Clarke's adventure, and fearing the effect which it might have on their Indian allies, they seemed determined to achieve a victory over him, and strike a retributive blow against the position which he then held.

[214] It is highly probable however, that the reputa-

---

[1] Col. Reuben T. Durrett, in his *Centenary of Louisville*, p. 47, says that Louisville at this time consisted of Clark's original block house, with eighteen cabins, on Corn Island, at the head of the rapids; a small fort at the foot of Third street, erected by Col. John Floyd in 1779; "a large fort on the east side of a ravine that entered the Ohio at Twelfth street, and a few rude log cabins scattered through the woods near the Twelfth street fort, all occupied by one hundred inhabitants, who had cleared and cultivated garden-spots around their humble cabins."—R. G. T.

tion which, the gallant exploits of Colonel Clarke had acquired for him, induced some doubts, in the minds of the
commanding officers, of the ultimate success of a movement against that post.[1] They changed their destination ;
and when their army arrived in their boats at the Ohio,
instead of floating with its rapid current to the point proposed, they chose to stem the stream ; and availing themselves of an uncommon swell of the waters, ascended the
river Licking to its forks, where they landed their men
and munitions of war.[2]

Not far from the place of debarkation, there was a
station,[3] reared under the superintendence of Captain Ruddle, and occupied by several families and many adventurers. Thither Colonel Byrd, with his combined army
of Canadians and Indians then amounting to one thousand men, directed his march ; and arriving before it on
the 22d of June, gave the first notice, which the inhabitants had of the presence of an enemy, by a discharge of
his cannon. He then sent in a flag, demanding the immediate surrender of the place. Knowing that it was impossible to defend the station against artillery, Captain
Ruddle consented to surrender it, provided the inhabitants
should be considered prisoners to the British, and not to
the Indians. To this proposition Colonel Byrd assented,
and the gates were thrown open. The savages instantly
rushed in, each laying his hands on the first person with
whom he chanced to meet. Parents and children, husbands and wives, were thus torn from each other ; and the

---

[1] The expedition was sent out by Maj. A. S. De Peyster, then British
commandant at Detroit. It was headed by Capt. Bird, with whom were
Simon, James, and George Girty. The force, as rendezvoused at Detroit, consisted of 150 whites, and 100 Indians from the Upper Lakes ;
they carried two cannon. They were joined on the Miami by Capt.
McKee, deputy Indian agent, and a large party of Indians, making the
force of savages amount to 700.—R. G. T.

[2] The original destination was Louisville, but en route the Indian
chiefs compelled Bird to first proceed against the forts on the Licking.—
R. G. T.

[214] [3] A station was a parallelogram of cabins, united by palisades
so as to present a continued wall on the outer side, the cabin doors opening into a common square, on the inner side. They were the strong
holds of the early settlers.

air was rent with sighs of wailing, and shrieks of agony. In vain did Captain Ruddle exclaim, against the enormities which were perpetrated in contravention to the terms of capitulation. To his remonstrances, Colonel Byrd replied that he was unable to control them, and affirmed, that he too was in their power.

That Colonel Byrd was really unable to check the enormities of the savages, will be readily admitted, when the great disparity of the Canadian and Indian troops, and the lawless and uncontrolable temper of the latter, are taken into consideration. That he had the inclination to stop them, cannot be [215] doubted—his subsequent conduct furnished the most convincing evidence, that the power to effect it, was alone wanting in him.[1]

After Ruddle's station had been completely sacked, and the prisoners disposed of, the Indians clamoured to be led against Martin's station, then only five miles distant. Affected with the barbarities which he had just witnessed, Colonel Byrd peremptorily refused, unless the chiefs would guaranty that the prisoners, which might be there taken, should be entirely at his disposal. For awhile the Indians refused to accede to these terms, but finding Colonel Byrd, inflexible in his determination, they at length consented, that the prisoners should be his, provided the plunder were allowed to them.—Upon this agreement, they marched forward. Martin's station, like Ruddle's, was incapable of offering any available opposition. It was surrendered on the first summons, and the prisoners and plunder divided, in conformity with the compact between Colonel Byrd and the savages.

The facility, with which these conquests were made, excited the thirst of the Indians for more. Not satisfied with the plundering of Ruddle's and Martin's stations, their rapacity prompted them to insist on going against Bryant's and Lexington. Prudence forbade it. The waters

---

[1] There seems to be abundant evidence that Bird, a competent officer, was humanely inclined; but he was quite in the power of his savage allies, who would brook little control of their passions. The number of prisoners taken at Isaac Ruddell's was nearly 300; about fifty more were taken at Martin's.—R. G. T.

were rapidly subsiding, and the fall of the Licking river, would have rendered it impracticable to convey their artillery to the Ohio. Their success too, was somewhat doubtful; and it was even then difficult to procure provisions, for the subsistence of the prisoners already taken.[1] Under the influence of these considerations, Colonel Byrd determined to return to the boats, and embarking on these his artillery and the Canadian troops, descended the river; while the Indians, with their plunder, and the prisoners taken at Ruddle's, moved across the country.

Among those who were taken captive at Ruddle's station, was a man of the name of Hinkstone, remarkable for activity and daring, and for uncommon tact and skill as a woodsman. On the second night of their march, the Indians encamped on the bank of the river, and in consequence of a sudden shower of rain, postponed kindling their fires until dark, when part of the savages engaged in this business, while the remainder guarded the prisoners. Hinkstone thought the darkness favorable to escape, and inviting its attempt. He resolved on trying it, and springing suddenly from them, ran a small [216] distance and concealed himself behind a large log, under the shade of a wide spreading tree. The alarm was quickly given, and the Indians, pursuing, searched for him in every direction. It was fruitless and unavailing. Hid in thick obscurity, no eye could distinguish his prostrate body. Perceiving at length, by the subsiding of the noise without the camp, that the Indians had abandoned the search, he resumed his flight, with the stillness of death. The heavens afforded him no sign, by which he could direct his steps. Not a star twinkled through the dark clouds which enveloped the earth, to point out his course. Still he moved on, as he supposed, in the direction of Lexington. He had

---

[1] The Indians had, contrary to Bird's expostulations, wantonly slaughtered all the cattle at Ruddell's Station, and this it was that caused the famine. With an abundance of food to sustain both prisoners and warriors, Bird might readily have carried out his purpose of uprooting nearly every settlement in Kentucky. There is nothing in his official report of the expedition, to warrant the statement that high water had any thing to do with the matter.—R. G. T.

mistaken the way, and a short space of time, served to convince him that he was in error. After wandering about for two hours, he came in sight of the Indian fires again. Perplexed by his devious ramble, he was more at fault than ever. The sky was still all darkness, and he had recourse to the trees in vain, to learn the points of the compass by the feeling of the moss. He remembered that at nightfall, the wind blew a gentle breeze from the west; but it had now, become so stilled, that it no longer made any impression on him. The hunter's expedient, to ascertain the direction of the air, occurred to him.—He dipped his finger in water, and, knowing that evaporation and coolness would be first felt on the side from which the wind came, he raised it high in the air. It was enough.—Guided by this unerring indication, and acting on the supposition that the current of air still flowed from the point from which it had proceeded at night, he again resumed his flight. After groping in the wilderness for some time, faint and enfeebled, he sat down to rest his wearied limbs, and sought their invigoration in refreshing sleep. When he awoke, fresh dangers encircled him, but he was better prepared to elude, or encounter them.

At the first dawn of day, his ears were assailed by the tremulous bleating of the fawn, the hoarse gobbling of the turkey, and the peculiar sounds of other wild animals. Familiar with the deceptive artifices, practised to allure game to the hunter, he was quickly alive to the fact, that they were the imitative cries of savages in quest of provisions. Sensible of his situation, he became vigilant to discover the approach of danger, and active in avoiding it. Several times however, with all his wariness, he found himself within a few paces of [217] some one of the Indians; but fortunately escaping their observation, made good his escape, and reached Lexington in safety, gave there the harrowing intelligence of what had befallen the inhabitants of Ruddle's and Martin's stations.

The Indians after the escape of Hinkstone, crossed · the Ohio river at the mouth of Licking, and, separating into small parties, proceeded to their several villages. The Canadian troops descended Licking to the Ohio, and this river to the mouth of the Great Miami, up which they ascended as far as it was navigable for their boats, and made their way thence by land to Detroit.

The Indian army destined to operate against North Western Virginia, was to enter the country in two divisions of one hundred and fifty warriors each; the one crossing the Ohio near below Wheeling, the other, at the mouth of Racoon creek, about sixty miles farther up. Both were, avoiding the stronger forts, to proceed directly to Washington, then known as Catfishtown, between which place and the Ohio, the whole country was to be laid waste.

The division crossing below Wheeling, was soon discovered by scouts, who giving the alarm, caused most of the inhabitants of the more proximate settlements, to fly immediately to that place, supposing that an attack was meditated on it. The Indians however, proceeded on the way to Washington making prisoners of many, who, although apprized that an enemy was in the country, yet feeling secure in their distance from what was expected to be the theatre of operations, neglected to use the precaution necessary to guard them against becoming captives to the savages. From all the prisoners, they learned the same thing,—that the inhabitants had gone to Wheeling with a view of concentrating the force of the settlements to effect their repulsion. This intelligence alarmed them. The chiefs held a council, in which it was determined, instead of proceeding to Washington, to retrace their steps across the Ohio, lest their retreat, if delayed 'till the whites had an opportunity of organizing themselves for battle, should be entirely cut off. Infuriate at the blasting of their hopes of blood and spoil, they resolved to murder all their male prisoners—exhausting on their devoted heads, the fury of disappointed expectation. Preparations to carry this resolution into effect, were immediately begun to be made.

The unfortunate victims to their savage wrath, were led [218] forth from among their friends and their families,—their hands were pinioned behind them,—a rope was fastened about the neck of each and that bound around a tree, so as to prevent any motion of the head. The tomahawk and scalping knife were next drawn from their belts, and the horrid purpose of these preparations, fully consummated.

"Imagination's utmost stretch" can hardly fancy a more heart-rending scene than was there exhibited. Parents, in the bloom of life and glow of health, mercilessly mangled to death, in the presence of children, whose sobbing cries served but to heighten the torments of the dying.—Husbands, cruelly lacerated, and by piece-meal deprived of life, in view of the tender partners of their bosoms, whose agonizing shrieks, increasing the anguish of torture, sharpened the sting of death. It is indeed

> ———"A fearful thing,
> To see the human soul, take wing,
> In any shape,—in any mood;"

but that wives and children should be forced to behold the last ebb of life, and to witness the struggle of the departing spirit of husbands and fathers, under such horrific circumstances, is shocking to humanity, and appalling, even in contemplation.

Barbarities such as these, had considerable influence on the temper and disposition of the inhabitants of the country. They gave birth to a vindictive feeling in many, which led to the perpetration of similar enormities and sunk civilized man, to the degraded level of the barbarian. They served too, to arouse them to greater exertion, to subdue the savage foe in justifiable warfare, and thus prevent their unpleasant recurrence.

So soon as the Indian forces effected a precipitate retreat across the Ohio, preparations were begun to be made for acting offensively against them. An expedition was concerted, to be carried on against the towns at the forks of the Muskingum; and through the instrumentality of Col's Zane and Shepard, Col. Broadhead, commander of the forces at Fort Pitt, was prevailed upon to co-operate in it.[1] Before however, it could be carried into effect, it

---

[1] Col. Daniel Brodhead was in command of the Eighth Pennsylvania Regiment. He succeeded McIntosh at Fort Pitt, in April, 1779.—R. G. T.

was deemed advisable to proceed against the Munsie towns, up the north branch of the Alleghany river; the inhabitants of which, had been long engaged in active [219] hostilities, and committed frequent depredations on the frontiers of Pennsylvania. In the campaign against them, as many of those, who resided in the settlements around Wheeling, as could be spared from the immediate defence of their own neighborhoods, were consociated with the Pennsylvania troops, and the regulars under Col. Broadhead. It eventuated in the entire destruction of all their corn, (upwards of 200 acres,) and in the cutting off a party of forty warriors, on their way to the settlements in Westmoreland county.

Very soon after the return of the army, from the Alleghany, the troops, with which it was intended to operate against the Indian villages up the Muskingum and amounting to eight hundred, rendezvoused at Wheeling. From thence, they proceeded directly for the place of destination, under the command of Col. Broadhead.[1]

When the army arrived near to Salem (a Moravian town,)[2] many of the militia expressed a determination to go forward and destroy it, but as the Indians residing there, had ever been in amity with the whites, and were not known to have ever participated in the murderous deeds of their more savage red brethren, the officers exerted themselves effectually, to repress that determination. Col. Broadhead sent forward an express to the Rev'd Mr. Heckewelder (the missionary of that place,)[3] acquainting

---

[1] Brodhead set out from Fort Pitt, April 7, 1781, with 150 regulars; at Wheeling he picked up David Shepherd, lieutenant of Ohio County, Va., with 134 militia, including officers; besides these were five friendly Indians, eager for Delaware scalps.—R. G. T.

[2] Salem, established by Heckewelder for his Indian converts, was on the west bank of the Tuscarawas, a mile and a half south-west of the present Port Washington.—R. G. T.

[3] John Gottlieb Ernestus Heckewelder was born at Bedford, England, March 12, 1743. Coming to Pennsylvania in 1754, he was at first a cooper, but later became an assistant to Charles Frederick Post, the Moravian missionary. In 1771, he first became an evangelist to the Indians, on his own account, and spent fifteen years in Ohio, where he assisted in the work of David Zeisberger. He was a man of learning, and made important contributions to the study of American archæology and

him with the object of the expedition, & requesting a small supply of provisions, and that he would accompany the messenger to camp. When Mr. Heckewelder came, the commander enquired of him, if any christian Indians were engaged in hunting or other business, in the direction of their march,—stating, that if they were, they might be exposed to danger, as it would be impracticable to distinguish between them and other Indians, and that he should greatly regret the happening to them, of any unpleasant occurrence, through ignorance or mistake. On hearing there were not, the army was ordered to resume its march, and proceeded towards the forks of the river.

At White Eyes plain, near to the place of destination, an Indian was discovered and made prisoner. Two others were seen near there, and fired at; and notwithstanding one of them was wounded, yet both succeeded in effecting their escape. Apprehensive that they would hasten to the Indian towns, and communicate the fact that an army of whites was near at hand, Col. Broadhead moved rapidly forward with the [220] troops, notwithstanding a heavy fall of rain, to reach Coshocton, (the nearest village,)[1] and take it by surprise. His expectations were not disappointed. Approaching the town, the right wing of the army was directed to occupy a position above it, on the river; the left to assume a stand below, while the centre marched directly upon it. The Indian villages, ignorant of the fact that an enemy was in their country, were all made prisoners without the firing of a single gun. So rapid, and yet so secret, had been the advance of the army, that every part of the town was occupied by the troops, before the Indians knew of its approach.

Successful as they thus far were, yet the expedition accomplished but a portion of what had been contemplated. The other towns were situated on the opposite side of the river, and this was so swollen by the excessive rains

---

ethnology. The last thirteen years of his life were spent in literary work. He died at Bethlehem, Pa., January 21, 1823.—R. G. T.

[1] Called in some of the contemporary chronicles, Goschocking.—R. G. T.

which had fallen and continued yet to deluge the earth, that it was impracticable to cross over to them; and Col. Broadhead, seeing the impossibility of achieving any thing farther, commenced laying waste the crops about Coshocton. This measure was not dictated by a spirit of revenge, naturally enkindled by the exterminating warfare, waged against the whites by the savages, but was a politic expedient, to prevent the accomplishment of their horrid purposes and to lessen the frequency of their incursions. When they fail to derive sustenance from their crops of corn and other edible vegetables, the Indians are forced to have recourse to hunting, to obtain provisions, and consequently, to suspend their hostile operations for a season. To produce this desirable result, was the object sought to be obtained by the destruction which was made of every article of subsistence, found here and at the Munsie towns, and subsequently at other places.

It remained then to dispose of the prisoners. Sixteen warriors, particularly obnoxious for their diabolical deeds, were pointed out by Pekillon (a friendly Delaware chief who accompanied the army of Col. Broadhead) as fit subjects of retributive justice; and taken into close custody. A council of war was then held, to determine on their fate, and which doomed them to death. They were taken some distance from town, despatched with tomahawks and spears, and then scalped. The other captives were committed to the care of the militia, to be conducted to Fort Pitt.

On the morning after the taking of Coshocton, an Indian, [221] making his appearance on the opposite bank of the river, called out for the "Big Captain." Col. Broadhead demanded what he wished. I want peace replied the savage. Then send over some of your chiefs, said the Colonel. May be you kill, responded the Indian. No, said Broadhead, they shall not be killed. One of their chiefs, a fine looking fellow, then come over; and while he and Col. Broadhead were engaged in conversation, a militiaman came up, and with a tomahawk which he had concealed in the bosom of his hunting shirt, struck him a severe blow on the hinder part of his head. The poor Indian fell, and immediately expired.

This savage like deed was the precursor of other, and perhaps equally attrocious enormities. The army on its return, had not proceeded more than half a mile from Coshocton, when the militia guarding the prisoners, commenced murdering them. In a short space of time, a few women and children alone remained alive. These were taken to Fort Pitt, and after a while exchanged for an equal number of white captives.

The putting to death the sixteen prisoners designated by Pekillon, can be considered in no other light, than as a punishment inflicted for their great offences; and was certainly right and proper. Not so with the deliberate murder of the chief, engaged in negotiation with Col. Broadhead. He had come over under the implied assurance of the security, due to a messenger for peace, and after a positive promise of protection had been given him by the commander of the army.—His death can, consequently, only be considered as an unwarrantable murder; provoked indeed, by the barbarous and bloody conduct of the savages. These, though they do not justify, should certainly extenuate the offence.

'The fact, that the enemy, with whom they were contending, did not observe the rules of war, and was occasionally, guilty of the crime, of putting their prisoners to death, would certainly authorize the practice of greater rigor, than should be exercised towards those who do not commit such excesses. This extraordinary severity, of itself, tends to beget a greater regard for what is allowable among civilized men, and to produce conformity with those usages of war, which were suggested by humanity, and are sanctioned by all. But the attainment of this object, if it were the motive which prompted to the deed, can not justify the murder of the prisoners, placed [222] under the safe keeping of the militia. It evinced a total disregard of the authority of their superior officer. He had assured them they should only be detained as prisoners, and remain free from farther molestation; and nothing, but the commission of some fresh offence, could sanction the enormity. But, however sober reflection may condemn those acts as outrages of propriety, yet so many and so great, were the barbarous excesses committed by the savages upon the whites in their power, that the minds of those who were actors in those scenes, were deprived of the faculty of discriminating between what was right or wrong to be practised towards them. And if acts, savouring of sheer revenge, were done by them, they should be regarded as but the ebullitions of men, under the excitement of great and damning wrongs, and which, in their dispassionate moments, they would condemn, even in themselves.

When, upon the arrival of Hinkston at Lexington, the people became acquainted with the mischief which had been wrought by the Canadian and Indian army,[1] every bosom burned with a desire to avenge those outrages, and to retort them on their authors. Runners were despatched in every direction, with the intelligence, and the cry for retribution, arose in all the settlements. In this state of feeling, every eye was involuntarily turned towards Gen. Clarke as the one who should lead them forth to battle; and every ear was opened, to receive his counsel. He advised a levy of four-fifths of the male inhabitants, capable of bearing arms, and that they should speedily assemble at the mouth of Licking, and proceed from thence to Chilicothe. He ordered the building of a number of transport boats, and directed such other preparations to be made, as would facilitate the expedition, and ensure success to its object. When all was ready, the boats with the provisions and stores on board, were ordered up the Ohio, under the command of Col. Slaughter.

In ascending the river, such was the rapidity of the current, that the boats were compelled to keep near to the banks, and were worked up, in two divisions—one near each shore. While thus forcing their way slowly up the

---

[1] Withers here reverts to the Bird invasion in the summer of 1780, and the escape of Hinkstone from his British captors, related *ante*, pp. 295–98. Clark's retaliatory expedition was made during August, 1780.— R. G. T.

stream, one of the boats, being some distance in advance of the others and close under the north western bank, was fired into by a party of Indians. The fire was promptly returned; but before the other boats could draw nigh to her aid, a number of those on [223] board of her, was killed and wounded. As soon however, as they approached and opened a fire upon the assailants, the savages withdrew, and the boats proceeded to the place of rendezvous, without farther interruption.

On the second of August, General Clarke took up the line of march from the place where Cincinnati now stands, at the head of nine hundred and seventy men. They proceeded without any delay, to the point of destination, where they arrived on the sixth of the month. The town was abandoned, and many of the houses were yet burning, having been fired on the preceding day. There were however, several hundred acres of luxuriant corn growing about it, every stalk of which was cut down and destroyed.

The army then moved in the direction of the Piqua Towns, twelve miles farther, and with a view to lay waste every thing around it, and with the hope of meeting there an enemy, with whom to engage in battle; but before they had got far, a heavy shower of rain, accompanied with loud thunder and high winds, forced them to encamp. Every care which could be taken to keep the guns dry, was found to be of no avail, and General Clarke, with prudent precaution, had them all fired and re-loaded— continuing to pursue this plan, to preserve them fit for use, whenever occasion required, and keeping the troops on the alert and prepared to repel any attack which might be made on them—during the night.

In the afternoon of the next day, they arrived in sight of Piqua, and as they advanced upon the town, were attacked by the Indians concealed in the high weeds which grew around. Colonel Logan, with four hundred men, was ordered to file off,—march up the river to the east, and occupy a position from which to intercept the savages, should they attempt to fly in that direction. Another division of the army was in like manner posted on the opposite side of the river, while General Clarke with the troops under Colonel Slaughter and those attached to the artillery, was to advance directly upon the town. The Indians seemed to comprehend every motion of the army, and evinced the skill of tacticians in endeavoring to thwart its purpose. To prevent being surrounded by the advance of the detachment from the west, they made a powerful effort to turn the left wing. Colonel Floyd extended his line some distance west of the town, and the engagement became general. Both armies fought with determined [224] resolution, and the contest was warm and animated for some time. The Indians, finding that their enemy was gaining on them retired unperceived, through the prairie, a few only remaining in the town. The piece of cannon was then bro't to bear upon the houses, into which some of the savages had retired to annoy the army as it marched upon the village.—They were soon dislodged and fled.

On reaching the houses, a Frenchman was discovered concealed in one of them. From him it was learned, that the Indians had been apprized of the intention of Gen. Clarke to march against Chilicothe and other towns in its vicinity, by one of Col. Logan's men, who had deserted from the army while at the mouth of Licking, and was supposed to have fled to Carolina, as he took with him the horse furnished him for the expedition. Instead of this however, he went over to the enemy, and his treason,

> ———" Like a deadly blight,
> Came o'er the councils of the brave,
> And damped them in their hour of might."

Thus forwarned of the danger which threatened them, they were enabled in a considerable degree to avoid it, and watching all the movements of the army, were on the eve of attacking it silently, with tomahawks and knives, on the night of its encamping between Chilicothe and Piqua. The shooting of the guns, convincing them that they had not been rendered useless by the rain, alone deterred them from executing this determination.

Notwithstanding that the victory obtained by Gen. Clarke, was complete and decided, yet the army under his command sustained a loss in killed and wounded, as great as was occasioned to the enemy. This circumstance was attributable to the sudden and unexpected attack made on it, by the Indians, while entirely concealed, and partially sheltered. No men could have evinced more dauntless intrepidity and determined fortitude than was displayed by them, when fired upon by a hidden foe, and their comrades were falling around them. When the "combat thickened," such was their noble daring, that Girty, (who had been made chief among the Mingoes,) remarking the desperation with which they exposed themselves to the hottest of the fire, drew off his three hundred warriors; observing, that it was useless to fight with fools and madmen. The loss in killed under the peculiar [225] circumstances, attending the commencement of the action, was less than would perhaps be expected to befall an army similarly situated;—amounting in all to only twenty men.

Here, as at Chilicothe, the crops of corn and every article of subsistence on which the troops could lay their hands, were entirely laid waste. At the two places, it was estimated that not less than five hundred acres of that indispensable article, were entirely destroyed.[1]

An unfortunate circumstance, occurring towards the close of the engagement, damped considerably the joy which would otherwise have pervaded the army. A nephew of Gen. Clarke, who had been taken, and for some time detained, a prisoner by the savages, was at Piqua during the action. While the battle continued, he was too closely guarded to escape to the whites; but upon the dispersion of the savages which ensued upon the cannonading of the houses into which some of them had retreated, he was left more at liberty. Availing himself of this change of situation, he sought to join his friends. He was quickly discovered by some of them, and mistaken for

---

[1] Butterfield, in *History of the Girtys*, p. 121, places the white loss at seventeen killed, and "a number wounded;" and the Indian loss at six killed and three wounded. Clark's nephew, Joseph Rogers, was killed on August 8, the day of the general engagement. Clark left Piqua. the 10th.—R. G. T.

an Indian. The mistake was fatal. He received a shot discharged at him, and died in a few hours.

Notwithstanding the success of the expeditions commanded by Col. Broadhead and Gen. Clarke, and the destruction which took place on the Alleghany, at Coshocton, Chilicothe and Piqua, yet the savages continued to commit depredations on the frontiers of Virginia. The winter, as usual, checked them for awhile, but the return of spring, brought with it, the horrors which mark the progress of an Indian enemy. In Kentucky and in North Western Virginia, it is true that the inhabitants did not suffer much by their hostilities in 1781, as in the preceding years; yet were they not exempt from aggression.

Early in March a party of Indians invaded the settlements on the upper branches of Monongahela river; and on the night of the 5th of that month, came to the house of Capt. John Thomas, near Booth's creek. Unapprehensive of danger, with his wife and seven children around him, and with thoughts devotedly turned upon the realities of another world, this gentleman was engaging in his accustomed devotions when the savages approached his door; and as he was repeating the first lines of the hymn, "Go worship at Emanuel's feet," a gun was fired at him, and he fell. The Indians [226] immediately forced open the door, and, entering the house, commenced the dreadful work of death. Mrs. Thomas raised her hands and implored their mercy for herself and her dear children. It was in vain. The tomahawk was uplifted, and stoke followed stroke in quick succession, till the mother and six children lay weltering in blood, by the side of her husband and their father—a soul-chilling spectacle to any but heartless savages. When all were down, they proceeded to scalp the fallen, and plundering the house of what they could readily remove, threw the other things into the fire and departed—taking with them one little boy a prisoner.

Elizabeth Juggins, (the daughter of John Juggins who had been murdered in that neighborhood, the preceding year) was at the house of Capt. Thomas, when the Indians came to it; but as soon as she heard the report of the gun and saw Capt. Thomas fall, she threw herself under the bed, and escaped the observation of the savages. After they had completed the work of blood and left the house, fearing that they might be lingering near, she remained in that situation until she observed the house to be in flames. When she crawled forth from her asylum, Mrs. Thomas was still alive, though unable to move; and casting a pitying glance towards her murdered infant, asked that it might be handed to her. Upon seeing Miss Juggins about to leave the house, she exclaimed, " Oh Betsy! do not leave us." Still anxious for her own safety, the girl rushed out, and taking refuge for the night between two logs, in the morning early spread the alarm.

When the scene of those enormities was visited, Mrs. Thomas was found in the yard, much mangled by the tomahawk and considerably torn by hogs—she had, perhaps in the struggle of death, thrown herself out at the door. The house, together with Capt. Thomas and the children, was a heap of ashes.[1]

In April, Matthias, Simon and Michael Schoolcraft left Buchannon fort, and went to the head of Stone coal creek for the purpose of catching pigeons. On their return, they were fired upon by Indians, and Matthias killed —the other two were taken captive. These were the last of the Schoolcraft family,—fifteen of them were killed or taken prisoners in the space of a few years. Of those who were carried into captivity, none ever returned. They were believed to have consociated with the savages, and from the report of others [227] who were prisoners to the Indians, three of them used to accompany war parties, in their incursions into the settlements.

In the same month, as some men were returning to Cheat river from Clarksburg, (where they had been to ob-

---

[1] I am informed by S. R. Harrison, of Clarksburg, W. Va., that the bodies of the victims were buried about five rods from the house, and " the graves are yet marked by the original rude stones." Mr. Harrison continues, " This burial ground, and also where the house stood, had never been disturbed until March, 1888—a hundred and seven years after the massacre—when the ground about the site of the house was plowed; many interesting relics were turned up, among them a compass and sun-dial in a copper case. I myself found a number of relics among the charred ruins of the house."—R. G. T.

tain certificates of settlement-rights to their lands, from the commissioners appointed to adjust land claims in the counties of Ohio, Youghiogany and Monongalia) they, after having crossed the Valley river, were encountered by a large party of Indians, and John Manear, Daniel Cameron and a Mr. Cooper were killed,—the others effected their escape with difficulty.

The savages then moved on towards Cheat, but meeting with James Brown and Stephen Radcliff, and not being able to kill or take them, they changed their course, and passing over Leading creek, (in Tygarts Valley) nearly destroyed the whole settlement. They there killed Alexander Roney, Mrs. Dougherty, Mrs. Hornbeck and her children, Mrs. Buffington and her children, and many others; and made prisoners, Mrs. Roney and her son, and Daniel Dougherty. Jonathan Buffington and Benjamin Hornbeck succeeded in making their escape and carried the doleful tidings to Friend's and Wilson's forts. Col. Wilson immediately raised a company of men and proceeding to Leading creek, found the settlement without inhabitants, and the houses nearly all burned. He then pursued after the savages, but not coming up with them as soon as was expected, the men became fearful of the consequences which might result to their own families, by reason of this abstraction of their defence, provided other Indians were to attack them, and insisted on their returning. On the second day of the pursuit, it was agreed that a majority of the company should decide whether they were to proceeded farther or not. Joseph Friend, Richard Kettle, Alexander West and Col. Wilson, were the only persons in favor of going on, and they consequently had to return.

But though the pursuit was thus abandoned, yet did not the savages get off with their wonted impunity. When the land claimants, who had been the first to encounter this party of Indians escaped from them, they fled back to Clarksburg, and gave the alarm. This was quickly communicated to the other settlements, and spies were sent out, to watch for the enemy. By some of these, the savages were discovered on the West Fork, near the mouth

of Isaac's creek, and intelligence of it immediately carried
to the forts.   Col. Lowther [228] collected a company of
men, and going in pursuit, came in view of their encampment, awhile before night, on a branch of Hughes'
river, ever since known as *Indian creek*.   Jesse and Elias
Hughs—active, intrepid and vigilant men—were left to
watch the movements of the savages, while the remainder
retired a small distance to refresh themselves, and prepare
to attack them in the morning.

Before day Col. Lowther arranged his men in order
of attack, and when it became light, on the preconcerted
signal being given, a general fire was poured in upon them.
Five of the savages fell dead and the others fled leaving
at their fires, all their shot bags and plunder, and all their
guns, except one.   Upon going to their camp, it was found
that one of the prisoners (a son of Alexander Rony who
had been killed in the Leading creek massacre) was among
the slain.   Every care had been taken to guard against
such an occurrence, and he was the only one of the captives who sustained any injury from the fire of the whites.[1]

In consequence of information received from the
prisoners who were retaken (that a larger party of Indians was expected hourly to come up,) Col. Lowther

---

[228] [1] As soon as the fire was opened upon the Indians, Mrs. Rony
(one of the prisoners) ran towards the whites rejoicing at the prospect
of deliverance, and exclaiming, " I am Ellick Rony's wife, of the Valley,
I am Ellick Rony's wife, of the Valley, and a pretty little woman too,
if I was well dressed." The poor woman, ignorant of the fact that
her son was weltering in his own gore, and forgetting for an instant that
her husband had been so recently killed, seemed intent only on her own
deliverance from the savage captors.

Another of the captives, Daniel Dougherty, being tied down, and
unable to move, was discovered by the whites as they rushed towards
the camp. Fearing that he might be one of the enemy and do them
some injury if they advanced, one of the men, stopping, demanded who
he was. Benumbed with cold, and discomposed by the sudden firing
of the whites, he could not render his Irish dialect intelligible to them.
The white man raised his gun and directed it towards him, calling
aloud, that if he did not make known who he was, he should blow a
ball through him, let him be white man or Indian. Fear supplying him
with energy, Dougherty exclaimed, "Loord Jasus! and am I too be
killed by white people at last!" He was heard by Col. Lowther and his
life saved.

deemed it prudent not to go in pursuit of those who had fled, and collecting the plunder which the savages had left, catching the horses which [229] they had stolen, and having buried young Rony, the party set out on its return and marched home—highly gratified at the success which had crowned their exertions to punish their untiring foe.

Some short time after this, John Jackson and his son George, returning to Buchannon fort, were fired at by some Indians, but fortunately missed. George Jackson having his gun in his hand, discharged it at a savage peeping from behind a tree, without effect; and they then rode off with the utmost speed.

At the usual period of leaving the forts and returning to their farms, the inhabitants withdrew from Buchannon and went to their respective homes. Soon after, a party of savages came to the house of Charles Furrenash, and made prisoners of Mrs. Furrenash and her four children, and despoiled their dwelling. Mrs. Furrenash, being a delicate and weakly woman, and unable to endure the fatigue of travelling far on foot, was murdered on Hughes' river. Three of the children were afterwards redeemed and came back,—the fourth was never more heard of. In a few days after, the husband and father returned from Winchester (where he had been for salt) and instead of the welcome greeting of an affectionate wife, and the pleasing prattle of his innocent children, was saluted with the melancholy intelligence of their fate. It was enough to make him curse the authors of the outrage, and swear eternal enmity to the savage race.

The early period in spring at which irruptions were frequently made by the savages upon the frontier, had induced a belief, that if the Moravian Indians did not participate in the bloody deeds of their red brethern, yet that they afforded to them shelter and protection from the inclemency of winter, and thus enabled them, by their greater proximity to the white settlements, to commence depredations earlier than they otherwise could. The consequence of this belief was, the engendering in the minds of many, a spirit of hostility towards those Indians; occasionally threatening a serious result to them. Reports too, were in circulation, proceeding from restored captives, at war with the general pacific profession of the Moravians, and which, whether true or false, served to heighten the acrimony of feeling towards them, until the militia of a portion of the frontier came to the determination of breaking up the villages on the Muskingum.[1] To [230] carry this determination into effect, a body of troops, commanded by Col. David Williamson, set out for those towns,

---

[1] The Moravian Indians were originally from the Susquehanna River. They moved to the Tuscarawas River in 1772, under the missionaries Zeisberger and Heckewelder, who built two villages on the eastern bank of that river, on land set apart for them by the Delawares: Schönbrunn, about three miles south-east of the present New Philadelphia, in what is now Goshen township, Tuscarawas County, O., and Gnadenhütten, lower down, in the outskirts of the present town of that name, in Clay township. The principal Delaware town, at that time, was some distance below, near the site of the present Newcomerstown; this was later moved to what is now Coshocton, at the confluence of the Tuscarawas and Walholding, which unite to form the Muskingum. At this time there was a Moravian village called Friedensstadt, on Beaver River, in what is now Lawrence County, Pa. In 1776 a new village for the accommodation of converts was established on the east bank of the Muskingum, two and a half miles below Coshocton, and called Lichtenau; William Edwards was the missionary in charge. In consequence of the disturbances on the border, Schönbrunn and Gnadenhütten were deserted in 1777, and all the teachers returned to Pennsylvania save Zeisberger and Edwards, who gathered the Indians together at Lichtenau; but in the spring of 1778, Gnadenhütten was re-occupied, with Edwards in charge. This was not for a long time, however, for in July we find Zeisberger, Heckewelder, and Edwards in charge of the union station at Lichtenau, the others being deserted. The spring of 1779 finds Edwards again at the resuscitated Gnadenhütten, Zeisberger re-occupying Schönbrunn with a small party, and Heckewelder at Lichtenau. Later in the season Zeisberger began New Schönbrunn on the west bank of the Tuscarawas, in what is now Goshen township, a quarter of a mile from the present Lockport, and a mile and a quarter south of New Philadelphia; thither he removed his flock in December. In the spring of 1780, Heckewelder abandoned Lichtenau, and took his converts to the west bank of the Tuscarawas, where he established Salem, in the present Salem township, a mile and a half north-west of Port Washington. In the autumn the Moravian villages were in general charge of Zeisberger, who traveled from one to the other; Gottlob Senseman being in charge of New Schönbrunn, Edwards of Gnadenhütten, and Heckewelder of Salem. It will thus be seen that at the time of the massacre, the Moravian villages were wholly in the valley of the Tuscarawas.— R. G. T.

in the latter part of the year 1781. Not deeming it necessary to use the fire and sword, to accomplish the desired object, Col. Williamson resolved on endeavoring to prevail on them to move farther off; and if he failed in this, to make prisoners of them all, and take them to Fort Pitt. Upon his arrival at their towns, they were found to be nearly deserted, a few Indians only, remaining in them. These were made prisoners and taken to Fort Pitt; but were soon liberated.

It is a remarkable fact, that at the time the whites were planning the destruction of the Moravian villages, because of their supposed co-operation with the hostile savages, the inhabitants of those villages were suffering severely from the ill treatment of those very savages, because of their supposed attachment to the whites. By the one party, they were charged with affording to Indian war parties, a resting place and shelter, and furnishing them with provisions. By the other, they were accused of apprizing the whites of meditated incursions into the country, and thus defeating their purpose, or lessening the chance of success; and of being instrumental in preventing the Delawares from entering in the war which they were waging. Both charges were probably, well founded, and the Moravian Indians yet culpable in neither.[1]

Their villages were situated nearly midway between the frontier establishments of the whites, and the towns of the belligerent Indians, and were consequently, convenient resting places for warriors proceeding to and from the settlements. That they should have permitted war parties after ravages to refresh themselves there, or even have supplied them with provisions, does not argue a disposition to aid or encourage their hostile operations. It was at any time in the power of those warring savages, to

_____

[1] Zeisberger and Heckewelder kept Brodhead continually informed, by letters, of the movements and councils of the hostiles. The position of the missionaries was one of exceeding delicacy, but the voluminous correspondence between them and Brodhead proves that the former were steadfast friends of the American colonies, and did effective service throughout the several years of disturbance on the frontier.— R. G. T.

exact by force whatever was required of the Moravian Indians, and the inclination was not wanting, to do this or other acts of still greater enormity. That the warriors were the better enabled to make incursions into the settlements, and effect their dreadful objects by reason of those accommodations, can not be questioned; the fault however, lay not in any inimical feeling of the christian Indians towards the whites, but in their physical inability to withhold whatever might be demanded of them.

And although they exerted themselves to prevail on other [231] tribes to forbear from hostilities against the whites, and apprised the latter of enterprizes projected against them, yet did not these things proceed from an unfriendly disposition towards their red brethren. They were considerate and reflecting, and saw that the savages must ultimately suffer, by engaging in a war against the settlements; while their pacific and christian principles, influenced them to forewarn the whites of impending danger, that it might be avoided, and the effusion of blood be prevented. But pure and commendable as were, no doubt, the motives which governed them, in their intercourse with either party, yet they were so unfortunate as to excite the enmity and incur the resentment of both, and eventually were made to suffer, though in different degrees, by both.

In the fall of 1781, the settlements of the Moravians were almost entirely broken up by upwards of three hundred warriors, and the missionaries, residing among them, after having been robbed of almost every thing, were taken prisoners and carried to Detroit. Here they were detained until the governor became satisfied that they were guiltless of any offence meriting a longer confinement; when they were released & permitted to return to their beloved people. The Indians were left to shift for themselves in the Sandusky plains where most of their horses and cattle perished from famine.[1]

---

[1] Brodhead's successful expedition against the Coshocton Indians, in April, 1781, led to preparations for a retaliatory foray. Headed by the renegade Capt. Matthew Elliott, a party of about 250 Indians,—mostly Wyandots, with chiefs Half King, Pipe, Snip, John and Thomas

Snake, and others—assembled at Gnadenhütten, for a talk with the Moravian teachers, preparatory to an expedition against Wheeling. They arrived August 17, and Zeisberger at once secretly sent a message of warning to Ft. Pitt, which threw the frontier into alarm, and caused the garrison at Wheeling to be fully prepared when the enemy appeared. A boy whom the Wyandots captured outside of Wheeling told them of Zeisberger's warning, and when the unsuccessful war party returned to Gnadenhütten (Sept. 2), vengeance was wreaked on the Moravians. The town was sacked that day, and the missionaries were kept as prisoners for several days. Finally they were released (Sept. 6), on promise that they remove their converts from the line of the warpaths. September 11, the Moravians and their teachers left Salem in a body, with but few worldly goods, for most of their property had been destroyed by the Wyandots. They proceeded down the Tuscarawas to the mouth of the Walhonding, thence up the latter stream and Vernon River, and across country to the Sandusky, where they arrived October 1, and erected a few huts on the east bank of the river, about two and a-half miles above the present Upper Sandusky. Fourteen days later, the missionaries were summoned to appear before the British commandant at Detroit, Major De Peyster. Zeisberger, Heckewelder, Edwards, and Senseman left for Detroit, October 25. De Peyster questioned them closely, and finally released them with the statement that he would confer with them later, relative to their final abode. They reached the Sandusky, on their return, November 22. Meanwhile, the winter had set in early; and in danger of starving, a party of the Moravians had returned to the Tuscarawas to gather corn in the abandoned fields; while there, a party of border rangers took them prisoners and carried them to Fort Pitt. Brig.-Gen. William Irvine, then in command, treated the poor converts kindly, and allowed them to go in peace, many returning to their old villages on the Tuscarawas, to complete their dismal harvesting.—R. G. T.

[232] CHAPTER XIII.

The revengeful feelings which had been engendered, by inevitable circumstances, towards the Moravian Indians, and which had given rise to the expedition of 1781, under Col. Williamson, were yet more deeply radicated by subsequent events. On the night after their liberation from Fort Pitt, the family of a Mr. Monteur were all killed or taken captive; and the outrage, occurring so immediately after they were set at liberty and in the vicinity of where they were, was very generally attributed to them. An irruption was made too, in the fall of 1781, into the settlement on Buffalo creek, and some murders committed and prisoners taken. One of these, escaping from captivity and returning soon after, declared that the party committing the aggression, was headed by a Moravian warrior.

These circumstances operated to confirm many in the belief, that those Indians were secretly inimical to the whites, and not only furnished the savages with provisions and a temporary home, but likewise engaged personally in the war of extermination, which they were waging against the frontier. Events occurring towards the close of winter, dispelled all doubt, from the minds of those who had fondly cherished every suggestion which militated against the professed, and generally accredited, neutrality and pacific disposition of the Moravians.

On the 8th of February 1782, while Henry Fink and his son John, were engaged in sledding rails, on their farm in the Buchannon settlement, several guns were simultaneously discharged at them; and before John had time to reply to his father's inquiry, whether he were hurt, another gun was fired and he fell lifeless. Having unlinked the chain which fastened the horse to the sled, the old man [233] galloped briskly away. He reached his home in safety, and immediately moved his family to the fort. On the next day the lifeless body of John, was brought into the fort.—The first shot had wounded his arm; the ball from the second passed through his heart, & he was afterwards scalped.

Near the latter part of the same month, some Indians invaded the country above Wheeling, and succeeded in killing a Mr. Wallace, and his family, consisting of his wife and five children, & in taking John Carpenter a prisoner. The early period of the year at which those enormities were perpetrated, the inclemency of the winter of 1781—2, and the distance of the towns of hostile Indians from the theatre of these outrages, caused many to exclaim, "*the Moravians have certainly done this deed.*" The destruction of their villages was immediately resolved, and preparations were made to carry this determination into effect.

There were then in the North Western wilderness, between three and four hundred of the christian Indians, and who, until removed by the Wyandots and whites in 1781, as before mentioned, had resided on the Muskingum in the villages of the Guadenhutten, Salem and Shoenbrun. The society of which they were members, had been established in the province of Pennsyivania about the year 1752, and in a short time became distinguished for the good order and deportment of its members, both as men and as christians. During the continuance of the French war, they nobly withstood every allurement which was practised to draw them within its vortex, and expressed their strong disapprobation of war in general; saying, "that it must be displeasing to that Great Being, who made men, not to destroy men, but to love and assist each other." In 1769 emigrants from their villages of Friedenshutten, Wyalusing and Shesheequon in Pennsylvania, began to make an establishment in the North Western wilderness, and in a few years, attained a considerable degree of prosperity, their towns increased rapidly in population, and themselves, under the teaching of pious and beneficent missionaries, in civilization and christianity. In the war of 1774, their tranquil and happy hours were interrupted, by reports of the ill intention of the whites along the frontier, towards them, and by frequent acts of annoyance, committed by war parties of the savages.

This state of things continued with but little, if any, intermission, occasionally assuming a more gloomy and portentious aspect, until the final destruction of their villages. In the spring of 1781, the principal war chief of the Delawares apprised the missionaries and them, of the danger which threatened them, as well from the whites as the savages, and advised them to remove to some situation, where they would be exempt from molestation by either. Conscious of the rectitude of their conduct as regarded both, and unwilling to forsake the comforts which their industry had procured for them, and the fields rendered productive by their labor, they disregarded the [234] friendly monition, and continued in their villages, progressing in the knowledge and love of the Redeemer of men, and practising the virtues inculcated by his word.

This was their situation, at the time they were removed to Sandusky, early in the fall of 1781. When their missionaries and principal men were liberated by the governor of Detroit, they obtained leave of the Wyandot chiefs to return to the Muskingum to get the corn which had been left there, to prevent the actual starvation of their families. About one hundred and fifty of them, principally women and children went thither for this purpose, and were thus engaged when the second expedition under Col. Williamson proceeded against them.

In March 1782, between eighty and ninety men assembled themselves for the purpose of effecting the destruction of the Moravian towns.[1] If they then had in

---

[1] One hundred and eighty-six men, mounted, from the Monongahela settlements. Early in March, 1782, they assembled under David Williamson, colonel of one of the militia battalions of Washington County, Pa., on the east bank of the Ohio, a few miles below Steubenville. The water was high, the weather cold and stormy, and there were no boats for crossing over to Mingo Bottom. Many turned back, but about two hundred succeeded in crossing. The expedition was not a "private" affair, but was regularly authorized by the military authority of Washington County; its destination was not the Moravian settlements, but the hostile force, then supposed to be on the Tuscarawas river. It seems to have generally been understood on the border that the Moravian towns were now deserted.—R. G. T.

contemplation the achieving of any other injury to those people, it was not promulgated in the settlements. They avowed their object to be the destruction of the houses and the laying waste the crops, in order to deprive the hostile savages of the advantage of obtaining shelter and provisions, so near to the frontier; and the removal of the Moravians to Fort Pitt, to preserve them from the personal injury which, it was feared, would be inflicted on them by the warriors. Being merely a private expedition, each of the men took with him, his own arms, ammunition and provisions; and many of them, their horses. They took up the line of march from the Mingo Bottom, and on the second night thereafter, encamped within one mile of the village of Gnadenhutten; and in the morning proceeded towards it, in the order of attack prescribed by a council of the officers.

The village being built upon both sides of the river, and the scouts having discovered and reported that it was occupied on both sides, one-half the men were ordered to cross over and bear down upon the town on the western bank, while the other half would possess themselves of that part of it which lay on the eastern shore. Upon the arrival of the first division at the river, no boat or other small craft was seen in which they could be transported across; and they were for a time, in some difficulty how they should proceed. What appeared to be a canoe was at length discovered on the opposite bank, and a young man by the name of Slaughter, plunging in swam to it. It proved to be a trough for containing sugar water, and capable of bearing only two persons at a time. To obviate the delay which must have resulted from this tedious method of conveying themselves over, many of the men unclothed themselves, and placing their garments, arms and ammunition in the trough, swam by its sides, notwithstanding that ice was floating in the current and the water, consequently, cold and chilling.

When nearly half this division had thus reached the western bank, two sentinels, who on the first landing had been stationed a short distance in advance, discovered and

21

fired at, one of the Indians. [235] The shot of one broke
his arm,—the other killed him. Directions were then sent
to the division which was to operate on the eastern side of
the river, to move directly to the attack, lest the firing
should alarm the inhabitants and they defeat the object
which seemed now to be had in view. The few who had
crossed without awaiting for the others, marched immediately into the town on the western shore.

Arrived among the Indians, they offered no violence,
but on the contrary, professing peace and good will, assured them, they had come for the purpose of escorting
them safely to Fort Pitt, that they might no longer be exposed to molestation from the militia of the whites, or the
warriors of the savages. Sick of the sufferings which they
had so recently endured, and rejoicing at the prospect of
being delivered from farther annoyance they gave up their
arms, and with alacrity commenced making preparations
for the journey, providing food as well for the whites, as
for themselves. A party of whites and Indians was next
despatched to Salem, to bring in those who were there.
They then shut up the Moravians left at Gnadenhutten, in
two houses some distance apart, and had them well guarded,
When the others arrived from Salem, they were treated in
like manner, and shut up in the same houses with their
brethren of Gnadenhutten.

The division which was to move into the town on the
eastern side of the river, coming unexpectedly upon one
of the Indian women, she endeavored to conceal herself in
a bunch of bushes at the water edge, but being discovered,
by some of the men, was quickly killed. She was the
wife of Shabosh, who had been shot by the sentinels
of the other division. Others, alarmed at the appearance of a party of armed men, and ignorant that a like
force was on the opposite side of the river, attempted to
escape thither.—They did not live to effect their object.
Three were killed in the attempt; and the men then
crossed over, with such as they had made prisoners, to
join their comrades, in the western and main part of the
town.

A council of war was then held to determine on the

fate of the prisoners. Col. Williamson having been much censured for the lenity of his conduct towards those Indians in the expedition of the preceding year, the officers were unwilling to take upon themseves the entire responsibility of deciding upon their fate now, and agreed that it should be left to the men. The line was soon formed, and they were told it remained with them to say, whether the Moravian prisoners should be taken to Fort Pitt or murdered; and Col. Williamson requested that those who were inclined to mercy, should advance and form a second link, that it might be seen on which side was the majority. Alas! it required no scrutiny to determine. Only sixteen, or at most eighteen men, stepped forward to save the lives of this unfortunate people, and their doom became sealed.[1]

From the moment those ill fated beings were immured in houses they seemed to anticipate the horrid destiny which awaited them; [236] and spent their time in holy and heartfelt devotion, to prepare them for the awful realities of another world. They sang, they prayed, they exhorted each other to a firm reliance on the Saviour of men, and soothed those in affliction with the comfortable assurance, that although men might kill the body, they had no power over the soul, and that they might again meet in a better and happier world, "where the wicked cease from troubling and the weary find rest." When told that they were doomed to die, they all affectionately embraced, and bedewing their bosoms with mutual tears, reciprocally sought, and obtained forgiveness for any offences which they might have given each other through life. Thus at peace with God, and reconciled with one another, they replied to those, who impatient for the slaughter had asked if they were not yet prepared, "Yes! We have commended our souls to God, and are ready to die."

---

[1] Contemporary accounts speak of a council of war, held in the evening, at which this question was decided. But a small majority voted for the butchery; Williamson himself was in the minority. Dorsey Pentecost, writing from Pittsburg, May 8, 1782 (see *Penn. Arch.*, ix., p. 540), says: "I have heard it intimated that about thirty or forty only of the party gave their consent or assisted in the catastrophe."—R. G. T.

What must have been the obduracy of those, who could remain inflexible in their doom of death, amid such scenes as these? How ruthless & unrelenting their hearts, who unmoved by the awful spectacle of so many fellow creatures, preparing for the sudden and violent destruction of life and asking of their God, mercy for themselves and forgiveness for their enemies—could yet thirst for blood, and manifest impatience that its shedding was delayed for an instant? Did not the possibility of that innocence, which has been ever since so universally accorded to their victims, once occur to them; or were their minds so under the influence of exasperation and resentment, that they ceased to think of any thing, but the gratification of those feelings? Had they been about to avenge the murder of friends on its *known authors*, somewhat might have been pardoned to retaliation and to vengeance; but involving all in one common ruin, for *the supposed offences* of a few, there can be no apology for their conduct,—no excuse for their crime.

It were well, if all memory of the tragedy at Gnadenhutten, were effaced from the mind; but it yet lives in the recollection of many and stands recorded on the polluted page of history.—Impartial truth requires, that it should be here set down.

A few of the prisoners, supposed to have been actively engaged in war, were the first to experience their doom. They were tied and taken some distance from the houses in which [237] they had been confined; despatched with spears and tomahawks, and scalped. The remainder of both sexes, from the hoary head of decrepitude, incapable of wrong, to helpless infancy, pillowed on its mother's breast, were cruelly & shockingly murdered; and the different apartments of those houses of blood, exhibited their bleeding bodies, mangled by the tomahawk, scalping knife and spear, and disfigured by the war-club and the mallet.[1]

---

[1] Lineback's Relation (*Penn. Arch.*, ix., p. 525) says: "In the morning, the militia chose two houses, which they called the 'slaughter houses,' and then brought the Indians two or three at a time, with ropes about their necks, and dragged them into the slaughter houses where

Thus perished ninety-six of the Moravian Indians. Of these, sixty-two were grown persons, one-third of whom were women; the remaining thirty-four were children.[1] Two youth alone, made their escape. One of them had been knocked down and scalped, but was not killed. He had the presence of mind to lie still among the dead, until nightfall, when he crept silently forth and escaped. The other, in the confusion of the shocking scene, slipped through a trap door into the cellar, and passing out at a small window, got off unnoticed and uninjured.

In the whole of this transaction the Moravians were passive and unresisting. They confided in the assurances of protection given them by the whites, and until pent up in the houses, continued cheerful and happy. If when convinced of the murderous intent of their visitors, they had been disposed to violence and opposition, it would have availed them nothing. They had surrendered their arms (being requested to do so, as a guarantee for the security of the whites,) and were no longer capable of offering any effectual or available resistance, and while the dreadful work of death was doing, "they were as lambs led to the slaughter; & as sheep before the shearers are dumb, so opened they not their mouths." There was but a solitary exception to this passiveness, and it was well nigh terminating in the escape of its author, and in the death of some of the whites.

As two of the men were leading forth one of the supposed warriors to death, a dispute arose between them, who should have the scalp of this victim to their barbarity. He was progressing after them with a silent dancing motion, and singing his death song. Seeing them occupied so closely with each other, he became emboldened to try an escape. Drawing a knife from its scabbard, he cut the

---

they knocked them down." This accords with Heckewelder's *Narrative*, p. 320, which says they were knocked down with a cooper's mallet. The victims included those converts living at Salem, who had peaceably come in to Gnadenhütten with their captors; but those at New Schönbrunn had taken the alarm and fled.—R. G. T.

[1] Later authorities put the total number at ninety—twenty-nine men, twenty-seven women, and thirty-four children.—R. G. T.

cord which bound him; and springing forward, aimed a thrust at one of his conductors. The cutting of the rope had, however, drawn it so [238] tightly that he who held it became sensible that it was wrought upon in some way; and turning quickly round to ascertain the cause, scarcely avoided the stab. The Indian then bounded from them, and as he fled towards the woods, dexterously removed the cord from his wrists. Several shots were discharged at him without effect, when the firing was stopped, lest in the hurry and confusion of the pursuit, some of their own party might suffer from it. A young man, mounting his horse, was soon by the side of the Indian, and springing off, his life had well nigh been sacrificed by his rashness. He was quickly thrown to the ground, and the uplifted tomahawk about to descend on his head, when a timely shot, directed with fatal precision, took effect on the Indian and saved him.

Had the Moravians been disposed for war, they could easily have ensured their own safety, and dealt destruction to the whites. If, when their town was entered by a party of only sixteen, their thirty men, aided by the youths of the village, armed and equipped as all were, had gone forth in battle array, they could have soon cut off those few; and by stationing some gunners on the bank of the river, have prevented the landing of the others of the expedition. But their faith in the sincerity of the whites— their love of peace and abhorrence of war, forbade it; and the confidence of those who first rushed into the town, in these feelings and dispositions of the Indians, no doubt prompted them to that act of temerity, while an unfordable stream was flowing between them and their only support.

During the massacre at Gnadenhutten, a detachment of the whites was ordered to Shoenbrun to secure the Moravians who were there. Fortunately however, two of the inhabitants of this village had discovered the dead body of Shabosh in time to warn their brethren of danger, and they all moved rapidly off. When the detachment arrived, nothing was left for them *but plunder.—This was secured,* and they returned to their comrades. Gnadenhutten was then *pillaged* of every article of value which could be easily removed; its houses—even those which contained the dead bodies of the Moravians—were burned to ashes, and the men set out on their return to the settlements.[1]

The expedition against the Moravian towns on the Muskingum, was projected and carried on by inhabitants of the [239] western counties of Pennsylvania,—a district of country which had long been the theatre of Indian hostilities. Its result (strange as it may now appear) was highly gratifying to many; and the ease with which so much *Indian* blood had been made to flow, coupled with an ardent desire to avenge the injuries which had been done them by the savages, led to immediate preparations for another, to be conducted on a more extensive scale, and requiring the co-operation of more men. And although the completion of the work of destruction, which had been so successfully begun, of the Moravian Indians, was the principal inducement of some, yet many attached themselves to the expedition, from more noble and commendable motives.

The residence of the Moravians ever since they were removed to the plains of Sandusky, was in the immediate vicinity of the Wyandot villages, and the warriors from these had been particularly active and untiring in their hostility to the frontier settlements of Pennsylvania. The contemplated campaign against the Moravians, was viewed by many as affording a fit opportunity to punish those savages for their many aggressions, as it would require that they should proceed but a short distance beyond the point proposed, in order to arrive at their towns; and they accordingly engaged in it for that purpose.

Other causes too, conspired to fill the ranks and form an army for the accomplishment of the contemplated objects.—The commandants of the militia of Washington and Westmoreland counties 'Cols. Williamson and Mar-

---

[1] Salem, New Schönbrunn and Gnadenhütten were all destroyed by fire. The whites returned home the following day, with ninety-six scalps—ninety Moravians and six outlying Indians. It seems certain that a few hostiles were with the Moravians at the time of the massacre.—R. G. T.

shall)[1] encouraged the inhabitants to volunteer on this expedition, and made known, that every militia man who accompanied it, finding his own horse and gun, and provisions for a month, should be exempt from two tours of militia duty; and that all horses unavoidably lost in the service, should be replaced from those taken in the Indian country. From the operation of these different causes, an army of nearly five hundred men was soon raised, who being supplied with ammunition by the Lieutenant Colonel of Washington county, proceeded to the Old Mingo towns, the place of general rendezvous—where an election was held to fill the office of commander of the expedition.[2] The candidates were Colonel Williamson and Colonel Crawford; and the latter gentleman being chosen immediately organized the troops, and prepared to march.

[240] On the 25th of May, the army left the Mingo towns, and pursuing "Williamson's trail," arrived at the upper Moravian town on the Muskingum (Shoenbrun,) where (finding plenty of corn of the preceding year's crop, yet on the stalk) they halted to refresh their horses. While here, Captains Brenton and Bean, discovered and fired upon two Indians; and the report of the guns being heard in camp, the men, in despite of the exertions of their officers, rushed towards the source of alarm, in the most tumultuous and disorderly manner.—Colonel Crawford, used to the discipline of continental soldiers, saw in the impetuosity and insubordination of the troops under his command, enough to excite the liveliest apprehensions for

---

[1] David Williamson, as previously seen, was a colonel of militia in Washington County, Pa.; James Marshal, as county lieutenant of Washington, was his superior officer.—R. G. T.

[2] The place of rendezvous was Mingo Bottom (the present Mingo Junction, O.), and the date May 20. It was the 24th before all were present. The volunteers numbered 480, of whom two-thirds were from Washington County; most of the others were from Fayette County, Pa., and a few from Ohio County, Va. In the vote for commander, William Crawford received 235, and Williamson 230. Four field majors were elected to rank in the order named: Williamson, Thomas Gaddis, John McClelland, and one Brinton. The standard modern authority for the details of this expedition, is Butterfield's *Crawford's Expedition Against Sandusky* (Cincinnati: Robert Clarke & Co., 1873).—R. G. T.

the event of the expedition. He had volunteered to go on the campaign, only in compliance with the general wish of the troops that he should head them, and when chosen commander in chief of the forces assembled at the Mingo towns, he is said to have accepted the office with reluctance, not only sensible of the impracticability of controlling men unused to restraint, but opposed to some of the objects of the expedition, and the frequently expressed determination of the troops, to spare no Indian whom accident or the fortune of war should place in their power.

From Shoenbrun the army proceeded as expeditiously as was practicable to the site of the Moravian village, near the Upper Sandusky; but instead of meeting with this oppressed and persecuted tribe, or having gained an opportunity of plundering their property, they saw nothing which manifested that it had been the residence of man, save a few desolate and deserted huts,—the people, whom it was their intention to destroy, had some time before, most fortunately for themselves, moved to the Scioto.

Discontent and dissatisfaction ensued upon the disappointment. The guides were ignorant of there being any Indian towns nearer than those on Lower Sandusky, and the men became impatient to return home. In this posture of affairs, a council of war, consisting of the field officers and captains, was held, and it was resolved to move forward, and if no enemy appeared that day, to retrace their steps. Just after this determination was made known, an express arrived, from a detachment of mounted men, which had been sent forward to reconnoitre, with information that about three miles in advance a large body of Indians had been discovered hastening [241] rapidly to meet them. The fact was, that Indian spies had watched and reported the progress of the expedition, ever after it left the Mingo towns; and when satisfied of its destination, every arrangement which they could make to defeat its object, and involve the troops in the destruction to which it was their purpose to consign others, was begun by the savages. Having perfected these, they were marching on to give battle to the whites.

Immediately upon the reception of this intelligence,

the army moved forward, and meeting the reconnoitreing party coming in, had proceeded but a short distance farther, when they came in view of the Indians hastening to occupy a small body of woods, in the midst of an extensive plain. The battle was then begun by a heavy fire from both sides, and the savages prevented gaining possession of the woods. A party of them having however, taken post in them before the whites came up, continued much to annoy the troops, until some of them, alighting from their horses, bravely rushed forward and dislodged them. The Indians then attempted to gain a small skirt of wood on Colonel Crawford's right; but the vigilance of the commanding officer of the right wing, (Major Leet) detected the movement, and the bravery of his men defeated it. The action now became general and severe and was warmly contested until dark, when it ceased for a time without having been productive of much advantage to either side. During the night, both armies lay on their arms; adopting the wise policy of kindling large fires along the line of battle, and retreating some distance behind them, to prevent being surprised by a night attack.

Early in the morning a few shots were fired, but at too great distance for execution. The Indians were hourly receiving reinforcements, and seemed busily engaged in active preparations for a decisive conflict. The whites became uneasy at their increasing strength; and a council of the officers deemed it expedient to retreat. As it would be difficult to effect this in open day, in the presence of an enemy of superior force, it was resolved to postpone it until night, making in the mean time every arrangement to ensure its success.—The killed were buried, and fires burned over the graves to prevent discovery,—litters were made for bearing the wounded, and the army was formed into three lines with them in the centre.

[242] The day passed, without an attack being made by the Indians. They were still seen to traverse the plains in every direction, and in large bodies; and not until the troops were about forming the line of retreat, did they seem to have any idea that such a movement was intended. They then commenced firing a few shots, and in a little

while it became apparent that they had occupied every pass, leaving open only that which led to Sandusky. Along this way, the guides conducted the main army, until they had passed the Indian lines about a mile; when wheeling to the left, they marched round and gained the trail of their outward march. Continuing in this they proceeded to the settlements without any interruption.— The savage warriors thinking it better to follow detached parties than the main army.

The few shots which were fired by the Indians as the whites were forming the line of retreat, were viewed by many as evidence that their purpose had been discovered, and that these were signal guns preceding a general attack. Under these impressions, the men in front hurried off and others following the example, at least one third of the army were to be seen flying in detached parties, and in different directions from that taken by the main body, supposing that the attention of the Indians would be wholly turned to this point. They were not permitted to proceed far under this delusive supposition. Instead of following the main army, the Indians pursued those small parties with such activity, that not many of those composing them were able to escape;—one company of forty men under a Captain Williamson,[1] was the only party detached from the principal body of the troops, fortunate enough to get with the main army on its retreat. Late in the night, they broke through the Indian lines under a heavy fire and with some loss, and on the morning of the second day of the retreat, again joined their comrades in the expedition, who had marched off in a body; in compliance with the orders of the commander-in-chief.

Colonel Crawford himself proceeded at the head of the army for some short distance, when missing his son, his son-in-law (Major Harrison) and two nephews,[2] he stopped to enquire for them. Receiving no satisfactory information respecting either of them, he was induced through

---

[1] Col. David Williamson.—R. G. T.

[2] His son John, his son-in-law Major William Harrison, and one of his nephews,—not two,—William Crawford. They were captured by the Indians and killed.—R. G. T.

anxiety for their fate to continue still, until all had passed on, when he resumed his flight, in company with doctor Knight[1] and two [243] others. For their greater security, they travelled some distance apart, but from the jaded and exhausted condition of their horses could proceed but slowly. One of the two men in company with the Colonel and doctor Knight, would frequently fall some distance behind the others, and as frequently call aloud for them to wait for him. Near the Sandusky creek he hallooed to them to halt, but the yell of a savage being heard near him, they went on and never again was *he heard of*. About day, Colonel Crawford's horse gave out and he was forced to proceed on foot, as was also the other of the two who had left the field with him and Knight. They continued however to travel together, and soon over-took Captain Biggs, endeavoriug to secured the safety of himself and Lieutenant Ashly, who had been so badly wounded that he was unable to ride alone. A heavy fall of rain induced them to halt, and stripping the bark from some trees, they formed a tolerable shelter from the storm, and remained there all night. In the morning they were joined by another of the troops, when their company con-sisted of six—Colonel Crawford and Doctor Knight, who kept about an hundred yards in front—Captain Biggs and Lieutenant Ashly, in the center; and the other two men in the rear. They proceeded in this way about two miles, when a party of Delawares suddenly sprang from their hiding places into the road, and making prisoners of Colonel Crawford and Doctor Knight, carried them to the Indian camp near to where they then were. On the next day the scalps of Captain Biggs and Lieutenant Ashly, were brought in by another party of Indians who had been likewise watching the road. From the encampment, they were led, in company with nine other prisoners, to the old Wyandot town, from which place they were told they would be taken to the new town, not far off. Before set-

---

[1] Dr. John Knight, surgeon to the expedition. He was captured, and sentenced to death, but after thrilling adventures finally escaped.— R. G. T.

ting out from this place, Colonel Crawford and Doctor
Knight were painted black by Captain Pipe, a Delaware
chief, who told the former, that he intended to have him
shaved when he arrived among his friends, and the latter
that he was to be carried to the Shawnee town, to see
some of his old acquaintance. The nine prisoners were
then marched off in front of Colonel Crawford and Doctor
Knight, who were brought on by Pipe and Wingenim,[1]
another of the Delaware chiefs. As they went on, they
passed the bodies of four of the captives, who had been
tomahawked and scalped on the way, and came [244] to
where the remaining five were, in time to see them suffer
the same fate from the hands of squaws and boys. The
head of one of them (John McKinley, formerly an officer
in one of the Virginia regiments) was cut off, and for some
time kicked about on the ground. A while afterwards
they met Simon Girty and several Indians on horseback;
when Col. Crawford was stripped naked, severely beaten
with clubs and sticks, and made to sit down near a post
which had been planted for the purpose, and around which
a fire of poles was burning briskly. His hands were then
pinioned behind him, and a rope attached to the band
around his wrist and fastened to the foot of a post about
fifteen feet high, allowing him liberty only to sit down, or
walk once or twice round it, and return the same way.
Apprehensive that he was doomed to be burned to death,
he asked Girty if it were possible that he had been spared
from the milder instruments of the tomahawk and scalping knife, only to suffer the more cruel death by fire.
" *Yes, said Girty, composedly, you must be burned Colonel.*"
"It is dreadful, replied Crawford, but I will endeavor to
bear it patiently." Captain Pipe then addressed the savages in an animated speech, at the close of which, they
rent the air with hideous yells, and immediately discharged
a number of loads of powder at the naked body of their
victim. His ears were then cut off, and while the men
would apply the burning ends of the poles to his flesh, the
squaws threw coals and hot embers upon him, so that in a

---

[1] Wingenund.—R. G. T.

little time he had too, to walk on fire. In the midst of these sufferings, he begged of the infamous Girty to shoot him. That worse than savage monster, tauntingly replied, "how can I? you see I have no gun," and laughed heartily at the scene.

For three hours Colonel Crawford endured the most excruciating agonies with the utmost fortitude, when faint and almost exhausted, he commended his soul to God, and laid down on his face. He was then scalped, and burning coals being laid on his head and back, by one of the squaws, he again arose and attempted to walk; but strength failed him and he sank into the welcome arms of death. His body was then thrown into the fire and consumed to ashes.[1]

Of the whole of this shocking scene, Doctor Knight was [245] an unwilling spectator; and in the midst of it was told by Girty, that it should be his fate too, when he arrived at the Shawanee towns. These were about forty miles distant; and he was committed to the care of a young warrior to be taken there. On the first day they travelled about twenty-five miles, and when they stopped for the night, the Doctor was securely fastened. In vain did he anxiously watch for an opportunity to endeavor to

[244] [1] Colonel Crawford was then about fifty years of age, and had been an active warrior against the savages for a great while. During [245] the French war, he distinguished himself by his bravery and good conduct, and was much noticed by General Washington, who obtained for him an ensigncy. At the commencement of the revolution, he raised a regiment by his own exertions, and at the period of this unfortunate expedition, bore the commission of Colonel in the Continental army. He possessed a sound judgment, was a man of singular good nature and great humanity, and remarkable for his hospitality. His melancholy sufferings and death spread a gloom over the countenances of all who knew him. His son, John Crawford, and his son-in-law, Major Harrison, were taken prisoners, carried to the Shawanee towns and murdered.

Comment by R. G. T.—Crawford was born in 1732, in Orange County, Va., of Scotch-Irish parentage. He made the friendship of Washington while the latter was surveying for Lord Fairfax, in the Shenandoah Valley, in 1749. Washington taught him his art, but in 1755 he abandoned it for a military life, and thenceforward was a prominent character on the frontier, often serving under Washington. From 1767 forward, his home was on the banks of the Youghiogheny, on Braddock's Road. Crawford fought in Dunmore's War, and throughout the Revolution did notable service on the Virginia border.

release himself from the cords which bound him. The Indian was vigilant and slept none. About day light they arose, and while the Indian was kindling a fire, the gnats were so troublesome that he untied his prisoner, and set him likewise to making a fire to relieve them from the annoyance. The doctor took a burning coal between two sticks, and going behind the Indian towards the spot at which he was directed to excite a smoke, turned suddenly around, and struck the savage with all his force. The Indian fell forward, but quickly recovering and seeing his gun in the hands of his assailant, ran off, howling hideously.—The anxiety of Doctor Knight, saved the life of the savage.—When he seized the gun, he drew back the cock in such haste and with so much violence as to break the main spring and render it useless to him; but as the Indian was ignorant of this circumstance, he continued his flight and the doctor was then enabled to escape. After a toilsome travel of twenty-one days, during which time he subsisted altogether on wild gooseberries, young nettles, a raw terrapin and two young birds, he arrived safely at Fort McIntosh—meagre, emaciated and almost famished.

Another instance of great good-fortune occurred in the person of John Slover,[1] who was also made prisoner after having travelled more than half the distance from the fatal scene of [246] action to Fort Pitt. When only eight years of age he had been taken by some Indians on New river, and detained in captivity for twelve years. In this time he became well acquainted with their manners and customs, and attached to their mode of living so strongly, that when ransomed by his friends, he left his Indian companions with regret. He had become too, while with them, familiar with the country north west of the Ohio, and an excellent woodsman; and in consequence of these attainments was selected a principal guide to the army on its outward march. When a retreat was prematurely began to be made by detached parties, he was some distance from

---

[1] John Slover, one of the guides to the expedition, was among the best known scouts of his day, on the Upper Ohio. His published *Narrative* is a prime source of information relative to the events of the campaign.— R. G. T.

camp, and having to equip himself for flight, was left a good way in the rear. It was not long however, before he came up with a party, whose horses were unable to extricate themselves from a deep morass, over which they had attempted to pass. Slover's was soon placed in the same unpleasant situation, and they all, alighting from them, proceeded on foot. In this manner they traveled on until they had nearly reached the Tuscarawa, when a party of savages from the way side, fired upon them. One of the men was killed, Slover and two others made prisoners, & the fifth escaped to Wheeling.

Those taken captive were carried first to Wachatomakah (a small town of the Mingoes and Shawanees,) from whence after having been severely beaten, they were conducted to a larger town two miles farther. On their arrival here, they had all to pass through the usual ceremonies of running the gauntlet; and one of them who had been stripped of his clothes and painted black, was most severely beaten, mangled, and killed, and his body cut in pieces and placed on poles outside the town. Here too, Slover saw the dead bodies of Col. McClelland, Major Harrison and John Crawford; and learned that they had all been put to death but a little while before his arrival there; and although he 'was spared for some time, yet every thing which he saw acted towards other prisoners, led him to fear that he was reserved for a more cruel fate, whenever the whim of the instant should suggest its consummation. At length an express arrived from Detroit with a speech for the warriors, which decided his doom. Being deciphered from the belt of wampum which contained it, the speech began by enquiring why they continued to take prisoners, and said, " Provisions are scarce and when you send in [247] prisoners, we have them to feed, and still some of them are getting off, and carrying tidings of our affairs. When any of your people are taken by the rebels, they shew no mercy. Why then should you? My children take no more prisoners of any sort, men, women, or children." Two days after the arrival of the express with this speech, a council of the different tribes of Indians near, was held, and it was determined to act in conformity with the advice of the Governor of Detroit. Slover was then the only white prisoner at this town; and on the morning after the council was dissolved, about forty warriors came to the house where he was, and tying a rope around his neck, led him off to another village, five miles distant. Here again he was severely beaten with clubs & the pipe end of the tomahawk, & then tied to a post, around which were piles of wood. These were soon kindled, but a violent rain falling unexpectedly, extinguished the flames, before they had effected him. It was then agreed to postpone his execution, until the next day, and being again beaten and much wounded by their blows, he was taken to a block house, his hands tied, the rope about his neck fastened to a beam of the building, and three warriors left to guard him for the night.

If the feelings of Slover would have permitted him to enjoy sleep, the conduct of the guard would have prevented it. They delighted in keeping alive in his mind the shocking idea of the suffering which he would have to endure, & frequently asking him "how he would like to eat fire," tormented him nearly all night. Awhile before day however, they fell asleep, and Slover commenced untying himself. Without much difficulty he loosened the cord from his arms, but the ligature around his neck, of undressed buffalo-hide, seemed to defy his exertions to remove it; and while he was endeavoring to gnaw it in vain, one of the sleeping Indians, rose up and going near to him, sat and smoked his pipe for some time. Slover lay perfectly still, apprehensive that all chance of escape was now lost to him. But no—the Indian again composed himself to sleep, and the first effort afterwards made, to loose the band from his neck by slipping it over his head, resulted in leaving Slover entirely unbound. He then crept softly from the house and leaping a fence, gained the cornfield. Passing on, as he approached a tree, he espied a squaw with several children lying at its root; and fearing that some of them might discover him and give the alarm of his [248] escape, he changed his course. He soon after reached a glade, in which were several horses, one of which he

22

caught; and also found a piece of an old rug, which afforded him his only covering until he reached Wheeling. This he was enabled to do in a few days, being perfectly acquainted with the country.

The town, from which Slover escaped, was the one to which Dr. Knight was to have been taken. The Indian who had him in charge, came in while Slover was there, and reported his escape—magnifying the Doctor's stature to gigantic size and attributing to him herculean strength. When Slover acquainted the warriors with the fact, that Doctor Knight was diminutive and effeminate, they laughed heartily at this Indian, and mocked at him for suffering the escape. He however bore a mark which showed that, weak and enfeebled as he was, the Doctor had not played booty when he aimed the blow at his conductor.—It had penetrated to the skull and made a gash of full four inches length.

These are but few of the many incidents which no doubt occurred, to individuals who endeavored to effect an escape by detaching themselves from the main army. The number of those, thus separated from the troops, who had the good fortune to reach the settlements, was small indeed; and of the many of them who fell into the hands of the savages, Knight and Slover are believed to be the only persons, who were so fortunate as to make an escape. The precise loss sustained in the expedition, was never ascertained, and is variously represented from ninety to one hundred and twenty.

Among those of the troops who went out under Col. Crawford, that came into Wheeling, was a man by the name of Mills.[1] Having rode very fast, and kept his horse almost continually travelling, he was forced to leave him, near to the present town of St. Clairsville in Ohio. Not liking the idea of loosing him altogether, upon his arrival at Wheeling he prevailed on Lewis Wetsel[2] to go with him to the place where his horse gave out, to see if they could not find him. Apprehensive that the savages would

---

[1] Thomas Mills. -R. G. T.

[2] Lewis Wetzel, a noted Indian fighter. See p. 161, *note.*—R. G. T.

pursue the fugitives to the border of the settlements, Wetsel advised Mills that their path would not be free from dangers, and counselled him to "prepare for fighting."

When they came near to the place where the horse had been left, they met a party of about forty Indians going towards [249] the Ohio river and who discovered Mills and Wetsel as soon as these saw them. Upon the first fire from the Indians Mills was wounded in the heel, and soon overtaken and killed. Wetzel singled out his mark, shot, and seeing an Indian fall, wheeled and ran. He was immediately followed by four of the savages, who laid aside their guns that they might the more certainly overtake him. Having by practice, acquired the art of loading his gun as he ran, Wetsel was indifferent how near the savages approached him, if he were out of reach of the rifles of the others. Accordingly, keeping some distance ahead of his pursuers whilst re-loading his gun, he relaxed his speed until the foremost Indian had got within ten or twelve steps of him. He then wheeled, shot him dead, and again took to flight. He had now to exert his speed to keep in advance of the savages 'till he should again load, & when this was accomplished and he turned to fire, the second Indian was near enough to catch hold of the gun, when as Wetsel expressed it, *"they had a severe wring."* At length he succeed in raising the muzzle to the breast of his antagonist, and killed him also.

In this time both the pursuers and pursued had become much jaded, and although Wetsel had consequently a better opportunity of loading quickly, yet taught wariness by the fate of their companions, the two remaining savages would spring behind trees whenever he made a movement like turning towards them. Taking advantage of a more open piece of ground, he was enabled to fire on one of them who had sought protection behind a sapling too small to screen his body. The ball fractured his thigh, and produced death. The other, instead of pressing upon Wetsel, uttered a shrill yell, and exclaiming, "no catch *him*, gun always loaded," returned to his party.

While expeditions were carrying on by the whites, against the Moravian and other Indians, the savages were prosecuting their accustomed predatory and exterminating war, against several of the settlements. Parties of Indians, leaving the towns to be defended by the united exertions of contiguous tribes, would still penetrate to the abode of the whites, and with various success, strive to avenge on them their real and fancied wrongs.

On the 8th of March as William White, Timothy Dorman and his wife, were going to, and in site of Buchannon fort, some guns were discharged at them, and White being shot through the hip soon fell from his horse, and was tomahawked, scalped and lacerated in the most frightful manner.[1]—Dorman and his wife were taken prisoners. The people in the fort heard the firing and flew to arms; but the river being between, the savages cleared themselves, while the whites were crossing over.

After the killing of White (one of their most active

---

[1] L. V. McWhorter informs me that White, who was a prominent settler, was once with others on a hunting expedition, when they surprised a small party of Indians. They killed several, but one active young brave ran off, with White close at his heels. The Indian leaped from a precipice, alighting in a quagmire in which he sank to his waist. White, with tomahawk in hand, jumped after him. In the struggle which ensued, White buried his weapon in the red man's skull. The victim's father was among those who escaped, and for a long time—McWhorter says "several years"—he lurked about the settlements trailing White. Finally, he succeeded in shooting his man, within sight of the fort. Mrs. White was an eye-witness of the tragedy. McWhorter claims that Withers is mistaken in saying that White was "tomahawked, scalped and lacerated in the most frightful manner." The avenging Indian tried to get his scalp, but an attacking party from the fort were so close upon him that he fled before accomplishing his object. McWhorter reports another case, not mentioned in Withers. One Fink was "killed by Indians in ambush, while letting down a pair of bars one evening, just in front of where the Buckhannon court-house now stands."—R. G. T.

and vigilant warriors and spies) and the capture of Dorman, it was resolved to abandon the fort, and seek elsewhere, security from the greater ills which it was found would befall them if they remained. This apprehension arose from the fact, that Dorman was then with the savages, and that to gratify his enmity to particular individuals in the settlement, he would unite with the Indians, and *from his knowledge of the* [251] *country, be enabled* to conduct them the more securely to blood and plunder. He was a man of sanguinary and revengeful disposition, prone to quarrelling, and had been known to say, that if he caught particular individuals with whom he was at variance, in the woods alone, he would murder them and attribute it to the savages. He had led, when in England, a most abandoned life, and after he was transported to this country, was so reckless of reputation and devoid of shame for his villainies, that he would often recount tales of theft and robbery in which he had been a conspicuous actor. The fearful apprehensions of increased and aggravated injuries after the taking of him prisoner, were well-founded; and subsequent events fully proved, that, but for the evacuation of the fort, and the removal of the inhabitants, all would have fallen before the fury of savage warriors, with this abandoned miscreant at their head.

While some of the inhabitants of that settlement were engaged in moving their property to a fort in Tygart's Valley (the others removing to Nutter's fort and Clarksburg,) they were fired upon by a party of savages, and two of them, Michael Hagle and Elias Paynter, fell. The horse on which John Bush was riding, was shot through; yet Bush succeeded in extricating himself from the falling animal, and escaped though closely pursued by one of the savages. Several times the Indian following him, would cry out to him, " *Stop, and you shall not be hurt—If you do not, I will shoot you,*" and once Bush, nearly exhausted, and in despair of getting off, actually relaxed his pace for the purpose of yielding himself a prisoner, when turning round he saw the savage stop also, and commence loading his gun. This inspired Bush with fear for the consequences, and renewing his flight he made his escape.　Edward Tanner, a mere youth, was soon taken prisoner, and as he was being carried to their towns, met between twenty and thirty savages, headed by Timothy Dorman, proceeding to attack Buchannon fort.　Learning from him that the inhabitants were moving from it, and that it would be abandoned in a few days, the Indians pursued their journey with so much haste, that Dorman had well nigh failed from fatigue.　They arrived however, too late, for the accomplishment of their bloody purpose; the settlement was deserted, and the inhabitants safe within the walls of other fortresses.

[252] A few days after the evacuation of the fort, some of its former inmates went from Clarksburg to Buchannon for grain which had been left there.　When they came in sight, they beheld a heap of ashes where the fort had been; and proceeding on, became convinced that the savages were yet lurking about.　They however, continued to go from farm to farm collecting the grain, but with the utmost vigilance and caution, and at night went to an out house, near where the fort had stood.　Here they found a paper, with the name of Timothy Dorman attached to it, dated at the Indian towns, and containing information of those who had been taken captive in that district of country.

In the morning early, as some of the men went from the house to the mill, they saw the savages crossing the river, Dorman being with them.　Thinking it best to impress them with a belief that they were able to encounter them in open conflict, the men advanced towards them,— calling to their companions in the house, to come on.　The Indians fled hastily to the woods, and the whites, not so rash as to pursue them, returned to the house, and secured themselves in it, as well as they could.　At night, Captain George Jackson went privately forth from the house, and at great hazzard of being discovered by the waylaying savages, proceeded to Clarksburg, where he obtained such a reinforcement as enabled him to return openly and escort his former companions in danger, from the place of its existence.

Disappointed in their hopes of involving the inhabit-

ants of the Buchannon settlements in destruction, the savages went on to the Valley. Here, between Westfall's and
Wilson's forts, they came upon John Bush and his wife,
Jacob Stalnaker and his son Adam. The two latter being
on horse back and riding behind Bush and his wife, were
fired at, and Adam fell. The old gentleman, rode briskly
on, but some of the savages were before him and endeavored
to catch the reins of his bridle, and thus stop his flight.
He however, escaped them all. The horse from which
Adam Stalnaker had fallen, was caught by Bush, and both
he and Mrs. Bush got safely away on him.

The Indians then crossed the Alleghany mountains,
and coming to the house of Mrs. Gregg, (Dorman's former
master) made an attack on it. A daughter of that gentleman, alone fell a victim to their thirst for blood. When
taken prisoner, [253] she refused to go with them, and
Dorman sunk his tomahawk into her head and then
scalped her. She however, lived several days and related
the circumstances above detailed.

After the murder of John Thomas and his family in
1781, the settlement on Booth's creek was forsaken, and
its inhabitants went to Simpson's creek, for greater security. In the Spring John Owens procured the assistance
of some young men about Simpson's creek, and proceeded
to Booth's creek for the purpose of threshing some wheat
at his farm there.—While on a stack throwing down
sheaves, several guns were fired at him by a party of twelve
Indians, concealed not far off. Owens leapt from the
stack, and the men caught up their guns. They could
not, however, discover any one of the savages in their
covert and thought it best to retreat to Simpson's creek
and strengthen their force before they ventured in pursuit
of their enemy. They accordingly did so, and when they
came again to Booth's creek, the Indians had decamped,
taking with them the horses left at Owens'. The men
however found their trail and followed it until night.—
Early next morning, crossing the West Fork at Shinns-
ton, they went on in pursuit and came within sight of
the Indian camp, and seeing some of the savages lying
near their fires, fired at them, but, as was believed without

effect. The Indians again took to flight; and as they were hastening on, one of them suddenly wheeled and fired upon his pursuers. The ball passed through the hunting-shirt of one of the men, & Benjamin Coplin (then an active, enterprising young man) returning the shot, an Indian was seen suddenly to spring into a laurel thicket. Not supposing that Coplin's ball had taken effect, they followed the other savages some distance farther, and as they returned got the horses and plunder left at the camp. Some time afterwards a gun was found in the thicket, into which the Indian sprang, and it was then believed that Coplin's shot had done execution.

In the same spring the Indians made their appearance on Crooked run, in Monongalia county. Mr. Thomas Pindall, having been one day at Harrison's fort, at a time when a greater part of the neighbourhood had gone thither for safety, prevailed on three young men, (Harrison, Crawford and Wright, to return and spend the night with him.) Some time after they had been abed, the females waked Mr. Pindall, and telling him that they had heard several times a noise very much [254] resembling the whistling on a charger, insisted on going directly to the fort. The men heard nothing, and being inclined to believe that the fears of the females had given to the blowing of the wind, that peculiar sound, insisted that there was no danger and that it would be unpleasant to turn out then, as the night was very dark. Hearing nothing after this, for which they could not readily account, the men rose in the morning unapprehensive of interruption; and the females, relieved of their fears of being molested by savages during the night, continued in bed. Mr. Pindall walked forth to the woods to catch a horse, and the young men went to the spring hard by, for the the purpose of washing. While thus engaged three guns were fired at them, and Crawford and Wright were killed. Harrison fled and got safely to the fort.

The females alarmed at the report of the guns, sprang out of bed and hastened towards the fort, pursued by the Indians. Mrs. Pindall was overtaken and killed, but Rachael Pindall, her sister-in-law, escaped safely to the fort.

In June some Indians came into the neighborhood of Clarksburg, and not meeting with an opportunity of killing or making prisoners any of the inhabitants without the town, one of them, more venturous than the' rest, came so near as to shoot Charles Washburn as he was chopping a log of wood in the lot, and then running up, with the axe, severed his skull, scalped him, and fled safely away. Three of Washburn's brothers had been previously murdered by the savages.

In August as Arnold and Paul Richards were returning to Richard's fort, they were shot at by some Indians, lying hid in a cornfield adjoining the fort, and both fell from their horses. The Indians leaped over the fence immediately and tomahawked and scalped them.

These two men were murdered in full view of the fort, and the firing drew its inmates to the gate to ascertain its cause. When they saw that the two Richards' were down, they rightly judged that Indians had done the deed; and Elias Hughes, ever bold and daring, taking down his gun, went out alone at the back gate, and entered the cornfield, into which the savages had again retired, to see if he could not avenge on one of them the murder of his friends. Creeping softly along, he came in view of them standing near the fence, reloading their guns, and looking intently at the people at the fort gate. Taking [255] a deliberate aim at one of them, he touched the trigger. His gun flashed, and the Indians alarmed ran speedily away.

A most schocking scene was exhibited some time before this, on Muddy creek in Pennsylvania. On the 10th of May as the Reverend John Corbly, his wife and five children were going to meeting, (Mr. Corbly being a short distance behind) they were attacked by a party of savages waylaying the road. The shrieks of Mrs. Corbly and the children, drew the husband and father to the fatal spot. As he was approaching, his wife called to him, "to fly." He knew that it was impossible for him to contend successfully against the fearful odds opposed to him, and supposing that his family would be carried away as prisoners, and that he would be enabled either to recover

them by raising a company and pursuing the savages, or
to ransom them, if conducted to the Indian towns, he complied with her wish, and got safely off, though pursued by
one of the savages. But it was not their intention to
carry them into captivity. They delighted too much, to
look upon the lifeblood flowing from the heart; and accordingly shed it most profusely. The infant in its
mother's arms was the first on whom their savage fury
fell,—it was tomahawked and scalped. The mother then
received several severe blows, but not falling, was shot
through the body, by the savage who chased her husband;
and then scalped. Into the brains of a little son, six years
old, their hatchets were sunk to the heft. Two little girls,
of two and four years of age, were tomahawked and
scalped. The eldest child, also a daughter, had attempted to
escape by concealing herself in a hollow log, a few rods from
the scene of action. From her hiding place, she beheld all
that was done, and when the bleeding scalp was torn from
the head of her last little sister, & she beheld the savages retiring from the desolation which they had wrought,
she crawled forth from concealment. It was too soon.
One of the savages yet lingered near, to feast to satiety on
the horrid spectacle. His eyes caught a glimpse of her as
she crept from the log, and his tomahawk and scalping
knife became red with her blood.

When Mr. Corbly returned, all his hopes vanished.
Which ever way he turned, the mangled body of some one
of his family was presented to his view. His soul sickened
at the contemplation of the scene, and he fainted and fell.
When he had revived, he was cheered with the hope that
some of [256] them might yet survive. Two of his
daughters had manifested symptoms of returning life, and
with care and attention were restored to him.

Thus far in the year 1782, the settlements only suffered
from the accustomed desultory warfare of the savages. No
numerous collection of Indians had crossed their border,—
no powerful army of warriors, threatening destruction to
the forts, those asylums of their safety, had appeared
among them.—But the scene was soon to change.

In August, there was a grand council convened at Chilicothe, in which the Wyandots, the Shawanees, the Min-goes, the Tawas, Pottowatomies, and various other tribes were represented.[1] Girty and McKee—disgraces to human nature—aided in their deliberations. The surrender of Cornwallis, which had been studiously kept secret from the Indians, was now known to them, and the war between Great Britain and the United States, seemed to them to be verging to a close.—Should a peace ensue, they feared that the concentrated strength of Virginia, would bear down upon them and crush them at once. In anticipation of this state of things, they had met to deliberate, what course it best became them to pursue. Girty addressed the council. He reminded them of the gradual encroach-ments of the whites;—of the beauty of Kentucky and its value to them as a hunting ground.—He pointed out to them the necessity of greater efforts to regain possession of that country, and warned them that if they did not combine their strength to change the present state of things, the whites would soon leave them no hunting grounds; and they would consequently, have no means of procuring rum to cheer their hearts, or blankets to warm their bodies. His advice was well received and they determined to continue the war.[2]

When the council was adjourned, the warriors pro-ceeded to execute its determinations. Two armies, the one of six hundred, and the other three hundred and fifty men, prepared to march, each to it assigned station—The larger was destined to operate against Kentucky, while the smaller, was to press upon North Western Virginia; and each was abundantly supplied with the munitions of war.[3] Towards the last of August the warriors who were

---

[1] The council was held at Wapatomica, in June. There were pres-ent representatives of the Ottawas, Chippewas, Wyandots, Delawares, Shawnees, Munsees, and Cherokees. Simon Girty came with the Wy-andots; Captain McKee was then a trader at Wapatomica.—R. G. T.

[2] See the alleged speech in Butterfield's *History of the Girtys*, pp. 190. 191.—R. G. T.

[3] The Kentucky party was under Capt. William Caldwell, who wrote, "I crossed the Ohio with three hundred Indians and rangers." Capts. McKee and Elliott, and the three Girtys were with the expedition.

348 _Withers's Chronicles_

to act in Kentucky, appeared before Bryant's station, south
of Licking river, and placed themselves under covert
during night,[1] and in advantageous [257] situations for
firing upon the station. so soon as its doors should be
thrown open.

There were at that time but few inhabitants occupying
that station. William Bryant, its founder, and one in
whose judgment, skill and courage, many confidently re-
posed for security from savage enormity, had been unfortunately discovered by some Indians near the mouth of
Cane run, and killed.—His death caused most of those
who had come to that place from North Carolina, to forsake the station, and return to their own country. Emigrants from Virginia, arriving some short time before, and
among whom was Robert Johnson, (the father of Richard
M. Johnson) to a certain extent supplied this desertion;
yet it was in respect to numbers so far inferior to the savage forces, that the most resolute shuddered in apprehension of the result.

The station too, was at that time, careless and inattentive to its own defence; not anticipating the appearance of a savage army before its gates. Indeed had the
Indians delayed their attack a few hours, it would have
been in almost an entirely defenceless condition; as the
men were on that morning to have left it, for the purpose
of aiding in the defence of another station, which was
then understood to be assailed by an army of Indians.
Fortunately however, for the inhabitants, as soon as the
doors of some of the cabins were opened in the morning,
the savages commenced the fire, and thus admonished
them of danger, while it was not yet too late to provide
against it.

The Indians in the attack on Bryant's station practised their usual stratagem, to ensure their success. It was
begun on the south-east angle of the station, by one hundred warriors, while the remaining five hundred were

_____

Caldwell crossed the river early in July, not far below the mouth of
Limestone creek—site of the present Maysville, Ky.—R. G. T.

[1] They arrived on the night of August 15.—R. G. T.

concealed in the woods on the opposite side, ready to take advantage of its unprotected situation when, as they anticipated, the garrison would concentrate its strength, to resist the assault on the south-east. But their purpose was fully comprehended by the garrison, and instead of returning the fire of the one hundred, they secretly sent an express to Lexington for assistance, and commenced repairing the pallisades, and putting themselves in the best possible condition to withstand the fury of the assailants. Aware that the Indians were posted near the spring, and believing that they would not fire unless some of the men should be seen going thither, the women [258] were sent to bring in water for the use of the garrison. The event justified their expectations—The concealed Indians, still farther to strengthen the belief, that their whole force were engaged in the attack on the south-east, forbore to fire, or otherwise contradict the impression which they had studiously sought to make on the minds of its inmates.

When a sufficiency of water had been provided, and the station placed in a condition of defence, thirteen men were sent out in the direction from which the assault was made. They were fired upon by the assailing party of one hundred, but without receiving any injury; and retired again within the pallisades. Instantly the savages rushed to the assault of, what they deemed, the unprotected side of the station, little doubting their success. A steady, well directed fire, put them quickly to flight. Some of the more desperate and daring however, approached near enough to fire the houses, some of which were consumed; but a favorable wind drove the flames from the mass of the buildings and the station escaped conflagration.

Disappointed of the expected success of their first stratagem, the assailants withdrew a short distance, and concealed themselves under the bank of the creek, to await the arrival of the assistance, which was generally sent to a besieged fort or station, arranging themselves in ambushment to intercept its approach.

When the express from Bryant's station reached Lexington, the male inhabitants had left there to aid in the defence of Holder's station, which was reported to be attacked. Following on their route, they overtook them at Boonesborough, and sixteen mounted, and thirty footmen were immediately detached to aid the inhabitants of Bryant's station. When this reinforcement came near, the firing had entirely ceased, no enemy was visible, and they approached in the confidence that all was well. A sudden discharge of shot from the savages in ambush, dispelled that hope. The horsemen however, passed safely by. The cloud of dust produced by the galloping of their horses, obscured the view and hindered the otherwise deadly aim of the Indians. The footmen were less fortunate. Two of them were killed, and four wounded; and but for the luxuriant growth of corn in the field through which they passed, nearly all must have fallen, before the overwhelming force of the enemy.

[259] Thus reinforced, the garrison did not for an instant doubt of safety; while the savages became hopeless of success by force of arms, and resorted to another expedient to gain possession of the station. In the twilight of evening, Simon Girty covertly drew near, and mounting on a stump from which he could be distinctly heard, demanded the surrender of the place. He told the garrison, that a reinforcement, with cannon, would arrive that night, and that this demand was suggested by *his humanity*, as the station must ultimately fall, and he could assure them of protection if they surrendered, but could not if the Indians succeeded by storm; and then demanded, if "they knew who was addressing them." A young man by the name of Reynolds, (fearing the effect which the threat of cannon might have upon the garrison, as the fate of Ruddle's and Martin's stations was yet fresh in their recollections,) replied, that he "knew him well, and held him in such contempt, that he had named a worthless dog which he had SIMON GIRTY; that his reinforcements and threats, were not heeded by the garrison, who expected to receive before morning such an auxiliary force as would enable them to give a good account of the cowardly wretches that followed him, whom he held in such contempt that he had prepared a number of switches with which to

drive them out of the country if they remained there 'till day."[1]

Affecting to deplore their obstinacy, Girty retired, and during the night, the main body of the Indian army marched off, leaving a few warriors to keep up an occasional firing and the semblance of a siege.[2]

Shortly after the retreat of the savages, one hundred and sixty men, from Lexington, Harrodsburg and Boonesborough, assembled at Bryant's station, and determined to pursue them.[3] Prudence should have prevailed with them to await the arrival of Colonel Logan, who was known to be collecting additional forces from the other station; but brave and fearless, well equipped, and burning with ardent desire to chastise their savage invaders, they rather indiscreetly chose to march on, unaided, sooner than risk suffering the enemy to retire, by delaying for other troops. But the Indians had no wish to retire, to avoid the whites. The trail left by them, to the experienced eye of Daniel Boone, furnished convincing evidence, that they were only solicitous to conceal their numbers, in reality to tempt pursuit.

[260] When the troops arrived at the Lower Blue Licks, they saw the only Indians, which had met their eye on the route. These were slowly ascending the ridge on the opposite side of the river. The party was halted, and Boone consulted as to what course it would be best to pursue. He was of opinion that the savage force was much greater, than most had been led to believe by the appearance of the trail, and anticipating pursuit, were then in ambush in the ravines; and he advised that the force be divided into two equal parts, the one, marching up the river, to cross it at the mouth of Elk creek, above

---

[1] The above incident is mentioned in none of the contemporary chronicles, and is probably fiction.—R. G. T.

[2] The attack was begun early in the morning of the 16th, and continued with more or less vigor until about 10 A. M. of the 17th. Caldwell then withdrew his force "in a leisurely manner." The attacking party lost five killed and two wounded, all Indians; the garrison lost four killed and three wounded.—R. G. T.

[3] A hundred and eighty-two, under Col. John Todd. Pursuit was commenced on the 18th.—R. G. T.

the upper ravine, while the other party should take a position below for the purpose of co-operating whenever occasion might require; but that neither party should by any means cross the river, until spies were sent out to learn the position and strength of the enemy.[1] The officers generally were inclined to follow the counsel of Boone, but Major McGary, remarkable for impetuosity, exclaiming, "Let all who are not cowards, follow me," spurred his horse into the river. The whole party caught the contagious rashness,—all rushed across the river. There was no order,—no arrangement—no unity or concert. None "paused in their march of terror," lest "we should hover o'er the path," but each, following his own counsel, moved madly towards the sheltered ravines and wooded ground, where Boone had predicted the savages lay hid. The event justified the prediction, and showed the wisdom of his counsel.

At the head of a chosen band of warriors, Girty[2] advanced with fierceness upon the whites, from the advantageous position which he covertly occupied, and "madness, despair and death succeed, the conflict's gathering wrath." The Indians had greatly the advantage in numbers, as well as position, and the disorderly front of the whites, gave them still greater superiority. The bravery of the troops for a while withstood the onset, and the contest was fierce and sanguinary 'till their right wing being turned, a retreat became inevitable. All pressed towards the ford, but a division of the savage army, foreseeing this, had been placed so as to interpose between them and it; and they were driven to a point on the river, where it could only be crossed by swimming. Here was indeed a scene of blood and carnage. Many were killed on the

---

[1] The battle occurred at 8 A. M. of August 19, a short distance north of the Lower Blue Licks, on the Licking river, in what is now Nicholas County.—R. G. T.

[2] The tendency among early Western chroniclers has been greatly to magnify the importance of Simon Girty. He was merely an interpreter on this, as on most other expeditions. Caldwell was in command. The British force now consisted of 200 Indians and 30 rangers. Some of the Indians had already left for their villages.—R. G. T.

bank; others in swimming over, and some were toma-hawked in the edge of the water. Some of those who had been foremost in getting across the river, wheeled and opened a steady fire upon the pursuers. Others, animated by the example, as soon as they reached the bank dis-charged their guns upon the savages, and checking them for a while enabled many to escape death. But for this stand, the footmen would have been much harrassed, and very many of them entirely cut off. As it was, the loss in slain was great. Of one hundred and seventy-six (the number of whites,) sixty-one were killed, and eight taken prisoners. Cols. Todd and Trigg,—Majors Harland and Bulger,—Capts. Gordon, McBride, and a son of Daniel Boone, were among those who fell. The loss of the sav-ages was never known;—they [261] were left in possession of the battle ground, and at leisure to conceal or carry off their dead, and when it was next visited by the whites, none were found.[1]

A most noble and generous act, performed by one of the whites, deserves to be forever remembered. While they were flying before the closely pursuing savages, Reynolds (who at Bryant's station had so cavalierly re-plied to Girty's demand of its surrender) seeing Col. Rob-ert Patterson, unhorsed and considerably disabled by his wounds, painfully struggling to reach the river, sprang from his saddle, and assisting him to occupy the relin-quished seat, enabled that veteran officer to escape, and fell himself into the hands of the savages. He was not long however, detained a prisoner by them. He was taken by a party of only three Indians; and two whites passing hurriedly on towards the river, just after, two of his cap-tors hastened in pursuit of them, and he was left guarded by only one. Reynolds was cool and collected, and only

---

[1] The British rangers lost one of their number by death; of their Indian allies, ten were killed and fourteen wounded. Of the Kentuck-ians, about seventy were killed, several badly wounded, and seven made prisoners. Caldwell continued his leisurely retreat to Upper Sandusky, which he reached September 24, the Indians meanwhile dispersing to their several homes.—R. G. T.

23

awaited the semblance of an opportunity, to attempt an escape. Presently the savage in whose custody he was, stooped to tie his moccason. Suddenly he sprang to one side, and being fleet of foot, got safely off.

The battle of the Blue Licks was fought on the 19th of August. On the next day Col. Logan, with three hundred men, met the remnant of the troops retreating to Bryant's station; and learning the fatal result of the contest, hurried on to the scene of action to bury the dead, and avenge their fall—if the enemy should be found yet hovering near. On his arrival not a savage was to be seen. Flushed with victory, and exulting in their revenge, they had retired to their towns, to feast the eyes of their brethren, with the scalps of the slain. The field of battle presented a miserable spectacle. All was stillness, where so lately had arisen the shout of the impetuous, but intrepid whites, and the whoop and yell of the savages, as they closed in deadly conflict; not a sound was to be heard but the hoarse cry of the vulture, flapping her wings and mounting into the air, alarmed at the intrusion of man. Those countenances, which had so lately beamed with daring and defiance, were unmeaning and inexpressive; and what with the effect produced on the dead bodies, by the excessive heat and the mangling and disfiguration of the tomahawk and scalping knife, scarcely one could be distinguished from another. Friends tortured themselves in vain, to find friends, in the huge mass of slain,—fathers to recognize their sons. The mournful gratification of bending over the lifeless bodies of dear relations and gazing with intense anxiety on their pallid features, was denied them. Undistinguished, though not unmarked, all were alike consigned to the silent grave, amid sighs of sorrow and denunciations of revenge.

An expedition against the Indian towns was immediately resolved upon, and in September, Gen. Clarke marched towards them, at the head of nearly one thousand men. Being discovered on their route and the intelligence soon spreading that an army from [262] Kentucky was penetrating the country, the savages deserted their villages and fled; and the expedition was thus hindered of its purpose of chastising them. The towns however were burned, and in a skirmish with a party of Indians, five of them were killed, and seven made prisoners, with the loss of only one man.[1]

The Indian forces which were to operate against North Western Virginia, for some time delayed their purpose, and did not set out on their march, until a while before the

---

[1] Gen. George Rogers Clark gave this official report of his expedition against the Shawnees, in a letter dated Lincoln, November 27, 1782: " We left the Ohio the 4th instant, with 1050 men, surprised the principal Shawanese Town in the evening of the 10th, and immediately detached strong parties to different quarters; and in a few hours afterwards two thirds of the towns were laid in ashes, and every thing they were possessed of destroyed, except such as were most useful to the troops, the enemy not having time to secrete any part of their property. The British trading post at the head of the Miami and Carrying Place to the waters of the Lakes, shared the same by a party of 150 horse, commanded by Col. Logan, and property to a great amount was also destroyed: the quantity of provisions burnt far surpassed any idea we had of their stores. The loss of the enemy was ten scalps, seven prisoners, and two whites retaken ; ours, one killed and one wounded.

" After laying part of four days in their towns, and finding all attempts to bring them to a general action fruitless, we retired, as the season was far advanced and the weather threatening. I could not learn by the prisoners that they had the least idea of General Irvin's design of penetrating into their country. Should he have given them another stroke at Sandusky, it will more than double the advantages already gained.

" We might probably have got many more scalps and prisoners-could we have known in time whether or not we were discovered, which we took for granted until getting within three miles when some circum, stances occurred that gave us reason to think otherwise, though uncertain.—Col. Floyd, with 300 men, was ordered to advance and bring on an action or attack the town, Major Wells with a party of horse being previously detached by a different route as a party of observation: although Col. Floyd's motion was so quick as to get to the town but a few minutes later than those who discovered his approach, the inhabitants had sufficient notice to effect their escape to the woods by the alarm cry being given, and which was repeated by all that heard it; of course our party only fell in with the rear of the enemy.

" I must beg leave to recommend the militia of Kentucky whose behaviour on the occasion does them honour, particularly their desire of saving prisoners."

The document is here given as found in Almon's *Remembrancer*, xvi., pp. 93, 94; but it has of course been edited, after the fashion of that day, for Clark's original letters abound in misspellings.—R. G. T.

return of those who had been sent into Kentucky. On their way, a question arose among them—against what part of the country they should direct their movements—and their division ou this subject, rising by degrees 'till it assumed a serious aspect, led many of the chiefs to determine on abandoning the expedition; but a runner arriving with intelligence of the great success which had crowned the exertion of the army in Kentucky, they changed that determination, and proceeded hastily towards Wheeling.

In the first of September, John Lynn (a celebrated spy and the same who had been with Capt. Foreman at the time of the fatal ambuscade at Grave creek) being engaged in watching the warriors paths, northwest of the Ohio, discovered the Indians marching with great expedition for Wheeling, and hastening to warn the inhabitants of the danger which was threatening them, swam the river, and reached the village, but a little while before the savage army made its appearance. The fort was at this time without any regular garrison, and depended for defence exclusively, on the exertions of those who sought security within its walls. The brief space of time which elapsed between the alarm by Lynn, and the arrival of the Indians, permitted only those who were immediately present to retire into it, and when the attack was begun to be made, there were not within its pallisades, twenty effective men to oppose the assault. The dwelling house of Col. Ebenezer Zane, standing about forty yards from the fort, contained the military stores which had been furnished by the government of Virginia; and as it was admirably situated as an out post from which to annoy the savages in their onsets, he resolved on maintaining possession of it, as well to aid in the defence of the fort, as for the preservation of the ammunition. Andrew Scott, George Green, Mrs. Zane, Molly Scott and Miss McCullough, were all who remained with him. The kitchen (adjoining) was occupied by Sam (a negro belonging to Col. Zane) and Kate, his wife.—Col. Silas Zane commanded in the fort.

When the savage army approached, the British colors

were waving over them; and before a shot was discharged
at the fort, they demanded the surrender of the garrison.
No answer was deigned to this demand, but the firing of
several shot (by order of Silas Zane) at the standard
which they bore; and the savages rushed to the assault.
A well directed and brisk fire opened upon them from
Col. Zane's house and the fort, soon drove them back.
Again they rushed forward; and again were they repulsed.
The number of [263] arms in the house and fort, and the
great exertions of the women in moulding bullets, loading
guns and handing them to the men, enabled them to fire
so briskly, yet so effectively, as to cause the savages to
recoil from every charge. The darkness of night soon
suspended their attacks, and afforded a temporary repose
to the besieged. Yet were the assailants not wholly inactive. Having suffered severely by the galling fire poured
upon them from the house, they determined on reducing
it to ashes. For this purpose, when all was quietness and
silence, a savage, with a fire brand in his hand crawled to
the kitchen, and raising himself from the ground, waving
the torch to and fro to rekindle its flame, and about to apply it to the building, received a shot which forced him to
let fall the engine of destruction and hobble howling away.
The vigilance of Sam had detected him, in time to thwart
his purpose.

On the return of light, the savages were seen yet en-
vironing the fort, and although for some time they delayed
to renew their suspended assault, yet it was evident they
had not given over its contemplated reduction. They
were engaged in making such preparations, as they were
confident would ensure success to their exertions.

Soon after the firing of the preceding day had subsided, a small boat, proceeding from Fort Pitt to the Falls
of Ohio with cannon balls for the use of the troops there,
put to shore at Wheeling; and the man who had charge of
her, although discovered and slightly wounded by the
savages, reached the postern and was admitted to the fort.
The boat of course fell into the hands of the enemy, and
they resolved on using the balls aboard, for the demolition
of the fortress. To this end they procured a log, with

a cavity as nearly corresponding with the size of the ball, as they could; and binding it closely with some chains taken from a shop hard by, charged it heavily, and pointing it towards the fort, in imagination beheld its walls tumbling into ruin, and the garrison bleeding under the strokes and gashes of their tomahawks and scalping knives. All things being ready, the match was applied.—A dreadful explosion ensued. Their cannon burst;—its slivers flew in every direction; and instead of being the cause of ruin to the fort, was the source of injury only to themselves. Several were killed, many wounded, and all, dismayed by the event. Recovering from the shock, they presently returned with redoubled animation to the charge. Furious from disappointment, exasperated with the unforseen yet fatal result, they pressed to the assault with the blindness of phrensy. Still they were received with a fire so constant and deadly, that they were again forced to retire; and most opportunely for the garrison.

When Lynn gave the alarm that an Indian army was approaching, the fort having been for some time unoccupied by a garrison, and Col. Zane's house being used as a magazine, those who retired into the fortress had to take with them a supply of ammunition for its defence. The supply of powder, deemed ample at the time, by reason of the long continuance of the savages, and the repeated [264] endeavors made by them, to storm the fort was now almost entirely exhausted, a few loads only, remaining. In this emergency, it became necessary to replenish their stock, from the abundance of that article in Col. Zane's house. During the continuance of the last assault, apprized of its security, and aware of the danger which would inevitably ensue, should the savages after being again driven back, return to the assault before a fresh supply could be obtained, it was proposed that one of their fleetest men should endeavor to reach the house, obtain a keg and return with it to the fort. It was an enterprise full of danger; but many of the chivalric spirits, then pent up within the fortress, were willing to encounter them all.

Among those who volunteered to go on this emprise,

was Elizabeth, the younger sister of Colonel Zane. She was then young active and athletic;—with precipitancy to dare danger, and fortitude to sustain her in the midst of it. Disdaining to weigh the hazard of her own life, against the risk of that of others, when told that a man would encounter less danger by reason of his greater fleetness, she replied—"and should he fall, his loss will be more severely felt. You have not one man to spare;—a woman will not be missed in the defence of the fort." Her services were accepted. Divesting herself of some of her garments, as tending to impede her progress, she stood prepared for the hazzardous adventure; and when the gate was opened, she bounded forth with the buoyancy of hope, and in the confidence of success. Wrapt in amazement, the Indians beheld her spring forward; and only exclaiming, "a squaw, a squaw," no attempt was made to interrupt her progress. Arrived at the door, she proclaimed her embassy. Col. Zane fastened a table cloth around her waist, and emptying into it a keg of powder, again she ventured forth. The Indians were no longer passive. Ball after ball passed whizzing and innocuous by. She reached the gate and entered the fort in safety.[1]

Another instance of heroic daring, deserves to be recorded [265] here. When intelligence of the investiture of Wheeling by the savages, reached Shepherd's fort, a party was immediately detached from it, to try and gain admission into the besieged fortress, and aid in its defence. Upon arriving in view, it was found that the attempt would be hopeless and unavailing, and the detachment consequently prepared to return. Francis Duke, (son-in-law to Colonel Shepherd) was unwilling to turn his back on a people, straitened as he knew the besieged must be, and declared his intention of endeavoring to reach the fort, that he might contribute to its defence. It was useless to disuade him from the attempt;—he knew its danger,

[1] [264] This heroine had but recently returned from Philadelphia, where she had received her education, and was totally unused to such scenes as were daily exhibiting on the frontier. She afterwards became the wife of Mr. McGlanlin; and he dying, she married a Mr. Clarke, and is yet living in Ohio.

but he also knew their weakness, and putting spurs to his horse, rode briskly forward, calling aloud, " open the gate,— open the gate." He was seen from the fort, and the gate was loosed for his admission; but he did not live to reach it.—Pierced by the bullets of the savages, he fell, to the regret of all. Such noble daring, deserved a better fate.

During that night and the next day, the Indians still maintained the seige, and made frequent attempts to take the fort by storm ; but they were invareiably repulsed by the deadly fire of the garrison and the few brave men in Colonel Zane's house. On the third night, despairing of success, they resolved on raising the siege; and leaving one hundred chosen warriors to scour and lay waste the country, the remainder of their army retreated across the Ohio, and encamped at the Indian Spring,—five miles from the river. Their loss in the various assaults upon the fort, could not be ascertained; but was doubtless very considerable. Of the garrison, none were killed and only two wounded,—the heroic Francis Duke was the only white who fell during the siege. The gallantry displayed by all, both men and women, in the defence of the fort, can not be too highly commended; but to the caution and good conduct of those few brave individuals who occupied Colonel Zane's house, its preservation has been mainly attributed.

In the evening preceding the departure of the savages from before Wheeling, two white men, who had been among them for several years, and then held commands in the army, deserted from them, and on the next morning early were taken prisoners by Colonel Swearingen, who, with ninety-five men, was on his way to aid in the defence of Wheeling fort, and the chastisement of its assailants. Learning from them [266] the determination of the savages to withdraw from Wheeling, and detach a portion of their force to operate in the country, he despatched runners in every direction to alarm the country and apprize the inhabitants of danger.[1] The intelligence was received by

---

[1] See p. 224, *note* 1, for reference to confusion between the two sieges of Wheeling, and the over-statement of early border historians.— R. G. T.

Jacob Miller when some distance from home, but apprehensive that the meditated blow would be aimed at the fort where he resided, he hastened thither, and arrived in time to aid in preparing for its defence.

The place against which the savages directed their operations, was situated on Buffaloe creek, twelve or fifteen miles from its enterance into the Ohio, and was known as Rice's fort. Until Miller's return there were in it only five men; the others having gone to Hagerstown to exchange their peltries, for salt, iron and ammunition. They immediately set about making preparations to withstand an assault; and in a little while, seeing the savages approaching from every direction, forsook the cabins and repaired to the blockhouse. The Indians perceived that they were discovered, and thinking to take the station by storm, shouted forth the war whoop and rushed to the assault. They were answered by the fire of the six brave and skilful riflemen in the house, and forced to take refuge behind trees and fallen timber. Still they continued the firing; occasionally calling on the whites to "*give up, give up. Indian too many. Indian too big. Give up. Indian no kill.*" The men had more faith in the efficacy of their guns to purchase their safety, than in the proferred mercy of the savages; and instead of complying with their demand, called on them, "as cowards skulking behind logs to leave their coverts, and shew but their yellow hides, and they would make holes in them."

The firing was kept up by the savages from their protected situation, until night, and whenever even a remote prospect of galling them was presented to the whites, they did not fail to avail themselves of it. The Indian shots in the evening, were directed principally against the stock as it came up as usual to the station, and the field was strewed with its dead carcases. About ten o'clock of the night they fired a large barn (thirty or forty yards from the blockhouse) filled with grain and hay, and the flames from which seemed for awhile to endanger the fort; but being situated on higher ground, and the current of air flowing in a contrary direction, it escaped conflagration. Collecting on the side of the fort opposite [267] to the fire, the

Indians took advantage of the light it afforded them to renew the attack; and·kept it up until about two o'clock, when they departed. Their ascertained loss was four warriors,—three of whom were killed by the first firing of the whites,—the other about sundown. George Folebaum was the only white who suffered. Early in the attack, he was shot in the forehead, through a port-hole, and instantly expired; leaving Jacob Miller, George Leffler, Peter Fullenwieder, Daniel Rice and Jacob Leffler, junior, sole defenders of the fort; and bravely and effectually did they preserve it, from the furious assaults of one hundred chosen savage warriors.

Soon after the Indians left Rice's fort, they moved across the hills in different directions and in detached parties. One of these observing four men proceeding towards the fort which they had lately left, waylaid the path and killed two of them on the first fire. The remaining two fled hastily; and one of them swift of foot, soon made his escape. The other, closely pursued by one of the savages, and in danger of being overtaken, wheeled to fire. His gun snapped, and he again took to flight. Yet more closely pressed by his pursuer, he once more attempted to shoot. Again his gun snapped, and the savage being now near enough, hurled a tomahawk at his head. It missed its object and both strained every nerve for the chase. The Indian gained rapidly upon him; and reaching forth his arm, caught hold of the end of his belt. It had been tied in a bow-knot, and came loose.—Sensible that the race must soon terminate to his disadvantage unless he could kill his pursuer, the white man once more tried his gun. It fired; and the savage fell dead at his feet.

Some time in the summer of this year, a party of Wyandots, consisting of seven warriors, (five of whom were, one of the most distinguished chiefs of that nation and his four brothers) came into one of the intermediate settlements between Fort Pitt and Wheeling, killed an old man whom they found alone, robbed his cabin, and commenced retreating with the plunder. They were soon discovered by spies; and eight men, two of whom were Adam and

Andrew Poe, (brothers, remarkable for uncommon size, great activity, and undaunted bravery) went in pursuit of them. Coming on their trail not far from the Ohio, Adam Poe, fearing an ambuscade, left his companions [268] to follow it, while he moved across to the river under cover of the high weeds and bushes, with the view to attack them in the rear should he find them situated as he expected.—Presently he espied an Indian raft at the water's edge, but seeing nothing of the savages, moved cautiously down the bank; and when near the foot, discovered the large Wyandot chief and a small Indian standing near and looking intently towards the party of whites, then some distance lower down the bottom. Poe raised his gun, and aiming surely at the chief, pulled trigger. It missed fire, and the snap betrayed his presence. Too near to retreat, he sprang forward; and seizing the large Indian by the breast, and at the same instant encircling his arms around the neck of the smaller one, threw them both to the ground. Extricating himself from the grasp of Poe, the small savage raised his tomahawk; but as he aimed the blow, a vigorous and well directed kick, staggered him back, and he let fall the hatchet. Recovering quickly, he aimed several blows in defiance and exultation,—the vigilance of Poe distinguished the real from the feigned stroke, and suddenly throwing up his arm, averted it from his head, but received a wound in his wrist. By a violent effort, he freed himself from the grip of the chief, and snatching up a gun, shot his companion through the breast, as he advanced the third time with the tomahawk.

In this time the large chief had regained his feet; and seizing Poe by the shoulder and leg threw him to the ground.—Poe however, soon got up, and engaged with the savage in a close struggle, which terminated in the fall of both into the water. Now it became the object of each to drown his antagonist, and the efforts to accomplish this were continued for some time with alternate success;— first one and then the other, being under water. At length, catching hold of the long tuft of hair which had been suffered to grow on the head of the chief, Poe held him under water, until he supposed him dead; but relaxing his hold too soon, the gigantic savage was again on his feet and ready for another grapple. In this both were carried beyond their depth, and had to swim for safety. Both sought the shore, and each, with all his might, strained every nerve to reach it first that he might end the conflict with one of the guns lying on the beach. The Indian was the more expert swimmer, and Poe, outstripped by him, turned and swam farther into the river, in the hope of avoiding being [269] shot by diving. Fortunately his antagonist laid hold on the gun which had been discharged at the little Indian, and he was enabled to get some distance into the river.

At this juncture, two others of the whites came up; and one of them mistaking Poe for a wounded savage attempting to escape, shot and wounded him in the shoulder. He then turned to make for shore, and seeing his brother Andrew on the bank, called to him to " shoot the big Indian." Having done this, Andrew plunged into the river to assist Adam in getting out; and the wounded savage, to preserve his scalp, rolled himself into the water, and struggling onward, sunk and could not be found.

During the continuance of this contest, the whites had overtaken the other five Indians, and after a desperate conflict, succeeded in killing all but one; with the loss of three of their companions.—A great loss, when the number engaged is taken into consideration.

[270] CHAPTER XVI.

The treaty of peace between the United States and Great Britain, which terminated so gloriously the war of the revolution, did not put a period to Indian hostilities.[1] The aid which had been extended to the savages, and which enabled them so successfully to gratify their implacable resentment against the border country, being withdrawn, they were less able to cope with the whites than they had been, and were less a hindrance to the population and improvement of those sections of country which had been the theatre of their many outrages. In North Western Virginia, indeed, although the war continued to be waged against its inhabitants, yet it assumed a different aspect. It became a war rather of plunder, than of blood; and although in the predatory incursions of the Indians, individuals some times fell a sacrifice to savage passion; yet this was of such rare occurrence, that the chronicles of those days are divested of much of the interest, which attaches to a detail of Indian hostilities. For several years, scarce an incident occurred worthy of being rescued from oblivion.

In Kentucky it was far otherwise. The war continued to be prosecuted there, with the wonted vigor of the savages.—The General Assembly of Virginia having, at the close of the revolution, passed an act for surveying the land set apart for her officers and soldiers, south of Green river, the surveyors descended to the Ohio, to explore the country and perform the duties assigned them. On their arrival they found it occupied by the savages, and acts of

---

[1] News of the preliminary articles of peace, which had been signed at Paris, November 30, 1782, did not reach Fort Pitt until May, 1783. In July following, De Peyster, British commandant at Detroit, gathered at that post the chiefs of eleven tribes as far south as the Great Miami and the Wabash, and informed them of the event.—R. G. T.

hostilities immediately [271] ensued. In December, 1783, the Legislature likewise passed an act, appropriating the country between the Scioto and Miami rivers, for the purpose of satisfying the claims of the officers and soldiers, if the land previously allotted, in Kentucky, should prove insufficient for that object. This led to a confederacy of the many tribes of Indians, interested in those sections of country, and produced such feelings and gave rise to such acts of hostility on their part, as induced Benjamin Harrison the Governor of Virginia, in November, 1784, to recommend the postponement of the surveys; and in January, 1785, a proclamation was issued, by Patrick Henry, (successor of Gov. Harrison) commanding the surveyors to desist and leave the country. A treaty was soon after concluded, by which the country on the Scioto, Miami, and Muskingum, was ceded to the United States.[1] In this interval of time, North Western Virginia enjoyed almost uninterrupted repose. There was indeed an alarm of Indians, on Simpson's creek in 1783, but it soon subsided; and the circumstance which gave rise to it (the discharge of a gun at Major Power) was generally attributed to a white man.

In 1784, the settlement towards the head of West Fork, suffered somewhat from savage invasion. A party of Indians came to the house of Henry Flesher, (where the town of Weston now is) and fired at the old gentleman, as he was returning from the labors of the field. The gun discharged at him, had been loaded with two balls, and both taking effect, crippled his arm a good deal. Two savages immediately ran towards him; and he, towards the door; and just as he was in the act of entering it, one of them had approached so closely as to strike at him with the butt end of his gun. The breech came first in contact with the facing of the door, and descending on his head, seemed to throw him forward into the house, and his wife closing

---

[1] The treaty was held at Fort McIntosh, at the mouth of the Beaver, early in January, 1785. The tribes represented were the Wyandots, Chippewas, Delawares, and Ottawas. The commissioners were Arthur Lee, Richard Butler, and George Rogers Clark. Col. Josiah Harmar was in charge of the troops.—R. G. T.

the door, no attempt was made by the savages to force it open. Still, however, they did not feel secure; and as soon as they became assured that the savages were withdrawn, they left the house and sought security elsewhere. Most of the family lay in the woods during the night,— one young woman succeeded in finding the way to Hacker's creek, from whence Thomas Hughes immediately departed to find the others. This was effected early next morning, and all were safely escorted to that settlement.

[272] The foregoing event happened in September, and in a few days after, as Daniel Radcliff was proceeding to the Brushy Fork of Elk creek on a hunting expedition, he was shot (probably by the Indians who had been at Flesher's,) tomahawked and scalped in a shocking manner.

In 1785, six Indians came to Bingamon creek, (a branch of the West Fork) and made their appearance upon a farm occupied by Thomas and Edward Cunningham. At this time the two brothers were dwelling with their families in separate houses, but nearly adjoining, though not in a direct line with each other. Thomas was then on a trading visit east of the mountain, and his wife and four children were collected in their room for the purpose of eating dinner, as was Edward with his family, in their house. Suddenly a lusty savage entered where were Mrs. Thomas Cunningham and her children, but seeing that he would be exposed to a fire from the other house, and apprehending no danger from the woman and children, he closed the door and seemed for a time only intent on the means of escaping.

Edward Cunningham had seen the savage enter his brother's house, and fastened his own door, seized his gun and stepping to a small aperture in the wall next the house in which was the Indian, and which served as well for a port hole as for the admission of light, was ready to fire whenever the savage should make his appearance. But in the other house was a like aperture, and through it the Indian fired at Edward, and shouted the yell of victory. It was answered by Edward. He had seen the aim of the savage only in time to avoid it,—the bark from the log close to his head, was knocked off by the ball and flew

into his face. The Indian seeing that he had missed his
object, and observing an adze in the room, deliberately
commenced cutting an aperture in the back wall through
which he might pass out without being exposed to a shot
from the other building.[1]

Another of the Indians came into the yard just after the
firing of his companion, but observing Edward's gun pointing through the port hole, he endeavored to retreat out of
its range. He failed of his purpose. Just as he was about
to spring over the fence, the gun was fired and he fell forward. The ball however only fractured his thigh bone,
and he was yet able to hobble over the fence and take
shelter behind a [273] coverlet suspended on it, before Edward could again load his gun.

While the Indian was engaged in cutting a hole in the
wall, Mrs. Cunningham made no attempt to get out. She
was well aware that it would draw down upon her head
the fury of the savage; and that if she escaped ·this, she
would most probably be killed by some of those who were
watching around, before the other door could be opened
for her admission.—She knew too, that it was impossible
for her to take the children with her, and could not brook
the idea of leaving them in the hands of the savage monster. She even trusted to the hope that he would withdraw, as soon as he could, without molesting any of them.
A few minutes served to convince her of the fallacy of this
expectation. When the opening had been made sufficiently large, he raised his tomahawk, sunk it deep into
the brains of one of the children, and throwing the scarcely
lifeless body into the back yard, ordered the mother to
follow after. There was no alternative but death, and she
obeyed his order, stepping over the dead body of one of
her children,[2] with an infant in her arms and two others

---

[1] L. V. McWhorter, well informed in the local traditions, writes:
" When the Indian sprang into the house, with drawn tomahawk, he
closed and for a few moments stood with his back to the door. Then,
while cutting an opening through the wall, he asked Mrs. Cunningham
how many men there were in the other house. She answered by holding up the extended fingers of both hands, indicating 10."—R. G. T.

[2] McWhorter: " Mrs. Cunningham related that the last she

screaming from horror at the sight, and clinging to her. When all were out he scalped the murdered boy, and setting fire to the house, retired to an eminence in the field, where two of the savages were, with their wounded companion.—leaving the other two to watch the opening of Edward Cunningham's door, when the burning of the house should force the family from their shelter. They were disappointed in their expectation of that event by the exertions of Cunningham and his son. When the flame from the one house communicated to the roof of the other, they ascended to the loft, threw off the loose boards which covered it, and extinguished the fire;—the savages shooting at them all the while, and their balls frequently striking close by.

Despairing of accomplishing farther havoc, and fearful of detection and pursuit, the Indians collected together and prepared to retreat. Mrs. Cunningham's eldest son was first tomahawked and scalped; the fatal hatchet sunk into the head of her little daughter, whom they then took by the arms and legs, and slinging it repeatedly against a tree, ended its sufferings with its life. Mrs. Cunningham stood motionless with grief, and in momentary expectation of having the same dealt to her and her innocent infant. But no! She was [274] doomed to captivity; and with her helpless babe in her arms, was led off from this scene of horror and of wo. The wounded savage was carried on a rough litter, and they all departed, crossing the ridge to Bingamon creek, near which they found a cave that afforded them shelter and concealment.[1] After night, they returned to Edward Cunningham's, and finding no one, plundered and fired the house.

When the savages withdrew in the evening, Cunning-

---

saw of her little daughter, was one quivering little foot sticking up over a log behind which she had been thrown."—R. G. T.

[1] McWhorter: "The cave in which Mrs. Cunningham was concealed is on Little Indian Run, a branch of Big Bingamon Creek, on which stream the tragedy took place. The cave is about two miles northwest of the site of the capture, and in Harrison County, W. Va."—R. G. T.

24

ham went with his family into the woods, where they remained all night, there being no settlement nearer than eight or ten miles. In the morning, proceeding to the nearest house, they gave the alarm and a company of men was soon collected to go in pursuit of the Indians. When they came to Cunningham's and found both houses heaps of ashes, they buried the bones which remained of the boy who was murdered in the house, with the bodies of his brother and little sister, who were killed in the field; but so cautiously had the savages conducted their retreat that no traces of them could be discovered, and the men returned to their homes.

Some days after, circumstances induced the belief that the Indians were yet in the neighborhood, and men were again assembled for the purpose of tracing them. They were now enabled to distinguish the trail, and pursued it near to the cave, where from the number of rocks on the ground and the care which had been taken by the Indians to leave no vestige, they could no longer discover it. They however examined for it in every direction until night forced them to desist. In thinking over the incidents of the day; the cave occurred to the mind of Major Robinson, who was well acquainted with the woods, and he concluded that the savages must be concealed in it. It was examined early next morning, but they had left it the preceding night and departed for their towns. After her return from captivity, Mrs. Cunningham stated, that in time of the search on the day before, the Indians were in the cave, and that several times the whites approached so near, that she could distinctly hear their voices; the savages standing with their guns ready to fire, in the event of their being discovered, and forcing her to keep the infant to her breast, lest its crying might point to the place of their concealment.[1]

In consequence of their stay at this place on account of their wounded companion, it was some time before they

---

[1] McWhorter: "Mrs. Cunningham stated that an Indian stood over her with an uplifted tomahawk, to prevent her from crying out. At times, the whites were upon the very rock above their heads."—R. G. T.

arrived [275] in their own country;[1] and Mrs. Cunningham's sufferings, of body as well as mind were truly great. Fatigue and hunger oppressed her sorely,—the infant in her arms, wanting the nourishment derived from the due sustenance of the mother, plied at the breast for milk, in vain—blood came in stead; and the Indians perceiving this, put a period to its sufferings, with the tomahawk, even while clinging to its mother's bosom. It was cast a little distance from the path, and left without a leaf or bush to hide it from beasts of prey.

The anguish of this woman during the journey to the towns, can only be properly estimated by a parent; her bodily sufferings may be inferred from the fact, that for ten days her only sustenance consisted of the head of a wild turkey and three papaws, and from the circumstance that the skin and nails of her feet, scalded by frequent wading of the water, came with her stockings, when upon their arrival at a village of the Delawares, she was permitted to draw them off. Yet was she forced to continue on with them the next day.—One of the Indians belonging to the village where they were, by an application of some sanative herbs, very much relieved the pain which she endured.

When she came to the town of those by whom she had been made prisoner, although receiving no barbarous or cruel usage, yet everything indicated to her, that she was reserved for some painful torture. The wounded Indian had been left behind, and she was delivered to his father. Her clothes were not changed, as is the case when a prisoner is adopted by them; but she was compelled to wear them, dirty as they were,—a bad omen for a captive. She was however, not long in apprehension of a wretched fate. A conference was soon to take place between the Indians and whites, preparatory to a treaty of peace; and

---

[1] McWhorter says local tradition has it that the Indians remained in the cave a night and a day; they departed before daylight, during the second night. Mrs. Cunningham related that just before leaving, the wounded brave was borne from the cave by his fellows, and she never again saw him; her opinion was, that he was then dead, and his body was sunk in a neighboring pool.—R. G. T.

witnessing an uncommon excitement in the village one evening, upon inquiring, learned that the Great captain Simon Girty had arrived. She determined to prevail with him, if she could, to intercede for her liberation, and seeing him next day passing near on horseback, she laid hold on his stirrup, and implored his interference. For a while he made light of her petition,—telling her that she would be as well there as in her own country, and that if he were disposed to do her a kindness he could not as his saddle bags were too small to conceal her; but her importunity at length prevailed, and he whose heart had been so long steeled [276] against every kindly feeling, every sympathetic impression, was at length induced to perform an act of generous, disinterested benevolence. He paid her ransom, had her conveyed to the commissioners for negotiating with the Indians, and by them she was taken to a station on the south side of the Ohio.[1] Here she met with two gentlemen (Long and Denton) who had been at the treaty to obtain intelligence of their children taken captive some time before, but not being able to gain any information respecting them, they were then returning to the interior of Kentucky and kindly furnished her a horse.

In consequence of the great danger attending a journey through the wilderness which lay between the settlements in Kentucky and those on the Holstein, persons scarcely ever performed it but at particular periods of the year, and in caravans, the better to defend themselves against attacks of savages. Notice of the time and place of the assembling of one of these parties being given, Mrs. Cunningham prepared to accompany it; but before that time arrived, they were deterred from the undertaking by the report that a company of travellers, stronger than theirs would be, had been encountered by the Indians, and all either killed or made prisoners. Soon after another party

---

[1] Mrs. Cunningham had been over three years with the savages, when she was taken to a great Indian conference held at the foot of the Maumee rapids, "at or near the site of the present Perrysburgh, Ohio." in the autumn of 1788. Girty brought the attention of McKee, then a British Indian agent, to the matter, and McKee furnished the trinkets which constituted the ransom.—R. G. T.

resolved on a visit to Virginia, and Mrs. Cunningham was furnished a horse belonging to a gentleman on Holstein (which had escaped from him while on a buffalo hunt in Kentucky and was found after his return,) to carry her that far on her way home. Experiencing the many unpleasant circumstances incident to such a jaunt, she reached Holstein, and from thence, after a repose of a few days, keeping up the Valley of Virginia, she proceeded by the way of Shenandoah, to the county of Harrison.[1] Here she was sadly disappointed in not meeting with her husband. Having understood that she had been ransomed and taken to Kentucky, he had, some time before, gone on in quest of her. Anxiety for his fate, alone and on a journey which she well knew to be fraught with many dangers, she could not cheerily partake of the general joy excited by her return. In a few days however, he came back. He had heard on Holstein of her having passed there and he retraced his steps. Arriving at his brother Edward's, he again enjoyed the satisfaction of being with all that was then dear to him on earth. It was a delightful satisfaction, but presently damped by the recollection of [277] the fate of his luckless children—Time assuaged the bitterness of the recollection and blessed him with other and more fortunate children.[2]

In October 1784, a party of Indians ascended Sandy river and passing over to the head of Clynch, came to the settlement near where Tazewell court house is now located. Going first to the house of a Mr. Davisson, they killed him and his wife; and setting fire to their dwelling, proceeded towards the residence of James Moore, sr. On their way they met Moore salting his horses at a *lick trough* in the woods, and killed him. They then went to the house and captured Mrs. Moore and her seven children, and Sally

---

[1] See McKnight's *Our Western Border*, pp. 714, 716.—R. G. T.

[2] Superstition was rife among the Scotch-Irish borderers. McWhorter writes: "On the day before the capture, a little bird came into Mrs. Cunningham's cabin and fluttered around the room. Ever afterwards, she grew frightened whenever a bird would enter her house. The fear that such an occurrence would bring bad luck to a household, was an old and widely-spread superstition."—R. G. T.

Ivens, a young lady who was there on a visit. Fearing detection, they immediately departed for Ohio with the prisoners; and in order to expedite their retreat, killed John Moore, jr. and the three younger children.

Upon their arrival at the Shawanee town on the Scioto (near the mouth of Paint creek) a council was held, and it was resolved that two of the captives should be *burned alive*, to avenge the death of some of their warriors who had been killed on the Kentucky river. This dreadful doom was allotted to Mrs. Moore and her daughter Jane,— an interesting girl about sixteen years of age. They were tied to a post and tortured to death with burning splinters of pine, in the presence of the remaining members of the family.

After the death of his mother and sister, James Moore was sent to the Maumee towns in Michigan, where he remained until December 1785,—his sister Mary and Sally Ivins remaining with the Shawanees. In December 1786, they were all brought to Augusta county in conformity with the stipulations of the treaty of Miami, and ransomed by their friends.[1]

In the fall of 1796, John Ice and James Snodgrass were killed by the Indians when looking for their horses which they [278] had lost on a buffalo hunt on Fishing creek. Their remains were afterwards found—the flesh torn from the bones by the wolves—and buried.

In a few days after Ice and Snodgrass left home in quest of their horses, a party of Indians came to Buffalo creek in Monongalia, and meeting with Mrs. Dragoo and her son in a corn field gathering beans, took them prisoners, and supposing that their detention would induce others to look for them, they waylaid the path leading

---

[277] [1] Mary Moore afterwards became the wife of Mr. Brown, a presbyterian preacher in Augusta. Her brother James Moore, jr., still resides in Tazewell county; and notwithstanding that he witnessed the cruel murder of his mother and five brothers and sisters by the hands of the savages, he is said to have formed and still retain a strong attachment to the Indians. The anniversary of the burning of Mrs. Moore & her daughter, is kept by many in Tazewell as a day of fasting and prayer, and that tragical event gave rise to some affecting verses, generally called " Moore's Lamentation."

from the house. According to their expectation, uneasy at their continued absence, Jacob Strait and Nicholas Wood went to ascertain its cause. As they approached the Indians fired from their covert, and Wood fell;—Strait taking to flight was soon overtaken. Mrs. Strait and her daughter, hearing the firing and seeing the savages in pursuit of Mr. Strait, betook themselves also to flight, but were discovered by some of the Indians who immediately ran after them. The daughter concealed herself in a thicket of bushes and escaped observation. Her mother sought concealment under a large shelving rock, and was not afterwards discovered by the savages, although those in pursuit of her husband, passed near and overtook him not far off. Indeed she was at that time so close, as to hear Mr. Strait say, when overtaken, "don't kill me and I will go with you;" and the savage replying "will you go with me," she heard the fatal blow which deprived her husband of life.

Mrs. Dragoo being infirm and unable to travel to their towns, was murdered on the way. Her son (a lad of seven) remained with the Indians upwards of twenty years,—he married a squaw, by whom he had four children,—two of whom he brought home with him, when he forsook the Indians.

In 1787 the Indians again visited the settlement on Buffaloe, and as Levi Morgan was engaged in skining a wolf which he had just taken from his trap, he saw three of them—one riding a horse which he well knew, the other two walking near behind—coming towards him. On first looking in the direction they were coming, he recognized the horse, and supposed the rider to be its owner—one of his near neighbors. A second glance discovered the mistake, and he siezed his gun and sprang behind a large rock,—the Indians at the same instant taking shelter by the side of a large tree.—As soon as his body was obscured from their view, he turned, and seeing the Indians looking towards the farther end of the [279] rocks as if expecting him to make his appearance there, he fired and one of them fell. Instantly he had recourse to his powder horn to reload, but while engaged in skinning the wolf the stopper had fallen out and his powder was wasted. He then fled, and one of the savages took after him. For some time he held to his gun; but finding his pursuer sensibly gaining on him, he dropped it under the hope that it would attract the attention of the Indian and give him a better chance of escape. The savage passed heedlessly by it. Morgan then threw his shot pouch and coat in the way, to tempt the Indian to a momentary delay. It was equally vain,—his pursuer did not falter for an instant. He now had recourse to another expedient to save himself from captivity or death. Arriving at the summit of the hill up which he had directed his steps, he halted; and, as if some men were approaching from the other side, called aloud, "come on, come on; here is one, make haste." The Indian not doubting that he was really calling to some men at hand, turned and retreated as precipitately as he had advanced; and when he heard Morgan exclaim, "shoot quick, or he will be out of reach," he seemed to redouble his exertion to gain that desirable distance. Pleased with the success of the artifice, Morgan hastened home; leaving his coat and gun to reward the savage for the deception practised on him.[1]

In September of this year, a party of Indians were discovered in the act of catching some horses on the West Fork above Clarksburg; and a company of men led on by Col. Lowther, went immediately in pursuit of them.[2] On the third night the Indians and whites, unknown to each other, encamped not far apart; and in the morning the fires of the latter being discovered by Elias Hughes, the detachment which was accompanying him fired upon the camp, and one of the savages fell. The remainder taking

---

[279] [1] At the treaty of Au Glaize, Morgan met with the Indian who had given him this chase, and who still had his gun. After talking over the circumstance, rather more composedly than they had acted it, they agreed to test each other's speed in a friendly race. The Indian being beaten, rubbed his hams and said, "*stiff, stiff; too old, too old.*" "Well, said Morgan, you got the gun by outrunning me then, and I should have it now for outrunning you;" and accordingly took it.

[2] McWhorter: "Alexander West was with Col. William Lowther on this expedition. They followed the Indians to the Little Kanawha River."—R. G. T.

to flight, one of them passed near to where Col. Lowther and the other men were, and the Colonel firing at him as he ran, the ball entering at his shoulder, perforated him, and he fell. The horses and plunder which had been taken by the savages, were then collected by the whites, and they commenced their return home, in the confidence of false security. They had not proceeded far, when two guns were unexpectedly fired at them, and John Bonnet fell, pierced through the body. He died before he reached home.[1]

[280] The Indians never thought the whites justifiable in flying to arms to punish them for acts merely of rapine. They felt authorized to levy contributions of this sort, whenever an occasion served, viewing property thus acquired as (to use their own expression) the "only rent which they received for their lands;" and if when detected in secretly exacting them, their blood paid the penalty, they were sure to retaliate with tenfold fury, on the first favorable opportunity. The murder of these two Indians by Hughes and Lowther was soon followed by acts of retribution, which are believed to have been, at least mediately, produced by them.

On the 5th of December, a party of Indians and one white man (Leonard Schoolcraft) came into the settlement on Hacker's creek, and meeting with a daughter of Jesse Hughes, took her prisoner. Passing on, they came upon E. West, Senr. carrying some fodder to the stable, and taking him likewise captive, carried him to where Hughes' daughter had been left in charge of some of their party.— Here the old gentleman fell upon his knees and expressed a fervent wish that they would not deal harshly by him.

---

[1] Another case of border superstition is related to me by McWhorter. Alexander West had been doing sentry duty most of the night before, and on being relieved early in the morning, sat with his back to a tree and, rifle across his lap, fell to sleep. On awakening he sprang to his feet and cried, "Boys, look out! Some of us will be killed to-day! I saw the *red doe* in my dream; that is the sign of death; I never knew it to fail!" When Bonnett fell, it was considered in camp to be a verification of the "red sign." Bonnett was carried by his comrades on a rude stretcher, but in four days died. His body was placed in a cleft of rock and the entrance securely chinked.—R. G. T.

His petition was answered by a stroke of the tomahawk, and he fell dead.

They then went to the house of Edmund West, Jun. where were Mrs. West and her sister (a girl of eleven years old, daughter of John Hacker) and a lad of twelve, a brother of West. Forcing open the door, Schoolcraft and two of the savages entered; and one of them immediately tomahawked Mrs. West. The boy was taking some corn from under the bed,—he was drawn out by the feet and the tomahawk sank twice in his forehead, directly above each eye. The girl was standing behind the door. One of the savages approached and aimed at her a blow. She tried to evade it; but it struck on the side of her neck, though not with sufficient force to knock her down. She fell however, and lay as if killed. Thinking their work of death accomplished here, they took from a press some milk, butter and bread, placed it on the table, and deliberately sat down to eat,—the little girl observing all that passed, in silent stillness. When they had satisfied their hunger, they arose, scalped the woman and boy, plundered the house—even emptying the feathers to carry off the ticking—and departed, dragging the little girl by the hair, forty or fifty yards from the house. They then threw her over the fence, and scalped her; but as she evinced symptoms of life, Schoolcraft observed "*that is not enough,*" when immediately one of the savages thrust a knife into her side, and they left her. Fortunately the point of the knife came in contact with a rib and did not injure her much.

Old Mrs. West and her two daughters, who were alone when the old gentleman was taken, became uneasy that he did not return; and fearing that he had fallen into the hands of savages (as they could not otherwise account for his absence) they left the house and went to Alexander West's, who was then on a hunting expedition with his brother Edmund. They told of the absence of old Mr. West and [281] their fears for his fate; and as there was no man here, they went over to Jesse Hughes' who was himself uneasy that his daughter did not come home. Upon hearing that West too was missing, he did not doubt but that both had fallen into the hands of Indians;

and knowing of the absence from home of Edmund West, Jun. he deemed it advisable to apprize his wife of danger, and remove her to his house. For this purpose and accompanied by Mrs. West's two daughters, he went on. On entering the door, the tale of destruction which had been done there was soon told in part. Mrs. West and the lad lay weltering in their blood, but not yet dead. The sight overpowered the girls, and Hughes had to carry them off.—Seeing that the savages had but just left them; and aware of the danger which would attend any attempt to move out and give the alarm that night, Hughes guarded his own house until day, when he spread the sorrowful intelligence, and a company were collected to ascertain the extent of the mischief and try to find those who were known to be missing.

Young West was found—standing in the creek about a mile from where he had been tomahawked. The brains were oozing from his head; yet he survived in extreme suffering for three days. Old Mr. West was found in the field where he had been tomahawked. Mrs. West was in the house; she had probably lived but a few minutes after Hughes and her sisters-in-law had left there.—The little girl (Hacker's daughter) was in bed at the house of old Mr. West. She related the history of the transactions at Edmund West's, Jun. and said that she went to *sleep* when thrown over the fence and was awaked by the scalping. After she had been stabbed at the suggestion of Schoolcraft and left, she tried to re-cross the fence to the house, but as she was climbing up she again went to sleep and fell back. She then walked into the woods, sheltered herself as well as she could in the top of a fallen tree, and remained there until the cocks crew in the morning.

Remembering that there was no person left alive at the house of her sister, awhile before day she proceeded to old Mr. West's. She found no person at home, the fire nearly out, but the hearth warm and she laid down on it. The heat produced a sickly feeling, which caused her to get up and go to the bed, in which she was found.—She recovered, grew up, was married, gave birth to ten children, and died, as was believed, of an affection of the head, occasioned by the wound she received that night. Hughes' daughter was ransomed by her father the next year, and is yet living in sight of the theatre of those savage enormities.

In March 1789, two Indians came to the house of Mr. Glass in the upper end of Ohio (now Brooke) county. They were discovered by a negro woman, who immediately exclaimed, "here are Indians." Mrs. Glass rose up from her spinning wheel, ran to the door, and was met by an Indian with his gun presented. She laid hold on the muzzle and turning it aside, begged that he would not kill, [282] but take her prisoner. He walked into the house and when joined by another Indian with the negro woman and her boy, about four years old, they opened a chest, took out a small box and some articles of clothing, and without doing farther mischief, departed with the prisoners,—Mrs. Glass and her child, two years of age, the negro woman and boy and her infant child. They had proceeded but a short distance when a consultation was held, and Mrs. Glass supposing from their gestures and frequent pointing towards the children they were the subject of deliberation, held forth her little boy to one of the savages and begged that he might be spared—adding, "he will make a fine little Indian after awhile." He signed to her to go on. The other savage then struck the negro boy with the pipe end of his tomahawk, and with the edge gave him a blow across the back of the neck, and scalped and left him.

In the evening they came to the Ohio river just above Wellsburg, and descended it in a canoe about five miles, to the mouth of Rush run. They drew the canoe some distance up the run and proceeding between one and two miles farther encamped for the night.—Next morning they resumed their march and about two o'clock halted on Indian Short creek, twenty miles farther.

When the savages came to the house of Mr. Glass he was at work in a field some few hundred yards off, and was ignorant that any thing extraordinary had occurred there, until in the afternoon.—Searching in vain for his wife, he became satisfied that she had been taken by the

Indians; and proceeding to Well's fort prevailed on ten men to accompany him in quest of them. Early next morning they discovered the place where the Indians embarked in the canoe; and as Mr. Glass readily distinguished the impression made by Mrs. Glass' shoe on the sand, they crossed the river with great expectation of being able to overtake them. They then went down the river to the mouth of Rush run, where the canoe was found and identified by some of Mr. Glass' papers, purposely left there by Mrs. Glass. From this place the trail of the Indians and their prisoners was plainly visible, and pursuing it, the party arrived in view of the smoke from their fire on Short creek, about an hour after the Indians had halted. Crossing slyly forward, when rather more than one hundred yards off they beheld the two savages attentively inspecting a red jacket which one of them held, and Mrs. Glass and her little boy and the negro woman and her child a few paces from them.—Suddenly the Indians let fall the jacket, and looked towards the men. Supposing they were discovered, they discharged their guns and rushed towards the fire. One of the Indians fell and dropped his gun, but recovering, ran about one hundred yards when a shot aimed at him by Major McGuire brought him to his hands and knees.—Mrs. Glass informing them that there was another encampment of Indians close by, instead of following the wounded savage, they returned home with all speed.

[283] In August five Indians on their way to the settlements on the waters of the Monongahela, met with two men on Middle Island creek, and killed them. Taking their horses they continued on their route until they came to the house of William Johnson on Ten Mile, and made prisoner of Mrs. Johnson and some children; plundered the house, killed part of the stock, and taking with them one of Johnson's horses, returned towards the Ohio. When the Indians came to the house, Johnson had gone to a lick not far off, and on his return in the morning, seewhat had been done, and searching until he found the trail of the savages and their prisoners, ran to Clarksburg for assistance. A company of men repaired with him imme-

diately to where he had discovered the trail, and keeping it about a mile, found four of the children lying dead in the woods. The savages had tomahawked and scalped them, and placing their heads close together, turned their bodies and feet straight out so as to represent a cross. The dead were buried and farther pursuit given over.

Other Indians, about the same time, came to the house of John Mack on a branch of Hacker's creek. He being from home, they killed all who were at the house. Two of the children, who had been sent into the woods to hunt the cattle, returning, saw a little sister lying in the yard scalped, and directly fled, and gave the alarm. In the morning some men assembled and went to ascertain the extent of the mischief. The house was no longer to be seen,—a heap of ashes was all that remained of it. The little girl who had been scalped in the yard, was much burned, and those who had been murdered in the house, were consumed with it. Mrs. Mack had been taken some distance from the house, tomahawked, scalped, and stripped naked. She was yet alive; and as the men approached, a sense of her situation induced her to exert her feeble strength in drawing leaves around her so as to conceal her nakedness. The men wrapped their hunting shirts about her, and carried her to a neighboring house. She lived a few days, gave birth to a child and died.

Some time after the murder of Mack's family, John Sims, living on a branch of Gnatty creek, seeing his horses come running up much affrighted, was led to believe that the Indians had been trying to catch them. In a few minutes, the dogs began to bark furiously in the corn field adjoining, and he became satisfied the savages were approaching. Knowing [284] that he could offer no effectual resistance, if they should attack his house, he contrived an artifice to deter them from approaching. Taking down his gun, he walked around the house backward and forward, and as if speaking to men in it, called out, *"Be watchful. They will soon be here, and as soon as you see them, draw a fine bead;"* Mrs. Sims in a coarse tone of voice and with feigned resolution, answering as she had been advised, " Never fear! let them once shew their yellow hides, and we'll pepper them." He would then retire into the house, change his garments, the better to support the deception, and again go forth to watch and give directions to those within. He pursued this plan until night, when he withdrew with his family to a place of safety. The Indians had actually been in the cornfield, and near enough to have shot Sims,—the place where they had been sitting being plainly discernible next morning. Sims' artifice no doubt drove them off, and as they were retreating they fired the house of Jethro Thompson on Lost creek.

In the spring of 1790, the neighborhood of Clarksburg was again visited by Indians in quest of plunder, and who stole and carried off several horses. They were discovered and pursued to the Ohio river, when the pursuers, being reinforced, determined to follow on over into the Indian country. Crossing the river and ascending the Hockhocking, near to the falls, they came upon the camp of the savages. The whites opened an unexpected fire, which killing one and wounding another of the Indians, caused the remainder to fly, leaving their horses about their camp.—These were caught, brought back and restored to their owners.

In April as Samuel Hull was engaged in ploughing a field for Major Benjamin Robinson, he was discovered by some Indians, shot, tomahawked, and scalped. The murder was first ascertained by Mrs. Robinson. Surprised that Hull did not come to the house as usual, to feed the horses and get his own dinner, she went to the field to see what detained him She found the horses some distance from where they had been recently at work; and going on, presently saw Hull lying where he had been shot.

[285] CHAPTER XVII.

Upon the close of the war of the revolution, many circumstances conspired to add considerably to the population of Kentucky; and her strength and ability to cope with the savages and repel invasion, were consequently much increased. Conscious of this, and sensible of their own condition, weakened by the withdrawal of their allies, the Indians did not venture upon expeditions against its inhabitants, requiring to be conducted by the co-operation of many warriors. They preferred to wage war in small parties, against detached settlements and unprotected families; and guarding the Ohio river and the "*wilderness trace*,"[1] to cut off parties of emigrants removing to that country. In all of those they were eminently successful. In the interval of time, between the peace of 1783 and the defeat of General Harmar, in 1790, it is inferred from evidence laid before Congress, that in Kentucky, not less than one thousand human beings were killed and taken prisoners. And although the whites were enabled to carry the war into the heart of the Indian country, and frequently with success, yet did not this put a stop to their enormities. When pressed by the presence of a conquering army, they would sue for peace, and enter into treaties, which they scarcely observed inviolate 'till those armies were withdrawn from among them.

In April 1785; some Indians hovering about Bear

---

[1] The "Wilderness Road" (or "trace") was the overland highway through Cumberland Gap. It was sometimes called "Boone's trace." From North Carolina and Southern Virginia, it was the nearest road to Kentucky; to those living farther north, the Ohio was the favorite highway. While the river was an easier path, it was more dangerous on account of Indians: but travelers of the early period who had come down the Ohio, preferred returning east by the Wilderness Road to poling up stream. See Thomas Speed's *Wilderness Road*, in the Filson Club publications (Louisville, 1886.)—R. G. T.

Grass, met with Colonel Christian and killed him. His loss was severely felt thoughout the whole country.[1]

In October of the same year, several families moving to the [286] country were attacked and defeated on Skegg's creek. Six of the whites were killed, and a number of the others made prisoners, among whom were Mrs. McClure and her infant. When the attack was begun, she secreted herself with four children in some bushes, which together with the darkness of the night, protected her from observation; and could she have overcome the feelings of a mother for her child, she might have ensured her own safety and that of her three other children by leaving her infant at some distance from them. She was aware of the danger to which its cries would expose her, and sought to prevent them by giving it the breast. For awhile it had that effect, but its shrieks at length arose and drew the savages to the spot. Three of her children were slain by her side.

On hearing of this disastrous event, Capt. Whitley collected twenty-one men from the nearer stations, and went in pursuit of the aggressors. He presently overtook them, killed two of their party, and retook the prisoners and the scalps of those whom they had slain.—So signal was his success over them.

In ten days afterwards, another company of *movers*, led on by Mr. Moore, was attacked, and in the skirmish which ensued, nine of their party were killed. Again Capt. Whitley went in pursuit of the savage perpetrators of this outrage, having thirty men to accompany him. On the sixth day of the pursuit, they overtook twenty mounted

---

[1] Col. William Christian, who served in Lord Dunmore's War. He was killed in April, 1786. John May, writing to Governor Henry from Crab Orchard, Ky.,,April 19, says: ["The Indians about the Wabash] had frequently been on Bear Grass, and Col. Christian, in order to induce others to go in pursuit of them, has upon every occasion gone himself. And last week he with about twenty men crossed the Ohio, and overtook three Indians, whom they killed; but his men not obeying his orders, which were to rush altogether on them, he with three others only overtook the Indians, and was so unfortunate as to receive a mortal wound himself and Capt. Isaac Kellar received another."—R. G. T.

Indians, some of whom were clad in the clothes of those they had slain; and who dismounted and fled upon the first fire. Three of them however were killed, and eight scalps and all the plunder were recovered.

In consequence of the many repeated aggressions of the savages, an expedition was this fall concerted against their towns on the Wabash, to be carried into immediate execution. Through the exertions of the county lieutenants an army of one thousand men, was soon assembled at Louisville[1] and placed under the command of Gen. Clarke, who marched directly for the theatre of contemplated operations—leaving the provisions and much of their munitions to be transported in boats. The army arrived near the towns, before the boats;—the men became dissatisfied and mutinous, and Gen. Clarke was in consequence, reluctantly forced to return without striking a blow.[2]

[287] When the army under Gen. Clarke marched from Louisville, Col. Logan knowing that the attention of the Indians would be drawn almost exclusively towards it, & other towns be left exposed and defenceless, raised a body of troops and proceeded against the villages on the Great Miami, and on the head waters of Mad river. In this campaign he burned eight large towns, killed twenty warriors and took between seventy and eighty prisoners.[3]

---

[1] The time for rendezvous was September 10, 1786 (letter of Col. Levi Todd to Governor Henry, August 29).—R. G. T.

[2] Clark was roundly scored in contemporary accounts, for being much of the time under the influence of liquor. His futile expedition was against the Indians around Vincennes, while Logan's party, which appears practically to have revolted from Clark, had a successful campaign against the towns on Mad River. See Green's *Spanish Conspiracy*, ch. v., and Roosevelt's *Winning of the West*, iii., *passim*.—R. G. T.

[3] Col. Benjamin Logan to Governor Randolph, Dec. 17, 1786: "Sept. 14, 1786, I received orders [from Clark] to collect a sufficient number of men in the District of Kentucky to march against the Shawnee's Towns. Agreeable to said orders I collected 790 men, and on the 6th of October I attacked the above mentioned Towns, killed ten of the chiefs of that nation, captured thirty-two prisoners, burnt upwards of two hundred dwelling houses and supposed to have burnt fifteen thousand bushels of corn, took some horses and cattle, killed a number of hogs, and took near one thousand pounds value of Indian furniture, and the

Among the troops led on by Col. Logan, was the late Gen. Lyttle (since of Cincinnati) then a youth of sixteen.[1] At the head of a party of volunteers, when the first towns on the Mad river were reduced, he charged on some of the savages whom he saw endeavoring to reach a close thicket of hazel and plum bushes. Being some distance in front of his companions, when within fifty yards of the retreating enemy, he dismounted, and raising his gun to fire, saw the warrior at whom he was aiming, hold out his hand in token of surrendering. In this time the other men had come up and were making ready to fire, when young Lyttle called to them, "they have surrendered; and remember the Colonel's orders to kill none who ask for quarters." The warrior advanced towards him with his hand extended, and ordering the others to follow him. As he approached, Lyttle gave him his hand, but with difficulty restrained the men from tomahawking him. It was the head chief with this three wives and children, two or three of whom were fine looking lads, and one of them a youth of Lyttle's age. Observing the conduct of Lyttle in preventing the murder of the chief, this youth drew close to him. When they returned to the town, a crowd of men rushed around to see the chief, and Lyttle stepped out of the crowd to fasten his horse. The lad accompanied him. A young man who had been to the spring to drink, seeing Lyttle with the Indian lad, came running towards him. The youth supposed that he was advancing to kill him, and in the twinkling of an eye let fly an arrow. It passed through Curner's dress, and grazed his side; and but for the timely twitch which Lyttle gave the lad's arm, would have killed him. His other arrows were then taken away, and he sternly reprimanded.

Upon the return of Lyttle to where the chief stood,

---

quantity of furniture we burnt I can not account for." The force was on duty "not above twenty-seven days . . . and I would venture to say the expenses will be found to be very moderate."—R. G. T.

[1] William Lytle, born in Carlisle, Pa., September 1, 1770. He came to Ohio with his father, at the age of ten, and subsequently became surveyor-general of the Northwest Territory. His father served as a captain in the French and Indian War, and as a colonel in the Revolution and headed a large colony to Ohio in 1780.—R. G. T.

he heard Col. Logan give orders that the prisoners must not be molested, but taken to a house and placed under guard for their [288] security; and seeing Major McGary[1] riding up and knowing his disposition, he called to him saying, " Major McGary, you must not molest those prisoners " and rode off. McGary mutteringly replied, " I'll see to that;" and dismounting, entered the circle around the prisoners. He demanded of the chief, if he were at the battle of the Blue Licks. The chief probably not understanding the purport of the question, replied affirmatively. McGary instantly seized an axe from the Grenadier Squaw, standing by and sunk it into his head. Lyttle saw the descending stroke and interposed his arm to prevent it or break its force. The handle came in contact with his wrist and had well nigh broke it. Indignant at the barbarous deed, with the impetuosity of youth he drew his knife to avenge it. His arm was arrested, or the steel would have been plunged into the heart of McGary. The bloody act of this man caused deep regret, humiliation and shame to pervade the greater part of the army, and none were more affected by it, than the brave and generous Logan.—When the prisoners were conducted to the house, it was with much difficulty the Indian lad could be prevailed upon to quit the side of Lyttle.

The commencement of the year 1786 witnessed treaties of peace with all the neighboring tribes;[2] but its progress was marked by acts of general hostility. Many individual massacres were committed and in the fall, a company of *movers* were attacked, and twenty-one of them killed. This state of things continuing, in 1787 the secretary of war ordered detachments of troops to be stationed at dif-

---

[288] [1] This name is sometimes written Magery. It is the same individual who caused the disaster at the Blue Licks in August 1782.

[2] The treaty with the Shawnees was negotiated January 30, 1786, at Fort Finney, near the mouth of the Great Miami, by George Rogers Clark, Richard Butler, and Samuel H. Parsons, commissioners. The treaty with the Wyandots, Delawares, Chippewas, and Ottawas was negotiated at Fort McIntosh, January 21, 1785, by Clark, Butler, and Arthur Lee. These treaties were of little avail, so long as British agents like McKee, Elliott, and Simon Girty lived among the Indians and kept them in a constant ferment against the Americans.—R. G. T.

ferent points for the protection of the frontier. Still the Indians kept up such an incessant war against it, as after the adoption of the federal constitution, led the general government to interpose more effectually for the security of its inhabitants, by sending a body of troops to operate against them in their own country.

While these things were doing, a portion of the country north west of the river Ohio, began to be occupied by the whites. One million and a half acres of land in that country, having been appropriated as military land, a company, composed of officers and soldiers in the war of the revolution, was formed in Boston in March 1786 under the title of the [289] " Ohio Company," and Gen. Rufus Putnam was appointed its agent. In the spring of 1788, he with forty-seven other persons, from Massachusetts, Rhode Island and Connecticut, repaired to Marietta, erected a stockade fort for security against the attacks of Indians, and effected a permanent settlement there.[1] In the au-

---

[1] The several states which, under their colonial charters had claims to territory beyond the Ohio River,—Virginia, New York, Connecticut, and Massachusetts,—had (1781-84) relinquished their several claims to the newly-formed United States, and the Ordinance of 1787 had provided for this Northwest Territory an enlightened form of government which was to be the model of the constitutions of the five states into which it was ultimately to be divided. There was formed in Boston, in March, 1786, the Ohio Company of Associates, and October 17, 1787, it purchased from Congress a million and a half acres in the new territory, about the mouth of the Muskingum. Many of the shareholders were Revolutionary soldiers, and great care was taken to select only good men as colonists—oftentimes these were the best and most prosperous men of their several localities. Gen. Rufus Putnam, a cousin of Israel, and a near friend of Washington, was chosen as superintendent of the pioneers. Two parties—one rendezvousing at Danvers, Mass., and the other at Hartford, Conn.—arrived after a difficult passage through the mountains at Simrall's Ferry (now West Newton), on the Youghiogheny, the middle of February, 1788. A company of boat-builders and other mechanics had preceded them a month, yet it was still six weeks more before the little flotilla could leave: " The Union Gally of 45 tons burden; the Adelphia ferry boat, 3 tons; & three log canoes of different sizes. No. of pioneers, 48." The winter had been one of the severest known on the Upper Ohio, and the spring was cold, wet, and backward; so that amid many hardships it was the seventh of April before they arrived at the Muskingum and founded Marietta, named for the unfortunate Marie Antoinette, for the love of France was still strong in the breasts of Revolutionary veterans.—R. G. T.

tumn of the same year, twenty families, chiefly from Essex and Middlesex counties in Massachusetts, likewise moved there, and the forests of lofty timber fell before their untiring and laborious exertions. Many of those who thus took up their abodes in that, then *distant* country had been actively engaged in the late war, and were used, not only to face danger with firmness when it came upon them; but also to devise and practice, means to avert it. Knowing the implacable resentment of the savages to the whites generally, they were at once careful not to provoke it into action, and to prepare to ward off its effects. In consequence of this course of conduct, and their assiduity and attention to the improvement of their lands, but few massacres were committed in their neighborhoods, although the savages were waging a general war against the frontier, and carrying destruction into settlements, comparatively in the interior.

In the winter of 1786, Mr. Stites of Redstone visited New York with the view of purchasing (congress being then in session there) for settlement, a tract of country between the two Miamies. The better to insure success to his project, he cultivated the acquaintance of many members of congress and endeavored to impress upon their minds its propriety and utility. John Cleves Symmes, then a representative from New Jersey, and whose aid Stites solicited to enable him to effect the purchase, becoming impressed with the great pecuniary advantage which must result from the speculation, if the country were such as it was represented to be, determined to ascertain this fact by personal inspection. He did so; and on his return a purchase of one million of acres, lying on the Ohio and between the Great and Little Miami, was made in his name. Soon after, he sold to Matthias Denman and others, that part of his purchase which forms the present site of the city of Cincinnati; and in the fall of 1789, some families from New York, New Jersey, and Redstone, descended the Ohio river to the mouth of the Little Miami. As the Indians were now more than ordinarily troublesome, forty soldiers under Lieut. Kersey, were ordered to join them for the [290] defence of the settlement.

They erected at first a single blockhouse, and soon after adding to it three others, a stockade fort was formed on a position now included within the town of Columbia.

In June 1789, Major Doughty with one hundred and forty regulars, arrived opposite the mouth of Licking, and put up four block houses on the purchase made by Denman of Symmes, and directly after, erected Fort Washington. Towards the close of the year, Gen. Harmar arrived with three hundred other regulars, and occupied the fort. Thus assured of safety, Israel Ludlow, (jointly interested with Denman and Patterson) with twenty other persons, moved and commenced building some cabins along the river and near to the fort.—During the winter Mr. Ludlow surveyed and laid out the town of Losantiville,[1] but when Gen. St. Clair came there as governor of the North Western Territory, he changed its name to Cincinnati.[2]

---

[290] [1] Perhaps there never was a more strange compound derivative term than this. Being situated opposite to the mouth of Licking, the name was made expressive of its locality, by uniting the Latin word *os*, (the mouth) with the Greek, *anti* (opposite) and the French, *ville*, (a town,) and prefixing to this union from such different sources, the initial (*L*) of the river. The author of this word, must have been good at invention, and in these days of *town making* could find ample employment for his talent.

[2] In 1788, John Cleves Symmes—uncle of he of "Symmes's Hole "— the first United States judge of the Northwest Territory, purchased from congress a million acres of land on the Ohio, lying between the two Miami Rivers. Matthias Denman bought from him a square mile at the eastern end of the grant, "on a most delightful high bank " opposite the Licking, and—on a cash valuation for the land of two hundred dollars—took in with him as partners Robert Patterson and John Filson. Filson was a schoolmaster, had written the first history of Kentucky, and seems to have enjoyed much local distinction. To him was entrusted the task of inventing a name for the settlement which the partners proposed to plant here. The outcome was "Losantiville," a pedagogical hash of Greek, Latin, and French: *L*, for Licking; *os*, Greek for mouth; *anti*, Latin for opposite; *ville*, French for city—Licking-opposite-City, or City-opposite-Licking, whichever is preferred. This was in August; the Fates work quickly, for in October poor Filson was scalped by the Indians in the neighborhood of the Big Miami, before a settler had yet been enticed to Losantiville. But the survivors knew how to "boom" a town; lots were given away by lottery to intending actual settlers, who moved thither late in December or early in January, and

In 1790, a settlement was made at the forks of Duck creek, twenty miles up the Muskingum at the site of the present town of Waterford; another fifteen miles farther up the river at Big Bottom, and a third at Wolf creek near the falls. These settlements were made on a tract of one hundred thousand acres, laid off into "donation" lots of one hundred acres, and gratuitously assigned to *actual settlers;* and at the close of the year they contained nearly five hundred men, of whom one hundred and seven had families.

Thus was the present flourishing State of Ohio begun to be occupied by the whites; and the mind cannot but be struck with astonishment in contemplating the wonderful changes which have been *wrought there*, in such brief space of time, by industry and enterprise. Where then stood mighty and unbroken forests, through which the savage passed on his mission of blood; or stalked the majestic buffaloe, gamboled the sportive deer, or trotted the shaggy bear, are now to [291] be seen productive farms, covered with lowing herds and bleating flocks, and teeming with

---

in a few months Judge Symmes was able to write that "it populates considerably."

A few weeks previous to the planting of Losantiville, a party of men from Redstone had settled at the mouth of the Little Miami, about where the suburb of California now is; and a few weeks later, a third colony was started by Symmes himself at North Bend, near the Big Miami, at the western extremity of his grant, and this the judge wished to make the capital of the new Northwest Territory. At first it was a race between these three colonies. A few miles below North Bend, Fort Finney had been built in 1785-86, hence the Bend had at first the start; but a high flood dampened its prospects, the troops were withdrawn from this neighborhood to Louisville, and in the winter of 1789-90 Fort Washington was built at Losantiville by General Harmar. The neighborhood of the new fortress became in the ensuing Indian war the center of the district. To Losantiville, with its fort, came Arthur St. Clair, the new governor of the Northwest Territory (January, 1790), and making his headquarters here, laid violent hands on Filson's invention, at once changing the name to Cincinnati, in honor of the Society of the Cincinnati, of which the new official was a prominent member— "so that," Judge Symmes sorrowfully writes, "Losantiville will become extinct." It was a winter of suffering for the Western Cincinnati. The troops were in danger of starvation, and three professional hunters were contracted with to supply them with game, till corn could come in from Columbia and other older settlements on the river.—R. G. T.

all the comforts of life.—And where then stood the town of Losantiville with its three or four little cabins and their twenty inmates, is now to be seen a flourishing city with its splendid edifices, and a population of 26,513 souls. Continuing thus progressively to improve, the mind of man, "pervading and far darting" as it is, can scarcely picture the state which may be there exhibited in the lapse of a few centuries.

The formations of those establishments north west of the Ohio river, incited the savages to the commission of such and so frequent enormities that measures were taken by the general government to reduce them to quiet and render peace truly desirable to them. While preparations were making to carry those measures into operation, detachments from the regular troops at Fort Washington were stationed at Duck creek, the Big Bottom and Wolf creek, for the security of the *settlers* at those places; and when every thing was prepared, Gen. Harmar, at the head of three hundred and twenty regulars, moved from his head quarters at Fort Washington, to the Little Miami, where the militia detailed for the expedition, were then assembled. The object was to bring the Indians, if posssible, to a general engagement; and if this could not be effected, to destroy their towns and crops on the Scioto and Miami.

On the last day of September 1790, the army then consisting of fourteen hundred and forty-three men, (of whom only three hundred and twenty were regulars) marched forward, and on the 17th of October reached the Great Miami village.[1] It was found to be entirely deserted and all the valuable buildings in flames—having been fired by

---

[1] Col. Josiah Harmar's militia were from Virginia, Kentucky, and Pennsylvania. He left Fort Washington (Cincinnati), October 3. At this time the Miami Indians had seven villages in the neighborhood of the junction of St. Joseph and St. Mary's, which streams unite to form the Maumee. The village which lay in the forks of the St. Joseph and the Maumee, was the principal; one in the forks of the St. Mary's and the Maumee, which was called Kekionga, had 30 houses; at Chillicothe, on the north bank of the Maumee, were 58 houses, and opposite these 18 houses. The Delawares had two villages on the St. Mary's, 45 houses in all, and a town on the St. Joseph of 36 houses.—R. G. T.

the Indians.   As it was apparent that the savages had but
recently left there, Col. Hardin was detached with two hundred and ten men, sixty of whom were regulars to overtake them.   Having marched about six miles, he was suddenly attacked by a body of Indians who were concealed
in thickets on every side of an open plain.   On the first
onset, the militia made a most precipitrate retreat, leaving
the few, but brave regulars to stand the charge.   The conflict was short but bloody.   The regular troops, over pow-
ered by numbers, were literally cut to pieces; and only
seven of them made their escape and rejoined the main
army at the Great Miami town.[1]

[292] Among those who were so fortunate as to escape
after the shameful flight of the militia, was Capt. Arm-
strong of the regulars.   He reached a pond of water
about two hundred yards from the field of action; and
plunging himself up to the neck in it, remained there all
night, a spectator of the horrid scene of a savage war
dance, performed over the dead and wounded bodies of his
brave soldiers.   The escape of ensign Hartshorn was perhaps owing entirely to a lucky accident.   As he was flying at his best speed he faltered over a log, which lay in
his path, and by the side of which he concealed himself
from the view of the savages.

Notwithstanding the disastrous termination of this
engagement, the detachment succeeded in reducing the
other towns to ashes, and in destroying their crops of corn
and other provisions; and rejoining the main army under
Gen. Harmar, commenced their return to Fort Washington.   Anxious to wipe off in another action, the disgrace
which he felt would attach to the defeat, when within
eight miles of Chilicothe, Gen. Harmar halted his men,
and again detached Col. Hardin and Major Wylleys, with
five hundred militia and sixty regulars, to find the enemy
and bring them to an engagement.

Early next morning, a small body of the enemy was

---

[1] A third expedition, under Maj. J. F. Hamtramck, went against the
Wabash Indians, successfully destroyed several deserted villages, and
reached Vincennes without loss.—R. G. T.

discovered, and being attacked, fled in different directions.—The militia pursued them as they ran in despite of orders; and when by this means the regulars were left alone, they were attacked by the whole force of the Indians, excepting the small parties whose flight had drawn off the militia. A severe engagement ensued. The savages fought with desperation; & when the troops which had gone in pursuit of those who fled upon the first onset, returned to take part in the engagement, they threw down their guns and rushed upon the regulars tomahawk in hand. Many of them fell, but being so very far superior in numbers, the regulars were at last overpowered. Their firmness and bravery could not avail much, against so overwhelming a force; for though one of them might thrust his bayonet into the side of an Indian, two other savages were at hand to sink their tomahawks into his head. In his official account of this battle, Gen. Harmar claimed the victory; but the thinned ranks of his troops shewed that they had been severely worsted. Fifty of the regulars and one hundred of the militia were killed in the contest, and many wounded. The loss of the Indians was no doubt considerable, [293] or they would not have suffered the army to retire to Fort Washington unmolested.[1]

Instead of the security from savage hostilities, which it was expected would result from Harmar's campaign, the inhabitants of the frontier suffered from them, more than they had been made to endure since the close of the war with Great Britain. Flushed with the success which had crowned their exertions to repel the invasion which

---

[1] In his report to the Secretary of War, October 29, 1790, Governor St. Clair said: ".I have the pleasure to inform you of the entire success of Gen. Harmar at the Indian towns on the Miami and St. Joseph Rivers, of which he has destroyed five in number, and a very great quantity of corn and other vegetable provisions. It is supposed that about two hundred of the Indians have likewise fallen in the different encounters that have happened between them and the detachment, for there has been no general action; but it has not been without considerable loss on our part. . . . Of the Federal troops, Major Wyllys and Lieutenant Frothingham and seventy-seven men; of the militia, Major Fontaine, Captain McMurtry, and Captain Scott, a son of General Scott, and seventy-three men, are among the slain."—R. G. T.

had been made into their country, and infuriated at the destruction of their crops and the conflagration of their villages, they became more active and zealous in the prosecution of hostilities.

The settlements which had been recently made in Ohio up the Muskingum, had ever after their first establishment, continued apparently on the most friendly terms with the Indians; but on the part of the savages, friendship had only been feigned, to lull the whites into a ruinous security. When this end was attained, they too were made to feel the bitterness of savage enmity. On the 2d of January 1791, a party of Indians came to the Big Bottom, and commenced an indiscriminate murder of the inhabitants; fourteen of whom were killed and five taken prisoners. The settlement at Wolf's creek escaped a similar fate, by being apprized of the destruction of Big Bottom by two men who got safely off in time of the massacre. When the Indians arrived there the next morning, finding the place prepared to receive them, they withdrew without making any serious attempt to take it.

On the 24th of April, John Bush (living on Freeman's creek,) having very early sent two of his children to drive up the cattle, became alarmed by their screams, and taking down his gun, was proceeding to learn the cause of it, when he was met at the door by an Indian, who caught hold of the gun, forced it from his grasp, and shot him with it. Bush fell across the threshold, and the savage drew his knife to scalp him. Mrs. Bush ran to the assistance of her husband, and with an axe, aimed a blow at the Indian with such force that it fastened itself in his shoulder, and when he jumped back his exertion pulled the handle from her hand. She then drew her husband into the house and secured the door.

In this time other of the savages had come up, and after endeavoring in vain to force open the door, they commenced shooting through it. Fortunately Mrs. Bush remained unhurt, although eleven bullets passed through her frock and some of [294] them just grazing the skin. One of the savages observing an aperture between the logs, thrust the muzzle of his gun thro' it. With another axe

Mrs. Bush struck on the barrel so as to make it ring, and, the savage on drawing it back, exclaimed *"Dern you."* Still they were endeavoring to force an entrance into the house, until they heard what they believed to be a party of whites coming to its relief. It was Adam Bush, who living close by and hearing the screams of the children and the firing of the gun, had set off to learn what had given rise to them, and taking with him his dogs, the noise made by them in crossing the creek alarmed the savages, and caused them to retreat, taking off the two children as prisoners. A company of men were soon collected and went in pursuit of the Indians; but were unable to surprise them and regain the prisoners. They however, came so nearly upon them, on the Little Kenhawa,[1] that they were forced to fly precipitately, leaving the plunder and seven horses which they had taken from the settlement: these were retaken and brought back.

In May, as John McIntire and his wife were returning from a visit, they passed through the yard of Uriah Ashcraft; and in a small space of time after, Mr. Ashcraft, startled by the sudden growling and springing up of one of his dogs, stepped quickly to the door to see what had aroused him. He had hardly reached the door, when he espied an Indian on the outside with his gun presented. Closing and making fast the door, he ascended the stairs that he might the better fire upon the unwelcome intruder; and after snapping three several times, and having discovered that there were other Indians in the yard, he raised a loud shout to apprize those who were within the sound of his voice, that he was surrounded by danger. Upon this the Indians moved off; and three brothers of McIntire coming to his relief, they all pursued the trail of the savages. About a mile from Ashcraft's, they found the body of John McIntire, tomahawked, scalped, and stripped; and concluding that Mrs. McIntire, was taken prisoner, they sent intelligence to Clarksburg of what had happened, and requested assistance to follow the Indians and recover the prisoner from captivity. The desired assistance was

---

[1] Thirteen miles below Marietta.—R. G. T.

immediately afforded; and a company of men, led on by Col. John Haymond and Col. George Jackson, went in pursuit. On Middle Island creek,[1] before they were aware of their proximity to the savages, they were fired upon by them, and [295] two of the party very narrowly escaped being shot.—A ball passed through the hankerchief on the head of Col. Haymond, and another through the sleeve of Col. Jackson's shirt. The fire was promptly returned, and the men rushed forward. The Indians however, made good their retreat, though not without having experienced some injury; as was discovered by the blood, and the throwing down some of the plunder which they had taken. It was here first ascertained that Mrs. McIntire had been killed,—her scalp being among the things left—and on the return of the party, her body was found some small distance from where that of her husband had been previously discovered.

Towards the last of June, another party of Indians invaded the settlement on Dunkard creek, in the county of Monongalia. Early in the morning, as Mr. Clegg, Mr. Handsucker, and two of Handsucker's sons were engaged at work in a cornfield near the house, they were shot at by some concealed savages, and Handsucker was wounded and soon overtaken. Clegg and Handsucker's sons ran towards the house, and the former entering it, defended it for a while; but confident that he would soon be driven out by fire, he surrendered on condition that they would spare his life and that of his little daughter with him. The boys passed the house, but were taken by some of the savages who were also concealed in the direction which they ran, and who had just made captive Mrs. Handsucker and her infant. They then plundered and set fire to the house, caught the horses and made off with the prisoners, leaving one of their company, as usual, to watch after their retreat.

When the firing was first heard, Mrs. Clegg being some distance from the house, concealed herself in the creek,

---

[1] Eighteen miles above Marietta, and one above St. Mary's, W. Va.— R. G. T.

under some projecting bushes, until every thing became quiet. She then crept out, but perceiving the Indian who had remained near the burning house, she took to flight; and he having at the same time discovered her, ran in pursuit. She was so far in advance, and ran so well, that the savage, despairing of overtaking her, raised his gun and fired as she ran. The ball just grazed the top of her shoulder, but not impeding her flight, she got safely off. Mr. Handsucker, his wife and child, were murdered on the dividing ridge between Dunkard and Fish creeks.[1] Mr. Clegg after some time got back, and upon the close of the Indian war, ransomed his two daughters.

[296] In the month of September Nicholas Carpenter set off to Marietta with a drove of cattle to sell to those who had established themselves there; and when within some miles from the Ohio river, encamped for the night.[2] In the morning early, and while he and the drovers were yet dressing, they were alarmed by a discharge of guns, which killed one and wounded another of his party. The others endeavored to save themselves by flight; but Carpenter being a cripple (because of a wound received some years before) did not run far, when finding himself becoming faint, he entered a pond of water where he fondly hoped he should escape observation. But no! both he and a son who had likewise sought security there, were discovered, tomahawked and scalped. George Legget, one of the drovers, was never after heard of; but Jesse Hughes succeeded in getting off though under disadvantageous circumstances. He wore long leggins, and when the firing commenced at the camp, they were fastened at top to his belt, but hanging loose below. Although an active runner, yet he found that the pursuers were gain-

---

[1] Dunkard Creek flows eastward into the Monongahela. Fish Creek flows southwestward into the Ohio, emptying 113 miles below Pittsburg, and 58 above Marietta. A famous Indian war-trail ran up Fish and down Dunkard—a short-cut from Ohio to the western borders of Pennsylvania and Virginia.—R. G. T.

[2] Soon after the establishment of Marietta, a rude wagon road was opened through the forest between that colony and Redstone (Brownsville, Pa.) This was the road Carpenter was following.—R. G. T.

ing and must ultimately overtake him if he did not rid
himself of this incumbrance. For this purpose he halted
somewhat and stepping on the lower part of his leggins,
broke the strings which tied them to his belt; but before
he accomplished this, one of the savages approached and
hurled a tomahawk at him. It merely grazed his head,
and he then again took to flight and soon got off.

It was afterwards ascertained that the Indians by
whom this mischief was effected, had crossed the Ohio
river near the mouth of Little Kenhawa, where they
took a negro belonging to Captain James Neal, and continued on towards the settlements on West Fork, until
they came upon the trail made by Carpenter's cattle.
Supposing that they belonged to families moving, they
followed on until they came upon the drovers; and tying
the negro to a sapling made an attack on them. The
negro availed himself of their employment elsewhere,
and loosing the bands which fastened him, returned to his
master.

After the defeat of General Harmer, the terrors and
the annoyance proceeding from Indian hostilities, still continued to harrass Kentucky, and to spread destruction
over its unprotected portions. Seeing that the expeditions
of the savages were yet conducted on a small scale, the
better to effect their purposes, the inhabitants had recourse
to other measures [297] of defence; and established many
posts on the frontier, garrisoned by a few men, to watch
the motions of the enemy, and intercept them in their progress, or spread the alarm of their approach. It was productive of but little benefit, and all were convinced, that
successful offensive war could alone give security from Indian aggression. Convinced of this, preparations were
made by the General Government for another campaign
to be carried on against them; the objects of which were
the destruction of the Indian villages between the Miamies;
the expulsion of their inhabitants from the country, and
the establishment of a chain of forts to prevent their return, until a general peace should give promise of a cessation of hostilities on their part. Means, deemed adequate
to the accomplishment of those objects, were placed by

Congress at the disposal of the executive, and of the army destined to effect them, he directed General Arthur St. Clair to take the command.[1]

It was some time before the troops detailed for this campaign, could be assembled at Fort Washington; but as soon as they rendezvoused there, the line of march was taken up.[2] Proceeding immediately for the principal establishments of the Indians on the Miami, General St. Clair had erected the Forts Hamilton and Jefferson,[3] and placing sufficient garrisons in each, continued his march. The opening of a road for the passage of the troops and artillery, necessarily consumed much time; and while it was in progress, small parties of the enemy were often seen hovering near, and some unimportant skirmishes took place; and as the army approached the Indian villages, sixty of the militia deserted in a body. To prevent the evil influence of this example, General St. Clair despatched Major Hamtrack at the head of a regiment, to overtake and bring them back; and the rest of the army moved forward.

On the night of the third of November, General St. Clair encamped near the Great Miami village, and notwithstanding the reduced state of the forces under his command, (by reason of the detachment of so large a body in pursuit of the deserters,) he proposed to march in the morning directly to its attack.[4] Having understood that the Indians were collected in great force, and apprehensive of a night attack, his men were drawn up in a square, and

---

[1] With Gen. Richard Butler, who was killed in the final battle, second in command.—R. G. T.

[2] Early in September, 1791. St. Clair had 2,000 men, fifty per cent less than had been promised him by the war department.—R. G. T.

[3] Fort Hamilton, a stockade with four bastions, was on the Big Miami, 24 miles from Fort Washington (Cincinnati), on the site of the present Hamilton, O. Fort Jefferson, built of logs laid horizontally, was six miles south of the present Greenville, O. The army left Fort Jefferson, October 24.—R. G. T.

[4] The army then numbered 1,400 men, and was encamped at the site of the present Fort Recovery, O., 55 miles away, as the crow flies, from the head of the Maumee, the objective point of the expedition.—R. G. T.

26

kept under arms until the return of day, when they were
dismissed from parade for [298] the purpose of refresh-
ment. Directly after, and about half an hour before sun
rise, an attack was begun by the Indians on the rear line,
and the militia there immediately gave way, and retreated,—
rushing through a battalion of regulars, to the very centre
of the camp. The confusion was great. Thrown into
disorder by the tumultuous flight of the militia, the utmost exertion of the officers could not entirely compose
the regulars, so as to render them as effective as they
would otherwise have been.

After the first fire, the Indians rushed forward, tomahawk in hand, until they were checked by the well directed aim of the front line ; which being almost simultaneously attacked by another body of the enemy, had to
direct their attention to their own assailants, and the action became general. The weight of the enemy being
brought to bear on the centre of each line where the
artillery had been placed, the men were driven with great
slaughter from the guns and these rendered useless by the
killing of the matrosses. The enemy taking advantage
of this state of things, pushed forward upon the lines, and
confusion began to spread itself in every quarter. A
charge was ordered, and Lieutenant Colonel Drake succeeded in driving back the Indians three or four hundred
yards at the point of the bayonet; but rallying, they returned to the attack, and the troops in turn gave way.
At this moment the camp was entered by the left flank;
and, another charge was directed. This was made by
Butler and Clark's battalions with great effect, and repeated several times with success; but in each of these
charges, many being killed, and particularly the officers,
it was impossible longer to sustain the conflict, and a retreat was directed.

To enable the troops to effect this they were again
formed into line, as well as could be under such circumstances, and another charge was made, as if to turn the
right flank of the enemy, but in reality to gain the road.
This object was effected; and a precipitate flight commenced which continued until they reached Fort Jeffer-

son, a distance of thirty miles, the men throwing away
their guns and accoutrements as they ran.

Great was the havoc done by the Indians in this engagement. Of the twelve hundred men engaged under
General St. Clair, nearly six hundred were left dead on
the field, and many were wounded. Every officer of the
second regiment [299] was killed in the various charges
made by it to retrieve the day, except three, and one of
these was shot through the body. Major General Butler
having been wounded, and carried to a convenient place to
have his wounds dressed, an Indian desperately adventurous, broke through the guard in attendance, rushed up,
tomahawked and scalped him, before his own life paid the
forfeit of his rashness. General St. Clair had many narrow escapes.[1] Early in the action, a number of savages
surrounded his tent and seemed resolved on entering it
and sacrificing him. They were with difficulty restrained
by some regular soldiers at the point of the bayonet.
During the engagement eight balls passed through his
clothes, and while the troops were retreating, having had
his own horse killed, and being mounted on a sorry beast,
"which could not be pricked out of a walk," he had to
make his way to Fort Jefferson as he could, considerably
in the rear of the men. During the action Adjutant Bul-
gess received a severe wound, but yet continued to fight
with distinguished gallantry. Presently a second shot
took effect and he fell. A woman who was particularly
attached to him had accompanied him in the campaign,
raised him up, and while supporting him in her arms, received a ball in the breast which killed her instantly.

The Chicasaws were then in amity with the whites,
and some of their warriors were to have co operated with
Gen. St. Clair, but did not arrive in time. There was

---

[1] He lay sick in his tent, when the action opened, but arose and
acted with remarkable courage throughout the fight. General Butler
was acting commandant while St. Clair was ill, and was credibly informed by his scouts, the night before the battle, of the proximity of the
enemy. But he took no precautions against surprise, neither did he
communicate his news to his superior. Upon Butler's head appears to
rest much of the blame for the disaster.—R. G. T.

however one of that nation in the engagement, and he killed and scalped eleven of the enemy with his own hands, and while engaged with the twelfth was himself killed, to the regret of those who witnessed his deeds of daring and of courage.

According to the statement of the Indians, they killed six hundred and twenty of the American troops, and took seven pieces of cannon, two hundred head of oxen, many horses, but no prisoners.[1] They gave their own loss in killed at only sixty-five; but it was no doubt much greater. Their force consisted of four thousand warriors, and was led on by a Missasago chief who had served with the British in the late war; and who planned and conducted the attack contrary to the opinion of a majority of the chiefs, who yet, having such confidence in his skill and judgment, yielded their individual plans and gave to him the entire control of their movements. He is reported to have caused the savages to forbear the pursuit of the retreating troops; telling them that they had killed enough, and it was time to enjoy the booty they had gained with the victory. He was then about forty-five years of age, six feet in height, and of a [300] sour, morose countenance. His dress was Indian leggins and moccasons, a blue petticoat coming half way down his thighs, and European waistcoat and surtout. His head was bound with an Indian cap, reaching midway his back, and adorned with upwards of two hundred silver ornaments. In each ear he had two ear rings, the upper part of each of which was formed of three silver meddles of the size of a dollar; the lower part consisted of quarters of dollars, and more than a foot in length; one from each ear hanging down his breast,—the others over his back. In his nose he wore ornaments of silver curiously wrought and painted.

Two days after the action the warriors from the Chic-

---

[1] The Americans lost 37 officers and 593 men, killed and missing, and 31 officers and 252 men, wounded. See *St. Clair Papers*, edited by William Henry Smith (Cincinnati: Robert Clarke & Co., 1882), for official details of the disaster. For Simon Girty's part, consult Butterfield's *History of the Girtys, passim.*—R. G. T.

asaw nation arrived at Fort Jefferson, under the command
of Piomingo, or the "Mountain Leader." On their march
they heard of the fatal battle, and saw one of the enemy;
who mistaking Piomingo's party for some of his own comrades, made up to them. He discovered the mistake when
it was too late to rectify it. Piomingo accosted him in harsh
tones, saying—"Rascal, you have been killing the whites,"
and immediately ordered two of his warriors to expand
his arms, and a third to shoot him. This was done and his
scalp taken.

After the disastrous termination of this campaign,[1]
the inhabitants of Kentucky were as much as, or perhaps
more than ever, exposed to savage enmity and those incursions which mark the bitterness of Indian resentment.
Soon after the retreat of the army under Gen. Sinclair,
a party of them came upon Salt river, where two men
and some boys were fishing; and falling suddenly upon
them killed the men and made prisoners of the boys.
They then liberated one of the boys, and giving him a
tomahawk, directed him to go home; shew it to his
friends; inform them what had been the fate of his companions, and what they were to expect for their own. The
threat was fearfully executed. Many families were entirely cut off and many individuals sacrificed to their fury.
Companies of Indians were constantly traversing the
country in secret, and committing depredations, wherever
they supposed it could be done with impunity. A remarkable instance of their failure and suffering in attempting to form an entrance into a house where was an
almost unprotected family, deserves to be particularly
mentioned.

On the 24th of December 1791, a party of savages attacked the house of John Merril, in Nelson county. Mr.
Merril, alarmed by the barking of the dogs, hastened to
the door to learn the cause.—On opening it, he was fired
at by two Indians and his leg and arm were both broken.
The savages then ran forward to enter the house, but be-

[1] St. Clair arrived at Fort Washington, on his return, November 8
—R. G. T.

fore they could do this, the door was closed and secured by Mrs. Merril and her daughter.   After a fruitless attempt to force it open, they commenced hewing off a part of it with their tomahawks, and when a passage was thus opened, one of them attempted to enter through it.   The heroic Mrs. Merril, in the midst of her screaming and affrighted children, and her groaning suffering husband, seized an axe, gave the ruffian a fatal blow, and [301] instantly drew him into the house. Supposing that their end was now nearly attained, the others pressed forward to gain admittance through the same aperture.   Four of them were in like manner despatched by Mrs. Merril, before their comrades were aware that any opposition was making in the house.   Discovering their mistake the survivors retired for awhile, and returning, two of them endeavored to gain admittance by climbing to the top of the house, and descending in the chimney, while the third was to exert himself at the door.   Satisfied from the noise on the top of the house, of the object of the Indians, Mr. Merril directed his little son to rip open a bed and cast its contents on the fire.   This produced the desired effect.—The smoke and heat occasioned by the burning of the feathers brought the two Indians down, rather unpleasantly; and Mr. Merril somewhat recovered, exerted every faculty, and with a billet of wood soon despatched those half smothered devils.   Mrs. Merril was all this while busily engaged in defending the door against the efforts of the only remaining savage, whom she at length wounded so severely with the axe, that he was glad to get off alive.

A prisoner, who escaped from the Indians soon after the happening of this transaction, reported that the wounded savage was the only one, of a party of eight, who returned to their towns; that on being asked by some one, "what news,"—he replied, "bad news for poor Indian, me lose a son, me lose a brother,—the squaws have taken the breech clout, and fight worse than the Long Knives."

The frequent commission of the most enormous outrages, led to an expedition against the Indians, carried on by the inhabitants of Kentucky alone.   An army of one thousand mounted volunteers was raised, and the command of it being given to Gen. Scott, he marched immediately for their towns.[1] When near them, he sent out two spies to learn the state of the enemy; who reported that they had seen a large body of Indians, not far from the fatal spot where St. Clair's bloody battle had been fought, enjoying themselves with the plunder there taken, riding the oxen, and acting in every respect as if drunk. Gen. Scott immediately gave orders to move forward briskly; and arranging his men into three divisions, soon came upon and attacked the savages. The contest was short but decisive.—Two hundred of the enemy were killed on the spot, the cannon and such of the other stores as were in their possession, retaken, and the savage forces completely routed. The loss of the Kentuckians was inconsiderable,—only six men were killed and but few wounded.

Gen. Scott on his return, gave an affecting account of the appearance of the field, where Gen. St. Clair had been encountered by the savages. "The plain," said he, "had a very melancholy appearance. In the space of three hundred and fifty yards, lay three hundred skull bones, which were buried by my men while on the ground; from thence for miles on, and the road was strewed with skeletons, muskets, &c." A striking picture of the desolation wrought there on the bloody fourth of November.

---

[1] This expedition under Gen. Charles Scott, one of the Kentucky committee of safety, was made in June, 1791, against the Miami and Wabash Indians. It was followed in August by a second expedition under Gen. James Wilkinson. In the course of the second campaign, at the head of 500 Kentuckians, Wilkinson laid waste the Miami village of L'Anguille, killing and capturing 42 of the savages.—R. G. T.

[302] CHAPTER XVIII.

Neither the signal success of the expedition under General Scott, nor the preparations which were being made by the general government, for the more rigorous prosecution of the war against them, caused the Indians to relax their exertions to harrass the frontier inhabitants. The ease with which they had overcome the two armies sent against them under Harmar and St. Clair, inspired them with contempt for our troops, and induced a belief of their own invincibility, if practising the vigilance necessary to guard against a surprise. To the want of this vigilance, they ascribed the success of Gen. Scott; and deeming it necessary only to exercise greater precaution to avoid similar results, they guarded more diligently the passes into their country, while discursive parties of their warriors would perpetrate their accustomed acts of aggression upon the persons and property of the whites.

About the middle of May, 1792, a party of savages came upon a branch of Hacker's creek, and approaching late in the evening a field recently cleared by John Waggoner, found him seated on a log, resting himself after the labors of the day. In this company of Indians was the since justly celebrated General Tecumseh, who leaving his companions to make sure of those in the house, placed his gun on the fence and fired deliberately at Waggoner. The leaden messenger of death failed of its errand, and passing through the sleeve of his shirt, left Waggoner uninjured, to try his speed with the Indian. Taking a direction opposite the house, to avoid coming in contact with the savages there, he outstripped his pursuer, and got safely off.

[303] In the mean time, those who had been left to operate against those of the family who were at the house, finding a small boy in the yard, killed and scalped him;

and proceeding on, made prisoners of Mrs. Waggoner and
her six children, and departed immediately with them, lest
the escape of her husband, should lead to their instant
pursuit. They were disappointed in this expectation. A
company of men was soon collected, who repaired to the
then desolate mansion, and from thence followed on the
trail of the savages. About a mile from the house, one of
the children was found where its brains had been beaten
out with a club, and the scalp torn from its head. A small
distance farther, lay Mrs. Waggoner and two others of her
children,—their lifeless bodies mangled in the most barbarous and shocking manner. Having thus freed themselves from the principal impediments to a rapid retreat,
the savages hastened on ; and the pursuit was unavailing.
They reached their towns with the remaining prisoners—
two girls and a boy—and avoided chastisement for the outrage. The elder of the two girls did not long remain with
them ; but escaping to the neighborhood of Detroit with
another female prisoner, continued there until after the
treaty of 1795. Her sister abided with her captors 'till the
close of the war; and the boy until during the war of
1812. He was then seen among some friendly Indians,
and bearing a strong resemblance in features to his father,
was recognized as Waggoner's captive son. He had married a squaw, by whom he had several children, was attached to his manner of life, and for a time resisted every
importunity, to withdraw himself from among them.
When his father visited him, it was with difficulty he was
enticed to return to the haunts of his childhood, and the
associates of his younger days, even on a temporary visit.
When however he did return to them, the attention and
kindly conduct of his friends, prevailed with him to remain, until he married and took up his permanent abode
amid the habitations of civilized men. Still with the feelings natural to a father, his heart yearns towards his children in the forest ; and at times he seems to lament that
he ever forsook them.[1]

---

[1] Drake, in *Aboriginal Races of North America* (15th ed.), p. 616, cites
the Waggoner massacre as "the first exploit in which we find Tecumseh
engaged." L. V. McWhorter sends me this interesting note, giving the

In the summer of this year, a parcel of horses were
taken from the West Fork, and the Indians who had
stolen them, being discovered as they were retiring, they
were pursued by Captain Coburn, who was stationed at

---

local tradition regarding the affair: "John Waggoner lived on Jesse's
Run, more than two miles above its junction with Hacker's Creek.
While engaged in burning logs in his clearing, he was sitting upon a
log, with a handspike lying across his lap. It was thought that Tecumseh mistook this tool for a gun, and was nervous. But three in number,
the Indians had entered the district with some trepidation. Over Sunday, while the settlers were holding religious services in West's Fort,
the savages lay in a neighboring ravine. The dogs of the settlement
barked furiously at them, and ran toward their hiding place, trying to
lead their masters; but the latter supposed that the animals had merely
scented wolves, hence paid no attention to them. Tecumseh was but
thirty paces from Waggoner when he fired, and it is singular that he
missed, for the latter was a large man and in fair view. Waggoner
sprang up and started for his cabin, a short distance only, but when
about fifteen yards away saw an Indian chasing one of the children
around the house. Waggoner was unarmed; his gun was in the house,
but he feared to enter, so ran for help to the cabin of Hardman, a
neighbor. But Hardman was out hunting, and there was no gun left
there. The screams of his family were now plainly heard by Waggoner, and he was with difficulty restrained from rushing back to help
them, unarmed. Jesse Hughes carried the news into the fort, and a
rescue party at once set out. Mrs. Waggoner and her three youngest
children had been carried across the ridge to where is now Rev. Mans-
field McWhorter's farm, on McKenley's Run, and here they were tomahawked and scalped. Henry McWhorter helped to carry the bodies to
the fort, but made no mention of their being 'mangled in the most barbarous and shocking manner.'"

The boy Peter, then eight years old, remained with the Indians
for twenty years. The manner of his return, as related to me by Mr.
McWhorter, was singular, and furnishes an interesting and instructive
romance of the border. One Baker, one of John Waggoner's neighbors,
went to Ohio to "squat," and on Paint Creek saw Peter with a band of
Indians, recognizing him by the strong family resemblance. Baker at
once wrote to the elder Waggoner, telling him of his discovery, and the
latter soon visited the Paint Creek band, with a view to inducing his
son to return home. But Peter was loth to go. He was united to a
squaw, and by her had two children. In tears, she bitterly opposed
his going. When finally he yielded to parental appeals, he promised her
he would soon be back again. When the time for his return to the
forest came, his relatives kept him under guard; when it had passed,
he was afraid to return to his Indian relatives, having broken his word.
Gradually he became reconciled in a measure to his new surroundings,
but was ever melancholy, frequently lamenting that he had left his
savage family. "Some time after his return to civilization," continues

the mouth of Little [304] Kenhawa with a party of men as scouts. Following them across the Ohio river, he overtook them some distance in the Indian country, and retaking the horses, returned to his station. Hitherto property recovered from the savages, had been invariably restored to those from whom it had been stolen; but on the present occasion a different course was pursued. Contending that they received compensation for services rendered by them in Virginia, and were not bound to treat without its limits in pursuit of the savages or to retake the property of which they had divested its rightful owners, they claimed the horses as plunder taken from the Indians, sold them, and divided the proceeds of sale among themselves—much to the dissatisfaction of those from whom the savages had taken them.[1]

In the course of the ensuing fall, Henry Neal, William Triplett and Daniel Rowell, from Neal's station ascended the Little Kenhawa in canoes to the mouth of the Burning Spring run, from whence they proceeded on a Buffoloe hunt in the adjoining woods. But they had been seen as they plied their canoes up the river, by a party of Indians, who no sooner saw them placed in a situation favoring the bloody purposes of their hearts, than they fired upon them. Neal and Triplett were killed, and fell into the river.— Rowell was missed and escaped by swimming the Kenhawa, the Indians shooting at him as he swam. In a few days

---

McWhorter, "an Indian woman, supposed to be his wife, passed through the Hacker Creek settlements, inquiring for Peter, and going on toward the East. She appeared to be demented, and sang snatches of savage songs. Peter never knew of her presence, nor would any one inform her of his whereabouts. He was reticent about his life among the Indians, and no details of that feature of his career became known to his white friends."

Tecumseh, who is said to have been born on Hacker's Creek, possibly at a village near the mouth of Jesse's Run, visited the white settlements there, after the peace, and told the whites of his experiences in connection with the Waggoner massacre.—R. G. T.

[1] It must be acknowledged that many of these militia forays against the Indians partook of the nature of buccaneering. The spoils were often considerable. Clark, in his Kaskaskia campaign (1778), captured so much booty, in property and slaves, that he declares his men were made "almost rich."—R. G. T.

after the dead were found in a ripple and buried. The Indians had not been able to draw them from their watery grave, and obtain their scalps.

During this year unsuccessful attempts were made by the general government, to terminate Indian hostilities by negotiation. They were too much elated with their recent success, to think of burying their resentments in a treaty of peace; and so little did they fear the operation of the governmental forces, and such was their confidence in their own strength, that they not only refused to nego-tiate at all, but put to death two of those who were sent to them as messengers of peace. Major Truman and Col. Hardin, severally sent upon this mission, were murdered by them; and when commissioners to treat with them, were received by them, their only answer was, a positive refusal to enter into a treaty.[1]

When this determination was made known to the President, every precaution which could be used, was taken by him to prevent the recurrence of these enormities which were daily committed on the [305] frontier, and particularly in the new state of Kentucky. Gen. St. Clair, after having asked that a court of enquiry should be held, to consider of his conduct in the campaign of 1791, and finding that his request could not be granted, resigned the command of the army, and was succeeded by Gen. Anthony Wayne. That the operations of the army might not be

---

[1] In the spring of 1792, Major Trueman, Colonel Hardin; and Mr. Freeman were dispatched from Fort Washington by different routes, to open peace negotiations, but they were murdered by the savages. Gen. Rufus Putnam, aided by Hekewelder, the Moravian, succeeded in bind-ing the Wabash and Illinois Indians to keep the peace. Later, Benja-min Lincoln, Timothy Pickering, and Beverly Randolph were ordered by the president to go to the Maumee to conclude a general treaty which Indians had declared their willingness to enter into. But the commis-sioners were detained at Niagara by sham conferences with Gov. John Graves Simcoe, of Canada, until the middle of July, when the Indians sent them word that unless they would in advance "agree that the Ohio shall remain the boundary between us," the proposed "meeting would be altogether unnecessary." The commissioners declined to ac-cept this ultimatum, and returned home. Meanwhile, General Wayne was prosecuting preparations for an active campaign against the hos-tiles.—R. G. T.

defeated as heretofore, by a too great reliance on undisciplined militia, it was recommended to Congress to authorize the raising of three additional regiments of regular soldiers; and the bill for complying with this recommendation, notwithstanding it was strenuously opposed by a stong party hostile to the then administration, was finally passed.[1]

The forts Hamilton and Jefferson, erected by Gen. St. Clair, continued to be well garrisoned; but there was some difficulty in supplying them with provisions—the Indians being always in readiness to intercept them on their way. As early as April 1792, they taught us the necessity of having a strong guard to escort supplies with safety, by a successful attack on Major Adair; who with one hundred and twenty volunteers from Kentucky, had charge of a number of pack horses laden with provisions. He was engaged by a body of savages, not much superior in number, and although he was under cover of Fort St. Clair, yet did they drive him into the fort, and carry off the provisions and pack horses. The courage and bold daring of the Indians, was eminently conspicuous on this occasion. They fought with nearly equal numbers, against a body of troops, better tutored in the science of open warfare, well mounted and equipped, armed with every necessary weapon, and almost under the guns of the fort. And they fought successfully,—killing one captain and ten privates, wounding several, and taking property estimated to be worth fifteen thousand dollars. Nothing seemed to abate their ardor for war. Neither the strong garrisons placed in the forts erected so far in advance of the settlements, nor the great preparations which were making for striking an effectual blow at them, caused them

---

[1] On a plain near the old French-Indian-English trading village, called Logstown (just below the present Economy, Pa., on the north side of the Ohio, 18 miles below Pittsburg), Wayne's army lay encamped from November, 1792, to Aprfl 30, 1793. The army was fancifully called the "Legion of the United States," and the camp was known as Legionville. From here, Wayne proceeded to Cincinnati, and took up his headquarters in Fort Washington.—R. G. T.

for an instant to slacken in hostilities, or check their movements against the frontier.

In the spring of 1793, a party of warriors proceeding towards the head waters of the Monongahela river, discovered a marked way, leading a direction which they did not know to be inhabited by whites. It led to a settlement which had been recently made on Elk river, by Jeremiah and Benjamin Carpenter and a few others from Bath county, and who had been particularly careful to make nor leave any path which might lead to a discovery of their situation, but Adam O'Brien moving into the same section of country in the spring of 1792, and being rather an indifferent woodsman, incautiously blazed the trees in several directions so as to enable him readily to find his home, when business or pleasure should have drawn him from it. It was upon one of these marked traces that the Indians chanced to fall; and pursuing it, came to the deserted cabin of [306] O'Brien: he having returned to the interior, because of his not making a sufficiency of grain for the subsistence of his family. Proceeding from O'Brien's, they came to the House of Benjamin Carpenter, whom they found alone and killed. Mrs. Carpenter being discovered by them, before she was aware of their presence, was tomahawked and scalped, a small distance from the yard.

The burning of Benjamin Carpenter's house, led to a discovery of these outrages; and the remaining inhabitants of that neighborhood, remote from any fort or populous settlement to which they could fly for security, retired to the mountains and remained for several days concealed in a cave. They then caught their horses and moved their families to the West Fork; and when they visited the places of their former habitancy for the purpose of collecting their stock and carrying it off with their other property, scarce a vestige of them was to be seen,—the Indians had been there after they left the cave, and burned the houses, pillaged their movable property, and destroyed the cattle and hogs.

Among the few interesting incidents which occurred in the upper country, during this year, was the captivity

and remarkable escape of two brothers, John and Henry
Johnson :—the former thirteen, the latter eleven years of
age.   They lived at a station on the west side of the Ohio
river near above Indian Short creek ; and being at some
distance from the house, engaged in the sportive amuse-
ments of youth, became fatigued and seated themselves on
an old log for the purpose of resting.   They presently
observed two men coming towards them, whom they
believed to be white men from the station until they approached so close as to leave no prospect of escape by
flight, when to their great grief they saw that two Indians
were beside them.   They were made prisoners, and taken
about four miles, when after partaking of some roasted
meat and parched corn given them by their captors, they
were arranged for the night, by being placed between the
two Indians and each encircled in the arms of the one
next him.

Henry, the younger of the brothers, had grieved much
at the idea of being carried off by the Indians, and during
his short but sorrowful journey across the hills, had wept
immoderately.   John had in vain endeavored to comfort
him with the hope that they should be enabled to elude
the vigilence of the savages, and to return to the hearth of
their parents and brethren.   He refused to be comforted.—
The ugly red man, with his tomahawk and scalping knife,
which had been often called in to quiet the cries of his infancy, was now actually before him ; and every scene of
torture and of torment which had been depicted, by nar-
ration, to his youthful eye, was now present to his terrified imagination, hightened by the thought that they were
about to be re-enacted on himself.   In anticipation of this
horrid doom for some time he wept in bitterness and affliction ; but

[307] "The tear down childhood's cheek that flows,
    Is like the dew drop on the rose ;—
    When next the summer breeze comes by
    And waves the bush, the flower is dry."—

When the fire was kindled at night, the supper prepared
and offered to him, all idea of his future fate was merged

in their present kindness; and Henry soon sunk to sleep, though enclosed in horrid hug, by savage arms.

It was different with John. He felt the reality of their situation.—He was alive to the anguish which he knew would agitate the bosom of his mother, and he thought over the means of allaying it so intensely, that sleep was banished from his eyes. Finding the others all locked in deep repose, he disengaged himself from the embrace of the savage at his side, and walked to the fire. To test the soundness of their sleep, he rekindled the dying blaze, and moved freely about it. All remained still and motionless,—no suppressed breathing, betrayed a feigned repose. He gently twitched the sleeping Henry, and whispering softly in his ear, bade him get up. Henry obeyed, and they both stood by the fire. "I think, said John, we had better go home now." "Oh! replied Henry, they will follow and catch us again." "Never fear that, rejoined John, we'll kill them before we go." The idea was for some time opposed by Henry; but when he beheld the savages so soundly asleep, and listened to his brother's plan of executing his wish, he finally consented to act the part prescribed him.

The only gun which the Indians had, was resting against a tree, at the foot of which lay their tomahawks. John placed it on a log, with the muzzle near to the head of one of the savages; cocked it, and leaving Henry with his finger to the trigger, ready to pull upon the signal being given, he repaired to his own station. Holding in his hand one of their tomahawks, he stood astride of the other Indian, and as he raised his arm to deal death to the sleeping savage, Henry fired, and shooting off the lower part of the Indian's jaw, called to his brother, *"lay on, for I've done for this one,"* seized up the gun and ran off. The first blow of the tomahawk took effect on the back of the neck, and was not fatal. The Indian attempted to spring up; but John repeated his strokes with such force and so quickly, that he soon brought him again to the ground; and leaving him dead proceeded on after his brother.

They presently came to a path which they recollected to have travelled, the preceding evening, and keeping along it, arrived at the station awhile before day. The inhabitants were however, all up and in much uneasiness for the fate of the boys; and when they came near and heard a well known voice exclaim in accents of deep distress, "*Poor little fellows, they are killed or taken prisoners,*" John replied aloud,—"No mother, we are here again."

When the tale of their captivity, and the means by which their deliverance was effected, were told, they did not obtain full credence. [308] Piqued at the doubts expressed by some, John observed, "you had better go and see." "But, can you again find the spot," said one. "Yes, replied he, I hung my hat up at the turning out place and can soon shew you the spot." Accompanied by several of the men, John returned to the theatre of his daring exploits; and the truth of his statement received ample confirmation. The savage who had been tomahawked was lying dead by the fire—the other had crawled some distance; but was tracked by his blood until found, when it was agreed to leave him, "*as he must die at any rate.*"

Companies of rangers had been for several seasons stationed on the Ohio river, for the greater security of the persons and property of those who resided on and near the frontier. During this year a company which had been sta-stationed at the mouth of Fishing creek,[1] and had remained there until its term of service had expired, determined then on a scout into the Indian country; and crossing the river, marched on for some days before they saw any thing which indicated their nearness to Indians. Pursuing a path which seemed to be much used, they came in view of an Indian camp, and observing another path, which likewise seemed to be much frequented, Ensign Levi Morgan was sent with a detachment of the men, to see if it would conduct them to where were others of the Indians, who soon returned with the information that he had seen another of their encampments close by. Upon the receipt of this intelligence, the Lieutenant was sent

---

[1] Fishing Creek enters the Ohio 128 miles below Pittsburgh. At its mouth is now the town of New Martinsville, W. Va.—R. G. T.

forward with a party of men to attack the second encampment, while the Captain with the residue of the company should proceed against that which had been first discovered, and commence an assault on it, when he should hear the firing of the Lieutenant's party at the camp which he was sent to assail.

When the second camp was approached and the men posted at intervals around it, awaiting the light of day to begin the assault, the Lieutenant discovered that there was a greater force of Indians with whom he would have to contend than was expected, and prudently resolved to withdraw his men without coming into collision with them. Orders for this movement were directly given, and the party immediately retired. There was however, one of the detachment, who had been posted some small distance in advance of the others with directions to fire as soon as the Indians should be seen stirring, and who, unapprized of the withdrawal of the others, [309] maintained his station, until he observed a squaw issuing from a camp, when he fired at her and rushed up, expecting to be supported by his comrades. He fell into the hands of those whom he had thus assailed; but his fate was far different from what he had every reason to suppose it would be, under those circumstances. It was the hunting camp of Isaac Zane, and the female at whom he had shot was the daughter of Zane; the ball had slightly wounded her in the wrist. Her father, although he had been with the Indians ever since his captivity when only nine years of age, had not yet acquired the ferocious and vindictive passions of those with whom he had associated; but practising the forbearance and forgiveness of christian and civilized man, generously conducted the wanton assailant so far upon his way, that he was enabled though alone to reach the settlement in safety. His fate was different from that of those, who had been taken prisoners by that part of the company which remained at the first camp with the Captain. When the Lieutenant with the detachment, rejoined the others, disappointment at the failure of the expedition under him, led some of the men to fall upon the Indian prisoners and inhumanly murder them.

Notwithstanding that preparations for an active campaign against the savages was fast ripening to their perfection, and that the troops of the general government had penetrated as far as to the field, on which had been fought the fatal battle of the fourth of November, 1791, and erected there Fort Recovery,[1] yet did they not cease from their accustomed inroads upon the settlements, even after the winter of 1793.—In March 1794, a party of them crossed the Ohio river, and as they were advancing towards the settlements on the upper branches of the Monongahela, met with Joseph Cox, then on his way to the mouth of Leading creek on Little Kenhawa, for a load of furs and skins which he had left there, at the close of his hunt the preceding fall. Cox very unexpectedly met them in a narrow pass, and instantly wheeled his horse to ride off. Endeavoring to stimulate the horse to greater speed by the application of the whip, the animal became stubborn and refused to go at all, when Cox was forced to dismount and seek safety on foot. His pursuers gained rapidly upon him, and he saw that one of them would soon overtake him. He faced the savage who was near, and raised his gun to fire; but nothing daunted, the Indian rushed forward. Cox's gun [310] missed fire, and he was instantly a prisoner. He was taken to their towns and detained in captivity for some time; but at length made his escape, and returned safely to the settlement.

On the 24th of July, six Indians visited the West Fork river, and at the mouth of Freeman's creek, met with, and made prisoner, a daughter of John Runyan. She was taken off by two of the party of savages, but did not go more than ten or twelve miles, before she was put to death. The four Indians who remained, proceeded down the river and on the next day came to the house of William Carder, near below the mouth of Hacker's creek. Mr. Carder discovered them approaching, in time to fasten his door; but in the confusion of the minute, shut out two

---

[1] This was an expedition made by Gen. James Wilkinson, second in command under Wayne, in December, 1793. He marched to the field from Fort Washington at the head of a thousand men, and left a garrison at the new fort.—R. G. T.

of his children, who however ran off unperceived by the
savages and arrived in safety at the house of a neighbor.
He then commenced firing and hallooing, so as to alarm
those who were near and intimidate the Indians.   Both
objects were accomplished.   The Indians contented themselves with shooting at the cattle, and then retreated; and
Mr. Joseph Chevront, who lived hardby, hearing the report of the guns and the loud cries of Carder, sent his own
family to a place of safety, and with nobleness of purpose,
ran to the relief of his neighbor.   He enabled Carder to remove his family to a place of greater security, although
the enemy were yet near, and engaged in skinning one of
the cattle that they might take with them a supply of
meat.   On the next day a company of men assembled, and
went in pursuit; but they could not trail the savages far,
because of the great caution with which they had retreated, and returned without accomplishing any thing.

Two days afterward, when it was believed that the Indians had left the neighborhood, they came on Hacker's
creek near to the farm of Jacob Cozad, and finding four
of his sons bathing, took three of them prisoners, and
killed the fourth, by repeatedly stabbing him with a bayonet attached to a staff.   The boys, of whom they made
prisoners, were immediately taken to the Indian towns and
kept in captivity until the treaty of Greenville in 1795.
Two of them were then delivered up to their father, who
attended to enquire for them,—the third was not heard of
for some time after, but was at length found at Sandusky,
by his elder brother and brought home.

After the victory obtained by General Wayne over
the Indians, [311] Jacob Cozad, Jr. was doomed to be
burned to death, in revenge of the loss then sustained by
the savages.   Every preparation for carrying into execution this dreadful determination was quickly made.   The
wood was piled, the intended victim was apprized of his
approaching fate, and before the flaming torch was applied
to the faggots, he was told to take leave of those who were
assembled to witness the awful spectacle.   The croud was
great, and the unhappy youth could with difficulty press
his way through them.   Amid the jeers and taunts of those

whom he would address, he was proceeding to discharge
the last sad act of his life, when a female, whose countenance beamed with benignity, beckoned him to follow her.
He did not hesitate. He approached as if to bid her fare-
well, and she succeeded in taking him off unobserved by
the many eyes gazing around, and concealed him in a wig-
wam among some trunks and covered loosely with a
blanket. He was presently missed, and a search immediately made for him. Many passed near in quest of the
devoted victim, and he could hear their steps and note
their disappointment. After awhile the uproar ceased,
and he felt more confident of security. In a few minutes
more he heard approaching footsteps and felt that the
blanket was removed from him. He turned to surrender
himself to his pursuers, and meet a dreadful death.—But
no! they were two of his master's sons who had been directed where to find him, and they conducted him securely
to the Old Delaware town, where he remained until carried to camp upon the conclusion of a treaty of peace.[1]

In a short time after the happening of the events at
Cozad's, a party of Indians made an irruption upon Tygart's Valley. For some time the inhabitants of that settlement had enjoyed a most fortunate exemption from
savage molestation; and although they had somewhat relaxed in vigilance, they did not however omit to pursue a
course calculated to ensure a continuance of their tranquillity and repose. Instead of flying for security, as they
had formerly, to the neighboring forts upon the return of
spring, the increase of population and the increased capacity of the communion to repel aggression, caused them
to neglect other acts of precaution, and only to assemble

---

[1] McWhorter says that the capture of the Cozad boys took place at
the mouth of Lanson Run, near Berlin, W. Va. The boy who was
killed was but six years of age; crying for his mother, an Indian
grasped him by the heels and cracked his head against a tree,—a favorite
method of murdering white children, among Indian war parties. "Jacob yelled once, after starting with the Indians, but was knocked down
by a gun in the hands of one of the savages. When he came to his senses,
a squaw was dragging him up hill by one foot. He remained with the
Indians for about two years, being adopted into a chief's family. He
died in 1862, in his eighty-ninth year."—R. G. T.

at particular houses, when danger was believed to be instant and at hand. In consequence of the reports which reached them of the injuries lately committed by the [312] savages upon the West Fork, several families collected at the house of Mr. Joseph Canaan for mutual security, and while thus assembled, were visited by a party of Indians, when perfectly unprepared for resistance. The savages entered the house awhile after dark, and approaching the bed on which Mr. Canaan was lolling, one of them addressed him with the familiarity of an old acquaintance and saying " how d'ye do, how d'ye do," presented his hand. Mr. Canaan was rising to reciprocate the greeting, when he was pierced by a ball discharged at him from another savage, and fell dead. The report of the gun at once told, who were the visitors, and put them upon using immediate exertions to effect their safety by flight. A young man who was near when Canaan was shot, aimed at the murderer a blow with a drawing knife, which took effect on the head of the savage and brought him to the ground. Ralston then escaped through the door, and fled in safety, although fired at as he fled.

When the Indians entered the house, there was a Mrs. Ward sitting in the room. So soon as she observed that the intruders were savages, she passed into another apartment with two of the children, and going out with them through a window, got safely away. Mr. Lewis (brother to Mrs. Canaan) likewise escaped from a back room, in which he had been asleep at the firing of the gun. Three children were tomahawked and scalped,—Mrs. Canaan made prisoner, and the savages withdrew. The severe wound inflicted on the head of the Indian by Ralston, made it necessary that they should delay their return to their towns, until his recovery; and they accordingly remained near the head of the middle fork of Buchannon, for several weeks. Their extreme caution in travelling, rendered any attempt to discover them unavailing; and when their companion was restored they proceeded on, uninterruptedly. On the close of the war, Mrs. Canaan was redeemed from captivity by a brother from Brunswick, in New Jersey, and restored to her surviving friends.

Thus far in the year 1794, the army of the United States had not been organised for efficient operations. Gen. Wayne had been actively employed in the discharge of every preparatory duty devolving on him; and those distinguishing characteristics of uncommon daring and bravery, which had acquired for him the appellation of "*Mad Anthony*," and which [313] so eminently fitted him for the command of an army warring against savages, gave promise of success to his arms.

Before the troops marched from Fort Washington, it was deemed advisable to have an abundant supply of provisions in the different forts in advance of this, as well for the supply of their respective garrisons, as for the subsistence of the general army, in the event of its being driven into them, by untoward circumstances. With this view, three hundred pack-horses, laden with flour, were sent on to Fort Recovery; and, as it was known that considerable bodies of the enemy were constantly hovering about the forts, and awaiting opportunities of cutting off any detachments from the main army, Major McMahon, with eighty riflemen under Capt. Hartshorn, and fifty dragoons, under Capt. Taylor, was ordered on as an escort. This force was too great to justify the savages in making an attack, until they could unite the many war parties which were near; and before this could be effected, Major McMahon reached his destination.

On the 30th of July,[1] as the escort was about leaving Fort Recovery, it was attacked by an army of one thousand Indians, in the immediate vicinity of the fort. Captain Hartshorn had advanced only three or four hundred yards, at the head of the riflemen, when he was unexpectedly beset on every side. With the most consummate bravery and good conduct, he maintained the unequal conflict, until Major McMahon, placing himself at the head of the cavalry, charged upon the enemy, and was repulsed with considerable loss. Maj. McMahon, Capt. Taylor and Cornet Terry fell upon the first onset, and many of the privates were killed or wounded. The whole savage force

---

[1] Thirtieth of June.—R. G. T.

being now brought to press on Capt. Hartshorn, that brave officer was forced to try and regain the Fort, but the enemy interposed its strength, to prevent this movement. Lieutenant Drake and Ensign Dodd, with twenty volunteers, marched from Fort Recovery and forcing a passage through a column of the enemy at the point of the bayonet, joined the rifle corps, at the instant that Capt. Hartshorn received a shot which broke his thigh. Lieut. Craig being killed and Lieut. Marks taken prisoner, Lieut. Drake conducted the retreat; and while endeavoring for an instant to hold the enemy in check, so as to enable the soldiers to bring off their wounded captain, himself received a shot in the groin, and the retreat was resumed, leaving Capt. Hartshorn on the field.

[314] When the remnant of the troops came within the walls of the Fort, Lieut. Michael, who had been early detached by Capt. Hartshorn to the flank of the enemy, was found to be missing, and was given up as lost. But while his friends were deploring his unfortunate fate, he and Lieut. Marks, who had been early taken prisoner, were seen rushing through the enemy, from opposite directions towards the Fort. They gained it safely, notwithstanding they were actively pursued, and many shots fired at them. Lieut. Marks had got off by knocking down the Indian who held him prisoner; and Lieut. Michael had lost all of his party, but three men. The entire loss of the Americans was twenty-three killed, and forty wounded.[1] The riflemen brought in ten scalps which were taken early in the action; beyond this the enemy's loss was never ascertained. Many of them were no doubt killed and wounded, as they advanced in solid columns up to the very muzzles of the guns, and were afterwards seen carrying off many of their warriors on pack horses.

At length Gen. Wayne put the army over which he had been given the command, in motion;[2] and upon its arrival at the confluence of the Au Glaize and the Miami of the

---

[1] The white loss, in killed, was 22, including Major McMahon.—R. G. T.

[2] The force started August 8. Besides the regulars, were about 1,100 mounted Kentucky militia, under Gen. Charles Scott.—R. G. T.

Lakes, another effort was made for the attainment of peace, without the effusion of blood. Commissioners were sent forward to the Indians to effect this desirable object; who exhorted them to listen to their propositions for terminating the war, and no longer to be deluded by the counsels of white emissaries, who had not the power to afford them protection; but only sought to involve the frontier of the United States in a war, from which much evil, but no good could possibly result to either party. The savages however felt confident that success would again attend their arms, and deriving additional incentives to war from their proximity to the British fort, recently erected at the foot of the rapids, declined the overture for peace, and seemed ardently to desire the battle, which they knew must soon be fought.

The Indian army at this time, amounted to about two thousand warriors, and when reconnoitered on the 19th of August were found encamped in a thick bushy wood and near to the British Fort. The army of Gen. Wayne was equal in numbers to that of the enemy; and when on the morning of the 20th, it took up the line of march, the troops were so disposed as to avoid being surprised, and to come into action on the [315] shortest notice, and under the most favorable circumstances. A select battalion of mounted volunteers, commanded by Major Price, moving in advance of the main army, had proceeded but a few miles, when a fire so severe was aimed at it by the savages concealed, as usual, that it was forced to fall back. The enemy had chosen their ground with great judgment, taking a position behind the fallen timber,[1] which had been prostrated by a tornado, and in a woods so thick as to render it impracticable for the cavalry to act with effect. They were formed into three regular lines, much extended in front, within supporting distance of each other, and reaching about two miles; and their first effort was to turn the left flank of the American army.

Gen. Wayne ordered the first line of his army to advance with trailed arms, to rouse the enemy from their

---

[1] Hence the popular name of the engagement, "Battle of Fallen Timbers."—R. G. T.

covert at the point of the bayonet, and when up to deliver
a close and well directed fire, to be followed by a charge
so brisk as not to allow them time to reload or form their
lines.   The second line was ordered to the support of the
first; and Capt. Campbell at the head of the cavalry, and
Gen. Scott at the head of the mounted volunteers were
sent forward to turn the left and right wings of the enemy.
All these complicated orders were promptly executed; but
such was the impetuosity of the charge made by the first
line of infantry, so completely and entirely was the enemy
broken by it, and so rapid the pursuit, that only a small
part of the second line and of the mounted volunteers
were in time to participate in the action, notwithstanding
the great exertions of their respective officers to co-operate
in the engagement; and in less than one hour, the savages
were driven more than two miles and within gunshot of
the British Fort, by less than one half their numbers.

Gen. Wayne remained three days on the banks of the
Miami, in front of the field of battle left to the full and
quiet possession of his army, by the flight and dispersion
of the savages.   In this time, all the houses and cornfields,
both above and below the British Fort, and among the
rest, the houses and stores of Col. McKee,[1] an English
trader of great influence among the Indians and which
had been invariably exerted to prolong the war, were consumed by fire or otherwise entirely destroyed.   On the
27th, the American army returned to its head quarters,
laying waste the cornfields and villages on each side of the
river for about fifty miles; and [316] this too in the most
populous and best improved part of the Indian country.

The loss sustained by the American army, in obtaining this brilliant victory, over a savage enemy flushed with
former successes, amounted to thirty-three killed and one
hundred wounded:[2] that of the enemy was never ascertained.   In his official account of the action, Gen. Wayne
says, "The woods were strewed for a considerable distance,

---

[1] Alexander McKee, the renegade, of whom mention has frequently
been made in foregoing pages.—R. G. T.

[2] Later authorities place the white loss at 107, killed and wounded.—
R. G. T.

with the dead bodies of the Indians and their white auxiliaries;" and at a council held a few days after, when
British agents endeavored to prevail on them to risk
another engagement, they expressed a determination to
" bury the bloody hatchet" saying, that they had just lost
more than two hundred of their warriors.

Some events occurred during this engagement, which
are deemed worthy of being recorded here, although not
of general interest. While Capt. Campbell was engaged
in turning the left-flank, of the enemy, three of them
plunged into the river, and endeavored to escape the fury
of the conflict, by swimming to the opposite shore. They
were seen by two negroes, who were on the bank to which
the Indians were aiming, and who concealed themselves
behind a log for the purpose of intercepting them. When
within shooting distance one of the negroes fired and
killed one of the Indians. The other two took hold of
him to drag him to shore, when one of them was killed,
by the fire of the other negro. The remaining Indian, being now in shoal water, endeavored to draw both the dead
to the bank; but before he could effect this, the negro who
had first fired, had reloaded, and again discharging his gun,
killed him also, and the three floated down the river.

Another circumstance is related, which shows the obstinacy with which the contest was maintained by individuals in both armies. A soldier and an Indian came in
collision, the one having an unloaded gun,—the other a
tomahawk. After the action was over, they were both
found dead; the soldier with his bayonet in the body of
the Indian,—and the Indian with his tomahawk in the
head of the soldier.

Notwithstanding the signal victory, obtained by General Wayne over the Indians, yet did their hostility to the
whites lead them to acts of occasional violence, and kept
them for some time from acceding to the proposals for
peace. In [317] consequence of this, their whole country
was laid waste, and forts erected in the hearts of their settlements at once to starve and awe them into quiet. The
desired effect was produced. Their crops being laid waste,
their villages burned, fortresses erected in various parts of

their country and kept well garrisoned, and a victorious army ready to bear down upon them at any instant, there was no alternative left them but to sue for peace.   When the Shawanees made known their wish to bury the *bloody hatchet*, Gen. Wayne refused to treat singly with them, and declared that all the different tribes of the North Western Indians should be parties to any treaty which he should make.   This required some time as they had been much dispersed after the defeat of the 20th of August, and the great devastation committed on their crops and provisions by the American army, had driven many to the woods, to procure a precarious subsistence by hunting.   Still however, to such abject want and wretchedness were they reduced, that exertions were immediately made to collect them in general council; and as this was the work of some time, it was not effected until midsummer of 1795.

In this interval of time, there was but a solitary interruption, caused by savage aggression, to the general repose and quiet of North Western Virginia; and that interruption occurred in a settlement which had been exempt from invasion since the year 1782.   In the summer of 1795, the trail of a large party of Indians was discovered on Leading creek, and proceeding directly towards the settlements on the head of the West Fork, those on Buchannon river, or in Tygart's Valley.   In consequence of the uncertainty against which of them, the savages would direct their operations, intelligence of the discovery which had been made, was sent by express to all; and measures, to guard against the happening of any unpleasant result, were taken by all, save the inhabitants on Buchannon.   They had so long been exempt from the murderous incursions of the savages, while other settlements not remote from them, were yearly deluged with blood, that a false security was engendered, in the issue, fatal to the lives and happiness of some of them, by causing them to neglect the use of such precautionary means, as would warn them of the near approach of danger, and ward it when it came.

Pursuing their usual avocations in despite of the warning which had been given them, on the day after the express had [318] sounded an alarm among them, as John Bozarth, sen. and his sons George and John were busied in drawing grain from the field to the barn, the agonizing shrieks of those at the house rent the air around them; and they hastened to ascertain, and if practicable avert the cause. The elasticity of youth enabled George to approach the house some few paces in advance of his father, but the practised eye of the old gentleman, first discovered an Indian, only a small distance from his son, and with his gun raised to fire upon him. With parental solicitude he exclaimed, "See George, an Indian is going to shoot you." George was then too near the savage, to think of escaping by flight. He looked at him steadily, and when he supposed the fatal aim was taken and the finger just pressing on the trigger, he fell, and the ball whistled by him. Not doubting but that the youth had fallen in death, the savage passed by him and pressed in pursuit of the father.

Mr. Bozarth had not attained to that age when the sinews become too much relaxed for active exertion, but was yet springy and agile, and was enabled to keep ahead of his pursuer. Despairing of overtaking him, by reason of his great speed, the savage hurled a tomahawk at his head. It passed harmless by; and the old gentleman got safely off.

When George Bozarth fell as the Indian fired, he lay still as if dead, and supposing the scalping knife would be next applied to his head, determined on seizing the savage by the legs as he would stoop over him, and endeavor to bring him to the ground; when he hoped to be able to gain the mastery over him. Seeing him pass on in pursuit of his father, he arose and took to flight also. On his way he overtook a younger brother, who had become alarmed, and was hobbling slowly away on a sore foot. George gave him every aid in his power to facilitate his flight, until he discovered that another of the savages was pressing close upon them. Knowing that if he remained with his brother, both must inevitably perish, he was reluctantly forced to leave him to his fate. Proceeding on, he came up with his father, who not doubting but he was killed when the savage fired at him, broke forth with the exclamation. "*Why George, I thought you were dead,*" and manifested, even in that sorrowful moment, a joyful feeling at his mistake.

The Indians who were at the house, wrought their work of blood upon such as would have been impediments to their [319] retreat; and killing two or three smaller children, took Mrs. Bozarth and two boys prisoners. With these they made their way to their towns and arrived in time to surrender their captives to Gen. Wayne.

This was the last mischief done by the Indians in North Western Virginia. For twenty years the inhabitants of that section of the country, had suffered all the horrors of savage warfare, and all the woes which spring from the uncurbed indulgence of those barbarous and vindicitive passions, which bear sway in savage breasts. The treaty of Greenville, concluded on the 3d of August 1795, put a period to the war, and with it, to those acts of devastation and death which had so long spread dismay and gloom throughout the land.

FINIS.

INDEX.

www.ingramcontent.com/pod-product-compliance
Lightning Source LLC
Chambersburg PA
CBHW022009110726
47901CB00006B/1455